MW00986776

The Phoenix

The Crossroad Publishing Company

The Phoenix

A Love That Endured the Winds of World War II

PETER M. KALELLIS

The Crossroad Publishing Company

The Crossroad Publishing Company
www.crossroadpublishing.com

Printed in December 2014

In continuation of our 200-year tradition of independent publishing, The
Crossroad Publishing Company proudly offers a variety of books with
strong, original voices and diverse perspectives. The viewpoints expressed in
our books are not necessarily those of The Crossroad Publishing Company,
any of its imprints or of its employees. No claims are made or responsibility
assumed for any health or other benefits.

Kalellis, Peter M., author.
The phoenix : a love that endured the winds of World War II / by Peter M.
Kalellis.
pages cm
ISBN 978-0-8245-2017-5 (alk. paper)
1. Lesbos Island (Greece)–Fiction. 2. Greece–History–Occupation,
1941-1944–Fiction. 3. Love stories. 4. Christian fiction.
5. Historical fiction. I. Title.
PS3561.A416516P48 2014
813′.54–dc23
2013051320

Cover design by: Ray Lundgren
Book design by: Thomson Digital

Books published by The Crossroad Publishing Company may be purchased
at special quantity discount rates for classes and institutional use. For
information, please email info@crossroadpublishing.com.

Printed in The United States of America

With genuine compassion, this novel is dedicated to young and older orphaned children who at a tragic time in their life lost either one or both parents. With deep respect, I also dedicate this story to his Eminence Metropolitan Iakovos, the inspired and inspiring Archbishop of Lesbos, Greece, who built and sustained as a safe and nurturing home the Mytilene Orphanage for Girls.

CHAPTER ONE

1934

THERE WAS LOVE at its budding, but would it last until the end? It was a disturbing dream, awakening her on a stormy dawn. All she knew was that when she blinked her eyes, her life would be somehow different. Wrapped in a light pink comforter, sixteen-year-old Nina Cambas propped her head up with an extra large pillow and watched the pine trees thrash in the frenzy of the nor'easter. A similar storm had occurred seven years before, but she was too young then to remember.

Her Aunt Pipina had said that nor'easters visited their island at least once every seven years at the beginning of March, causing huge problems. As the windows vibrated, Nina felt the chill, and trembling, pulled her comforter up under chin. Her aunt told her not to be afraid, for their house was as strong as a Venetian castle. Dark clouds scudded across the sky, but nothing suggested that strange things would soon be happening all over the island. She closed her eyes, musing and recounting minute by minute, inch by inch, the previous evening at the shore. Embraces and kisses, as if time were endless; she could still feel the tingling through her body.

Two sets of footprints had converged on the Aegean shore that bordered an inlet where a white fishing boat was anchored. Nina and her boyfriend, a barefooted fisherman whom her father had forbidden her to see, had reached the boat only a few minutes before he was to set out. She could hear her heart pounding at the thought of saying, *My father doesn't want me to have any contact with you,* and she could hear the echo of her father's voice, *You're my daughter. Think of the reputation of our family.*

Father, Stephen is just a good friend, she told him the day Stephen had taken her for a boat ride.

He's a penniless fisherman—not our kind.

Don't fishermen have souls?

They're barefooted fate-chasers.

Stephen is different.

I don't want you to be seen with him. Do you hear?

Nina never hated anyone, but that day she had hated her father. She could not understand his attitude. He was a stubborn man. Lately, he had stopped buying fish from Stephen, who always brought his best catch to him. Why was her father so set against him? She was only sixteen and not even thinking of marriage, although she and her girlfriends many times talked and giggled about getting married some day and strolling along the seashore with their babies on sunny afternoons.

The sun had set, gold-leafing the mountaintops and sending through silvery olive trees a veil of vapor toward the sea. A line of fishing boats, all white, like huge swans, with lit lanterns were about to sail across the inlet toward the sea for their night catch. That's how most islanders made a living. On the brink of tears, Nina watched the boats, one behind the other, sailing away, and sighed.

"Stephen, please don't go."

"I have to. Dad has been out of work. If I don't go fishing . . ."

"I could give you some money."

"That's very generous, but . . . ." Sadly, Stephen perused the area; there wasn't a soul around. His eyes darkened. *I wish I didn't have to go,* he thought, as he put his arms around Nina and held her tightly. "You're the sweetest, most beautiful girl on the island, and I love you."

"I love you, too," she whispered.

He kissed her gently. "I'll see you tomorrow."

"Stephen, please hold me and kiss me again." What she was not able to articulate was, *Embrace me and kiss me and get the most of me, for my father will not permit this to continue.* She wept.

"You're beautiful even when you cry, but please dry your tears and know that I love you."

She nodded, forcing a smile. On her way home, each step became a thought. *What if some evil eyes saw us kissing and reported the scene to my father? I'll never hear the end of it.*

When she returned to her room, she found a note in Aunt Pipina's handwriting: *Your father was looking for you. Where were you? He was worried.*

Quickly, Nina peeled off her clothes, slipped under her comforter, and tried to think what she could tell her father if someone had told him where she had been. When she opened her eyes, the room looked different. She ran her fingers through her long, dark brown hair, letting the tresses cascade over her budding breasts, and let out a deep sigh. In spite of the thick storm windows, she could hear the wind howling outside. Oh, God! If Stephen is still out at sea, he may be in danger. Feeling the comfort and warmth of the bed, she blinked to dismiss bad thoughts. The Byzantine icon of the Virgin Mary on her bedroom wall looked alive under a flickering vigil light, creating wraith-like shadows. Nina's fears increased by the moment, thinking of Stephen at sea. Her teary eyes were riveted on Mary's icon. She could discern the faint shadow of a small ship hanging under the icon. Stephen had carved it for her from wood from a lemon tree. Again she thought of his gentle touch and sweet kisses and how much she would love to marry him someday.

Stephen used to go fishing with his father, but lately, since his father had become sick, he went alone. *He's too young and inexperienced to manage a boat,* many of his father's colleagues said. But Stephen was a strong nineteen-year-old man who loved the sea. On the screen of her mind, she could see Stephen's radiant face as he arrived each morning, happy with his catch of silvery fish squirming in large baskets. She smiled at the image, but her mind echoed, *Girls of your age don't go out alone.* It was her father's voice, followed by her aunt's benevolent antiphon: *How old-fashioned can you be, dear brother? You cannot keep her in a cage. She's a big girl now.* What Pipina didn't dare to verbalize was her awareness that Nina had become a woman. Sometimes Pipina spoke to him boldly, but when his temper was at high tide, she, too, would run. *Why is Father so old-fashioned? He has traveled; he has spent many, many years in America. Why is he so strict? I'm not going to do anything to embarrass him,* Nina thought.

The windows rattled madly from the wind, and Nina curled up among her pillows. Apollo, her tiny black kitten, yawned, showing his pink tongue, and then, tucking his head under his front paws, went back to sleep. In the next room her father was snoring, asleep like a stone. It appeared that he was a satisfied man, sliding into wealth and settling into his golden years. But in the opposite room, his sister, Pipina, knew that her brother was not at all settled. He was a good man, a loving father, but his daughter's feelings for Stephen did not sit well with him. Not a sound came from either her father's or aunt's room. Everyone was still asleep except Nina, shivering at the thought of Stephen at sea. She tossed the comforter to the foot of her bed and sat up. Apollo stretched luxuriously and looked up at her with sleepy eyes.

"Go back to sleep," Nina said. "Just be glad you're a cat and you don't have to go fishing for your food." She slipped out of bed and went to the window to look at the storm-battered island. Villagers of all ages, like scattered sheep, emerged from their homes and headed toward the harbor—not an unusual sight for Sunday evenings, but why did they rush so early this Monday morning? She opened the window. The air carried the salty weight of the sea, muffling the noise and shouting of the people, "God help us! Somebody's boat returned unmanned and empty."

Stratya, who periodically ran errands for the Cambas family, this morning rushed eagerly to tell Pipina the sad news. Mind and body in utter shock, Nina listened to her raspy voice, shaking her head, refusing to believe what she heard. *Not my Stephen,* she thought. With tears and sighs she ran to her room.

4

Capsized and cracked, Stephen's boat was tossing about, prow dipping among the rocks. Stephen had vanished. Could he have drowned? There was no sign of him anywhere. None of the other fishermen had seen him. The news spread like wildfire.

In fear, people gathered around his boat, looking for signs of comfort. A woman in black cried bitterly. "No-oo-oo," she screamed. "My boy, my precious son, where are you?" In shock, with eyes full of loathing, she looked at the sea, cursed the waves, and fell, burying her face in her hands on the wet sand. Firmly making their way through the throng, Papavasile, the village priest, and Mother Superior of St. Mary's Convent reached the grieving mother and compassionately lifted her to her feet. Sorrow veiled the swarthy faces of the islanders. In the evening, people swarmed to the church to pray. Everyone was there, everyone except Nina Cambas, who wept in her room alone. With red and swollen eyes, Nina pressed her fingers against her temples to contain her headache. How could her father forbid her to go to the church service for Stephen? She could not understand him or his reasoning. Anger at her father mounted to rage. Furiously, she stalked around the house like a caged animal. She yanked the window open, almost at the point of jumping out. The darkness that followed the storm was thick and sinister. A black night was shutting down the village on the day she had lost that young, blond fisherman. She wanted to die. *Maybe Stephen has not drowned. He might come back.* She looked at the icon and whispered, "Oh God, bring him back!" She wept. Dark sadness, like a stifling blanket, shrouded the village by morning. Life itself had been suspended. Neither human nor animal sound disturbed the stillness. Only the church bell could be heard in the distance clocking the hour.

Through olive and pine trees Nina trudged along a winding trail bordering the shore. She saw the rising breakers crashing against the rocks. *One of those waves could carry Stephen ashore.*

CHAPTER TWO

1941

POSEIDON BLEW STIFF winds from the north, sending mountainous waves splashing against the Aegean islands. Wiping the salt water off his face, Captain Vincent Thompson thundered, "I've never seen such a menace, not even in the Atlantic."

Watching the captain wrestling during the stormy hours, Dan Cohen, his first mate, asked, "Sir, shall I send an S.O.S. to other ships in the area?"

"Are you that much afraid?" shouted the captain.

"No, sir."

"We're not far from land, right on schedule, March first, just as I said," the captain insisted.

As the turbulence persisted, Cohen brought a mug of freshly brewed coffee. "It's very hot, captain," he said. "I'll take over the rudder so you can have a chance to breathe."

Balancing the mug, the captain sipped heartily, cherishing the warmth. His eyes were on his first mate; he was glad to have a man like Cohen on his crew, not only because he could act as an interpreter, but also because he had relatives in Lesbos who might be of help. Grasping the rudder, Cohen followed the compass like a professional. A handsome man with a mariner's wide stance, he stood rock ribbed and anxious, studying the distant shore. He guided the vessel toward the hardly visible land where eventually they would be able to dock.

When the captain handed back the empty mug, ready to reclaim the rudder, Cohen grinned. He was about to tease the captain. It was on the tip of his tongue to ask, *What about the muses that we're going to meet on the island?* But the glint in old Cap'n Vince's eyes made him think again. A younger man, Cohen always cherished the captain's tales of exotic places and beautiful women. *Muses,* the captain called them. Whether these events were real or fictitious was of no consequence; they helped to fill the time during the long sea journeys, and that was reason enough for their telling. Cohen was a good listener and looked to the captain as a father figure; he would do anything to please him. In Thompson's presence he felt accepted and appreciated. He could sense that, even in the toughest times, among his mates he was the captain's favorite. When he first met him and told him about his origins and his fluency in the Greek language, the captain raised his thick eyebrows, sizing him up from head to foot. His blue eyes sparkled. His face was lean, the skin creased and weathered. He wore a close-cropped beard. His strong irregular features were dominated by piercing eyes, which followed the stars at night and spotted whales during the day. Pirates had learned to give a wide berth to his ship.

"You may be the man I need," said the captain. "But you don't look like the Greeks I know. You look Scandinavian to me." He chuckled.

"Half Greek, sir, and half German, but as a whole, I'm an American," Cohen said.

"Son, do you like the sea?"

"Yes, sir!"

On the way to Lesbos, as Cohen shared his story with the captain, he saw a father's love in his eyes. *Had my father been alive, he would probably look like Thompson,* he thought. Before his fourteenth birthday, Dan Cohen had lost his father in a fire accident aboard a ship. It was a horrible death, a tragedy that Cohen refused to discuss. His mother, a dedicated German wife, adopted his father's Greek culture and insisted that Dan go to the Greek school and learn the language well. *Some day,* she said, *you will visit Uncle Thano, your father's brother, and you will meet other relatives in Greece.*

Although Dan Cohen insisted on being the man of the house and taking care of his mother, she stressed the value of education. After high school, he attended the Naval Academy in Annapolis, Maryland. In his third year at the Academy his mother was killed by a car as she tried to cross Main Street in Miami, Florida. Sad and devastated, Cohen continued his education and graduated with honors. The look in Thompson's face was empathic. "Cohen," he said, "your journey through life has just begun."

The captain perused the horizon, and smiled. "By the way, if your father was Greek, how did you get the name Cohen?"

"It's a long story, sir."

"I knew a famous lawyer in Boston with the same name."

"No relationship, captain." They looked at each other and smiled.

"Okay, Cohen, let's get to work," he commanded. Haughty and invincible, the captain towered on the deck. Sharp, blue eyes, shaggy hair bleached almost colorless by years of sun and salt, added a ruggedness to his New England features. He surveyed his prized purchase, the *North Star.* He had bought it a year ago at an auction in Italy from the only heir of the renowned ship owner, Grasparelli. Within nine months, the two-masted ship had paid for itself. Now, she wrestled in the brine beyond the island of Chios, three hours away from Lesbos, her hold crammed with empty barrels to be filled with olive oil.

For Dan Cohen, this particular island evoked conflicting emotions: excitement about the possibility of meeting his father's kin and a tinge of fear that his Uncle Thano might not even be around. He could have been drafted and sent to Albania to fight the Greek war against the Italians. What if his uncle revealed something about his father that he did not want to hear? What if the islanders suspected he was a spy who happened to know their language? What if they reacted in a hostile manner toward the captain? After all, there was a war being fought.

"Gentlemen, we should be in Lesbos by morning hours," bellowed the captain. As a liaison, Cohen had to make sure that the *North Star* was loaded with choice olive oil. That would make his captain a happy man. As a merchant marine, Thompson often went to Mediterranean countries to purchase tobacco and rare wines, but olive oil was the product that brought him the greatest profit. Several times, he had crossed the Atlantic in search of this wonderful oil. This time, he would purchase the best oil for a fine customer, the Crinos Corporation in New York.

Thompson switched on the radio, and among deafening static he discovered an Italian station playing music from the late thirties. He was enjoying a familiar tune, "La Paloma." The rhyming verses were being rendered in Italian, German, and then in Greek, which Dan was able to interpret. *Makrya thai na fygo manam sti xenitia. When I go to a foreign land, pray to God for my safe return.* He smirked. It may be appropriate, but not reassuring. The song sent the captain's mind to distant shores. He thought of his mother and how determined she had been to make him a priest like her brother. But young Vincent Thompson had liked girls too much. His face lit up as he recollected the mischief of his youth. Nostalgic, he turned the knob of the radio to silence the past. He searched for the latest news, but there was nothing. Under a starless sky lay the dark sea, impregnated with moist air and fog, and avalanches of cotton, a mist too dense to penetrate. Savage waves leapt and descended upon the deck. Below, the mechanic and his assistant vigilantly eyed the engine, which made erratic sounds. Fearlessly, the captain held on to the rudder, growling commands at his six-man crew, until a monumental wave nearly foundered the vessel. Suddenly, a loud cracking sound resounded through the thick air. The mast crashed down onto the deck. "Oh, my leg!" Thompson yelled. A muffled gagging sound came from the captain's throat, pain contorted his face, and his hand fell from the rudder. Had he not been shielded by an iron barrel beside him, both his legs would have been shattered by the broken pole. Masses of water rolled over the deck. Two sailors rushed to lift the mast off his leg. The engine died. Cohen gripped the rudder as the ship, its lights no longer functioning, climbed the waves slowly. Tiny Tom, the second mate, hoisted the broken mast. "Are you alright, sir?"

"Of course I'm alright." With a ferocious look, the captain insisted he felt no pain, but Cohen saw his expression, which belied his words.

"Lean on me, sir," Cohen said, and both men waded across the deck.

Then, "I'll manage by myself," said the captain. "You see that the engine gets started." He limped toward his cabin and felt the stiffness in his bones. *Captain's a tough man,* Dan thought. An image of the captain had formed in his mind when Thompson described the vicious Atlantic storms he had survived, and it had been accurate.

Dan Cohen remembered the day he was interviewed by Vince Thompson. With a duffle bag over one shoulder and a guitar over the other, he had ridden on a Greyhound bus from Florida to New Orleans. In his search for a career as a merchant marine, he had come across some prominent features in the *Mariner*. The picture and name of a seafarer caught his eye: Captain Vincent Thompson, born in 1888 in Boston, Massachusetts, went to sea as a child, became master of his own ship, the *Atlantis,* at twenty-four. Pilot and skipper, he has crossed the Atlantic several times; has a reputation of absolute fearlessness.

CHAPTER THREE

1941

NINA JUMPED OUT OF BED, FRIGHTENED AWAKE BY A RECURRING NIGHTMARE. At daybreak on Tuesday, a day in early March, another storm was swirling over the Aegean Sea with menacing force. In her thin nightgown, Nina flicked her window shutters closed and hurried barefoot to her aunt's bedroom.

Aunt Pipina, awake but still under her covers, whispered, "Child, don't be scared. We have seen storms like this before. Don't be afraid. Just lie next to me here until you are warm. You're shivering. It's too early to get up."

"This seems to be an unusually terrible storm," Nina said, feeling her heart beat. From the large window that faced sea and mountains, she could see the angry winds, which uprooted trees, broke their branches, hurled them into the air, and dropped the debris on the rooftops by the shore. Nina snuggled next to her aunt, still scared of the dream that had awakened her.

"Aunt Pipina, aren't you scared?"

"No." Bad weather never bothered her.

Nina caressed her aunt's face.

"I need to get up and go to church, light candles, and pray for better weather and for peaceful times." Pipina's voice held a sad tone.

"Lesbos is so far away. Do you think we'll be in danger?"

"Only God knows that," Pipina answered as she rolled out of bed, leaving her shape outlined in the sheets.

Nina found Pipina's bed warm and comforting. Though awake, she was still shaken by her dream. Closing her eyes, she remembered: *She was coming home through a howling rainstorm. Her hair was wet and rain dripped down the nape of her neck, trickled down her spine, and crept into her clothes. She was shivering. She heard a voice coming from the barn. Mourtos, her father's manager, stood at the door holding a raincoat. "What are you doing out in the rain? You'll catch pneumonia," he said and dragged her into the barn. He covered her with his coat and held her tightly. "Let me warm you up, sweet Nina," he said and began to kiss her.*

"Get away from me," she screamed. "Your breath smells like the barn."

She awoke startled, soaking in her own perspiration; she could still smell the odor of the barn. Pipina, dressed for church, returned to her bedroom. "Child, you'd better stay in bed for a while. You look terribly pale."

The storm gradually abated; the heavy rain became a thin drizzle and allowed the sun to shine through in soft colors.

Nina sat by the window, watching the cloud formations. Suddenly, her eyes caught sight of her father and Manolis Mourtos. A compellingly handsome man, twenty-nine years old. He was dressed in a lumber jacket and faded jeans. He shook hands with her father and smiled. Nina's father loved Mourtos like a son. Having barred the gate behind them, both men climbed into the wagon harnessed to two mares and headed toward the olive groves. Nina shook her head. *My father would have liked me to be a boy,* she thought. *He would have taken me into the fields and taught me man's work, picking olives. The way he fusses over Mourtos, he treats him like a son. If he only knew the way he looks at me! Lust all over his face! If Papa saw that, he would kill him.*

Momentarily she scanned the fields, a vignette of younger years surfacing in her mind. She was about five, small and frail, a time when Mourtos always accompanied Aunt Pipina and her niece on their journeys to distant places. On one long walk from the mountain of St. Elias on a warm May evening,

Mourtos offered to carry her. Gently, he knelt and adjusted her arms around his neck and gingerly hoisted her onto his shoulders. She loved him, especially when he gave her rides like that. On this day, however, Mourtos was breathing heavily. He caressed her thighs with unusual firmness. Nina didn't think much about it until, as he was bringing her down from his shoulders, she felt him pressing her little body against his heaving chest. He tickled and kissed her neck, and her stomach tightened. "Put me down! You're hurting me!" she screamed. "Mourtos, I don't like you anymore. You smell like onions."

"My shoulders are tired, my sweet," he said blushing. "I'll carry you in my arms."

"I don't want that," Nina said, and clung to her aunt.

From that day onward, Nina distrusted Mourtos, She never spoke of that day to anyone. Over the years of loyal service Mourtos gave to her father's olive groves, Nina developed a distant respect for him. She realized how appreciative her father was to have such a devoted manager and friend. As for Aunt Pipina, she had a tender spot in her heart for Mourtos. She had practically raised him from the time he was a little boy until he reached manhood. He was a friend who never said no to her. But their friendship made Nina somewhat jealous, especially when Pipina praised his virtues. *Lucky is the woman who will marry him some day. He will make a wonderful husband.*

Nina agreed, but had no interest in marrying him. She would never love a man other than Stephen. *I loved only once in my life,* she told herself, and she believed that, for she was determined not to relive such sorrow again.

Regardless of what her father and aunt wished for her, she had decided to devote her life to the church and maybe eventually become a nun. Through her nightgown, she felt a chill in her body; she shivered and hurried back to her room to dress more warmly. Apollo, now a huge black cat, sleeping in his special spot at the foot of her bed, opened his eyes, gave her a don't-disturb-me look, and went back to sleep.

Dismissing thoughts about her father and Mourtos, Nina tied her hair back and slipped into a thick robe. She thought of her father's favorite toy, which was never to be touched by anyone—a telescope he had purchased from Athens. Mischief and curiosity took hold of Nina. As she entered her father's room, deep in a closet she found the hidden treasure, the telescope. She lugged it carefully to the balcony, adjusted it on a tripod, and took a moment to calm her thumping heart. *If my father knew,* she thought, *he'd have a fit.* She looked through the strong lens. "I can see the whole world!" she exclaimed. The town of Moria lay at the foot of a beautiful lavender mountain with two distinct peaks. Midway to the top of the eastern crest nestled St. Mary's Convent. One hundred and fourteen carved stone steps led to a plateau where the pristine chapel stood like a seagull gazing at the ocean below. The land around the convent was desertlike, but the hardworking nuns had turned it into a rich garden of trees, fruits, and flowers.

Nina halted in her survey of the landscape. A strange sight at sea attracted her attention, and she refocused the lens on a large vessel dragging into the harbor of Mytilene, the capital city of Lesbos. One of the two masts stood straight and tall; the other was a mere jagged stump protruding from the deck. At the waterfront, islanders thronged the quay. Nina returned the telescope to the mountains for a while, watching glorious mountain life, goats, sheep, and donkeys. The silvery olive trees added an earthy scent to the air, diffusing the kitchen aromas of pepper, bay leaves, oregano, and garlic that filled the stone-paved streets. Pots of azaleas, carnations, and leafy sweet basil decorated the balconies. Young women with braided hair, colorful handmade dresses, and leather sandals scurried home with ceramic pitchers of cold water, drawn from a nearby well. Nina could spend hours observing the scenery, but something made her turn the telescope back to the broken mast. *Definitely not a Greek ship,* she thought. Scanning the vessel, she discovered the name, *North Star.*

CHAPTER FOUR

NEAR 2:00 P.M. THAT SAME DAY, after a long stay in her garden pruning rosebushes, hungry and tired, Nina left lightheaded. She lost her balance and nearly fell as she climbed the stairway to her room. She took a glimpse of her face in the mirror. No color. With clothes on she crawled in her bed. Aunt Pipina overheard Nina's hurried steps and followed her.

"Child, is anything wrong? You look so pale."

"I'm a little dizzy."

Pipina touched Nina's forehead. "I think you're running a fever," she said. She excused herself and came back quickly, applying home remedies, compresses of vinegar to reduce the fever and chamomile for a dry throat. She sat next to her bed and watched Nina fall into a deep sleep.

Wednesday at dawn, Pipina checked her niece's forehead. The fever was gone. Relieved, she decided to go to church. Although she had slept very little the previous night, she wanted to attend morning services.

Papavasile, Moria's priest, entered St. Basil's Church to commence the Office of Matins, a service he performed each morning of his priestly life. Something was different this morning. Approaching the sanctuary, he saw a million pieces of glass shattered over the altar. An olive tree branch had fallen through a stained-glass window and landed before the icon of Christ.

In shock, Papavasile began to remove the glass, repeating to himself, "Jesus Christ conquers and defeats all evil."

On weekdays, church attendance was minimal, but Papavasile maintained the melody of the liturgy and smiled when he saw Alexis beside Dimitri, the cantor. The six-foot man with the perfect mustache was mumbling verses. He had come to church today to get holy water to sprinkle over his remodeled American café, or, as he called it, his *Kafeneion,* which, apart from its excellent coffee, served the best wine in town. By the time Pipina arrived, more than seventy people, more women than men, occupied the front part of the church. Pipina took her usual place near the cantor, where she enjoyed humming the Byzantine chant. Nodding pleasantly at the cantor, Dimitri, Papavasile's future son-in-law, she opened her prayer book. As the priest intoned the litany of peace, he paused. Silence prevailed. *Is something wrong with Papavasile?* whispered some elderly women. Pipina turned toward the priest with concern. She noticed his meditative expression. In reverie, she closed her eyes. She felt sure that he, like many other men in Moria, was thinking about the encroaching Nazis.

Papavasile noticed more wrinkles in his hands as he turned the pages of the Bible. *Soon this war against Mussolini's injustice will be over, which has been scourging our homeland for the past five months. Rifles, machine guns, and cannons will stop firing, and the young men will return home. Marriages will occur, cradles will be filled with babies, and I will perform many christenings. Then I will no longer wear dark purple vestments, the color of mourning, but bright colors of green, red, sky blue, and gold. New life and joy will return to my flock in Moria. Already we are mourning the loss of eleven men killed in Albania.* With a bittersweet smile, he petitioned the icon of Christ, "Enough of this, Lord."

Pipina, vivacious in her middle fifties, was the last to leave the church. She longed to talk to the priest. Over her left arm she carried a folded purple cloth she had embroidered for the altar. Lent had already started, and she had vowed to make this offering to the glory of God. Gratefully, the priest thanked her and asked about Nina.

"She will be in church next Sunday," she said with evident affection in her hazel eyes as she kissed the priest's hand. Spiritually lifted, she hurried home to tell her niece that Papavasile had asked for her.

Pipina was a stunning, distinguished woman. Tall, fine-boned, and slender, her honey-streaked silver hair was swept up into an elegant bun, making her appear taller. Time had encircled her gently, had enriched and deepened her beauty as the years tiptoed past her. Her eyes and face reflected a past of transfiguring, even painful events. Grief had left its scars on both sides of her mouth. Time had left at least a few footprints in its passage. Pipina's curious nose could smell, at a distance, any strange thing on the island. On her way back home, she saw the *North Star* in the harbor. The American flag waved at the top of the mast. *Perhaps our American allies are here to protect us from this crazy war,* she thought.

Before sunset, Pipina sat on her balcony facing the Aegean Sea and the mountains of Turkey at the far end. This hour was sweet on the small island. The breeze wafted the evening balsam of the pines. Slowly sipping the traditional demitasse of Greek coffee, she indulged in thought. *What am I to do with my niece? Girls of her age ought to be married. Like pears when they get to be too ripe, they lose their taste. Nobody wants them,* she worried. *My stubborn brother thinks no man in Moria is worthy to marry his daughter. We have Manolis Mourtos, a handsome, honest man. Could my brother truly consider him as his son-in-law or is he hoping for a prince to come along on a white steed? Who could sway his mind?* Pursing her lips tightly, she smirked. *Nina suffers and runs to the convent for comfort. What can an aunt do? Please, God, show me the way.* She made the sign of the cross upon herself.

Nina had closed herself in her bedroom again and refused to eat. *Nina needs a doctor.* Determined to discover the cause of Nina's depression, Pipina finally sent Mourtos to the city of Mytilene to ask Dr. Joseph Andrew to make a house call. Not being a mother herself, her maternal instincts found fulfillment in Nina. Savoring the last drop of coffee, she thought, *My niece is tormented, Lord,* and crossing her hands over her breast to soothe her anguish, she wondered, in the tradition of older Greek women, whether her brother's sins as well as her own were the cause of Nina's condition.

Caught up in a nightmarish memory of childhood, a frenzy of excess, her chest pain became real. Her prayers referred to the Penitential Psalm: *I know my transgression, O Lord, and my sin is ever before me.* Clouds, like wisps of cotton, trailed across the indigo sky. Pipina observed the formations in her search for some significant sign. As she stood up to return to her chores, she felt blood rushing in her ears, her heartbeat, the pulse in her wrist, and a tinge of lingering pain in her lower back. Pipina found her niece buried awake under the covers. "You look rested," she lied.

"But I feel so weak."

Worried, Pipina touched her forehead and said, "Do you think you still have a fever? Last night you were sizzling."

Nina shook her head. "No. I have no strength to get out of bed."

"I'll make you something to eat."

"I don't feel like eating anything."

Pipina, concerned about Nina's paleness, said, "You may need some fresh air."

"Not today."

"But I saw Mourtos preparing the horses. He said he could take you for a ride by the sea."

"No, thank you. I don't feel well. I need to sleep for a while."

"Then I'll tell him you won't be going," Pipina said. She wanted her niece to be with Mourtos and tried to encourage such opportunities to get her out of her room.

"You may as well stay put this evening. Dr. Andrew may be visiting us," Pipina said. "It's time that he took a good look at you." She could tell that Nina was annoyed that her aunt had sent for the doctor without asking her first.

"He has been our family doctor since you were a child," Pipina said, trying to disguise her deep concern.

"He can't do anything for me," Nina protested.

"It won't hurt to have an examination, child. Maybe he can take a look at my old bones also," she added with a grin.

"Good, Aunt Pipina! Then he can examine you."

Smiles enveloped both women as they embraced each other. "Aunt Pipina, I love you so much."

CHAPTER FIVE

THAT MORNING, Captain Thompson had limped on deck to view the harbor. Although the pain in his injured leg was excruciating, he refused to accept Cohen's advice to go to the hospital. He was in agony when he moved, but he maintained an invincible look in his eyes. Sixty-one years old, Captain Thompson was alive to see yet another war.

Each day, Hitler's mechanized army furrowed through European towns and cities. However, to the captain and his crew, who spent most of their days at sea, the reality of war was somewhat remote. The blue Mediterranean waters where Thompson explored had not seen a single Nazi. Until the previous day, he had scoffed at Hitler's campaign to conquer Europe. But after midnight, a message in Morse code reached his ship. He had already played his part in the First World War; he did not want a part in this one. His interests were simply commercial: tobacco, olive oil, white marble, and anything else that would ensure his American dream—a wealthy retirement.

Cohen worried after hearing the news. "We are on an extremely important mission, the Aegean Alliance. We are at war," the captain said, sighing as he sat on the stool that Cohen had brought for him. "We're in the war. At 2:00 a.m., we were drafted into the U.S. Navy." From his shirt pocket, he pulled out a folded piece of yellow paper.

"Read this," he said. "I was hoping not to have to show this telegram to anyone."

Cohen read silently.

Captain Vincent Thompson:

Your trip to Greece and the Middle East has been approved on one condition. Stop. If and when America declares war on Germany, your ship and crew will be under the command of the U.S. Navy. Stop. Meanwhile, photograph the islands and search for strategic spots for our military bases in the Aegean.

Cohen folded the telegram and handed it back while observing the captain's face. Silently, he watched and waited, wondering what the captain was thinking. The gleam in the captain's eye was not one of fear or disappointment. It was a gleam that traveled to his past, when he had joined the Navy as a young man. He had always loved adventure.

The captain lit his pipe, leaned back, and exhaled a cloud of smoke. He said, "World War I, that's when I nearly lost my life in a shipwreck. A young sailor with your looks, risking his own life, ran through fire and rescued me."

Listening to Thompson's recollection, Dan thought of his father and how he, too, had risked his life to save a stranger. Recalling his father's death triggered unexpected sadness. The nonsense of war was beyond comprehension, killing young men and leaving behind widows and orphans.

"The chances of them coming to the Greek islands are remote," the captain said. In a grimace of pain he tried to stand on his injured leg. It felt stiff.

"Let me give you a hand, captain," said Cohen.

"I'll be okay." A proud man, the captain towered over his ship as he took a few limping steps. Then, with a commanding hand, turning back to his first mate the gruff sea wolf said, "There's a lot of work to do here. Don't worry about me. I want you to go out there and find a timber tall and straight to be fashioned into a mast."

"In the meantime, we'll bind this broken foremast until the ship can be dry-docked and repaired," said Tiny Tom, who approached from a nearby cabin.

"Good," the captain said. "And all you sailors are to behave while you're ashore. Stretch your legs, but keep your pants on."

"Yes, sir." Cohen saluted, then winked slyly at Tiny Tom. The aging and ageless captain, whose eyes were as dark blue as the oceans he had crossed, looked at his men with pride. "In every port there is love, and in every port there is trouble."

"We'll be careful," Cohen said.

———

Early the next morning, Cohen stood on deck, scanning the swarthy faces of the islanders on the pier and grasped at some familiar phrases as they shouted to each other. His eyes were filled with wonder. He understood well enough what they were saying:

"*Then enai Ellines*" (This crew isn't Greek).

"*Eglezi-British*" (maybe).

"*Rossi*" (Russians)?

"*Ohi, Americani, re*" (No, Americans).

Cohen saw a young boy pointing at him, and he waved, smiling pleasantly.

"*Yiassas paidia*" (Hi, boys).

"I know some English," said Takis, a teenager with big brown eyes, wearing a white shirt, short blue pants, and sandals. The harbor was a favorite rendezvous for him and his three friends every morning on their way to school.

"Go on, Americanaki. Ask that sailor," one of his friends said, pushing him forward.

"Hey, sailor. Are you British or American?" Takis asked, trying his English.

"American," shouted Cohen and pointed to their flag.

"I'm American, too," Takis said proudly.

"You are? You look Greek to me."

"I'm Greek, but I was born in America and that makes me an American."

"So what are you doing here?

"I was going to ask you the same question," said Takis.

"The captain wants to fill the *North Star* with olive oil."

"Why? Don't you have oil in America?"

Impressed with Takis' ability to speak English but anxious to go, his friends grabbed him by the arm and said, "Come on, Americanaki. We'll be late for school!"

Cohen perused the island, drinking in the sight. What he saw made his heart leap. Color was everywhere, from the bobbing blue boats to the white-washed houses with their flower-filled window boxes, to the emerald and purple hills. *There's something special about this island.* Not a cloud in the sky, and every tree, shrub, and flower bathed in sunlight and morning crispness.

Perched at the side of a curving slope, Moria, a suburb of Lesbos, was nestled among clusters of olive and fruit trees. A town of matchless serenity, Moria combined impressive traditional and modern houses of limestone with red ceramic rooftops. *My Uncle Thano probably lives in one of those houses. I hope I can find him. I wonder if he'll recognize me.* Dan recounted those few but treasured times when his father told him about Lesbos. *Someday, when you are old enough, you might go to Lesbos and meet my brother and his family. There are beautiful girls on the island. You might even marry one of them and bring her to America.* Stratis Papadopoulos, his father, had been sixteen when he left Lesbos to seek his fortune in America. He was the son of a priest named Daniel. Stratis had to explain to Americans that Greek Orthodox priests are allowed to marry. Stratis Papadopoulos learned his name was not one an American could remember or even pronounce. When a New England captain hired him to work on a transatlantic ship, it was with the stipulation that he would change his name. Stratis Papadopoulos went to the nearest library and asked, "What's the correct name for the son of a priest?" The librarian, a rabbi's wife, had replied matter-of-factly, "Cohen." It was then that his father adopted the name Charles Cohen. Five years later, he married Rita, a German maid aboard the ship. Life on the ship was secure. Food, clothing, and money were abundant. The birth of a son made the couple's contentment complete. Charles and Rita had plans to return to Lesbos someday and build a house with a big yard filled with trees and flowers.

Now, as he took in Lesbos' beauty, he wondered, *Have I come to Lesbos to fulfill my father's wish and carry on his dream? Have I come to his native land to rekindle my belief in a God who directs destiny?*

Eager for shore leave, the sailors secured the ropes, and the islanders looped them around the stanchions. All the while, Cohen cautioned his mates in an imitation of the captain's voice: "Keep your pants on."

Cohen returned to his cabin to estimate the damage suffered by the ship and to outline the necessary repairs. Through a skylight opening onto the lower deck, he heard Thompson's commands and the sailors' raucous laughter, and then a heavy groan and limping steps outside his door. Thompson came in and sat down in an armchair riveted to the floor as his first mate placed a low wooden stool with a pillow under his injured foot.

"It's so swollen. Does it hurt much, sir?"

"No. I'm not worrying about this old leg of mine. It's my age I'm thinking about. I'm getting old, Danny."

"Does a seaman ever get old, captain?"

"Today I feel old," he responded, concealing his agony.

"Sir, we must get you to a hospital. That leg needs care."

The captain, comforted by the attention, filled and lit his pipe. Puffing out clouds of smoke, eyes sharp, he asked, "When are you going to take photographs of the island?"

"In a couple of days. Let me tour the island, make a few inquiries about oil. I don't want to look suspicious."

The captain stretched the injured leg, fingers twined on his pipe. "I need pictures of potentially strategic places on this island."

"I have enough film and a good camera."

"Good."

"Let's hope the Nazis won't come this far, at least not until we have left."

"Enemy aircraft have been flying over the Aegean islands," the captain said and frowned. Before embarking on this trip, he had been told by Merchant Marine Enterprises that he was in danger. Hitler had threatened to conquer all of Europe. At the time, Thompson had laughed and said,

"Hitler won't last three months. Besides, he wouldn't think of the Aegean islands."

"I'll make sure to discover strategic spots," Cohen said, bringing the captain back to the matter at hand.

"You said your father grew up on this island?"

"Yes, sir. I have an uncle somewhere here. His name is Thano."

"Then you must find him."

"That's what I plan to do, captain."

"The villagers will think you are just a visitor, looking for a relative."

Cohen nodded with a smile. His father often spoke about his big mustached brother who wore a turban and was a great storyteller. He felt excited at the prospect of finding him, and wondered if he would resemble his father. "I don't know if he'll be of any help to our mission."

The captain cleared his throat. "Well, let's get back to the olive oil. I want the best you can find on the island."

"Aye, sir."

The captain drew on his pipe, but kept his eyes on Cohen.

"Nobody will suspect oil merchants."

"Aye, sir," Cohen repeated. His heart swelled with devotion to Captain Thompson. He was proud the captain had entrusted him with their secret mission. Thompson frowned as struggled to get up from his chair. Cohen reached out to help him, but the captain shook his head. "I'll manage," he said. "Now, keep your eyes open for a new mast."

"I think I've spotted one already, captain," Cohen said.

CHAPTER SIX

MOURTOS RETURNED FROM MYTILENE and announced to Pipina that Dr. Andrew would be arriving at the Cambas estate around 4:00 p.m. Concerned, he asked if there was something seriously wrong with Nina. Pipina sensed beyond any form of loyalty Mourtos' deeper feelings for her niece and said, "Nina is in her room resting, but she will be alright. Don't worry. Tomorrow or the next day, get the mares ready and plan to take her for a long ride. She needs to get out of the house and get some fresh air."

Thrilled by her suggestion, he said, "You're a wonderful aunt. I'll take Nina anywhere she wants to go."

Mourtos had been thirteen when Cambas hired him as an errand boy. Pipina had called him *Parayio,* an endearment meaning "like a son." Tall, thin, and swarthy, he looked older than thirteen. Nina was not more than six then, and he carried her on his shoulders. Affectionately, he called her *Boubouki,* rosebud. Now, almost twenty-nine, Mourtos was an exceptionally good-looking man. His Boubouki had indeed blossomed, and he secretly nurtured his attraction to her in his heart. But Pipina knew his secret. He no longer loved a little girl; he was incurably in love with a woman who kept her distance from him. *Even though she is very rich and I am very poor, my wealth lies in my honesty,* Mourtos told himself. He knew that Pipina trusted him, and he hoped that at some future date she would be happy to have him as her nephew. Even now he wished he could call her Aunt Pipina, but his peasant heart respected boundaries. He must not jeopardize his relationship with his boss.

That night, before the doctor's visit, Pipina went to her bedroom and lit a candle; she was determined to remain on her knees in prayer until it burned out. On her knees in front of the icon of Jesus, Pipina remained silent for a long time. Eyes focused on the face of Jesus, she prayed, "Show my niece the way, dear Lord. Send a caring man to love and to cherish her. It's time for her to leave this household and make her own family." Her heart waited for the Lord's voice. "Unless you have other plans for her," she said, sensing a tingling in her chest. The icon suddenly took on a reddish color, and what appeared to be drops of perspiration fell from the forehead of Jesus. "Lord, You agonize with me . . . but You do have a plan for all of us. But what is your plan for Nina?" Pipina covered her face with her hands and let her head touch the floor as she whispered, "Hasten Your help and bring peace to our tormented souls."

When she lifted her head, the whole scene of her niece's confession unfolded before her eyes and Pipina knew exactly what had occurred, for she had seen the white robe hidden in the back of Nina's closet.

———

Eight months before, Nina returned from a fifteen-day retreat at St. Mary's Convent. It was an annual retreat, attended by many young women. Nina had confessed her secret love to Mother Superior, an elderly nun known for her spirituality. "Oh, Holy Mother, I have lost the greatest love I have ever known. Since his death seven years ago, my heart has been tormented," she wept.

"But seven years ago you were so young!"

"Old enough to be in love with a beautiful young man. I wanted to marry him someday, but he was drowned at sea."

Her eyes widening, Mother Superior said, "You don't mean Stephen the fisherman?"

"Yes," said Nina with an agonized smile. "I had such intense feelings for him. Often, against my father's orders, I snuck out to be with him. He was older, but it didn't matter to me. Secretly, he taught me how to ride a horse. He told me of his sea adventures, he sang to me, I still hear the echo of his voice in my mind, and he made me laugh. Then one evening, shortly before his fatal fishing trip, we kissed, and . . . ." Tears flowed down her cheeks. "We were not seen, except by the moon that had just risen over the mountaintop."

"A kiss is sign of love, not a sin," Mother Superior said.

"But there is more, Holy Mother." Nina sighed, wiping her eyes.

"Go on, child. Our loving God is also a merciful Father."

"After we kissed, I wanted more. I wanted him to take me on his boat and make love to me. I begged him."

"Did he?" The sound of her voice evoked guilt.

"No. I longed to surrender my whole body to him, but he said, 'No, my sweet Nina, we are not ready for this kind of love yet.' Passionately, he took me in his arms and caressed me for a long time."

Mother Superior shook her head and said, "Sometimes what seems like surrender isn't surrender at all, my dear. It is what is going on in our souls. It is about accepting our life and being true to it, whatever the pain, because the pain of not being true to it is far, far greater."

"Wise words, Holy Mother. But my pain is deep, and I only feel some relief when I think that my soul belongs to Stephen and to God."

"Nina, I know you respect me. I know you find comfort in our convent. I have seen your eyes during our services, but what you need is to trust the voice of your soul." She blinked and said, "What do you think brings you here so often?"

Nina remained silent, as her eyes observed Mother Superior's world. A fragrant smell of incense permeated the simple paneled cell, which contained old oak furniture—a narrow bed, a dresser, two chairs, a small sofa—a large icon of Christ on the wall, and a small oil lamp on a shelf. The simplicity was soothing. She could not articulate an answer to Mother Superior's question.

Mother Superior pulled a pair of spectacles from the inner pocket of her cassock and adjusted them to her oval face. She looked at Nina, but her perceptive nature scanned Nina's soul. "You have had two significant losses in your life. You lost your mother at an early age, and at the prime of your youth, you lost your first and only love. To be true to this pain, your soul is seeking healing. No one can possibly do that for you except the Great Healer."

"Holy Mother, what do you suggest I do?"

"Have you ever thought of joining our convent?"

"Many times. I know there is peace here, but my father doesn't want to hear about it."

Sensing Nina's sincerity, Mother Superior said, "Our Loving Father in heaven has a plan for you."

Making the sign of the cross on herself, Nina said, "I believe He does, Holy Mother, but what is it? Will I ever know?"

Mother Superior lifted herself from the chair, her knees creaking, and from her dresser she unfolded a pure white robe, a belt, and a veil. "Put this on for a few minutes and see how you feel."

Hesitantly, Nina put on the robe, covered her head, and tied the ends of the veil under her chin. Mother Superior watched her with a genuine smile and said, "He makes our souls whiter than snow. This is the code for a novice. How does it feel?"

Nina smoothed the robe against her body and said, "I don't know how to explain it. But I feel a calming under my skin, throughout my body. It feels good."

"It's the enveloping grace of God. Take it home with you, and when you visit us again, you can wear it while you are here. It's a gift to remind you of our talk. And when you feel sad or unhappy, put it on. It will bring you peace, the peace of God, peace that surpasses all understanding."

"Thank you." Nina reached out, took Mother Superior's hand, and kissed it.

———

Pipina, a religious woman herself, was sympathetic to her niece's longing for comfort, but she couldn't help but wonder why a beautiful woman like Nina would want to be a nun and remain barren. Orphan or poor girls of the island found the convent a secure resort, but not her niece. She had more wealth than all the other girls of the island combined. Nina needed a man who would walk and make the ground tremble, a solid, handsome, robust man who would love her. Then she would definitely forget about the convent and Stephen.

An epidemic had left Lesbos with a large number of orphaned children in desperate need of shelter. Papavasile was able to place eleven orphans with a few caring families. Archbishop Iakovos took eight to his home, yet there were still others roaming in the streets. Nina asked her father to house a few orphans in their villa, but he didn't think it was a good idea. It was then she told her aunt, "When I become a nun, I can open many doors. I could appeal to the wealthy of Lesbos and ask them to contribute for the orphans." Pipina nodded, but her reaction was lukewarm. When she told her brother that Nina had thoughts of becoming a nun, he did not consider his daughter's involvement with the convent to be serious. *Her idea of becoming a nun will wear off,* he thought. Pipina did not tell him that Nina also entertained fantasies of becoming the head of an orphanage.

One day before noon, Cambas had returned home unexpectedly. Pipina had gone shopping. He came to pick up a purchase order he had been working on the previous evening to sell a thousand gallons of olive oil. In the master bathroom, he found his daughter dressed in a nun's cassock, glowing and standing in front of the mirror, lost in thought. She had covered her beautiful hair with a white silk hood, almost hiding her smiling face, making her eyes and thin, Sapphic nose look like a Byzantine icon. He could hardly control his emotions. "Take that thing off!" he shouted furiously. "I don't ever want to see you in that silly garment again—ever! Do you understand?"

"Father, how can you say such a thing?" Nina stared at him wide-eyed. She remained still, holding her tears back.

"Off! Off!" he shouted, until she took off the hood and fled crying in fright to her own bedroom.

CHAPTER SEVEN

THAT NIGHT, IMPECCABLY DRESSED in his dark gray suit and red tie, Costas Cambas welcomed Dr. Joseph Andrew to his home. His smile hid the nagging discomfort he felt in his stomach. He could not admit to himself his fear that something was mentally wrong with his only heir. Pipina led the doctor into Nina's room. She had faith in this heavy-set, ruddy-faced man, with eyebrows so bushy they looked like misplaced mustaches. An odor of medicine followed in his wake. He pulled his stethoscope from his medicine bag, puffed out his cheeks, and said, "My! My! You are prettier than ever, Miss Nina Cambas, but why so pale? What is wrong?" He placed the stethoscope under her bra before she had a chance to answer.

"Do you keep this thing in an icebox?" She shivered with a giggle.

Pipina had joined her brother and anxiously waited in his study. An antique mahogany grandfather clock ticked monotonously in the hallway. Hands folded behind his back, Cambas paced by his desk and looked at his watch. Nineteen minutes had passed since she had brought the doctor to Nina's room, and it seemed like nineteen hours. Another five minutes passed before the doctor came out of Nina's room to meet Cambas and Pipina in his study. Their sad faces revealed profound concern.

"Relax, it's nothing too serious," the doctor said. "Nina will be up and around in no time. But if I might speak to you privately, Mr. Cambas." Pipina left the room, closing the door behind her, realizing that a man-to-man talk was important to her brother. But she paused behind the door, hoping to hear what the doctor would say to her brother, but he spoke too softly.

Dr. Andrew gazed out the window. The dark sky was studded with stars. He sat down on a walnut chair and, crossing his legs, sized up the oil merchant while admiring the molded paneling and his hand-carved furniture. A man of power who possesses wealth and is well respected in his town. Small vials of olive oil were arrayed on Cambas' desk, samples, the doctor thought. He noticed family pictures on the walls and a recent portrait of Nina, which hung crookedly on the wall behind the desk.

Cambas lowered himself into his favorite leather chair. "Doctor, what is the matter with my daughter? Tell me, and I'll do anything." He felt the blood draining from his face.

Dr. Andrew reassured him at once that Nina was in good physical condition, but, "I shall not speak in riddles. You have a pressing problem on your hands, Mr. Cambas."

"Doctor, please tell me the truth. I want to know." Seeing the doctor in deep thought, raised brows, a trace of concern in his eyes, he worried.

"It's a case of latent adolescent confusion, hormonal changes, and depression. She needs help." *How can I explain adolescent maladjustment to a wealthy oil merchant?*

Cambas' jaw dropped. "What kind of medical mumbo-jumbo is that?" he asked.

"Are you aware that your daughter is determined to become a nun?"

Cambas scowled and sank back in his chair. *How could this silly notion be affecting her health?* "I know Nina finds the idea of devoting herself to the convent appealing. But she will soon outgrow this ridiculous fantasy, don't you think?"

"It is possible she may not," the doctor divulged. "Her desire seems very strong, and she is extremely upset that you might oppose her plans."

In utter disbelief of the diagnosis, Cambas vowed to take his daughter to Athens and find better doctors. He remained silent for what seemed a long time. Then he got up and, with his hands folded behind his back, paced the length of his desk, aware that his black shoes were squeaking. He ran his hand nervously over his neatly combed hair, then smoothed his salt-and-pepper mustache. With a heavy heart, he glanced out the window, pondering the diagnosis. His head shook disapprovingly. Pulling a rope, a drape covered the window, closing out the world. He straightened a framed picture on the wall behind his desk, a photograph of Nina taken on her first day at Arsakio, a girls' school in Athens. A soft smile crossed his face as he recalled Nina's excitement, a zest for adventure the camera had captured. Then Cambas thought of the time when he had first reprimanded Nina for her wish to become a nun. His leather chair puffed as he sat down again. Beads of sweat trickled down his forehead, and he wiped his face with a large white handkerchief. He noticed the doctor move in his chair.

"But why, Doctor Andrew? The convent is for poor or neglected girls," he said, accentuating each word. "How could she possibly leave me and everything I have created for her?"

"If we believe in human destiny, someday she must leave you."

Unconvinced, Cambas nodded. "Yes, but I cannot bear to think of it."

"For her sake, you must."

"I should permit her to carry out this impulsive desire?" He felt his face flushing.

Dr. Andrew smiled, pulled out his watch, and looked at the time. He could not stay much longer, and he wished to go. *It may astonish Cambas, but I must tell him my true diagnosis.* He looked straight into Cambas' eyes and said, "Everyone in the town of Moria knows you have discouraged young men from courting Nina. You probably think no man in Lesbos is good enough for her, and so you have overprotected her. I don't blame you. She's not just pretty, she has a beautiful heart. But now you must set your daughter free." The doctor's face glowed with a grace Cambas had not seen in him before. He stared at him, his mouth too dry to speak.

"I'm sorry, but I must tell you what a fool you have been, a loving fool, my dear man," the doctor said. "Although you have given Nina everything, you have denied her the most important thing that can happen to a young woman. You have denied her the chance to fall in love."

Cambas wanted to jump up and shout at the doctor. His insides quivered with rage. *How dare this old wizard presume to tell* me *how to be* a *father!* But deep inside, he knew Dr. Andrew had a good point. So he held his tongue and waited for the doctor to speak again.

"Many people suffer slow death, Mr. Cambas. Without love, they lose the will to live. Let your daughter meet a nice young man and get married. It's time."

"But Nina is not well," said Cambas, rising from his chair. "Didn't you see how pale she is? And she looks sad most of the time."

"That's true, and love is the medicine I have prescribed. Good night, Mr. Cambas." The doctor walked out the door and gently closed it behind him.

Cambas thought for a while, rubbing his neck. It hurt.

CHAPTER EIGHT

CONFUSED, COSTAS CAMBAS took several hesitant steps back and forth before pausing again in front of the window. As he pulled the drapes completely open, he saw the portico's light subdued. The doctor's voice echoed in his mind, *You have denied her the chance to fall in love.* The force of those words pierced him, pushing at the limit of his tolerance and composure. His tormented soul knew that he was strict and overprotective. "Pipina!" he shouted.

The door opened, and his sister crept in apprehensively and asked, "What did the doctor say?"

"Pipina, Dr. Andrew is insane."

"You look upset."

"Enraged. You call a medical man for advice, and he turns out to be a matchmaker."

"What do you mean?"

"Let your daughter fall in love. Love has magical healing powers," he mimicked the doctor's voice.

My dear brother, it's about time someone told you about love, Pipina thought.

"Don't you have anything to say?" he asked with a scowl.

She knew that he wanted her to agree with him, but she did not answer him. Costas Cambas was usually an even-tempered man, and it frightened her now to see his distress. Inhaling deeply, she searched his eyes.

"Let Nina fall in love, and she will be alright," he scratched his forehead and mumbled again the doctor's advice.

"He might have a good point," Pipina said.

"Ha. You don't know. He could have prescribed the same medicine for you."

"Nonsense," said Pipina with a glare of annoyance. Her brother didn't flinch, but returned her stare, until she backed down, shaking her head and thinking what to say.

Costas, her only sibling, was not in the habit of emoting. She had watched over him after his wife, Mercina, had died and seen him almost paralyzed with grief. Unlike other men, he had decided never to remarry. Although Pipina thought he needed a wife and Nina needed a mother, he did not believe he could love another woman. When he felt lonely, he sought out Pipina, and he relied on her advice. Her brother not only respected her but counted on her to raise Nina and to run his home. Pipina was largely responsible for the high esteem that the islanders had for Costas Cambas, the olive oil merchant, and everybody knew it. That esteem was so great that it let them forgive him for going off to America, and even accepting citizenship of that faraway country.

Cambas watched Pipina, whose face was roughened with grief. Despite his agitation, he was determined to hear her out.

"The doctor is a smart man." She crossed herself. "Thank God for bringing him our way. He knows what he is talking about. He is not old-fashioned like us, and he is honest. Nina must get married and leave behind this boring, archaic existence. This is only for us, the old fossils."

"Splendid," said Cambas. "You and the doctor are convinced you have all the answers, but you are forgetting something very important. Over the last few weeks, you have visited every shrine and every festivity on the island to offer vows and prayers for Nina's health. Have you prayed for what you really believe will make her well?"

"What are you talking about?" she asked.

"A man!" Cambas erupted. "A man good enough for our Nina."

"I always think of men, for Nina, I mean."

"We only need one man, but a good one."

Pipina hesitated for a moment. "You're right," she confessed. "My dear brother, why search for water outside when the fountain is in our own backyard?"

"Leave your riddles alone and tell me what's on your mind."

"What's wrong with Manolis Mourtos? He's honest, healthy, handsome, and hardworking. Besides, he loves you like a father."

"I hope you are joking."

"Not at all."

"Nonsense," shouted Cambas. "Are you out of your mind? If it weren't for me, Mourtos would be a mere peasant."

"Shame on you. How can you talk like that about Mourtos, who adores you and loves our family? He would make a great husband."

"If you like him so much, maybe you should marry him," Cambas said, mocking her.

"You're being ridiculous. But if I were Nina's age, I would marry him tomorrow."

Pipina knew when to stop a risky conversation. Her brother's defiance told her she had made a mistake in even mentioning Mourtos. "I'd better go and check on dinner." She knew he would be unwilling to talk to her that evening. Over dinner, he would glare at her once or twice and harrumph. He would withdraw behind a newspaper, munching on walnuts, finally retiring to his bedroom with a grumpy "Good night." She braced herself for such an evening, but for the moment she would leave him alone in his study. As she held the doorknob, her irritation at his stubborn pride got the better of her.

"You know, my dear brother, were it not for you, we would all be mere peasants."

His eyes flashed with anger, but before he could react, Pipina had vanished. Despite his ire, he could not help but smile at her spirit and wit. *Women!*

Cambas sighed. *Ah, Pipina, we have been through so much together.* His mind shuttled back to the time when the two of them had gone to live with their uncle Demetrios, their father's brother. When he was only fourteen and Pipina twelve, their father had been killed in Asia Minor by the Turks. Two years earlier, their mother had died of tuberculosis soon after the Greek-Turkish war of 1912. Demetrios, a bachelor and the oldest brother in the Cambas family, had a beautiful, palatial home a stone's throw from the beach. Because he also had a full-time maid who could look after him, he was chosen as their guardian. Costas and Pipina had been traumatized by their parents' deaths. They clung to each other from the day they learned their mother had also died. With deep affection, Costas was very protective of Pipina. She was terrified of storms, and whenever wind and rain gripped the island, he would hold and kiss her until she grew calm. With her dark eyes and honey-colored hair, Pipina was a lovely girl, and she blossomed into womanhood at a young age.

Akakios, a monk well known on Lesbos for his prophecies, predicted the island would someday sink into the sea. It so happened that on her thirteenth birthday, Pipina woke to torrential rains. By evening, the rivers had over-flowed their banks. Brother and sister were alone in the vast mansion by the sea, for Demetrios had gone to his farm in Moria. Three of his sheep had died, and he went to see what he could do. Costas and Pipina sat in the living room by the fireplace eating roasted chestnuts, dried figs, and walnuts. Pipina had made a pot of sage tea, and Costas discovered a bottle of cognac. "A few drops will make our tea taste better," he had said.

"Oh, good," said Pipina, licking her lips. To quiet her fear of the howling winds, she was trying to be festive.

"Happy birthday, my dear sister." Costas kissed her on both cheeks.

She leaned gratefully against his shoulder. Suddenly a thunderous sound seized the house, causing fear and casting Pipina into his arms.

"This must be the end. We'll drown!" she cried.

"Kyrie Eleison," he whispered. Pipina joined him in asking the Lord for mercy. After what seemed like hours, the two realized no water was entering the house. Costas crept to the door and peeked out. A rickety wooden shack where their uncle stored his fishing tools had collapsed. "We're going to drown," he said, teasing his sister. But the rain gradually ceased. "We're not going to drown," Pipina repeated.

That night, Costas and Pipina slept in the same bed. Having drunk what was left in the bottle, they snuggled together for warmth, and Pipina kept tickling and teasing her brother. He pinned her arms to the bed, and she struggled, laughing. As they wrestled and giggled, they rubbed their bodies together. Soon, the wrestling stopped. Insatiable desire had scared the young pair.

"Dear God, forgive me," Pipina said, and both wallowed in heavy guilt feelings and swore never to reveal their sinful experience.

Costas Cambas shook his head to vanquish the memory. It had only been one scary night, he did not hurt his sister, but he was still tormented by guilty thoughts. A burning sensation in his stomach kept him striding across the room and glancing out of the window, forcing away the memory.

CHAPTER NINE

COHEN FINALLY PERSUADED the captain to get medical attention for his leg. He hired an old 1926 Ford that had been converted into a taxi and took him to Bostaneion, the only hospital in Lesbos, situated on top of a hill overlooking the Aegean Sea. The administrator, realizing that the patient was an American, drafted the best personnel available. The captain was immediately taken to an airy room with a large window facing the sea. Cohen stayed with him until a doctor and an English-speaking nurse arrived. The nurse, a shapely, rosy-cheeked brunette, interpreted the doctor's questions, and when the captain heard her British accent, his ears perked up and healing began. He looked at his mate with a teasing twinkle in his eyes, and Cohen knew the captain's thoughts: *I wouldn't mind spending a few weeks here, provided I had this nurse by my bedside.*

In the afternoon, Cohen took the same taxi and drove along the shore road. He gazed at the turquoise waters of the Aegean and felt the velvety air soothing his soul. The parting words of the captain still echoed in his ears: *Now you're in charge of the* North Star. *We have a mission—photos, contacts, strategic posts, and a ship to carry several barrels of the best olive oil.* Mindful of his responsibilities, Cohen also felt empowered by the trust that Captain Vincent Thompson had put in him.

In the evening, Cohen and Tiny Tom dropped into Alexis' American Café. It appeared to have been recently renovated. Cohen instantly noticed the American flag and Franklin D. Roosevelt's portrait, complete with presidential smile and cigar, hanging in a prominent place above a tall marble table. He elbowed his colleague and both men smiled. *But why is a guitar hanging beside the flag?* he wondered. It must be special.

Alexis was in his early forties and still single. When asked if he'd ever settle down and marry, his answer was unpretentiously simple: As soon as Manoula, my dear Mama, finds me the right bride I'll get married. His close friends knew of his attachment to his mother, Zographia, a gracious woman with deep dimples in both her cheeks and a surprisingly smooth face.

Alexis was behind a marble counter sampling a new bottle of Johnny Walker Red Label. Politely, he put his glass down and extended his hand to welcome the strangers. "Please be seated, gentlemen. I'll be with you shortly," he said. The sailors sat at a small table near a window. There was an unfinished mural on the wall across from them. Gathered around a cauldron, four teenage boys were singing folk songs and intermittently giggling. Alexis introduced them as the Moria Quartet. Nikos the barber and Apostolos the butcher were drinking ouzo and munching on salty olives and slices of cucumber. Another serious group at a corner table was playing cards. Villagers with swarthy faces and bright eyes filled the chairs and tables for a friendly chat or a drink, which good-natured Alexis provided. Their curious eyes looked at the sailors and wondered what they were doing in Moria.

Dan Cohen and Tiny Tom looked around curiously and marveled at the neatness of the café. They admired the local artifacts and the array of foreign liquor displayed on a marble shelf.

Tiny Tom licked his lips and said, "Not a bad place. We'll be coming back here again."

Dan Cohen said, "A place like this nurtures the spirit of these freedom-loving people."

Takis, one of the Moria Quartet, asked, "Hey, Americans, would you like to hear a Greek song?"

"Surely, but how much do you charge?

"Oh, nothing for the Americans."

"Then sing, boy." Cohen said. He recognized the boy. "It's the kid who spoke to me in English the day we anchored," he told Tiny Tom.

As Takis and his friends sang, Dan Cohen improvised a translation:

> At the place where we first met l shall plant an evergreen tree,
> To proclaim through the year my ever-growing love for thee.
> Let your hair become a ladder, a ladder that I may climb,
> To climb a bit closer, and kiss your tender neck a while.

A thunderous applause followed as the quartet bowed. Someone in the audience made a comment, and the rest laughed.

At a loss, Tiny Tom asked, "Cohen, what are they smirking about?"

"Someone said that you must weigh at least a ton without your clothes on."

"Crazy Greek! Let's get the hell out of here before I start a fight."

"Relax! I like it here. Let's have a couple of drinks before we go," Cohen said.

A strange and emaciated man holding a bundle of small brushes and a shallow tray of paint entered the café. He nodded good evening to Alexis and settled himself in a wicker chair. The noise subsided as some patrons gathered around him to watch him finishing the fresco on the wall. His payment tonight would be a dish of okra stew and a glass of wine.

"Come closer and see our local talent," Alexis said to the sailors. "You may have many wonders in America, but you don't have a Gregori."

"He seems to have a talent with color," Cohen said.

Alexis served Apostolos, the bulbous-nosed butcher, and Nikos, the bald-headed barber, a tray heaped with sizzling lamb chops. "Tender as a woman's heart," Alexis said.

Tiny Tom's eyes followed the tray as he sniffed the barbecued meat, while Cohen watched the artist at work. The barber, with mischief in his eyes, pulled a pair of snipping scissors from his pocket. To amuse the crowd, he snipped off a piece of the artist's pant cuff. The crowd laughed, but Gregori continued painting, ignoring his surroundings.

"Gentlemen." Alexis came to the sailors' table with a big bowl of grilled octopus, a dish of olives, and a bottle of retsina. "Enjoy your visit on our beautiful island."

"*Efharisto,*" Cohen said.

"Thank you," Tiny Tom said, filling his glass with wine. The octopus he would not touch; he looked away. Cohen's attention was still fixed on the emerging painting. In a moment of admiration he saw the figure in the fresco come alive—a gorgeous young woman. He felt at home among the islanders. He crunched on the juicy tentacle and washed it down with retsina. *Delicious,* he thought, but the retsina went straight into his veins. His heartbeat quickened, his spine tingled, and his face glowed. As he savored another glass, he studied the faces of the islanders. *Could one of them be my Uncle Thano?* He hadn't looked him up yet, but he planned to search for him as soon as the captain felt better.

"How can you eat that thing?" Tiny Tom asked in disgust.

"Try it. It's good, tender and tasty."

"It looks like a snake with chicken pox."

"Your loss," said Cohen. Alexis turned a spotlight on Gregori's fresco. The artist glanced at his audience with indulgence, then resumed his task of painting the girl's flowing gown and giving her the seductive expression of a young woman in love. He mixed some new colors on his palette, and next to the woman he outlined the shape of a handsome young man. Cohen finished his second glass of wine, and feeling a bit tipsy, he imagined himself coming to life on the tavern wall. There were his face, shoulders, muscles, and long fingers. *The man does look like me,* he thought.

But the youth in the picture was dressed in a loose blue tunic tied at the waist with a gold cord. Dan Cohen summoned Alexis to ask about the artist, but really he wanted to know about his uncle.

"Come, sit with us and have some wine," said Cohen.

"Do you like the painting?" Alexis asked.

"Very much."

Alexis poured himself a glass of retsina and popped a couple of olives into his mouth.

"Tell me about Gregori," Cohen said.

"He is about sixty-eight years old, and he is one of Lesbos' rare treasures. He can play the violin and he can sing. He is rather eccentric. Sometimes you'll see him dressed as a soldier or as Alexander the Great," Alexis chuckled. "He refuses to take money for his work. He'd be insulted if you offered him any. He works for a plate of food or a glass of wine or just for the joy of it. He has painted in houses, churches, and coffee shops all over Lesbos."

"What if I bought him some new clothes?" Cohen asked.

Alexis touched Cohen's arm. "I guarantee that if you proposed something like that, he'd leave my fresco unfinished."

After translating the conversation to Tiny Tom, Cohen asked, "Alexis, what's that painting all about?"

"The girl in the picture is a real person. I think Gregori is in love with her, but he would never admit it. She's one of the loveliest women on our island." Alexis leaned in closer and whispered, "If you ever met this gorgeous creature, you would want to take her to America." With a gleam in his eyes, he downed his retsina and added, "Though you probably have plenty of beautiful girls in America."

"We do, we do," Cohen said.

Alexis went on. "The story Gregori is telling in the painting is from a famous Greek epic, a poem written in 1650, which we all learn in school. It's the story of two lovers, Aretoussa and Erotokritos, like Romeo and Juliet.

"It is set in ancient Athens, and tells of a king's daughter, who falls in love with her father's trusted counselor, a foreigner. Despite the king's respect for Erotokritos, he does not consider him good enough for Aretoussa. Erotokritos is banished, and much sadness ensues. One day, he comes back, the lovers are reunited, and love triumphs."

Cohen studied the nearly finished painting. "He's a very good artist, a great one." *If only I could have a painting like this and take it back to America,* he thought.

In the days that followed, the sailors hit every promising spot in town. They were amazed to see the taverns crowded, and they gazed at the groups of friends enjoying wine, spicy foods, and music. They liked to watch the jovial faces around the tables, chattering and laughing, celebrating life and having fun. A town of fewer than two thousand people, Moria had a child's heart.

Cohen's knowledge of the language and his affinity with Greek customs particularly endeared him to the islanders. Within a few days, he and Tiny Tom made a few friends, but Alexis stole their hearts. They loved him.

While the captain was being treated at the hospital, the two of them, along with the ship's mechanic, assistant mechanic, and cook, cleaned and painted the *North Star*. At night they drank, danced, and sang in Alexis' café or roamed the alleyways of Moria.

CHAPTER TEN

A DISTANT *DONG* from St. Basil's belfry shook up the little town of Moria. It was the day of All Souls.

Nina yawned and clasped her hands behind her head, staring out the window. The sky smiled. Peeling off the covers, she felt a chill and swiftly tiptoed to her closet. Slowly she removed her pink nightgown, fingering her breasts and grinning. She recalled the day she had run naked into her aunt's room and screamed, "Aunt Pipina, look, I have bumps!" She opened the closet door and wrapped herself in a fluffy pink kimono, feeling its embrace of cotton softness.

The long talk with Dr. Andrew last Friday night had given her great relief. She tied her torrent of chestnut-colored hair with an azure velvet ribbon. Nature had endowed her with beauty, a flawless face, a statuesque body vibrating with energy. Nina flung open the window, cherished the morning aura, and surveyed the garden below. *It is a great day for tennis or volleyball or even swimming, but the water is still icy cold. Maybe I'll visit the convent. Well, maybe not today.*

At the east end of the garden, two tall pines waved like huge brushes painting the sky's infinite canvas. A soothing fragrance filled her lungs. She walked along the hallway to her father's room; it was safe to use his telescope as he was out of town. On the balcony overlooking the harbor, she panned the telescope from St. Mary's Convent to the docks, then focused on the ship, the *North Star,* flying the American flag. Men moved swiftly, carrying brushes and pails of water for swabbing the deck.

Pipina had been up since dawn, doing the housework.

"Aunt Pipina, come," Nina called. "Look. Have you seen the big ship in the harbor? It's called the *North Star.* It's flying an American flag. Look at the seamen."

"I 've seen it."

"It's beautiful," Nina said. "Why has it anchored in Lesbos?"

"Child of God, don't you see I'm busy?" Pipina had her own rituals. A woman of her age had other things to do in the morning hours. Arranging her brother's room, changing his sheets, and dusting were priorities. *Above all, it's Saturday of All Souls, it's a church day!* she thought.

Pipina was never meant to manage an estate. She had always wanted to become a teacher or a priest's wife, but had refashioned herself to satisfy her brother's needs.

"Come, Aunt Pipina," Nina giggled. "I can see things."

"God help us," he said and joined Nina on the balcony.

"The fair sailor with the blond hair looks very serious."

Unable to resist, Pipina laughed and put her arm around Nina. "Perhaps he is disappointed," she said after looking through the glass. "I imagine there are other ports more exciting than Lesbos."

"They've been in a storm. The foremast is broken," Nina noticed. "They're lucky to be alive. God has led them here. I hope our people will be good to them." Nina's heart palpitated, a strange surge.

Pipina smiled. "Don't worry about them. Sailors have a way of providing for themselves."

But Nina gasped and drew back from the telescope.

"I think that sailor looked right at me." She blushed.

"Silly girl, he couldn't possibly see you."

"He saw me. I know he did. Oh, I feel so ashamed for spying on them like this."

"Nonsense," Pipina said. "The sailors would be flattered if they knew a pretty girl like you was watching them."

Nina laughed. "Then I shall spy some more." She embraced and kissed her aunt. "I love you, Aunt Pipina."

"And I shall get back to work, while you, young lady, must get dressed. I have a lot to do before we go to church. What would Papavasile think if we didn't get to church on time?" The priest's opinion of her was vitally important. Pipina was now fifty-seven years old, and she had never missed a service. For forty years, she had nurtured a secret love for Papavasile.

When she was seventeen, she had mustered up the courage to confess to Papavasile the sin she and her brother had committed, drinking cognac and getting drunk. The priest had reassured her of Christ's forgiveness. After years of guilt, Pipina had finally felt at peace. Touched by the priest's warmth, she had been overwhelmed by gratitude and love for him. Then and there, she had vowed to remain celibate for the rest of her life. Later, when her brother needed her help raising Nina, Pipina became convinced that her decision never to marry was God's will. Some of her peers pitied her because she was not married and did not know the happiness of having children of her own, but Pipina had no regrets. She crossed herself gratefully and dusted her brother's room, cherishing her fondness for Papavasile. Even from a distance she felt fulfilled.

Now her thoughts were about her niece. *If only Nina could find a man to love and marry, I would feel my efforts rewarded.* Day and night, she prayed for this. When Nina was married, Pipina planned to enter the convent and free herself from earthly cares. Leaning against the bedpost, she watched Nina still gazing intently through the telescope.

What's the attraction at the harbor? There's nothing there but sailors and merchants. At least she is regaining an interest in life, she thought.

When both women were ready, Mourtos, in a charcoal suit, well-groomed and proud, drove them to church in Costas Cambas' ornate carriage, drawn by two mares.

"Slow down, Mourtos," she said. The carriage had to pass through the market where merchants displayed their fresh produce—cane baskets stacked with fresh zucchini, eggplants, parsley, string beans, apples, walnuts, chestnuts, and almonds. Slabs of red meat protected with cheesecloth hung on the butchers' hooks.

Occasionally, as Mourtos cracked his whip, he glanced obliquely at his boss's sister and daughter. Rich and gorgeous Nina wore a white, long-sleeved dress woven of organically developed silk, and an intricate lace scarf covered her shoulders. Her long hair flowed in soft waves. An embroidered handkerchief peeked out of the pocketbook that rested in her lap. Pipina was in her usual well-pressed black Sunday dress, her head covered with the traditional thin black veil, tied under her chin. Holding a shiny black purse, she looked forward to seeing Papavasile and hearing his melodic chant. Across from Alexis' American Café, Pipina saw Apostolos, the big-bellied butcher, swatting at flies that were after the meat, and cursing. "Why did God make flies, anyway?" he shouted.

"Why did God make *you*?" replied Anthony, the fat baker, as he balanced a tray of hot loaves of bread on his bald head. Gently Pipina elbowed her niece and said softly, "These two characters are rough but honest, and we need them . . . fresh meat and good bread."

From a narrow alley emerged Despina, dressed in a tight, short blue skirt and sleeveless blouse, defining her best features. She passed by the carriage, glanced at Mourtos, and walked next to the baker. She seemed to be in a hurry. Drooling over her dancing rear hemispheres, the baker lost his balance, and the loaves tumbled into the street. Head thrown back, Despina smiled at the butcher and winked at him seductively.

Noticing that her aunt's face turned sour, Nina asked, "Is something wrong?"

"No, child. It's that woman. I wish I had not seen her on my way to church. May God forgive me."

Nina knew of Despina's bad reputation but made no comment. As the carriage rolled along, she saw two sailors in white uniforms who were caught in the merry hubbub of the market. They seemed to be drinking in the scene and gaping at the merchandise. The sailors gazed at the carriage as it passed by and stood aside to make way. "Look," said Nina, clutching Pipina's hand. "It's the fair-haired sailor. The one I saw through the glass this morning. Mr. Mourtos, stop for a second," she said firmly.

"Hush, girl," said Pipina. "What would the people say if they saw us talking to strangers?"

"It's only polite to say 'good morning.' Besides, how else will foreigners truly know they are in Greece unless we show them how welcome they are?"

"There is no time for hospitality. We don't want to be late for church."

Mourtos frowned at the idea but he obeyed despite Pipina.

"Now I've seen me an angel," whispered Tiny Tom.

"A Greek goddess," said Cohen and proceeded to say in Greek, "*Kalimera sas.*"

Surprised to hear a foreigner greet them in their own language, Nina replied, "*Kalimera sas Kyree,* (Good morning to you, sirs). Are you Greek?"

"Americans," replied Cohen, looking into Nina's eyes. The sweet tremor in her voice had made his heart flutter.

What an exquisite young woman. This must be one of the muses the captain spoke of. He interpreted her words to Tiny Tom, and then turned his attention to Pipina.

"Pardon the imposition, ma'am," Cohen said politely in Greek. "We have survived a storm at sea, and we're here to search for a big pine tree. We need it for our mast."

Pipina pursed her lips, for she did not trust sailors. *Why was he talking to her about this tree? What did she know about masts?* However, she couldn't help but be pleased at the young man's good manners, his grasp of the native tongue, and his charming accent. Out of the corner of her eye she could see a look of distaste on Mourtos' face. The mares must have sensed his annoyance; one of them pawed the stony street with her front hoof and the other neighed impatiently. Mourtos shook the leather reins, and the tiny bells around the mares' necks jingled.

"Just a moment, Mr. Mourtos." Nina touched his arm. The sailors in white uniforms had an inexplicable impact on her. One of them was a huge man, built like an oak tree, with powerful limbs. He had small blue eyes in a round, weather-beaten face. Beside him stood the fair-haired sailor, who had beautiful green eyes and was smaller in stature, but with similar tanned skin from long days at sea. She felt the weight of his interest in her as he could not take his eyes off her. Responding with an unexpected feeling, Nina looked at him. "It's church day! Have you been to church yet to thank God for bringing you safely ashore?"

"I'm afraid not," Cohen said. "Sailors don't make it to church often, ma'am."

"Then I doubt God will lead you to the pine tree you need." With feigned disapproval, Nina waved for Mourtos to move on, and the carriage left the men behind.

"Okay, Greek, explain what that angel said. Was she cross with us?" Tiny Tom said.

"No," Cohen assured him. "She wasn't angry. She only said we were going the wrong way."

"Would you teach me some Greek words?"

"I don't think your Italian-Irish brain could learn Greek," Cohen chided.

"But I'm a good lover. And I can sing, too," said Tiny Tom, who proceeded to sing the American National Anthem.

"The islanders will think we've escaped from a mental institution," Cohen said. Both men watched the carriage that carried the two women to church and decided to follow them.

CHAPTER ELEVEN

A CHURCH OF ELEGANT SIMPLICITY, peeling but impressive, and bordered by a symmetrical array of cypress trees, stood as a perpetual fortress at the entrance of the town. A structure of fine line in the Byzantine style, St. Basil's Church was built in the middle of the eighteenth century. The omnipresent town pillar—Papavasile, the priest of Moria—tended to his people's spiritual needs there.

The two seamen apprehensively entered the awesome church. Smelling the sweetness of incense, they stood in wonder, admiring an ebony altar screen holding thirty-three Byzantine icons depicting the life of Jesus. Twelve narrow Roman windows, six on each side of the church, symbolic of the twelve apostles, let in ample light. The lit candles before the icon of St. Basil were small and thin. The middle-aged priest was dressed in purple vestments.

Cohen had never before experienced such a warm atmosphere. Ecstatic at the sight, Tiny Tom took small steps, following Cohen. Ebullient men and women in their best clothes curiously eyed the sailors. Several women were pregnant; others held babies at their breasts. There were no young men among the congregation. They had been drafted from Lesbos and were currently fighting in Albania against the fascist Italians. All congregants, with their hair neatly combed and shoes shined, heeded Papavasile, who chanted hymns with passion as he stood facing the effigy of Christ on the cross above the altar.

Spellbound, Cohen and Tiny Tom observed the priest's mannerisms, conferring blessings, making the sign of the cross over the people. Tall, with a slender body, hollow cheeks, long gray beard, and deep-set eyes, he resembled a prophet of old times. His flock, mostly fishermen, olive pickers, and olive merchants with their wives and children, had grown to love him and depend upon his wise counsel. For Father Vasile was not just a spiritual leader who baptized, married, and buried people, but a protector, a real caring father figure who promoted love and peace. When he chanted in a mournful tone "Memory Eternal," a throbbing commotion occurred among the women. It was a prayer for the eleven Moria men who had died in the Albanian war.

Nina and other young women were upstairs in a loft behind a lattice. They could see and hear the services, but they could not be seen. From a superior position she could see the sailors, but they could not see her.

In vain Cohen looked for the beautiful muse he had seen in the carriage. *She must be somewhere among the assembly,* he thought, but suddenly he caught sight of the woman in black, alone. *What happened to her gorgeous young companion?* He nudged Tiny Tom, who was leaning against a church column, yawning. The melody of the cantor had mesmerized him. Cohen could hardly understand the ecclesiastical Greek, but he enjoyed the Byzantine chant. As a young boy, he had been familiar with it, since his mother would take him to St. Nicholas Greek Orthodox Church in Tarpon Springs, Florida.

Four teenage boys harmonized with the cantor, whose voice dominated. Tiny Tom whispered in Cohen's ear, "Aren't they the boys we met at the American Café?"

"Yes, that's them." Still, his eyes kept searching for the pretty girl in the carriage, and not finding her, they rested upon the altar. A parade of amber candles, some burning low and some freshly lit, glowed in front of the icons, to symbolize mortal life.

As the services came to an end, the congregation, young and old, approached the priest in single file to receive his blessing and a small piece of blessed bread. The two sailors were last in line, and when they reached Papavasile, he beamed. It was obvious they were guests, and he invited them to his home for coffee after the service. He gave Cohen one piece of bread and as he took a profound look at Tiny Tom, he handed him three large pieces.

Tiny Tom put all three into his mouth at once. "Delicious homemade bread," he said. "This church is very interesting."

"The Greeks are traditionalists," Cohen said. "Their ceremonies date back two thousand years."

"How do you know all this?"

"My dad used to tell me all kinds of stories." His eyes brimmed joyfully.

CHAPTER TWELVE

AFTER some personal hospitality at his rectory, Papavasile strolled with the sailors toward the marketplace. He wanted to introduce the guests to some of the upstanding citizens of Moria. For March, the weather was mild. Bright sunshine accentuated the colors of the blossoming almond trees on the way. At the American Café, Alexis welcomed the priest and jovially said to the sailors, "It's good to see you again."

"Have you been here before?" Papavasile asked.

"We surely have. The sign . . . the *American Café*!"

"Alexis loves America. Look at the décor," the priest said.

Alexis served them three pieces of *galactoboureko* sprinkled with cinnamon and honey, hot from the oven. Tiny Tom devoured a piece of the syrupy pastry and licked his lips, as Alexis poured three cups of mountain tea. The priest and his guests savored the tea silently. Alexis wanted to know the purpose of their visit, but he preferred to wait for the right time to ask Cohen. Realizing that the big sailor had no knowledge of Greek, he reached out to him with a smile and a hearty handshake.

"Papavasile, do you happen to know someone by the name Thanasi? He is my uncle," Cohen said. "He's my father's brother, but I don't even know what he looks like or where he lives."

"Oh, we have many Thanasis in Moria," the priest said, "but none named Cohen."

"Papadopoulos is his real name," Cohen explained. "When my father came to America, he had to change his name. Americans can't easily pronounce long Greek names."

"Thanasi Papadopoulos? Of course I know him," the priest said, pleasantly surprised. "We call him Barba-Thano. Your grandfather, Father Daniel, was a priest in St. Basil's for forty years." Papavasile stroked his beard. "I'll take you to your uncle's house, if you like."

"Thank you, that would be great," said Cohen. But he noticed a sad gleam in the priest's eyes that he was unable to understand. "Too much trouble?"

"Not at all. But I must warn you, Barba-Thano is a troubled man."

"Mentally?" Cohen asked with evident concern.

"Emotionally. Grief-stricken. You may not want to hear about it."

"Please. He's my uncle."

Tiny Tom eyed Alexis and pointed to the dish. He wanted another piece of that sweet pastry. Cohen ordered another *galactoboureko* for his colleague, which Alexis quickly brought him. In two bites, Tiny Tom devoured it like a seal and stood up. "I need to stretch my legs, so I'll take a walk in the market," he said.

"Are we boring you, big man?" Cohen asked.

"It's all Greek to me," he said, and shook the priest's hand good-bye.

"Remember what the captain told us," Dan said.

"How can I forget?" Tiny Tom winked. "I'll keep my pants on."

Moving his chair closer to Cohen, the priest said, "Your uncle Barba-Thano had one misfortune after another. About eight years ago, his parents died. Then he lost his wife, leaving him with a teenage daughter, Demetria."

"That must have been difficult."

"It was not easy, but Demetria turned out to be a fine young woman. Then she married, and within a year she had twins."

"That probably brought some comfort."

"It did wonders for him. Barba-Thano used to carry the twins and bring them to church. Then one day a letter came from America announcing your father's death. Your uncle was devastated. He adored your father."

"My father always spoke of his brother."

"I know," Papavasile said, and reached to take Cohen's hand into his own. "But sometimes, misfortune . . ."

"You mean there is more?" Cohen asked.

"The memorial service in church today . . . One of the eleven men who died in the war against Italy was Andrew, your uncle's son-in-law, leaving behind Demetria, a pregnant wife, and two fatherless children."

"That's too much to bear."

"It is one of the ironies of life," the priest said. "During a battle in Albania, Andrew had stopped to bandage the wounds of a soldier, when a piece of shrapnel threw him on top of his comrade. He died almost immediately. That wounded soldier survived to tell us the story."

"That's the saddest story I've ever heard," Cohen said, sensing an unusual tightness in his stomach. He began to wonder if he should ask his uncle to help the American mission.

Papavasile went on. "Your uncle no longer comes to church. Since his son-in-law died, he has withdrawn from society. Nobody knows where he is or what he does. But I know that every afternoon he spends time with his grandchildren so that Demetria can go to work."

It is amazing how quickly one can go from one place to another in a little town like Moria. Cohen and Papavasile left the café and arrived at Barba-Thano's house within a few minutes. A pine tree towered over the wall that bordered the house. *This must be the tree my father used to climb, looking for nests,* Cohen thought. The priest knocked at the door. Cohen perused the surrounding walls and flowers as his heart pounded in anticipation. It opened, and Barba-Thano appeared, surprised by the unexpected visit.

"Papavasile, welcome. What an honor!" His bluish eyes responded warmly. "And who is this young man?" He extended his hands, welcoming both visitors.

"This is your nephew from America," the priest said.

"God Almighty with all your saints!" Shock showed in his withering face. Thirty seconds passed while Barba-Thano gazed at his nephew in ecstasy. *Little Danny, whose picture I have next to my holy icons. My brother's little boy, now a grown man and a sailor!* Embracing his nephew, he kissed him on both cheeks. Steeped in emotion, in a choking voice he said, "Well, don't just stand here. Come inside. I happen to have cooked something special today. Every day is the Lord's day, but this one He made for me. I feel blessed. Please join me."

Noon was approaching and Papavasile had some errands to do, so he excused himself and left. Cohen followed his uncle into the house. There was a scent of bay leaf and spices. A bit shorter than his father, his uncle was dark, with fine high cheekbones that gave him a brooding nobility. He wore a black shirt and a pair of patched gray pants.

"Barba-Thano, what in the world are you cooking?" Cohen asked, sniffing the sweet and spicy fragrance that came from the kitchen.

"I had a premonition," Barba-Thano said.

The house sat atop a hill on the west side of the village, facing the harbor. From the window Cohen saw a magnificent sight. In wonder his eyes scanned the whole house, loving its simplicity and classical beauty.

His uncle had cooked *lago-stifado,* rabbit stew, a meal he was planning to take to his widowed daughter and her children later that evening. Near the window was a table, covered with a white-and-blue-striped tablecloth. Two wicker chairs sat opposite each other.

"Please sit," Barba-Thano said. "I will be right back."

As he recalled the story the priest had told him, Cohen looked through the window at the distant sea, wondering how he could be of help to his uncle, a man stricken by ill fate. When Barba-Thano returned from the kitchen, holding a large pot of stew, he appeared to be the luckiest man in Moria. "I'm thrice blessed, dear nephew," he said, eyes beaming. "God has sent my brother's son to bring me some joy." He left again and quickly returned with bowls, forks, and two glasses of red wine.

"Thank you," said his nephew with a gentle smile, and he took a profound look at his uncle. He was a fairly stout man, like his father, of swarthy complexion like most of the islanders. His eyes were blue, like the sky over the Aegean Sea. He filled his nephew's plate with a few shapely chunks of rabbit meat, small onions, and potatoes glazed golden. He mumbled a brief grace, made the sign of the cross, and said, "Welcome."

Looking in each other's eyes, both men silently raised and clinked their glasses.

"Welcome to your father's homeland," Barba-Thano said. "May God rest his soul." His smile was joyous, yet tinged with grief. As the wine reached his bloodstream, Cohen's heart beat with excitement and sorrow. On the wall, a portrait of his uncle's wife, covered with a black veil, evoked grief. *How could a man with* so *many losses appear the image of contentment?* Cruel fate had carved deep wrinkles in Barba-Thano's face. In his eyes Cohen saw pain, which his uncle tried to hide as he sipped his wine.

For a while, not a word passed between them; there was only the sound of silverware clinking on their plates. Cohen slowly sipped his wine, drawing maximum pleasure from the aroma.

"Excellent wine," he said. "Is it local?"

"Very local. Every year I use my own grapes to make a few gallons."

"My father told me many stories about you, but he didn't tell me you could also make wine."

"A lucky man, your father. But I guess, perhaps, not as lucky as he should have been. He didn't live long enough to realize his dream. I remember how happy he was leaving our island for America. He wrote wonderful letters, sent us money, but . . . his dream was to return to Lesbos wealthy and to make a life here."

"Uncle Thano, why is there so much pain in our lives?"

"Does anyone really know the answer, dear nephew? Sometimes pain results from human error. Wars are a result of human greed and thirst for power and control. Hurricanes, storms, and earthquakes are acts of nature, and death is part of life. What else can I tell you? I barely finished elementary school. I'm an illiterate man."

"Your words are wise," Cohen said. "But tell me one more thing. Why does God allow so much pain? The priest told me your story. I feel so bad for you."

"Try to understand that God is a loving Father. Our losses, our pain and suffering are not His will. God created us for joy, and when bad things happen, He gives us courage and strength to endure our pain and rebuild our lives."

"Honestly, I don't understand this part of life."

"Someday we'll know. The Almighty upstairs," he pointed to the sky, "He has plans for us, all of us. If and when we get to heaven, we'll find out," he giggled. "Now, it's time for a bit more wine, don't you think?" He rose and went into the kitchen.

Cohen's eyes followed the old-timer as dreams and imaginary dramas unfolded in his brain—life with his parents when he was younger, devastating portraits of their sudden deaths, and now his mission with the *North Star*. Should he involve his uncle with the American mission in Lesbos? How could he ask him for help? He rehearsed some lines in his head, but when his uncle returned to the table with another carafe of wine, Cohen felt at a loss for words. Noticing mischief in those dark bluish eyes, he said, "Uncle, you're a wonderful man."

Barba-Thano refilled the glasses before sitting. From a leather pouch, he retrieved a pinch of tobacco and tissue paper, which he rolled into a cigarette. As he lit and drew a few times on the cigarette, he said, "This is a bad habit. I hope you don't smoke." Cohen shook his head no.

His uncle paused, scratched his head, and said, "I have a good thought. Don't laugh at me when I tell it to you, okay?"

Cohen nodded and brought the wine glass to his lips.

"Since you have no other relatives in America, can you see yourself making a home here on this beautiful island and having a family? That was your father's dream." He took a gulp of wine, wiped his lips, and said, "In our little town of Moria, even the stones smile. We're simple yet happy people. You'll be a happy man here, and you will give your old uncle much joy."

"That's a very nice thought, but America is my birthplace. I grew up there. It's where I belong, Uncle Thano."

"Of course that's where you first saw the light, and you must love it." He leaned closer to his nephew and said, "But what if you find a beautiful girl here and get married?" He winked. "Then the Papadopoulos name will continue to live on. Would that be so bad?"

"Your idea is noble and a bit romantic, I must say. But I have a mission to fulfill, a duty to my own country."

"A mission? Is that why you came to Lesbos? For a mission? I thought you came to meet your father's brother." He giggled to hide his disappointment.

Cohen conceded with a nod, and placing an arm around his uncle's shoulder, he summarized the purpose of his mission, exactly as Captain Thompson had told him. He explained that, initially, the captain had come to Lesbos to buy olive oil, but things had changed.

"This is the right island for olive oil," Barba-Thano said with pride.

"I'm sure you have a great deal of knowledge about olive oil, but I am more interested in other areas. Would you be willing to acquaint me with areas on the island that could serve for military bases? I would also need the names of people who can be trusted."

"That much I can do."

"Rest assured that you will be rewarded by the American government."

"America has been good to our country. It will be an honor for me to do my part. Please don't be concerned about rewarding me. I have my reward already. You came to see me."

"But the captain is a generous man. He will insist on paying you."

"Tell the captain that America has always helped Greece. It's time for Greece, as small as she is, to return the favor. Tell him that your uncle will help, but will not accept money. Maybe I'll accept some American cigarettes or tobacco if you happen to have any on board."

In the hour that followed, Barba-Thano told Cohen of some of the peak strategic points of the island, places that neither eagles nor snakes could invade. Then lighting a torch, Barba-Thano took Cohen into his basement and showed him one of the most secret shelters in the world. Nature had carved an underground rock into a maze. It was dark, cold, and moldy. "Four hundred years under Turkish dominance, and not a single Turk has ever entered this cavernous place. Here your grandfather stored wine, olive oil, and perishable food."

On one wall Cohen saw an array of old and unusual guns. "What are these?" he asked.

"Those are some of the weapons we used to fight against the Turks to liberate Lesbos."

"I would love to have one of those guns to take back to America as a souvenir."

"Take any one you like, but let me polish it. I'll have it ready for you when you come back to see me again."

"The captain will be pleased to know that such a hiding place exists. It's a perfect place to store weapons and ammunition, even a radio transmitter," Cohen said as he picked a doubled-barreled shotgun from the wall. A knot formed in his stomach as he worried about proposing such a risky plan to his uncle.

"Nobody in this town knows about this place, not even the devil himself," Barba-Thano said with a smile inching across his face. "And if you can use it, I'll give you a key to the basement." Escorting his nephew out, he said, "There is an old bench under the pine tree. Let's sit there for a few minutes so I can think of a few good people who could be of help to you."

"I only need one or two names initially. Maybe three."

"First and foremost, watch for a snake that circulates in our town. His name is Cara-Beis, and should he come near you just walk away. He can be a leech. He may try to sell you the whole island. Usually he walks around with a friend, another leech, named Lambis. Avoid them."

"I'll be careful."

"A good man to meet is Costas Cambas. And talking about olive oil, he produces the largest amount, enough to serve all of Europe."

"The captain wants a shipload, several barrels."

"Then Cambas is your man in terms of quality.'

"Tell me about him."

"He lived many years in America. He's the wealthiest man on the island, and he has a heart of gold. He gives jobs to people. He may give you a good bargain and may even be sympathetic to your mission. But like me, he has had a misfortune. His wife died and left him with a little girl. Of course now she's a big girl, very beautiful and kind. I think her name is Nina.

"She and your cousin Demetria are the same age, and they were in the same class in elementary school."

Back in the dining area, Barba-Thano took another sip of his wine, and shaking his head, added, "Cambas is a good man, but his sister, Pipina, is a saint. When my wife died, she was here every day, bringing me hot meals and homemade bread."

"Cambas sounds like a good contact," Cohen said.

"Of course, there are some less wealthy people who could be of help—like the café owner, Alexis. He's shrewd but honest, and he loves America so much that he renamed his tavern American Café."

"I met Alexis," Cohen said. "My colleague and I enjoyed his café. Also, earlier today, Papavasile took us there."

"Papavasile is another good man you must get to know. He's the pillar of Moria, a walking saint who is always available to anyone who needs help."

"A gentle soul and very hospitable," Cohen said. "He brought my colleague and me to his home for coffee. I met his wife and son."

"Yes, Christos, a fine young man. He is priestly material, like his father." Barba-Thano said. "Someday he may succeed his father."

After glancing warmly at his nephew, he added, "I have thought of something better than a gun to give you."

"The gun is just fine," Cohen said, not wanting to take advantage of his uncle's generosity.

Barba-Thano led the way into another room, a multicolor-carpeted den. He unlocked an old oak trunk and pulled out what resembled a baby wrapped in a woolen blanket. Carefully, he unfolded the blanket, uncovering a handmade mandolin. "Your father made this out of a gourd, and he played it."

"My father made this?" Cohen asked and took the mandolin in his hands. Gently, he tested the strings. They were intact and made a sweet sound. Caressing the instrument and feeling a vibration in his spine, he said, "I'd like to take this to America." His eyes glowed with a bittersweet emotion.

"It's all yours," said Barba-Thano, reaching into the trunk, "and here, this book was also your father's. It's a love story."

"My father read love stories?"

"This one, yes, but in secret. Papa-Daniel, your grandfather, was very strict. A priest, you know!" he said with a glitter in his eye.

"It must be a good story."

"Danny, it's a story of unfulfilled love, and parents who control the destiny of their children."

"Uncle Thano, you must have read it."

"I did, secretly, too," he said with a smile. "Young and beautiful Hermione committed suicide because her father did not allow her to marry Emilio, the man of her dreams. Emilio suffers a slow death on Hermione's grave."

"It's not a story I want to read, but the book belonged to my father and I would like to have it as a keepsake," Cohen said. The lid creaked as Barba-Thano closed the trunk. Then a sudden idea knocked at the door of his memory. "My dear nephew," he said, reopening the trunk, "there is something else I want you to have, from your grandfather."

Cohen sat on a low, cushioned stool, browsing through the book and watching his uncle searching the trunk. "Here it is. I found it." He withdrew a box lined with cedar wood and containing a small golden chalice wrapped in a burgundy velvet cloth. "My father and mother shared wine from this cup on special occasions. It was their tradition. When I got married, I continued the tradition. But now your aunt is no longer with me," he said, shaking his head.

"And you want me to have such a precious cup?" Cohen felt it was not quite right to accept this heirloom.

"Why, don't you like it?"

"I do, but . . ."

"Some day, when you get married, you and your bride can drink wine from this cup and remember your roots."

"Thank you," Cohen said, deeply touched.

One hand resting on his knee and the other still searching the contents of the trunk, Barba-Thano exclaimed, "Oh, I found something else. Here it is." He brought out a yellowish envelope containing pictures that his father had sent from America. Pointing to one particular picture, he said, "Here you look like an angel from a Christmas card—blond, sky-blue eyes, and long curly hair—little Danny. My neighbors couldn't believe you were my brother's son."

"Eyes and hair I took from my mom," Cohen said.

"I know. I have their wedding picture. Your mother was beautiful. But you, your body, you've grown to be just like your father."

Cohen viewed the pictures and relived his childhood. He looked at Barba-Thano with admiration. He saw a disarmingly gentle smile on his uncle's face. It was apparent to him that he was a man of awesome strength. He had survived one tragedy after another. That's why the priest had said, *Barba-Thano is a troubled man. In no way would I bring more trouble into this man's life.*

At that very moment, Cohen made a decision. *I will not endanger my uncle's life under any circumstances. The captain might think we should involve my uncle in our mission, but to hide weapons in his uncle's home is out of the question. If the Nazis ever came to Lesbos or if an enemy smelled something questionable, his life and his daughter's life would be at risk.*

"Nephew, you seem to be far away. Is something worrying you?"

"No. I'm thinking what a remarkable man you are. I wish my father was still around." Cohen stood up. "It's time to get back to the ship."

"You're not leaving so soon, are you?" Barba-Thano also stood. "But I understand. You're here on a mission. I hope you'll come back to see me again. Demetria would love to meet you."

Kissing his uncle on the cheek, Cohen said, "I'll be back."

When Cohen returned to the *North Star,* Tiny Tom was nowhere to be seen. *He must still be carousing in town. I hope he doesn't get lost,* he thought.

But Tiny Tom was too big a guy to get lost. He meandered along some narrow alleys and remote roads. Walking through narrow streets made him feel taller. Impressed by the simple little all-white houses, with red doors and curtained windows with colorful flowers, he memorized landmarks so that he could find his way back to the harbor. Suddenly a door opened and a voluptuous woman wearing a low-cut dress and with mountainous breasts snatched him into her house. He did not resist. *This must be one of those muses the captain talked about,* he thought. *She's one of those good women destined to make a man happy. How lucky can I get!*

"My name is Despina, or Despinaki," she said. "You is American."

"My name is Tiny Tom," he said, still wondering what was about to happen.

Jovially pointing to a red velvety couch, Despina said, "Sit and I'll bring you a drink."

Tiny Tom looked around. The house was small but spotless, with wall-to-wall carpeting, leather chairs on the other side of the room, and a table in front of a pale green wall decorated with pictures.

She took a bottle of cognac from a closet, filled two glasses, and handed one to Tiny Tom, which he eagerly accepted. He touched her glass with his and said, "Cheers!"

After the second glass, he surrendered. At dawn, he woke up in Despina's arms. He tried to remember how he got there, but other thoughts clouded his memory. *Dear God, what a night! How am I going to tell Cohen about this?*

CHAPTER THIRTEEN

MONDAY, MARCH 25, WAS Greek Independence Day. It commemorates the day when Bishop Germanos of Patras raised the flag of revolution over the monastery of *Agia Lavra,* or Holy Fire, in Peloponnese. The cry of "Freedom or Death!" became the motto of the revolution, as Greeks valiantly fought against the Turks, who had occupied their country for four hundred years. In 1829, Greece was finally liberated from the Turkish yoke. Ever since, Greek Independence Day is celebrated throughout the country with patriotic parades, traditional costumes, and displays of the flag. Evening dinner gatherings in town squares follow as families and friends enjoy regional dishes and folk dances. They toast *"Zito I Ellatha"* (Long live Greece!) with local wines.

The hours could not pass quickly enough for Dan Cohen and Tiny Tom. They had agreed that in the early afternoon, they would be where the action was—the center of Moria.

The *North Star* was cradled in the waveless harbor. The first golden rays of the sun slanted through the mountain forests, reaching Moria's whitewashed cottages. Cohen's eyes glittered as he perused the rows of little houses, like strings of lovely pearls, perched on the slope. The sky was a radiant blue and the air deliciously cool. He felt invigorated by the fragrance of the silvery olive trees and the fan-shaped emerald leaves of the palms.

Enchanting Aegean Sea! Never before had he inhaled air as clean and seen water so pure. He leaned over the rail. The turquoise water reflected his image, and through it he could decipher colorful pebbles, intriguing shapes of coral on the seabed. By four o'clock, the two sailors, dressed impeccably in their naval uniforms with gold buttons, stripes, and shined shoes, wandered throughout Moria, absorbing the sights and sounds. The streets were freshly cleaned and washed. Front doors were adorned with myrtle branches and pots of colorful begonias, and fragrant basil adorned the windowsills. Cohen noticed some young women eyeing them from behind the window curtains.

At the town square, the Moria Quartet carried bundles of myrtle to decorate the area of the celebration. The two stopped to see what the boys were up to.

"You American! The name of me is Takis. Remember me?"

"I remember you," Cohen said. "You speak English!"

"Few words," Takis said, a glimmer of pride in his big eyes. His friends approached saying, "Ask the sailors if they are coming to the festival this evening."

"You coming to festival? Lots fun," Takis said.

"Will there be many girls?" asked Tiny Tom.

"Many . . . many . . . You come?"

"Count us in."

Around 5:00 p.m. the town square overflowed with islanders of all ages in their festive clothes. Long communal tables were draped with snow-white tablecloths garlanded with flowers. Several women had prepared seafood platters, and delicious dairy and cheese dishes.

Alexis saw the sailors from a distance and, waving his hand, invited them to draw closer. Cohen looked around for his uncle. He was nowhere to be seen. Then he approached Alexis, who seemed to be in charge of the preparations, and asked, "Have you seen Barba-Thano?"

"I don't think he'll be coming," Alexis said. "He's still grieving."

Unassumingly, the people took their places. The food smelled inviting. Smiles and casual amenities set the mood for the occasion, as the crowd waited for the priest to offer the invocation. No etiquette was followed. A few red-cheeked men, known as the wine fathers, were sampling the demijohns to make sure the wine had matured, feeling the spirit moving in their veins. Alexis surveyed the area and said to the Americans, "Tonight, you are our guests. Come, I have a place for you." He led them to the dais.

"Would you be able to introduce us to Mr. Costas Cambas?" Cohen asked.

"No problem," Alexis said. "How did you hear of him?"

"My uncle praised him a lot, and by the way, he thinks highly of you."

Alexis hardly said thank-you. He saw the priest arriving, followed by the mayor and the town's dignitaries proceeding toward the dais. Costas Cambas, the olive-oil tycoon, was seated beside the mayor. Alexis invited the American sailors to sit on the right-hand side of the priest. Papavasile made room for them and asked a Greek-American of Moria, Asimakis, Takis' father, to keep the sailors company.

Cohen felt excited at being part of the festivities, but beneath his joyful smile lurked an awareness of his mission. He wanted to become acquainted with some prominent citizens who could help the purpose of the *North Star*.

As the revelry reached a crescendo, Papavasile extended his arms upward, the garrulous crowd stood up, and silence prevailed. It was time for grace:

"Bless, O Lord, the food and drink of Your people, and bring peace to our world. Amen."

The audience remained standing, and Papavasile requested a minute's silence for the eleven men who had died recently in the Albanian war.

Tiny Tom, who understood nothing of what was going on, seemed curiously happy. He caught the eye of a few islanders and repeated several Greek words he had learned: *Kalispera sas m'aresi to nesi sas.* (Good evening, I like your island.) To him the island was an oasis of Mediterranean brunettes, gorgeous looking with big brown eyes and golden skin. Nudging Cohen's knee while he was eyeing the girls, he said, "Danny, I'd love to marry one of them!"

"My uncle said I should marry a girl from Moria and make my home here," said Cohen.

"Then I could visit you," Tiny Tom said.

"Captain Thompson would love the idea!"

"What would he say if we both married Greek girls and settled here?"

Cohen paid no attention to what Tiny Tom was mumbling on about. His sight was drawn to two women who had just arrived. He has seen them the first day he and his friend had been in town. He wondered if he could ever get closer to them, especially to the younger one. Slowly he sipped his wine to quiet down his beating heart, but his eyes followed the enchanting beauty. *She is gorgeous,* he thought.

Cambas' sister, Pipina, and her niece sat on the dais, too, surveying faces and gestures. Pipina's heart thumped like a teenager's as she tried to catch the eye of the priest. She smiled and hoped that the festivity would bring her nearer to him. That was all she wanted. To chat with him, to be close enough to smell his curly, bushy beard, to see the coarse weave of his cassock, and to love him just by looking at him. *Why couldn't he be mine,* she thought, realizing the futility of her yearning. Papavasile was a married priest, and she had no desire to cast a shadow on his married life.

Cambas' daughter, Nina, said a quick good-bye to her aunt and joined her girlfriends to discuss plans for the traditional dances. She met with Eleni, who had made a name for her dancing skills, and asked her to take the lead this evening. Although four years younger than Nina, Eleni had an athletic physique and an extraordinary ability to do the intricate steps of the *Kalamatiano* and *Tsamiko*.

Moria's perennial bachelor, Alexis, paced back and forth, filling glasses with wine. Then he carried a shallow baking tin heaped with sizzling tyropeta, triangles of phyllo dough filled with feta cheese, eggs, olive oil, and herbs, and with a teasing twinkle in his gray-blue eyes he placed it in front of Papavasile and said, "Father, this is so good that a mother wouldn't want to share it with her child."

Tiny Tom, perpetually hungry, put a whole tyropeta in his mouth and devoured it like a seagull while reaching for another piece. Cohen was watching Nina and attempting to catch her eye.

Realizing that he had failed to introduce the American sailors officially to his compatriots, Alexis combed his hair, unrolled his sleeves, buttoned his shirt, and rushed to the dais. Resting a friendly hand on Cohen's shoulder, he said, "I'm sorry."

Cohen looked at him, puzzled.

"*Prosochi . . . prosochi prakalo!*" Alexis shouted. When he had everyone's attention, he said, "Loving people of Lesbos, our town of Moria is privileged this evening to welcome members of the crew of the *North Star,* Mr. Dan Cohen and Mr. Tiny Tom. Mr. Cohen happens to be of Greek origins. He's Barba-Thano's nephew. His father, Stratis Papadopoulos, was born in Moria and went to America many years ago."

There was some whispering among the audience. *Is Alexis drunk already? Cohen? Could a man with blond hair and blue eyes be Greek?*

"*Ysihia,*" (silence), Alexis shouted.

"Let's wish our American friends a most pleasant stay and smooth sailing in their travels." Alexis lifted his glass high as the crowd burst into thunderous applause. Still holding his glass, Alexis scanned the audience. He caught sight of beautiful Nina Cambas. He leaned forward and whispered to Cohen's ear, "My friend, the girls are already looking at you." His thick eyebrows pointed at Nina. "A very beautiful girl cannot keep her eyes off you."

"Seriously?" Cohen said.

"I've been watching her ever since I introduced you."

Cohen kept looking around and felt like a little boy who hears for the first time a little girl's sweet voice saying, *I love you.* He blushed. His heart pounded, and as his eyes searched discreetly for Nina, thoughts whizzed like bullets through his brain. *I'm here on a serious mission. How many of these islanders can I trust, and how many would be willing to help? I have no time for girls right now.*

Alexis came back and refilled all the glasses of the dais. Cohen set his eyes on him, thinking, *Perhaps I can trust him.* He turned toward Tiny Tom, who was absorbed with the commotion, and said, "Are you having a good time, lover boy?"

Alexis had noticed the way Cohen had looked at him and came over. "My American friend, is everything okay?"

Cohen nodded.

"Something is on your mind, I can tell," Alexis giggled.

"Nothing, really. I just asked my mate if he had a good time."

Unconvinced, Alexis pulled up a chair next to Cohen and said, "Greeks are people of many passions; either they love you or they hate you. They know no middle way, no flattery, no diplomacy. I want you to know that I like you a lot. I liked you the very first time you came into my café. But I feel bad about your friend. He doesn't speak Greek, and I don't speak English."

Cohen clutched Alexis' hand. "I'm so glad to have a friend like you," he said.

"Thank you," Alexis said. "I hope we get to know each other better." He raised his glass and clinked it with Cohen's and Tiny Tom's glasses. "*Stin Ygia sas,*" (To your health), he said.

Cohen seized the moment to plant the seed of his mission. Softly, he asked, "Can we get together tomorrow evening? There's something I need to talk to you about."

"It would be my honor," Alexis said.

"Could you meet me at St. Basil's? I'd like Papavasile to be with us, if that's alright with you."

"Name the hour," Alexis said.

CHAPTER FOURTEEN

ALEXIS CLAPPED HIS HANDS. The Moria Quartet got the message, and the singing began, accompanied by Takis' harmonica. Nina and her girlfriends, dressed in white silk blouses and dark blue pleated skirts above the knee, gracefully synchronized their steps, landing in a squat position on the balls of their feet. Nina, holding a white handkerchief in her right hand, hopped on her left foot while raising her right leg with the knee bent, a skill she had mastered.

The sailors studied the reaction of the audience, but their interest was fixed on the dexterity of the dancers. Cohen wondered if he would be able to get closer to Nina after the dance and possibly strike up a conversation. He could not take his eyes off her. She seemed proud of her dancing skills.

Throughout the dance she sensed that the blond sailor was staring at her. Watching him surreptitiously, she felt a need to impress him. But her thoughts of him—*Who is he? Why is he here? Is he as good as he looks?*—caused her to miss a few steps.

"Nina, are you okay?" Eleni asked.

"Oh, yes, I'm fine." She blushed.

"The sailors are looking at you."

"They are? Well, let them look."

When the quartet had completed a couple of songs, Alexis asked another group of musicians to join in. Melodies of guitars, violins, and a clarinet stimulated the spirit of the celebrants. The strings of a bouzouki, an instrument that resembles a mandolin with a long arm, introduced a different dance, the *Zeibekiko*, which combines both smooth and leaping steps.

Cambas' manager, Manolis Mourtos, stepped forward to dance. The resonance of the bouzouki strings vibrated inside his head. Glancing around, he looked in Nina's direction, fully aware that if Cambas ever knew his intentions about his only daughter he would fire him on the spot. Despite that sinking thought, his heart sang like a choir of birds. So he took a red kerchief out of his back pocket and stood up to convey his feelings to the one he secretly loved. To the delight of the spectators, he performed the most athletic dance that any of them had ever seen. As his legs crossed and tipped above the level of his head, his arms sprang and fingers snapped. With enough wine in his bloodstream, he felt the true meaning of exhilaration and relief. His face cracked in an enormous, insuppressible grin. *Oh, Mr. Cambas, my* effendi, *I want to marry your beautiful daughter,* he thought, oblivious for the moment of the impossibility of his aspiration. As he danced, he noticed how persistently the blond sailor was looking at Nina, and his heart pounded with envy. A maelstrom of emotions evoked a disturbing conflict between old loyalty to his boss and the possibility of a rival. *Nobody else could love Nina as much as I do,* he thought.

The musicians swaggered, running their fingers over the strings of their instruments. Cohen, after staring at Nina, looked at Mourtos' performance, and Mourtos looked back at him with loathing. *Man, if you have your eyes on this girl, forget it fast. I'll kill anyone who dares to touch the one I love. Life imprisonment doesn't scare me.* He threw a handful of coins at the musicians, indicating that they should play another *Zeibekiko* song. This time he jumped high, performed a somersault, and landed on his feet. As the crowd applauded, more revelers joined the dancing circle.

The *Hasapiko*, the butchers' dance, followed. It dated back more than a thousand years, and was invented by butchers, who were known as *hasapis*.

Later, it was renamed as a sailors' dance. Alexis approached Cohen and Tiny Tom, pulling them by the hands. "Come! This is a sailors' dance," he said.

"But we don't know the steps," Cohen protested.

"Never mind. You'll learn them as you dance."

Tiny Tom, who had had one too many drinks, began to do random steps, boasting his newfound knowledge of Greek and repeating like a parrot, "*M'aresi to nesi sas,*" (I love your island). He extended his hand to congratulate the girls, who giggled graciously and blushingly returned the greeting, "Welcome to our island."

As the music played, men and women aligned themselves with the sailors, arms over the shoulders of their partners, making a big circle. It was a lively dance, and the islanders encouraged the sailors with shouts of "*Opa, opa,*" and clapping and laughing whenever they missed a step.

When the *Kalamatiano* dance was convened, all the younger women joined the circle and Cohen found himself between Nina and Eleni. Nina felt goose bumps move up her arms when this young sailor held her hand. Eyes gleaming and heart pounding, she wondered, *What fate has brought this handsome sailor to dance next to me?* But she cherished the moment.

Mourtos, still sweating from his rigorous dance, had stepped to the side. When he saw the sailor and Nina holding hands and dancing, he dashed abruptly to wedge himself between them.

He looked ferociously at the sailor's face and said, "Foreigner, you're crossing the line and I don't like it."

"Is there a problem?" Cohen smiled apprehensively.

"You're getting under my skin."

Protectively, Tiny Tom jumped between Cohen and Mourtos. Ready to throw a couple of punches, he asked his colleague, "Is this character causing any trouble?"

"Take it easy, big guy. Remember, we're guests," Cohen said, unable to understand the attitude of this angry man.

Nina saw the envy in Mourtos' eyes and overheard what he said to the sailor. Annoyed, she pulled him aside and said, "I want you to go back to your table right now. Do you understand?"

Afraid that his boss might be watching the intrusion, Mourtos retreated, and Nina clasped Cohen's hand affectionately as the dance continued.

"Are you enjoying yourself?" she asked.

"Beyond description." Cohen squeezed her hand.

"You find Lesbos to be a special place?"

"Yes, ma'am, very special." He observed her dancing steps and tried to imitate them. "My name is Dan Cohen," he added.

"Mine is Nina Cambas," she replied.

"I'm pleased to meet you, Miss Cambas." Their eyes engaged with prolonged smiles. *This must be the daughter of the Costas Cambas my uncle mentioned,* he thought.

The moon slipped slowly behind the mountain, veiling Moria in a thin, dark haze. Instantly, four kerosene lanterns from four different directions gave abundant light, turning the night into day. The quartet emerged from a corner, carrying torches. Alexis had drafted them to set fire to a bundle of twigs around the tree, symbolizing the burning of the enemy forces who had enslaved them for centuries. A man of passion for God and compassion for his people, Papavasile saw a glow of joy in the faces around him, and his heart moved with gratitude. These were his spiritual sons and daughters, and he wanted them to enjoy the life of freedom.

As the merrymakers sprang to their feet, Alexis shouted, "Time for church! Papavasile is now expecting all of us at Vespers, if you really want to go to heaven."

In small groups, the islanders headed for St. Basil's. Cohen and Tiny Tom followed the crowd. After a brief service, the priest and the congregants hugged each other and said, "We can thank God for the gift of freedom." Then they approached the sailors and shook their hands in theirs and wished them a happy stay on the island.

The evening service concluded with the traditional sacred dance in the cobblestone churchyard. This time, the priest was the leader. Although his long black robe limited his movements, he danced with grace and sang:

> *Christ is the tree,*
> *And the Virgin Mary is the root,*

The Apostles are the branches,
Who bear the fruit.

A festive week and a long day of celebration had ended. In the silence of that night, a soft serenade could be heard as the Moria Quartet sang:

Life, my love, is like a flower,
At autumn shedding its leaves,
Don't postpone your joy, dear,
Till sweet springtime leaves.

Mellowed to the bone, Cohen and Tiny Tom walked slowly to their ship. Many lanterns brightened the narrow streets on the way. Balconies were festooned with colorful flowers. An enchanting peace had veiled the island. Now Cohen understood his father's longing for his homeland. *Paradise revisited,* he thought. *How could I prolong our stay?*

Tiny Tom interrupted his reverie. Nostalgic, he burst out in a raucous song that even he could not understand: *Despina . . . Despinaki . . .* (Hurry up, come to me!)

"Shut up, big guy." Cohen put his hand over Tiny Tom's mouth, but he pulled his hand down and screamed: "I want to go to that woman—now." He insisted. He had a strange feeling that part of his heart belonged in her bedroom.

"You must have forgotten what happened to you the last time you went there."

"I want to go back," Tiny Tom said. *Despina . . . Despinaki . . . I think I'm in love.*

"And I think you are drunk," Cohen said.

CHAPTER FIFTEEN

ON TUESDAY MORNING at ten o'clock, Captain Thompson returned to the *North Star,* in spite of his swollen leg being encased in a heavy cast. Bravely, he limped up the gangplank, and once on the deck he resumed his authority, and every crew member knew it. Standing in line, they welcomed him and wished him a speedy recovery. With a jovial smile, he expressed his gratitude.

Last in line was Dan Cohen, who embraced the captain. "I have some good news, sir."

Raising a curious eyebrow, the captain pointed to his cabin. They slowly made their way there. They sat down, the captain lit his pipe, and clearing his throat he inquired, "What's the good news?"

"Papavasile is the priest of Moria. He was of great help. He introduced me to Alexis, the owner of the American Café in Moria."

"Oh, there is such a thing?" The captain drew on his pipe and coughed.

"Yes, sir. Alexis seems to be a good man. He favors America."

The captain nodded approvingly.

"I met my uncle. He told me about certain people I could trust, including these two men, Alexis and Papavasile. Last night, I was with them, and a third reputable man, Costas Cambas, who might sell us the olive oil. They could be supportive."

"Great start," the captain said.

Cohen wanted to share his entire experience on the island, meeting fun-loving people, the good time that he and Tiny Tom had at the festival, but when he saw the agony on the captain's face as he tried to reposition his leg, he decided to spare him the details.

"Don't close the oil deal unless the price is right."

"I'll see if I can trace other oil merchants so I can compare prices."

Sensing the captain's satisfaction with the news, Cohen debated in his mind whether to tell him that he had danced with a beautiful woman last night at the festival. But he could almost hear the captain's warning: *Watch out, Cohen. Sailors fall in love in each port.* Nervously, he tapped his pants and reached into his pocket. "Captain, I'm sorry. I almost forgot to give you this note. It came before dawn today."

The captain shook his head, his face grave as he read the Morse code.

"Is something wrong, sir?"

"Wrong? No." The captain remained silent for a few seconds. "Let me translate the code for you." With the end of his pipe, he pointed at each dot: "As of 2:00 a.m. this morning, the *North Star* and its crew are officially members of the Office of Strategic Services (OSS). Stop. Ship and crew are now irrevocably under the command of the U.S. Marine Force. Stop. Scour neighboring islands, trace secure hiding places for weapon storage. Stop. Stay alert for further information. Stop. Admiral William L. Bell."

The captain narrowed his eyes. *What now?* He struck a match against his cast to relight his pipe. After a few puffs, he said, "Cohen, we are in it! I have had a premonition that the U.S. is going to declare war against Germany."

Cohen waited to hear more about the captain's concerns.

"It's officially not just oil we should be looking for—although we need a full cargo to avoid any suspicion from possible enemies. We need to deal with more serious issues."

"Captain, I'm meeting Alexis and Papavasile at St. Basil's Church tonight at eight."

"Good, let me know their reaction when you mention our mission."

From a distance, Cohen could see St. Basil's Church surrounded by cypress trees. He walked toward it slowly.

His eyes revealed a heavy heart, for yesterday's joy at the festival had become today's agony. *Are you enjoying yourself? Do you find our island to be a special place?* Nina's voice echoed in his head. *What a beautiful woman!* He imagined her sparkling emerald eyes, her gorgeous face, her flowing dark brown hair, and her voice speaking English with a slight Greek accent.

Why do I feel like this? It's a good thing I didn't mention my fascination to Captain Thompson. I can just hear him saying, "Get over it, Cohen. We're at war."

That evening, Dan Cohen caught the scent of sweet basil as he entered the church. He was about to reveal his plans to Alexis and to Papavasile, that the *North Star* and its crew had been commissioned to find strategic areas on the island for American bases. In dim candlelight, Papavasile was standing before the icon of Christ, completing his evening prayers. Cohen could hear the priest's solemn voice:

Lord and Master of my life, give me the spirit of prudence, humility, patience, and love. Grant that I may see my faults and sins and not judge my brothers and sisters. Amen.

As the steeple clock chimed the hour of eight, Alexis arrived. He was anxious over the secret that the American had to share with him. *I bet this handsome American sailor wants a personal favor. Could he be love-stricken, and would like me to be a matchmaker?* He smiled, recalling how this good-looking sailor kept his eyes on Cambas' daughter at the festival.

Cohen thanked Alexis for agreeing to meet him. There was not a soul around, and he felt this was a choice place to disclose the details of his mission in the presence of the priest. Crossing himself, the priest invited the two men to approach the altar.

"Good news from a far country is like cool water to a thirsty soul," he said, quoting the Bible.

For a split second, Cohen hesitated, skeptical that his disclosure was really "good news." But interpreting the wishes of his captain, he explained the dual nature of their visit to Lesbos: how it had started as a commercial venture and evolved into a war enterprise. He reassured the men that now, in addition to purchasing olive oil, the *North Star* was there to secure the safety of Lesbos.

"America is our faithful ally," Papavasile said. "We'll do anything in our power to help you accomplish your mission."

Glowing with patriotism, Alexis said, "Tell us what you wish and it shall be granted."

"We may have to store ammunition and weapons."

The priest scratched his beard.

Alexis said, "I have the perfect hiding place. Not even the devil could find it."

"My uncle Thano offered a unique place. But he has had enough trouble. I don't want to add more to it."

"Should that accursed creature, Hitler, come this far, we are all doomed," Alexis cautioned.

"He won't last long," Cohen said with a chuckle, disguising his concern. *I might be exposing these innocent folks to the possibility of a real catastrophe,* he thought.

Papavasile held onto his long beard as he looked penetratingly at Cohen's face. He shook his head and spoke with depth. "We must meet again." He turned to Alexis and said, "It would be good for us to know more details about your mission."

"As you wish," Cohen said.

Cohen returned to the ship around ten o'clock. He found the crew vigilant and ready to weigh anchor. He saw Tiny Tom dressed in fatigues and heard the engines running. "The captain wants to see you, lover boy."

Looking at him askance, Cohen said, "What's going on, big guy? Are we going somewhere?"

"We're all going somewhere," Tiny Tom said sadly.

"At midnight we are to sail to Chios, a small island three hours away," Captain Thompson advised them.

"But, captain, we haven't replaced the mast yet, sir," Cohen said anxiously.

"It doesn't matter. It's a short ride. We'll pretend we're testing the engines. A small vessel will meet us there," the captain continued with simulated confidence and attempted to light his pipe. Behind the puffs of smoke his mind searched for words to conceal his true feelings. He wanted no part of another war, but now he had no choice. "We are to receive a supply of weapons and bring them back to Lesbos by dawn. We need to do this job within twenty-four hours. Things are more serious than I thought."

By dawn, the *North Star* had returned to Lesbos carrying twelve cases of weapons. In the bustle of the harbor, hardly anyone noticed that the ship, heavy with the load, was several inches deeper in the water.

CHAPTER SIXTEEN

AS THE WEATHER became warmer, the islanders met outside Alexis' café, where they sat under an oak tree. It was their daily ritual to savor a drink while discussing the latest events: who was getting engaged or married; whose goat had given birth to two kids; whose mare should be bred with the butcher's donkey; deaths, thefts, and infidelities. Today, the topic was the *North Star* and the friendly American sailors in town. When Alexis told his patrons that Dan Cohen was Barba-Thano's nephew, Cara-Beis, the leech of Moria, said, "I don't believe that story. Have you ever seen a fair-haired, blue-eyed male around here? A blond Greek, hah!" he mocked. "I'll bet he's a spy!"

"Nonsense," Alexis said. "Dan Cohen is not a spy. He's an American of Greek descent. Barba-Thano and Dan's father, Stratis Papadopoulos, are brothers. Cohen is Stratis' son. But in America people Americanize their names. Papadopoulos made his name Cohen."

"You're just pro-American," Cara-Beis said, pinching his nose and laughing with evident sarcasm.

"Enough of this," Alexis said, scowling at Cara-Beis. He knew of his pro-Nazi notions.

"Okay, phil-American, I'll see you later," said Cara-Beis and walked away. At some distance, he caught sight of Dan Cohen walking along with the priest's son, Christos. Outside Cambas' warehouse, they paused and chatted for a few seconds, and after a friendly handshake they parted. Cohen looked around the marketplace, waved good-bye to Christos, and entered the warehouse. Cunning Cara-Beis lingered for a few minutes behind a column outside. "Something is going on," he said to his friend, Lambis. "Why would the American sailor visit Cambas' place?" His schemes unfolded with the speed of light, configuring the purpose of this visit. It was not just a social matter. In perusing the harbor, he had noticed an array of steel barrels on the deck of the *North Star*. "Could the Americans want a cargo of olive oil?"

"Cara-Beis, you're a smart man," his friend Lambis said, tapping him on the shoulder. "You always figure things out."

"If olive oil is what they are after," Cara-Beis bit his lip, his mind soaring to grand heights, "I could strike a good bargain, purchase every ounce of oil available in Moria, mark up the price, and resell it to the *North Star*."

Lambis' mouth remained open. Thinking of the potential of such a sale, he said, "Do you think you can pull it off?"

Grabbing Lambis by the arm and squeezing it, he replied, "Just stand by me, brother, keep your mouth shut, and listen to what I have to say."

In a pinewood-paneled office, Dan Cohen found Costas Cambas sitting behind an oak desk. Cambas stood and extended his hand. "Welcome again," he said jovially and offered a chair. "Sorry I couldn't chat with you at the festival . . . too noisy. But I noticed you had a grand time."

"Yes, I did. Thank you." Cohen sat down and observed Cambas and his world with no small measure of curiosity. The eyes of the merchant were bright with the same vitality he had noted in the eyes of the other islanders. He was a noble man in his early sixties, crisply dressed in a gray suit and claret-colored tie. Silver-rimmed glasses magnified his sparkling blue-green eyes, and thick silver hair spilled onto his forehead and over his big ears. A prominent Greek nose overshadowed his thick salt-and-pepper mustache, which matched the tufts of his graying eyebrows. Spread on the wall behind him was a colorful oil painting of a suspension bridge, and on his right was a striking picture of

Cambas standing close to a woman almost his equal in height. *It's the girl I saw at the festival. I danced with her!*

Pointing to the oil painting, Cohen said, "That must be the Brooklyn Bridge."

"That's correct. An engineering marvel of its time—built by Washington A. Roebling in 1883," Cambas said proudly.

Impressed by Cambas' detailed knowledge, Cohen said, "I've noticed a pro-American spirit in Moria."

"What do you mean?"

"Well, I saw a big portrait of President Roosevelt at the American Café."

"Right," Cambas said with a slight irritation in his voice. "We have an epidemic in Lesbos called communism. Equal distribution of properties, equality of all material possession, that's the theme that prevails on this island, but nobody really knows what communism is all about. Yet the current is strong, and lately I hear rumors that we have a few Hitlerites in our town, too."

"The freedom-loving Greeks are flirting with such ideas? That's absurd," Cohen said.

"With war in Europe and the promises of Hitler, some of my lazy compatriots live in a fantasy world. Hitler will make a perfect life for them, and they expect free meals. Nonsense. They have no idea how destructive this new Napoleon is," Cambas said seriously.

Cohen listened with some interest, but his mind was on how he was going to present his interest in purchasing olive oil and also tell him about their mission.

"One man in this town defies those rebels with their ideas," Cambas said, proudly shaking his head. "That brave man is Alexis. When he remodeled his tavern, he renamed it the American Café. When I saw that sign I gave him the portrait of Roosevelt, and he was very happy. It cost him the loss of a few customers, but he didn't mind."

He filled two glasses with water from a ceramic pitcher and signaled to his guest to have a drink. "I'm glad you enjoyed the festival." Cambas said.

"My friend and I had a great time."

"Well, in this part of the world people don't like to work too much, but they know how to have fun." Cambas smiled. "Celebration of life is an integral part of our culture. Since ancient days, *to Efzin,* good living, has been our axiom. We have more feast days during the year than actual working days. That's why this country is so poor."

He leaned forward and held up his fist as if he were holding the reins of a horse. "America taught me a lesson: hard work, good pay," he said. "I worked honestly and hard and got well paid." He pointed at the Brooklyn Bridge with great esteem. "When I came back to the island, I applied the American system: teamwork and proper reward. Of course, I found the right workers, stood by their side, and worked equally hard next to them."

Sensing an unmistakable sincerity in Cambas' voice, Cohen explained the dual purpose of his visit. He mentioned that Papavasile had spoken very highly of him.

"You came to the right place," Cambas said. His eyes gleamed with the shrewdness of a businessman. He had a knack for sniffing out profitable business deals. But this evening, it was not just profit he was after. He had seen the American sailors mixing and dancing with his countrymen, and he was impressed. But he was also wondering why a ship with the American flag had anchored in Lesbos. He had a surge of good feelings about Dan. *Americans are good people. I'll do anything to help their mission,* he thought.

Although their dialogue started in Greek, Cambas insisted on speaking English. "My friend," he said, "I rarely get a chance to practice my English." He spoke reasonably well, with a charming accent, pronouncing each word with precision, slurring his "r"s and producing a harsh "h" sound. Having spent two decades in America, he considered himself Greek-American, and the people of Moria identified him as Cambas, the Americanos.

"Let's start with the olive oil," Cambas said. "Come with me." He lit a kerosene lamp and opened the fireproof door that led to another part of the warehouse. Cohen saw a symmetrical line of cement-covered tanks with wooden lids. The odor was heavy but not unpleasant, and the edifice was impeccable. "I have the best-quality oil and the best price on the island."

Cohen did not respond immediately, although he was impressed with what he saw. He needed to have Captain Thompson's approval before he could make any deal.

When Cohen left Cambas' warehouse, he thought, *This is one man I can trust.* He took a shortcut and walked uneasily down a dark side street, feeling a little tense. A soft throb of starlight illuminated his steps as he headed toward Alexis' café. As the captain had suggested, he would need to check out oil prices with more than one merchant.

He found two men at the American Café sitting by the window facing the street. Outside, streetlights shone on the marketplace, and people were going about their business. Alexis welcomed Cohen and secretly told him, "Ignore those two by the window. They are the curse of our town, Cara-Beis and Lambis." One of the names rang a bell in Cohen's mind. Alexis winked and brought to their table two glasses, a carafe of ouzo, and a plate of cucumber-tomato salad tossed in olive oil and vinegar, and garnished with feta cheese and sprinkled liberally with oregano.

Preoccupied with his schemes, Cara-Beis smiled and bowed his head in a form of greeting when he saw Cohen. *Now the mouse has come to the trap,* he thought. He ate and drank greedily, but the effects of alcohol fired his brain. In his deliriously happy fantasy he visualized himself selling to the *North Star* any cargo of oil he wished. Downing another glass of ouzo, he said, "Lambis, I swear to you, we're going to be rich."

"Too much ouzo!" Lambis laughed.

"Trust me," he said, tapping his forehead to signify his wisdom. Seeing Dan Cohen chatting with Alexis was a good sign. He took a couple of deep breaths, threw back his shoulders, and wiped his lips, ready to present himself as a giant in the oil business. His eyes widened in anticipation of impressing the foreigner.

"Join us, Mister American," Cara-Beis said while he made space at his table. "Have a drink with us," he said, and ordered Alexis to bring an extra glass and another carafe of ouzo.

"No drinks tonight," Cohen said politely, but he accepted a seat.

"My name is Cara-Beis, and this is my friend, Lambis. Welcome to our island."

"Thank you, gentlemen. My name is Dan Cohen, but my Greek name is Daniel Papadopoulos."

"So you're Greek," Cara-Beis said, assuming interest.

"Greek-American," Cohen said, fully aware that this man's hospitality had some ulterior motive.

"Too much drink at the festival?" Cara-Beis grinned.

"It was fun," Cohen said, but suddenly recalled his uncle's warning about Cara-Beis and eyed him suspiciously. On the left side of his temple was a purple, crescent-shaped scar, a kick from a mule that had left him marked for life. He wore a soldier's cap slightly off center to hide the scar, along with a khaki shirt, pants, and army boots. The customers in the café watched the American talking to Cara-Beis and wondered what was going on.

"People have been talking about you, Mr. Cohen!" With a false smile, Cara-Beis raised his eyebrows. And savoring another sip of ouzo, he said, "Of course, you made many girls jealous when you held Cambas' daughter by the hand and danced next to her."

"Did they tell you that?" Cohen chuckled. In spite of what his uncle had told him, he decided to be polite. He did not want to make any enemies during his visit.

Cohen decided to take the lead. "I'm interested in filling *the North Star* with good-quality olive oil."

"If the *North Star* is interested in olive oil," Cara-Beis said, assuming a merchant's attitude, "I'll fill your ship with the best-quality oil as soon as you give me the go-ahead." Cara-Beis sounded convincing. His face beamed as he boasted of his accomplishments in the oil business.

"We'll talk again," Cohen said, preparing to leave. "I need to get back to the ship."

Eagerly Cara-Beis asked, "Do we have a deal? No one else can give you the price per barrel that I plan to offer you."

"I can't make any promises yet."

"I'll be here tomorrow waiting." When Dan Cohen waved good-bye and left, Cara-Beis threw a fat wallet on the table and ordered drinks for everyone in the café. Full of himself, he stood and glanced around the room.

"*Stin Ygia sas,*" (to your health), he said, lifting his glass high. "I represent the hard-working people of Moria, not wealthy drones. Comrades, bottoms up!"

On his way to the ship, Cohen noticed that the warehouse was still lit up. He decided to go back and tell Cambas about the offer Cara-Beis had made to him.

"I hope you don't have to buy even a thimbleful of oil from that man or from anyone else." Cambas stood up and walked around his desk with firm, determined steps. In his hand he held a vial of golden oil, which he gave to Cohen and said, "Still warm, fresh from the press. Smell it."

Gently Cohen sniffled the oil and smiled. "It's very fragrant. May I taste it?"

"Of course," Cambas said, "but wait a second." In a covered basket were two loaves of freshly baked whole-wheat bread, which he had intended to take home. He twisted off a handful of the crunchy corner and gave it to his potential buyer. "The Greek way . . . Pour a few drops of oil on this and see if you like it."

Cohen did as he was told. Pleased with the taste, he nodded and said, "I've never had anything as tasty as this." Savoring the oiled bread, he felt a surge of confidence in the accomplished merchant.

"My friend, people who cook their food with my oil soar high to heavens." His eyes flashed with pride. He reached out and clasped Cohen's hand and said, "Come to my home on Sunday after church. I want you to experience what my olive oil does to food."

"I'd like that. Thank you." Cohen's face brightened.

"You'll enjoy meeting my sister, Pipina, and my daughter, Nina. She speaks English better than I do. That's my whole family."

"I appreciate the invitation, Mr. Cambas. Thank you." Cohen decided not to mention that he had already met Nina and danced with her.

"On Sunday you can tell me the latest about America the beautiful, and I'll tell you about a strategic spot that might interest you. It happens to be in one of my olive groves. You might like to see it."

"You're a good man, Mr. Cambas. You think of everything, but you may have to give me directions to your house."

"Easy! Near the west end of the harbor, follow the path to the two tall pines. You can't miss it. You'll see an iron gate, the only gate in the area. I'll be waiting for you. Shall we say, around noon?"

"Aye, I'll be there," Cohen said, and the two men shook hands and parted.

On the way back to the harbor, Cohen could not wait to update Captain Thompson on the special contact he had made with Cambas. He had seen the two pines. One of them would make a perfect replacement for the mast. Now he had another reason for visiting the oil tycoon. Before the oil agreement was signed and sealed, he would ask that one of the pine trees be included in the purchase of the oil. Cambas might even feel honored to know that one of his trees would become the *North Star*'s new mast.

CHAPTER SEVENTEEN

ON THE FOLLOWING SUNDAY, MARCH 31, Cohen set out excitedly for Cambas' house at noon. The sea breeze brushed against his white uniform. On both sides of the street, flowers decorated Moria's doors and windowsills. Guided by the two tall pine trees, their feathery tops swaying and reaching the skyline, he spotted the imposing iron gate. His heart beat with anticipation; he was delighted that Cambas invited him. Captain Thompson thought it was a unique opportunity to close the oil deal.

Cambas' house was one of the most beautiful villas on the island. A mosaic of brown, blue, and black sea-washed pebbles formed a huge bird, the phoenix, about fifty feet before a striking marble stairway. The bird pointed the way to the steps, which led up to the main door.

When Cohen arrived at the gate, he pulled a chain attached to a bell. Soon two men appeared at the door at the top of the steps. As the gate opened, Cohen walked toward them. When he reached the mosaic he paused and took a profound look at the bird, then walked around it. He did not want to step across it. Later Cohen would learn that the phoenix is the symbol of rebirth and resurrection.

Meanwhile, Cambas had come down the steps and was eagerly saying, "Welcome! Welcome, my American friend."

"Thank you," Cohen said, and the two warmly shook hands.

"I want you to meet my manager, Manolis Mourtos," Cambas said, as both men walked up the marble steps.

Cohen recognized the dancer at the festival who wanted to stop him from dancing with Nina. With a lukewarm glance, he said, "Hello."

The two exchanged a polite hello, but Mourtos' eyes examined the stranger from head to toe. Feeling threatened by the sailor's goodwill and impeccable appearance, he felt a nag of envy. *This fair-skinned foreigner was the one who had danced next to Nina at the festival. He had tried to stop him. He did not like him then, and he did not like him now. What is he doing here?* Giving Cohen a peevish look, he buttoned his leather jacket with annoyance and ran down the steps.

Cambas was dressed in a stylish worsted coat the color of chestnut. His neckpiece was perfectly tied, and a striped waistcoat hugged his solid ribs. A man of wealth, he wanted to display it in a reserved fashion. He ushered his guest into the vast dining room area, where a varnished walnut table was set for four. Grecian ceramic plates, ornate silverware, and cream-colored home-woven napkins decorated the table. Above this attractive arrangement, a crystal chandelier sparkled. The floor was covered with a strikingly colorful Persian rug. A tall woman dressed in black came out of the kitchen carrying the welcoming fragrance of dinner. Cohen could smell the aroma of spices mingling together.

"Mr. Cohen, this is my sister, Pipina."

"I'm happy to meet you," said Cohen, aware of who this woman was.

"The pleasure is mine." She hesitated, piercing him with her eyes as she extended her hand, not admitting that they had met before.

"Mr. Cohen is the first mate of the *North Star*," Cambas said jovially.

"What an honor!" Pipina said. Graciously, she welcomed her guest. Her dark brown eyes shone with joy. *Of course I have seen this man before. . . .* She excused herself to serve dinner. As she laid out the platters on the kitchen counter and arranged the food, she remembered vividly when she had first seen the sailor. *It was on the way to church weeks ago, and at the festival.* She was

92

delighted to see him there, holding hands with Nina and dancing, She had also noticed how Mourtos stood between them.

The March sun peeked through a large window, brightening the area where they sat enveloped in a golden glow. With pursed lips, Cambas stared at his pocket watch, which he took out of a velvet case. Presumably, a man of power expected punctuality. It was 12:45 p.m.

"Pipina," he boomed, "we shall wait no longer. Church was over a couple of hours ago. Nina ought to be here by now." He slipped the watch back into its case and returned it to the lower pocket of his waistcoat.

Silently Cohen observed his host's eyes while wondering where his daughter could be.

"My women have difficulty being on time, and I detest cold soup."

"Your soup will be steaming hot," Pipina said, as she emerged from the kitchen again. She made several swift trips to the kitchen, bringing in assorted dishes of delicacies and a tricolored salad sprinkled with feta cheese. The fragrance of kolokythokeftedes, Greek zucchini balls, and mousaka was intoxicating. Following signals from her brother, Pipina opened a cabinet beneath a China closet where special dishes and crystal were stored. She brought out a bottle of aged wine, a rare forty-year-old bottle from Cyprus reserved for important guests, and filled their glasses, pouring only a few drops for herself.

Both men clinked their glasses, saluting each other and savoring the wine. "Great wine," said Cohen, indulging in a second sip. Cambas downed his first glass and had a refill. Pipina ate politely, satisfied that the two men were enjoying her cooking. She could tell that her brother was in a rare mood of kindness. *Obviously he likes this guest very much.*

Cambas' tongue loosened after the second glass of wine. He lost the reserve he normally displayed in the company of strangers. He already liked everything he had seen about Dan Cohen. He admired his posture, height, facial expression, and daring spirit. Until now, he had met no man who would cross the Atlantic and seek his oil. He knew the deal with the *North Star* would be closed within days. Confident, he refilled the glasses. *God would grant me the greatest bliss if my daughter met a man like this one and fell in love with him,* he thought. *Then she would forget all this nonsense about becoming a nun.* With a glow of fatherly affection, he smiled at Cohen, took another sip of wine, and let his mind wallow in fantasy. *I wouldn't mind at all having a man like him as my son-in-law.*

The good wine created a cheerful spirit, and Costas Cambas felt mellow and talkative. With nostalgic eyes, he said, "My friend, I miss America. I wake up some nights, and in front of my eyes I see the Statue of Liberty." Cohen's nod of enjoyment encouraged him to continue. "How old are you? Excuse me for asking."

"Twenty-eight."

"At your age I was a maitre d' at the Washington Hotel in Washington, D.C. One day I had the good fortune to serve the president of the United States. Imagine me, a village boy, an olive-picker, serving food to the president of the U.S.A. What a thrill!" His eyes brimmed with joy.

"Remarkable! How old were you when you went to America?"

"Seventeen." Sadness came over Cambas' face. "Crazy age. The island could not contain me. I wanted to go to America to make my fortune. Twenty years later, when I was thirty-seven, I came back and married a woman from Moria. Then, back to America again! I was in love with America the beautiful! As fate would have it, my wife had a miscarriage and died, and I was left with a three-year-old girl." He paused, in deep thought for a few seconds, then took a sip of wine. *That my wife had a miscarriage and died was not the whole truth,* he thought. "So I said, Goodbye America, and came back to Lesbos to be with my sister for the sake of my daughter."

"I'm sorry to hear that. It must have been a hard time for you," Cohen said.

"Very hard," he said.

"But you seem to like it here," Cohen said.

"Yes, but I wish I had stayed in the U.S.A. There are more opportunities there."

"But you seem to be a wealthy man."

"Well, I'm grateful."

"What about your daughter?"

"I've tried to raise her like an American girl. I had a tutor teach her English. Of course my sister has been like a mother to her . . . ." A sudden anxiety appeared in his eyes. Pipina was busy in the kitchen. He shouted, "Pipina, where in the world is your niece?"

She came to the table, a sizzling spinach pie in her hands. She cut it into small slices and put a piece on each plate as an appetizer. "I left her with some of her friends after church services. They must still be talking. You know how girls are," Pipina said.

"On Sundays I expect all of us to eat together as a family. I want to be listened to in this house."

"Don't worry, she knows that."

"Pipina, I expect some discipline."

"Of course you do!" she said, rolling her eyes and smiling.

"By the way, the mousaka is well-peppered today, Pipina, so we may need an extra bottle of wine."

Cohen saw Pipina pursing her lips to conceal her reaction. As he studied his hosts, he noticed a strong resemblance between brother and sister. Both had similar faces and thick eyebrows.

"Let's enjoy the day. Nina should be here soon," Pipina said, keeping her eyes on her guest, and wishing her brother had better manners. *My brother's bark is worse than his bite.* She had a lot of influence on him, but in the presence of others she allowed him to have the last word. She poured more wine as her brother shook his head. *Women. They always side with each other.*

As he sipped the wine, Cohen examined his surroundings. Cambas and Pipina's tastes were impeccable; their wealth was apparent but never flaunted. Heavy chintz drapes kept out curious eyes, as did the gates and well-tended hedges that surrounded the mansion. Suddenly there was the sound of running footsteps, and Pipina and Cohen turned their heads toward the door.

Rushing up the stairway, Nina arrived, red-faced and panting. Cambas glared at her as she entered the dining room. She realized by his expression how much her tardiness had annoyed him. Wetting her lips with her tongue, she said, "I'm very sorry. I hope I haven't kept you waiting."

When she saw Cohen's face, she swallowed her shock, lowered her eyes, and sat hesitantly in the fourth chair. "I'm truly sorry for being late!"

"Mr. Dan Cohen, this is my daughter, Nina."

"*Kalos orisate.* Welcome." Nina smiled, instantly recognizing the sailor and holding back a chuckle. *How clumsily he had danced.*

"Thank you. Happy to meet you, ma'am." As he reached out to shake her hand, he felt a hot flush coming over his face and could hear the palpitations of his heart.

"We met at the festival," Nina said.

"Of course," Cohen said, as he took a bite of *spanakopita* spinach pie, nearly choking at the pleasant sight of her. Slowly bringing his glass to his lips, he looked at her as the wine trickled down his throat, giving him one of the most blissful moments of his life.

With an anxious heart and some confusion, Nina's eyes shuttled between her father and his guest, then she glanced at her aunt. Pipina had that calculating look on her face; Nina could read her matchmaking spirit.

Near the end of the meal, Cohen offered a toast to his hosts, thanking them for the delicious meal, but he was finding it difficult to think of eventually leaving this desirable company. *Would this merchant ever allow his daughter out of his sight?* he wondered.

"Mr. Cohen, tell us what the Americans think of Hitler." Cambas was more interested in finalizing the oil transaction than discussing politics, but his style was subtlety.

"They don't think he will last long."

"Would they ever go to war against Germany?"

"Americans never attack unless they are attacked, and I don't think Hitler would dare."

"That lunatic can't be trusted. Yesterday his army crossed the Greek border."

"Do you think the Nazis will come as far as Lesbos?" Nina asked in a worried voice, looking at both men with concern.

"What would they want from this island?" Pipina shrugged.

Cambas opined, "I don't think they would be interested in Lesbos unless olive oil is what they are after. Which reminds me . . ."

Pipina's face spelled *No business talk on Sundays.* Attuned to his sister's slightest mood, Cambas heeded her message and bowed to her superior sense of the social graces. Turning to Nina, he changed the subject.

"Where were you, young lady? The church was over hours ago."

Nina whispered to her father, "I was visiting my friend Maria. You probably don't know, but she is ill. She looks so pale and weak. Perhaps later today I'll bring her some food," she added, toying with her spoon.

"And you should be back on time."

"Yes, Father."

Meanwhile, Pipina explained Greek tradition during Lent, trying to make her guest feel at home. Cohen's eyes met Nina's several times, and on each occasion she smiled faintly and looked down at her food or gazed nervously out the window. The sun radiated from the cloudless sky. Cohen was entranced by Nina's beautiful face, white neck, dark brown eyes, long lashes, and long dark tresses. He sipped a little more wine each time their eyes met. Their minds wrestled to guess each other's thoughts. Nina wanted to believe that his demeanor was genuinely pleasant. Unlike the young men of the island, he was strikingly good-looking. She was fascinated with his blond hair, tanned skin, and bluish-hazel eyes. It was easy for her to understand why she was so attracted to him.

"My friends have been talking about the *North Star* and the American sailors," she said.

"They have?" he smiled. "My friend and I saw you on your way to church the first Sunday we were ashore. I said we were looking for a pine tree. Do you remember? And you told us we were going the wrong way."

Nina, impressed at his ability to speak Greek, could not take her eyes off his eyes. She shook her head. But the way she looked at him made him wonder, *Does she like me?*

Pipina said tartly, "Nina, you've studied English. Let's hear you speak to our guest. He's come thousands of miles to be here." But Nina's lashes remained charmingly closed like wings over her eyes.

Cohen watched her hand movements, the velvety softness of youth and shyness, and his ears began to ring. He avoided eye contact and kept talking to her father, simply because his heart was pounding. Despite the conservative design of her dress, he noticed her body almost shone through the cloth with exceptional sensuality. Whatever thoughts were crossing her mind made her blush, and he watched a red surge come over her face.

"You must have met our priest. Our people love him," said Nina, unable to think of a more interesting topic.

"Aye, ma'am. Papavasile is a very good man! He invited my first mate and me for coffee. Then he took us to the American Café." Cohen was careful not to reveal how well he knew the priest.

Pipina felt her face turn poppy-red. Anything pertaining to Papavasile made her heart quiver. Though her love for the priest was great, she would carry her feelings for him to the grave. No human soul would ever suspect her secret. She could see her niece interacting flirtatiously with their guest. Her hands and lips both quivered.

Cohen's knife fell on the floor, and he swore under his breath. But as he leaned under the table to retrieve it and saw Nina's statuesque legs, he was spellbound. *What a gorgeous creature. Definitely a muse!* He smiled.

As he finished his wine, he began to feel intense heat pulsing through his limbs. A persistent itch in the center of his body made him shift positions on his chair. A sweet fantasy swept him away from his gracious hosts. *What if I could marry this gorgeous creature that's sitting across from me?* Sweat trickled down his spine. He imagined himself on the *North Star,* with his arms clasped around Nina's waist, smelling her hair in the ocean breeze, touching her cheek, pressing his chest against her breasts. He visualized all the nights they would travel on the sea, searching the sky for their lucky star. He saw his cabin and sensed the scent of a woman like Nina sharing his bed, a woman he would kiss and hold in his arms and make love to, and who would be the mother of his children! His fantasy left him tongue-tied.

Their eyes met, and what he saw in hers made his heart thump and interrupted his daydream. In his tenure of travel with Captain Thompson he had seen many beautiful women, but Nina was extraordinarily different. She had an angelic face, a sweet countenance, a smile, but melancholy in her eyes. Woe and wonder wrestled within him. Maybe he should say something, but he felt speechless.

Cambas came to his rescue. "I'm drinking alone," he said. He sipped the last drop of his wine and picked up the carafe to refill the glasses. Cohen covered his glass with his hand. "That's enough for me, Mr. Cambas. Thank you."

"Just another drop, Mr. Cohen!"

"How did you get the name Cohen?" Nina asked.

"It's a long story," he said.

"I know it's not Greek."

"Of course it is," he teased. In a more serious tone he said, "Actually, when my father went to America, he decided to change his name for convenience. Your father can tell you that Americans cannot pronounce long Greek names—like Papadopoulos, for example. So he changed it."

"Really?" With incredulity in her eyes, Nina said, "So you are Greek?"

"Of course he is," her father said.

"On my father's side, yes. My mother was German-American."

She realized that Cohen's fair skin and light hair probably came from his mother's side. She asked, "Do your parents live in the United States?"

"They died some years ago."

"I'm sorry."

Nina looked at her father and then at Cohen. She noticed a sudden shrewd look in her father's face, and she rolled her eyes, signaling to her aunt that something was going on. Pipina's antennae were up, and she nodded back gracefully. Without a word being spoken, the two women understood that Cambas probably wanted to be alone with his guest. Both women excused

99

themselves to take the dishes to the kitchen. Nina picked up the guest's dish as well as her own. She had not eaten much, and she saved the remainder on her plate for Apollo, who meowed in the kitchen. Another thought was in Nina's mind: She wanted her father to like this man.

When the two men were alone, Cambas suggested to his guest that if he would like to visit the lumber mill, he could arrange for transportation.

"Tomorrow is a good day for me," Cohen said. "Would I be able to take some pictures?"

"No problem, just bring your camera," said Cambas.

This will be a good opportunity to seek out foxholes, Cohen thought.

When the women returned to the dining area, Cambas said, "Mourtos will drive our guest to the mill tomorrow."

"Father, may I go, too?" asked Nina. "It's over two years since I was there."

"Of course, if you want to," Cambas said and rose from the table. "Now Mr. Cohen and I will stretch our legs, and I'll show him our garden."

"Nina can show Mr. Cohen the garden," Pipina said as she gathered up the rest of the dishes and silverware.

"No, no," said Cambas, walking toward the back door that led to the garden. "We need to have a man-to-man talk."

"But you look tired." Pipina stared at him. "Remember, Dr. Andrew advised you to rest after meals. It's your heart I'm concerned about," she said firmly.

Cambas put a white woolen cap on his head and nodded for Cohen to go out first. "I'm not in the least tired, and there is nothing wrong with my heart. What is the matter with you?"

Pipina widened her eyes, disappointed that her brother did not catch her point. Their guest was already outside.

"Alright, go." Then she deliberately dropped a handful of knives and forks on the floor and leaned forward to retrieve them. "Oh, my back again! My miserable back. Just give me a hand . . . and . . . ." She squeezed her brother's hand and moaned. Cohen heard the noise and rushed back. "Can I help you?" He leaned down and picked up the silverware.

Pipina handed the tray to her brother and said, "Take this to the kitchen and then go to your garden." She sounded exasperated. She looked at Nina, winked with a smile, and said, "Nina, please show Mr. Cohen our garden. Your father will join you shortly."

Cambas' eyes were full of suspicion as he carried the tray into the kitchen. This was a woman's job; he was not in the habit of carrying dishes. When they were alone in the kitchen, Pipina shook her head and whispered through her teeth, "Won't you ever give her a chance? Can't you see they enjoy each other's company? Did you notice the gleam in her eyes? I think she likes our guest!"

"A fine aunt you are," grumbled Cambas. "A cunning matchmaker."

Amused at Pipina's clever ruse, he said, "I guess Nina can practice her English with the American."

CHAPTER EIGHTEEN

THE GARDEN DOOR opened with a faint squeak, and Nina's eyes invited Cohen to follow her. Together they entered a colonnade of white sculptured pillars whose marble roof afforded ample shade from the sun. This charming arcade led to a colorful, pebble-paved path. Nina, who knew every inch of the garden, nimbly strolled along, pointing out her favorite flowers. Cohen trailed awkwardly, thinking, *If the captain could only see me with this gorgeous woman he might be jealous.* But the captain's voice echoed in his brain: *Keep your pants on.* Occasionally, he stumbled on a tree root or a sudden hillock. *It's easier to walk on the deck of a ship,* he thought. The salty smell of the Aegean Sea became stronger, but not unpleasant. Cohen reached for her hand, and they descended a long, steep stairway cut into the rocks. Nina beamed, recalling his strong grip as they danced at the festival. With every heartbeat, her thoughts for him caused unexpected feelings.

At the bottom of the stairway lay a massive stone that bordered the sea. Cambas had spent a fortune to have this rock leveled and to create this patio to please his daughter. The long, flat surface was covered with a sky-blue-and-white-striped awning as protection from the summer sun. Bamboo chairs and a table had been permanently affixed to the stone.

Nina had remained unspoiled, although her father showered her unstintingly with his generosity. What still delighted Cambas was that she picked a fresh rose from their own garden every Friday evening and placed it on the desk in his library.

The young couple walked in the garden for a long time as Nina explained the history of every statue and piece of artwork they passed. As the first statue of the mythical phoenix appeared among laurel and myrtle bushes, Nina explained how the bird would die, and in the fourth year it would rise from its own ashes as a symbol of resurrection. "The phoenix has become our symbol in Lesbos," she said.

Sappho's statue, a masterpiece of white Pentelic marble elaborately sculptured, evoked greater attention. She explained that Sappho, poet and philosopher, was the pride of the island.

"In college, I learned that Sappho was a lover of women. Is that true?"

"Yes," Nina said. "But not in the way people think. Some scholars have distorted Sappho's motives."

"Why would they do that?"

"I don't know. All I know is that she wanted to raise the morale of women in her time. Sometime in the sixth century B.C., after being educated in Sicily, she returned to Lesbos and founded a school of music and etiquette. All her students were young girls."

"But her poems were erotic?"

"Wedding songs, love songs praising the virtues of young brides."

Cohen realized he had been bested. Nina was far more knowledgeable on the subject than he was. He also enjoyed listening to her distinct articulation of English. Impressed, he asked, "How did you learn all this?"

"During one of his trips to Athens, my father brought me back a twelve-volume encyclopedia of Greek mythology, written in English, with full-color illustrations. I'll show it to you when we get back."

"And you speak the language so well."

"Thank you," she said. "I had a professor from England. He was such a good man."

"I love the British accent," Cohen said.

"Is it different?"

"Distinct."

"I heard you talking Greek with my father. You do well."

"I try, but I need practice."

"At least you can communicate with our people."

"Beautiful people—and this is a wonderful island," Cohen said.

"Of course, we do have some good people—and some bad ones. But we have poets, artists, and renowned teachers that were born and lived here," she said with a charming look, and with pride.

"And you, of course," he smiled.

"Of course!" she confirmed with a chuckle.

Her heart quivered at his smile, and she wondered what he thought of her. He looked serene and inspired by the beautiful surroundings. He moved closer to her and said, "I can see how the magic of this place could turn someone into a poet." He stooped down and picked a bunch of wild violets. He touched them to his lips and gave them to her, eyeing the expression on her face.

"For me?" Nina almost gasped when she met his gaze. The sun seemed caught in his smile, coloring his eyes, reflecting the sky. Her long, delicate fingers caressed the flowers as her heart began to pound intensely from the unforeseen attraction she felt to this stranger. An image crossed her mind, of two sailors on her way to church. The initial mysterious feeling that had stirred within her then was now so much more vivid and real. For half a second, she closed her eyes. A river of emotions flowed within her, reminding her of Stephen, her first love. Had he lived, he would now be as old as her guest. When she opened her eyes and looked at him, she sensed a likeness to Stephen. *Is God trying to tell me something?*

"You seem to have something on your mind. Are you okay?"

"Oh, I'm fine," Nina answered, not wishing to reveal that his eyes reminded her of the young man she once loved dearly. Behind an evergreen hedge, a hidden waterfall whispered an unending song. As the two walked silently together, the sound of the waterfall died away, and Nina could hear the murmur of the sea waves. Soon they reached the thick stone wall that protected the garden from the sea. A row of peach trees, fully blossomed, looked like brides.

Cohen observed with interest the trees and bushes, flowers and rocks, but his eyes spontaneously followed Nina's movements. Accidentally, their bodies brushed against each other. Then Nina lost her balance and stumbled, but Cohen instantly grabbed her lest she fall and hurt herself. Holding her in his arms, he asked if she was alright.

"I'm just fine," she said again, giggling. "I haven't stumbled on this path since I was three." Her warm and pulsating body in his arms fired the blood in his body. He wanted to continue holding her. But gently she pulled away, although she wanted his manly embrace to last longer.

Beneath the branches of an almond tree, they gazed across the Aegean Sea. Butterflies flitted in the sunshine, and mating birds sang sweet love calls. Under the trees, the grass was so thick that Nina longed to lie down and stretch out. She pulled her shawl off her shoulders and spread it on the grass. "Sit on this," she said. "Otherwise your white uniform will turn green."

"Then I would look like an Irish sailor," he said. "Don't worry, I have another one in my cabin," he laughed.

Nina sat down, leaning back against the trunk of a tree and made space for Cohen. He sat near her feet and gazed at her eyes, speculating on her thoughts. She saw the look in his eyes and quickly pulled her skirt over her knees. Somehow she felt as if she had become a crystal case in which all her thoughts, feelings, and desires were arrayed for his inspection. In spite of her excitement, a trace of melancholy lingered in her eyes.

Although she had everything, her face revealed that something was missing in her life. *If I could only read his mind. Could he ever give up the sea and live on the island? Why am I attracted to seamen?* She thought of Stephen and the fatal night when she had begged him not to go fishing. *Why am I thinking of these things? What about my plan to become a nun?* Entangled thoughts caused confusion in her mind.

Cohen indulged in his own reverie. These moments in the garden were taking precedence over his dual mission on the island. He got up and stretched his arms. A few dry leaves were sticking to his pants, but Nina brushed them off. When she stood closer to him he smelled the scent of her hair and wanted to engulf her in his arms. But afraid she might get scared, he hesitated. His attention was attracted to something on the tree. He reached high and carefully pulled down a branch. Excited by his discovery, he said, "Look, a bird's nest!"

"How beautiful," she said. "Three tiny blue eggs."

Gently he allowed the branch to ascend, and with a child's curiosity he said, "What is it that causes birds to build such intricate nests?"

"Well, where else can they keep their babies? Humans build houses," Nina answered and began to walk.

"Your home is a palace."

"My father's dream."

"What's your dream?"

"I don't know." Averting her gaze from him, Nina looked far across the harbor at the cream-colored buildings of the Convent of the Virgin Mary. Glistening among the olive groves, it was a place of peace and prayer.

At that moment, Cohen reached out and took her hand into his own. It felt cold. "Are you cold?" he asked. His eyes penetrated her gaze. Gently, she pulled her hand back. "You seem sad."

"No," Nina said, eyelashes lowered.

"What are you staring at?" he asked softly.

Cohen felt he had reached the point of telling her what was in his heart and mind, but he could not express it in words.

After moments of thoughtful silence, Nina said, "Do you see that building?" she pointed to it. "It's a convent, and it's where I would like to go some day, to give my life to God."

"You?" Cohen asked, totally surprised.

"Yes. I have wanted to become a nun ever since I was a teenager."

A sudden chill ran down his spine unlike anything he had ever felt before. His lips opened, closed, and quivered, then he said, "A nun, why? No, no, you mustn't. You can't."

"Why not?" she asked, hoping that he would say what she wanted to hear—*I love you and want to be my wife.* But he did not.

"Are you trying to escape the realities of life?" he asked, finally finding his tongue. "The good, the evil, the world's endless adventures? Why?" Disappointment saddened his face.

"I'm not sure I understand what you are asking."

"Well, I'll tell you." Cohen's mouth felt dry. He licked his lips. "Have you ever known the love of a man? Is there no hunger in you for a child?"

For a minute, his eyes held hers, and Nina saw in his an unfathomable passion. She was dumbfounded. Three years of college education in Athens, private tutoring by highly esteemed teachers on the island, and she could not utter a word. His words seemed to fill an emptiness in her heart that she had felt since Stephen's death.

"Isn't there a yearning in your heart for your own home, for a man's embrace, for a child of your own? For the joy of having the man you love come home to you at the end of the day?"

She heard the excitement and conviction in his voice, but also a sensitivity that he might have said too much, since they had only known one another for a short time. It was the first time Nina had ever heard such words from a man. She saw anguish in his face and said, "Yes, there is a longing in my heart for a home and for children, hundreds of children, but not the kind of home you mean. When I become a nun, I intend to gather all the orphans and the neglected little children of this island and make a home for them. I'll teach them things and provide them with warmth, protection, and love."

Cohen drew closer to her. He reached for her hand, and this time she allowed him to take it. Both their hearts beat faster, both their hands felt warmer. "That's a remarkable idea! But why must you become a nun to help children?"

His fingers gripped hers tightly, and she realized that the mere touch of his hand was altering her whole world. She felt as if another person were being born within her, a woman who knew herself and who unabashedly desired a man. For the first time since Stephen's death, she was seized by an uncontrollable yearning for physical contact, a kiss. She wanted this handsome sailor to hold her tight, but the very thought frightened her. Nervously, she tried to pull her hand back, but he would not let it go and she did not mind. Flushed, she stared again at the other side of the harbor. The slanting rays of the sun struck the convent, making it glow like a jewel.

"What's the attraction to that place? Tell me, are you trying to escape something? Tell me the truth."

"Please don't talk like that." Nina remained silent for a few seconds. Sadness around her heart caused her whole body to feel numb. Confused, she slowly pulled her hand away from his and began to walk along the pebble path leading back to the house. Unable to understand a young and beautiful woman's desire to become a nun, Cohen moved beside her, and both walked in silence until the path brought them to a small orange grove where they paused.

Nina feigned smelling the white and purple blossoms. "Mmm, delicious," she said to change the subject and break the tension between them. Cohen found a long reed from a nearby bush, threaded fragrant orange blossoms through it, and made a necklace.

"That's so pretty," she said. But when he tried to garland her neck, the reed broke and all the blossoms scattered at her feet.

"Oh dear!" she giggled.

"I'm sorry." Cohen took her hand again, and this time held it close to his side. She walked slowly, still holding his hand. There was only a little more distance to the house, and he felt agony constricting his chest. He wanted to tell Nina that life was too rich to run away from, that there was beauty and value in every tear shed for a loved one, in every despondent thought, in every joy or sorrow. He realized they were getting close to the house and that he could no longer afford to wait. Gently, he drew her under the shade of an orange tree and placed his hands on her arms.

"Are you sure it is the will of God for one as beautiful as you to live behind the convent walls?"

Nina shivered like a wild bird caught in a cage. Affectionately, Cohen shook her shoulders and embraced her tightly, demanding an answer.

"I made a vow to myself . . . I . . . I've never thought of anything else," she said weakly. She quaked in his arms, and a cry arose within her, the cry of a woman who did not want to face life alone, whose heart had another unrealized yearning. She wanted strong shoulders to lean on and needed a man as surely as nature needed God.

Seeing her wavering, he said gruffly, "No, you don't belong in a convent. You were born to love and be loved by a man." A shiver down his spine triggered a sudden vitality within, a life force that he needed to translate into action. If he did not express to her that very moment the warmth that he felt in her presence, he could lose her forever. With his hands on the small of her back, he pressed her to himself and kissed her hungrily, shooting desire through her body as she helplessly opened her mouth to his probing tongue.

Nina was in shock that a guest in her father's house would dare to pull her toward him and cover her mouth with his, but she was also pleasantly curious about the feeling it evoked in her, and she did not resist. As she was absorbed by his kisses, he took her hand in his and led it to explore his body. Timidly she began stroking his hair and caressing his cheeks. Holding her even tighter to himself, she felt his throbbing heart against her breasts and his manhood against her thighs. Momentarily frightened, she yanked herself away. Eyes blazing anger, she said, "You are terrible . . . a terrible man!"

Leaving him unsettled and wandering in the garden, she ran into the house and upstairs to her room. Her father was dozing in his study, but Pipina heard her footsteps and went after her. "Is there anything the matter, child? What's wrong?"

Nina fell into her aunt's arms, hoping that she would understand, as she sobbed.

"Don't cry, child. It hurts me to see you in tears. Tell me what happened?"

"I hate him, just hate him," Nina said angrily and fell on her bed, burying her tearful face in the pillow.

"What did that beast do to you?" demanded Pipina.

Nina turned to her aunt with a trace of resentment in her eyes. "He's not a beast . . . and he didn't do anything to me. I just hate him."

"Yes, yes, dear, I'm sure you do," said Pipina. She closed Nina's door and stood for a moment outside her room. "Oh, my aching back." She laughed, cocked her head upward, and winked at God.

Cohen remained in the garden ruminating for minutes. If Nina told her father what happened under the orange tree, he would feel terribly embarrassed. Apprehensively, he returned to his hosts, and found Pipina serving coffee to her brother.

"Oh, Mr. Cohen," Cambas said with a chuckle, "I mean, my American friend, did you like the garden?"

Before he could answer, Pipina said, "How about a cup of Greek coffee?"

"No, thank you," he said, his heart racing. "I really must return to the ship." He bowed, avoiding Pipina's eyes. "Thank you for your hospitality. Everything was exceptional." He shook Cambas' hand and then his sister's and said, "Your garden is a real paradise."

"Well, I'm glad you like our garden, I mean, Nina's garden," she said. "Come back and visit us again."

"Thank you, I will," he replied, suspecting her cunning look to be an invitation.

CHAPTER NINETEEN

LATE THAT NIGHT, the full moon unfolded its silvery veil over the island. In a daze, Cohen stretched himself out in a long chair on the deck of the *North Star* and rocked in the Aegean's calm and rhythmic waves. He cradled a shiny old guitar in his arm and mused. It was his companion during the long sea voyages. He had strummed the strings tenderly on the day his mother died, when at first he could not cry. But in later days, the sound of the guitar unleashed hot tears, as he visualized his mother's tragic end.

As the breeze caressed his face, he felt her presence, sitting close beside him. For a second, glimpses of her blonde hair, sky-blue eyes, light skin, and tall, slender body paraded through his mind. Responding to his fingertips, the strings of his guitar harmonized a comforting tone, words that he could tell her—his trip to Lesbos, meeting wonderful people, his Uncle Thanos, Cambas and his family. But a sudden thought about meeting Nina brought him back to reality—back to a ship with a broken mast anchored in a Greek island to purchase olive oil and to search for possible sites for military posts.

The island bathed in the springtime moonlight caused his eyes to moisten, but tears would not come. Thoughts of wanting to stay here and make his home on Lesbos danced in his mind. He had no reason to return to America. He thought of his father's dream, to return to his homeland someday. Why did he leave Lesbos in the first place? Maybe it's the destiny of humans to explore other lands, to seek their purpose elsewhere. Cambas had done it. He left his island, gone to America, made his fortune, and come back a wealthy man. He admired Cambas, a man he thought he could trust and whose advice could be valuable. Now he wanted more than oil and help for his mission. He wanted Cambas' daughter to fall in love with him so that he could marry her. *Perhaps I overstepped the mark in the garden,* he thought. *But I could not help myself. It was love at first sight, and I wanted to confess my love to her, but could not find the words.*

"*Agape mou, agape mou,*" he whispered. "My love, my love." Far off, the silhouette of the two pine trees leading to the Cambas estate seemed taller, growing by the moment. The captain's voice resounded in his mind, *Have fun, but don't fall in love in a foreign land. In every harbor there could be someone to love, but a sailor's first love is the sea. Anything else is a betrayal.*

Cohen had fallen in love a few times in his travels, but he could not remember ever feeling as he did about Nina. He longed to see her again. Strumming his guitar, his mind wandered back to the garden where he and Nina had walked that afternoon. What destiny had brought him five thousand miles away from home? He raised his eyes upward as if the sky had the answer. Above the mast of the *North Star,* twinkling millions of stars filled the dark blue sky. But Cohen could hear Captain Thompson's voice echoing: *Stars are like great ideals and lofty ambitions, unattainable under any circumstances. But stars help us, the seafarers, to reach our destination.*

Spotting a star that blazed brighter than the others, he softly began to sing an impromptu song:

> *Little star, the brightest in the sky,*
> *I wish I could wrap you up in a box,*
> *Tie a golden ribbon around,*
> *And send you to my love tonight!*

How many stormy nights had he searched the sky for a special star. Seeing it now, he felt a joyous tremor in his chest. "This song is for another star," he muttered to himself, "a very special woman I cannot erase from my mind."

Go to sleep, my sweet star,
Let your eyelids rest;
You shone your beams upon me
And I've been forever blessed.

Cohen had a flair for melodies, but never before he had been able to write a song that rhymed. An unusual spell had come over him tonight. In a moment of ecstasy, more verses flowed from his lips like a rivulet and the singing continued:

Sleep, my heavenly angel,
And dream about me,
Then tell me in the morning
What you dreamed of me.
When dawn comes in its glory,
Tenderly open your eyes;
Send me a beam of love,
Fill my heart with smiles.

At midnight the moon slid behind a huge dark cloud. A chill in the air sent him back to his cabin. He lied on his narrow cot and reflected. *Could I really care so much for someone I have just met? Is it possible to fall in love after one kiss, a kiss I imposed upon her? It doesn't make sense. It must be infatuation or I must be nuts. Perhaps I have been too many days at sea and I'm not thinking clearly.*

He jumped up from his bed and went to the mirror that hung crookedly above a porcelain sink. He turned on the water full force and put his head under it. His thoughts were making him groggy. Cool water dripped from his thick hair onto his shoulders and chest. He looked at himself in the mirror and mumbled, "Either I'm falling in love or I'm losing my mind."

Turning away from the mirror, a troubling notion challenged him—the truth. *Women have always been a game for me. Do I think I am Don Juan? That I must have any beautiful woman I meet?*

Numbly, he ran his fingers over his face and through his hair and sat on his cot in obvious confusion. From a stack of old magazines, he picked up one and turned the pages absentmindedly, focusing on nothing. He put down the magazine and grabbed the guitar again, unable to push Nina out of his mind. He rested the guitar in his arm, visualizing the stunning woman he had kissed in her father's garden. His fingers touched the strings making awkward sounds, but he could no longer play the guitar or sing. Obsession had found room in his heart. He kept telling himself this could not be happening to him. *How could I think of settling down in one port with one girl? Insanity,* he thought. *A sailor could love a girl in every port, as many girls as there are waves in the sea. I must be reliving my adolescent life, but I'll have recovered by morning.*

On his way to the bathroom, Tiny Tom heard the strings and knocked on Cohen's cabin. He pushed the door open and found Cohen sitting on the cot hugging his guitar and looking depressed.

"You still up?"

"I can't sleep."

"Why not?"

"I don't know."

Tiny Tom smiled knowingly. "Get some sleep, lover boy. There's lots of work to be done tomorrow."

"I can't sleep."

"You must be thinking about the Greek goddess?"

"What if I am?"

"Get over it, lover boy," Tiny said and waved goodnight.

"Wait a minute," Cohen said. "A couple of nights ago, you were not on the ship."

"Danny Cohen, we'll talk about that tomorrow," Tiny Tom said and left quickly. He was not about to discuss his visit to Despina.

CHAPTER TWENTY

COCKS ANNOUNCED THE BREAKING OF DAWN. Nina buried her head in her pillow to shut out the noise. She had hardly slept. A tempest of feelings tangled inside her, and her pulse throbbed in her temples. Each time she closed her eyes she saw the young sailor and heard his voice. She rolled her tongue over her lips and thought she felt his scent. A war had erupted between heart and logic. Yesterday's stranger turned out to be this morning's suitor. How could this be? But his kiss was different. Stephen was the young man who had introduced her to kissing. But nothing could compare to the sailor's kiss. When their bodies touched, she felt electrified. But a life with him was unrealistic. He was just a sailor visiting the island for his own personal purposes. Soon he would leave her. She was glad she had called him a terrible man. *He probably stalks women in every port.* She couldn't make herself believe it, and she felt a tinge of guilt for even doubting his intentions. She cast a serious glance at the icon of the Virgin Mary that hung on the wall next to her bed. It seemed that the Blessed Mother's kind, sensitive eyes were staring back at her. *"Panagia,* Most Holy One, Mother of Jesus, show me the way," she prayed under her breath.

A gusty wind blew the window panels open, and the icon crashed to the floor, its glass broken. In shock, Nina screamed.

Pipina dashed in, partially dressed, her hair tousled. Seeing the fallen icon, she shivered with fear and crossed herself as she gently picked it up. "Jesus Christ conquers and disperses all evil," she whispered with evident fear.

Nina rose and knelt down by her aunt. "Why did this happen?" she asked in fear.

"I don't know, child," Pipina whispered. "I just don't know. Go to bed, it's still early."

Nina nodded and returned to bed, covering herself with a soft silk quilt that she pulled over her head. In the dark under the cover, she felt weak with fatigue and slept deeply.

It was nearly eight o'clock when she finally woke up to a room filled with soft sunlight. The windows overlooking the village offered a panoramic view of Moria bustling with activity. A flock of white sheep pattered by on their way to the hills. Two elderly women swept almond and plum tree leaves from the narrow street. A sudden urge within sent her to her wardrobe. She donned a pleated skirt, a cream blouse, a pair of boots, and out of the house she dashed. Half an hour later, the sailor, casually dressed in civilian work clothes with his camera slung over his shoulder, arrived near the two pine trees. He looked pleasantly surprised to see Nina waiting for him in the carriage. Mourtos, standing by the mares, glanced at the sailor with evident envy. His boss had asked him to bring Nina and their guest to the mill.

"I didn't think you would come," Cohen said, concealing his excitement as he climbed into the back of the carriage and sat beside her.

"I made a promise. I am keeping it," she said in a mock serious tone. Without looking at Mourtos, she motioned for him to drive on. Upset that the sailor sat next to Nina, he whipped the mares a bit too harshly to vent his anger. The harness bells rang gaily, and the carriage rolled away.

Cohen busied himself adjusting the lens of his camera, getting it ready to take pictures. Then he leaned back in the carriage and looked at Nina's face. Her skin was as white as cream, her cheeks a light rose color, framed by her long, chestnut-brown hair. When the carriage made an abrupt sharp turn, her hair brushed against his face. He took a deep breath, inhaling her aroma, and felt both happy and miserable. He wanted to put his arm around her waist, but he didn't dare.

Sensing his silence to be anxiety, she said, "Are you enjoying the scenery, Mr. Cohen?"

"Aye, ma'am," he replied, focusing his camera on her profile. He snapped a picture, and then another one.

Nina turned to look him straight in the eyes. Strong undefined feelings were waking within her, sitting next to a man whose presence had kept her awake last night. In the dreamlike radiance of the morning she felt exuberant. Her lips quivered, wanting to kiss him, her heart palpitated as the sailor leaned close to her. Cohen allowed his knee to touch hers, but he pulled it back apologetically, given her the impression that the motion of the carriage caused him to touch her. More honestly, he wanted to snuggle closer, to hug and kiss her, but the disapproving glances from her father's manager spelled *Sailor, behave,* reminding him that he was Cambas' guest.

"What's the matter, ma'am?" Cohen said softly. "Can't you smile a bit so I can take another picture?"

Nina remembered his steely arms around her and shifted in her seat, pulling slightly away from him. Summoning courage, she faced him with feigned irritation. "Alright, take another picture, Mr. Cohen, but just one more."

He clicked his camera twice. "Thank you, ma'am."

"Do you always have to call me 'ma'am'? I do have a name, you know."

"Aye, ma'am," he said. "I could call you Nina."

"Only my friends and those who love me call me Nina."

"May I also be your friend, ma'am?"

"A friend is someone you can trust."

"Aye, ma'am."

She turned toward him. "I can't stand hearing you call me ma'am, ma'am, all the time." She had to stifle her laughter. "Call me Nina."

"Now that we're friends, don't call me Mr. Cohen anymore. You may call me Danny. All my friends do," he teased.

The carriage stopped before Nina could reply. At the sight of Cambas, Cohen jumped down from his seat and attempted to assist Nina from the carriage. Shaking her head, she preferred to step down herself. Mourtos observed how her eyes followed the sailor.

As Cohen and Cambas shook hands, Mourtos walked away from the carriage. Jealousy boiled within him. He picked up a stick, angrily broke it in two, and forcefully threw the pieces on the ground.

Cambas showed his guest the lumber mill, which was built close to a mountain stream. He pointed to a crevice between two towering rocks and winked. Cohen understood. Casually, he took a couple of pictures and said, "Promising." Gingerly he climbed up the rock where he could see the abyss below, a perfect shelter for artillery, he thought. On the opposite side lay the Aegean Sea, its blue water bordering Asia Minor. His surroundings filled him with awe, and his love of Lesbos grew.

Among a forest of pines, over a dozen hard-working men were stripping logs and finishing them into planks. Cohen thought about how much time and labor could be saved with just one American electric saw. After a polite "good morning" to her father's workers, Nina took a stroll toward a tiny chapel located on the hilltop. She went in, lit a candle, sat in prayer, and thought about Cohen being with her father.

Cambas was jolly and enthusiastic, addressing each employee with a personal touch and introducing his guest. Taking time and treating them as members of his company was the secret of his success. *Teamwork was a strategy he had learned in America,* Cohen thought. He took several snaps of Cambas talking with his workers and explaining to him the intricacies of his lumber business. "Will I see you again tomorrow? Come and take some more pictures." Cambas clapped Cohen on the shoulder and whispered, "These fellows will spread the word through our little town that you are interested in lumber."

"That's great," said Cohen. "Good lumber, Mr. Cambas," he said in a louder voice. "I'll be back tomorrow." He snapped a few more pictures of the workers, who paused and smiled.

"I'll expect you," replied Cambas with a hearty laugh.

Cohen looked toward the carriage. For one exquisite moment, he saw Cambas' daughter climbing in the carriage. She looked back at him and their eyes locked. Mourtos noticed it and was ready to kill the sailor.

On the ride home, again he sat beside Nina in the backseat. Surprisingly, she felt warm and friendly now. She could see how much her father liked him. Ignoring Mourtos' jealousy, she turned to Cohen and said, "You took a lot of pictures."

"Fascinating place," he said. "Mountains and trees, magnificent sights."

"Danny," she said in a sweet tone, "if you think this area is magnificent, wait until you see the highest mountain in Lesbos."

"Will you take me there?" he asked, anticipating a yes.

"I'm not sure, but I'll think about it," Nina replied flirtatiously.

"Maybe tomorrow?"

"Maybe," she said, aware that her "maybe" was a qualified yes. In her heart she wanted to be with Danny Cohen longer and get to know him better.

CHAPTER TWENTY-ONE

The next day, Nina woke up with an unusually strong sense of sadness. She yearned to be with Danny, but she also knew that the *North Star* would not be anchored in Lesbos forever. Then she would be left behind to deal with good memories and local gossip. She thought of their first walk in the garden together that memorable Sunday, how he had grabbed and kissed her. She couldn't help but wonder if he did that with every girl he met. Even now, the memory made her blush. *How dare he, a guest in my father's house, do such a thing?* Still she could not get him out of her mind.

With a strange tightness in her chest, she felt the need for fresh air. She pushed open the window, and the morning sea breeze slipped into her room. She took a deep breath, and as she exhaled, she saw on the far horizon St. Elias Mountain enveloped in gray mist. She remembered that when they were on their way back from the lumberyard the previous day, she had told him about the magnificent sight of the highest mountain on the island, and that Danny had wished to be taken there. Later, when she shared the idea with her aunt, she realized her father would not readily approve such a trip. Pipina, however, liked her niece's plan. *"Philoxenia,* befriending a stranger, is a virtue in our homeland," she said. "Something tells me that you like the sailor."

"I don't hate him. I'm just trying to be polite."

"Well, you offered to take him to the mountain. That's being polite?" Pipina said, well aware of her Nina's emerging yet shy feelings.

Apprehensively, Nina asked, "Do you think my father will allow this?"

"You know your father, but I'm more concerned about the gossiping tongues of Moria. They can be vicious." Both aunt and niece were concerned that people would see Nina alone with the American sailor and gossip would be rampant.

"I'd better forget it then."

After a moment's thought, Pipina offered, "Well, would you object if I followed you from a distance as a chaperone?"

"Object? Aunt Pipina, you're a saint."

"I don't know about that. I'm just being practical. In this part of the world, reputation is a capital virtue," Pipina said. "You know what the villagers believe: *It's better to lose an eye than to stain your name.* You don't want your father's reputation to be at stake."

When she saw Danny on her doorstep, her fear of possible gossip melted away with his warm greeting. She felt a sweet sensitivity permeating her body and heart. Seeing him again dressed in casual civilian clothes with a small knapsack and a camera hung over his shoulder, hair impeccably combed, face and eyes radiant in anticipation of seeing her, she became ecstatic.

Pipina had instructed Mourtos to have the mares and a donkey harnessed and ready. Danny helped Nina to mount. Mourtos kept watching them out of the corner of his eye as they took off and felt sickened. His stomach muscles tightened. But when he saw Pipina following them, he was somewhat relieved. His next task was to see his boss, but he had no desire to do that. "Mr. Cambas," he said, "I won't be able to work today. I need to go home and lie down. I have an upset stomach."

"Why don't you ask Pipina to make you some soup?" offered Cambas.

"Pipina is already out with Nina and the American, but I'll be okay. I don't think I could eat anything at this time." He already knew that he needed a shot of that special spicy cognac that Despina reserved for him.

Despina had seen Nina and Danny riding past her house, and she was glad, for that meant that the heat would be off her for a while. Now the busy tongues in Moria would be occupied in gossiping about Cambas' wealthy daughter running around with an American sailor. And her boyfriend, Mourtos, would have to give up any ideas about his boss's daughter. Maybe she'd even spice it up a bit and tell Mourtos that she saw the rich girl whoring around with a sailor.

CHAPTER TWENTY-TWO

ON HORSEBACK, NINA AND DANNY rode through an alley of stucco houses with brightly painted wooden shutters and orange tiled roofs, built on the rising hills. Further down in the neighborhood, snow-white cottages sparkled in the March sun.

"This place looks like a postcard," Danny said.

"You must have more beautiful houses in America, and big buildings, skyscrapers."

"Nothing like Moria."

"You're just saying that."

"Honestly . . ."

Nina's mare began to gallop ahead, leaving Pipina half a kilometer behind. Danny spurred his mare to catch up. The cobbled alleyways contrasted sharply with the startling green of new spring grass along the walkways. Sea breezes swept across the open heath, bringing the fragrance of blossoming olive trees, orange groves, and laurels. Shepherds tending flocks of goats and sheep stood and waved their hands in a salute. St. Elias came into view at the very top of the mountain, a white stone chapel with a bell tower, picturesquely perched like a benevolent guardian angel. As the two mares galloped closer to each other, Nina said with evident pride, "According to an ancient myth, Lesbos was first inhabited by the descendants of Makareus."

"Who was he?" Danny asked, edging his mare closer to Nina's.

"He was a son of the Sun. That's why, even in the dead of winter, there is rarely a day when the sun doesn't shine on our island," Nina explained.

Pipina's donkey was still far behind at the foot of the mountain. The young couple dismounted and stretched their arms and legs near the chapel. Relieved, their mares neighed and began to graze. Exhilarated by their scenic ride, Nina and Danny rested under an olive tree and silently looked at each other, deep in thought. Two colorful butterflies landed on a red poppy near Danny's feet. He reached out to catch one, but Nina grabbed his hand.

"Leave them alone," she said with a twinkle in her eyes. "Maybe they love each other."

"Maybe they're mates," Danny said.

"Most likely," said Nina with a wistful smile, keeping her eyes on the man she'd begun to adore.

When their eyes met, the gleam in his eyes stirred her blood. Tenderly, she reached out and touched his cheek with the tips of her fingers. He caught her hand and entwined his fingers with hers, pulling her closer. Nina did not resist. He gave her a prolonged kiss. She learned how pleasurably sweet his kiss could be, and with eyes closed, she caressed the back of his head and neck. Kissing feverishly, they rolled together on nature's velvety carpet. In a moment of silence, Nina looked around introspectively.

"Danny, do you think people can predict the future?" she asked, with a tremor in her voice.

"I doubt it," he said.

"It's been said that some people have a sixth sense."

"Do you really believe that?" Danny asked.

She did not answer, for at that moment, Pipina arrived on her donkey. "I would have been here sooner if I had been riding a turtle," she laughed, happy to see the couple together. A seasoned woman, Pipina studied her niece and the sailor. Their eyes held that special gleam. She wanted to leave them alone on the mountaintop so that they could take full charge of nature's glory, but she was concerned about any evil eyes that might be around.

"Aunt Pipina, I'm starving," Nina said. "Did you bring anything to eat?"

Pipina shook her head. "But I have an idea. After we offer our prayers in St. Elias' Chapel, let's take our guest to Petalidi, the Mussel. He would love it, and it's not that far."

"The Mussel?" Danny asked excitedly. "What's it like?"

"It's an isolated inlet shaped like a mussel shell. My brother gave it as a dowry to our niece Toula when she married Panagiotis, a sailor who gave up the sea and settled down." Eyes downcast, Pipina was aware of the subtle seeds she was planting.

"It sounds interesting," said Danny.

"Well, those lovebirds built an inn and a tavern right on the beach that serves quality seafood. They make a good living. They are beautiful people."

"What are we waiting for?" Danny said. "I'll untie the mares."

"Aunt Pipina, you are an angel." Nina kissed her on both cheeks.

"Oh, I don't know about that, but I'll get my Pegasus ready," said Pipina.

Danny and Nina rode through the orchard-filled valley of Moria. Pipina lagged behind at a safe distance, giving the young lovers a bit of private time. The sun grew progressively warmer, and as they passed groves of orange and lemon trees, the citrus scents filled the air. The mares knew these roads well. Nina could close her eyes and surrender to the blissful sensation of being carried along through the perfect spring day.

The journey took them past the small seaport of Panagiouda. Nina saw the delight in Danny's eyes when he caught sight of the fishing craft—rowboats and sailboats in soft, chalky pastels of various hues. "When I was younger," she said, shaking the reins to tell the mare to move on, "I used to draw pictures of pretty boats with tall masts and colorful sails, but I never visualized a vessel as big as yours."

"Maybe you ought to draw a picture of the *North Star.*"

"I could try, but I wouldn't want you to laugh if I didn't do a good job."

"It would be a masterpiece," Danny said, "and I would hang it in my cabin."

"Is that a promise?" she giggled.

"Yes, it is."

"I haven't drawn anything for ages, but for you . . ."

The sparkling beach was laced with coffee shops and taverns selling the delicious locally made ouzo. The open, cobblestone walk was alive with merchants catching up on gossip as they sold their wares: goat cheese, fresh fish and fruits, salty black olives, wine, and vibrant handmade crafts.

They were still perusing the goods when Pipina arrived. Soon, the three continued on the last leg of their journey. The mares whinnied when they neared their destination. At the sound, Nina jumped off her mare with delight. "We're here," she said.

"So this is Petalidi. It's gorgeous." Danny was awestruck by the shimmering blue water and virgin sand. Under a hill stood Toula's inn and tavern. On top of the hill was a tiny white chapel.

"It's a glorious beach," Danny said.

"It's very special to my father. Do you see that rock out there, far from the shore? He calls it his island and swims out to it each time we come here."

"Have you ever gone that far?"

"Oh, yes," Nina laughed. "The summer I became seven years old I said, 'Daddy, I'm coming with you,' and he said, 'You go first, and I'll follow you.' He probably wanted to protect me."

"Of course."

"I swam it without any difficulty."

"So you've been a swimmer since you were seven?"

"Since I was three."

"I would really like to swim to your father's island."

"Not today, Danny, it's too cold. Nobody swims in March."

"It can't be colder than the Atlantic." Danny took off his shoes, rolled up his pants to his knees, and waded into the water. "It's perfect," he said. "Next time we come here, we must bring our bathing suits."

CHAPTER TWENTY-THREE

OVERWHELMED WITH JOY by her niece's obvious interest in the American sailor, Pipina decided to have a talk with her brother. Apprehensively, she told him that she suspected a strong attraction between Nina and Cohen. She emphasized that Nina had finally become interested in a special man, which would put an end to all thoughts about the convent and becoming a nun. It was time to discuss the matter with Papavasile before Moria's evil tongues began to spread rumors.

They met the priest in his study, a modest home adjacent to the church, amply illuminated by a skylight and purified by the scent of incense. Through a small window behind him, a gentle breeze and the rays of the setting sun entered, falling on the pink azalea plant on the sill. Behind a small desk, Papavasile waited to hear the purpose of their visit. He indicated they could sit on the velvety sofa opposite him. His well-combed hair blended into his grayish beard, and his fatherly face was radiant. Pipina's heart palpitated fast as thoughts came into her mind. *Had Christ lived to be in his sixties, He might have looked just like Papavasile.*

Although a religious woman, Pipina did not want to see her niece resort to life in a convent or become an old maid like her. Nina was too beautiful and too loving to cover her body or her fate with a nun's cassock and deprive herself of a family, children, and a man she could truly love who could genuinely love her. The priest agreed with Pipina. It was time for Cambas' family to increase in size, time for Nina to consider marriage and bring joy to her household.

As a caring father, Cambas saw Danny Cohen as a better choice than most of the other men he had considered as potential sons-in-law. This Greek-American sailor was assertive, intelligent, and a solid man. He would make a good husband. But would he ever think of settling down in Lesbos? This was a serious question.

Brother and sister admitted to their worries about Cohen and Nina being seen together, which would stir malicious gossip. They were anxious to hear his advice. The priest took a sharp look at them and could see their concern. Pipina, who was friendlier with the priest than her brother, asked him for guidance. In silence and deep thought the priest shook his head with concern. "We cannot really control the destiny of our children," he said. "If there is genuine love, they will know what to do." His words evoked Pipina's deeper feelings. She truly loved this man and knew that he, too, had high respect for her. But her loving feelings had to be confined within the walls of reality. She had learned that sometimes even genuine love remained unfulfilled. He was a priest, already married with a family. Her love for him had to remain dormant. After a silent moment she opined, "I know my niece. Nina's love knows no boundaries. She would be happy to marry this man."

"My dear people," he said with a smile and gentle voice, "the American sailor that Nina happens to like and goes out with seems to be a fine young man. I met him when he first arrived. He came to our church, and then we had coffee together. To my surprise, I found out that he is of priestly origins and from this island. Daniel Papadopoulos, his grandfather, was a priest at St. Basil's.

"If they truly love each other, make it official," said the priest.

"What do you mean?" Cambas asked.

"Explain to the American that in our tradition, an engagement is considered a testing period," the priest said.

"But what if he wants to settle down in America with Nina?" Cambas asked.

"That's a possibility that you must accept. Of course you'll miss her. But if she loves him strongly enough, she will follow him wherever he goes. That's why the engagement serves a purpose, as a test of love."

Cambas' blood was rising fast. Although he loved America, to have his only daughter live five thousand miles away would be unbearable! His face had turned red.

Noticing her brother's anxiety, Pipina searched for a more viable solution.

"Papavasile," she said, "we know it's the destiny of a woman to follow her man, but what if Danny Cohen decides to make Lesbos his home?"

Cambas sighed, relieved at the thought. With a loving gleam in his eyes, he looked at his ageless sister. Instantly, his mind improvised endless possibilities. He could get Danny Cohen to be his partner, give the young couple a hefty dowry, and provide money to help his future son-in-law follow his noble dreams. *Maybe the priest could convince Danny to make his home in Moria,* he thought.

The priest's eyes subtly moved between brother and sister. He had the highest regard for the Cambas family, but their request for advice on such a sensitive issue put him on the spot. Even the idea of the engagement he'd proposed sounded risky. He turned to Pipina and said, "This is the period of Holy Lent. We need to pray hard that God's plan may be revealed to both Nina and Danny." Out of the corner of his eye he could detect Cambas' nervousness.

"Dear friends," he said, "suppose you continue to treat this young man as a guest, and when Nina goes out with him, have your manager Mourtos chaperone them."

Pipina shook her head. "That won't do." She knew Mourtos yearned for Nina, and she did not wish to subject him to such torment. Turning to her brother and grabbing his hand she said, "Papavasile is right. A chaperone might silence some bad mouths. I volunteer my services. I'll keep an eye on them. The American sailor will have to be made aware of the local customs."

Later that night, Mourtos dropped into Cambas' warehouse, distraught. He had heard Cara-Beis badmouthing Cambas at Alexis' tavern and got into a fistfight with him.

"Don't worry about that worm," Cambas said.

"*Afendi,* boss, that snake was telling everybody that you are allowing your daughter to . . . you know what!" Mourtos mumbled, "To go out with the American for personal business purposes."

"What else did he say?"

"He said the American sailor might be a spy."

"Why are you so upset? You know Cara-Beis is scum."

"I'm concerned about your reputation."

"Let me worry about that and don't get into any fights," Cambas advised. "Pipina will take care of things."

———

In the days that followed, the young couple took advantage of Pipina's offer to chaperone, and they visited several scenic sights. Remaining in the background, Pipina heeded her brother's caution to be vigilant yet discreet. All this was fine with Nina. In her heart she knew that each time they took a little trip, Pipina would undoubtedly look the other way to allow her some privacy with Danny. A week later the weather was warmer. It was a Thursday morning when Pipina saw Danny waiting at the iron gate with a smile. "Our guest is here," she said to her niece and signaled him to come up the stairway.

"Good morning, ladies," Danny bowed politely.

"You look very happy," Pipina said.

"Well, I'm in good company."

"Perhaps we can go to Petalidi again," Nina said.

"I've got my bathing suit on and I'm ready to go. A great day for swimming, isn't it?" He looked to Nina for a response.

"Not for me," she said. "My first swim will be on the first day of May."

"That doesn't mean that Danny shouldn't enjoy a dip."

"What's got into you, Aunt Pipina? The sea is still ice cold."

"Not for a sailor with Greek blood in his veins," Pipina said with a smile.

Through mountain laurels and myrtle bushes, the mares and the donkey found their way to Petalidi within the hour. When Danny, Nina, and Pipina dismounted by the sea, Panayiotis, Toula's husband, greeted them and took the animals to a fenced stall. In the tavern, Toula, a beautiful gray-haired woman who spoke with a lilting voice, had arrayed mussels on two ceramic platters. "You chose a good day to come," she said. "These are fresh out of the sea, and we get them only on Thursdays." Panayiotis entered the kitchen, rolled up his sleeves, and out of a bucket he pulled two red snappers.

"Those look as if they're still alive," Pipina said.

"I'm happy you're here," Toula said gracefully. "You will have mussels for hors d'oeuvres with a little ouzo if you wish, and Panayiotis will broil the snappers for you."

Pipina and Nina turned their gaze upon Danny for approval. "Good idea," he said, grateful for their hospitable spirit. "But before I eat this delicious meal, I'm going to take a swim in the sea. Anybody care to join me?"

Nina pretended to shiver. "I'll sit by the shore and watch you." Side by side, they walked toward the inlet. Danny bent down, found a little flat pebble, and forcefully skimmed it over the smooth sea. They watched it skip like a butterfly over the surface of the water, making circles.

"One, two, three, four, five, six, seven," Danny counted.

Nina picked a grayish blue pebble and said, "Let me try!" But as she prepared to throw it, she noticed a white cross etched upon it. A shiver in her spine held her back.

"Danny, look at this."

"A pretty stone!" he said.

"I'm going to keep it as an amulet," she said.

Danny picked up another flat pebble. "Throw this one. I want to see how many circles you can make."

Meanwhile, peering from inside the tavern, the two women discussed the natural grace that Danny and Nina exuded. As Toula cleaned the fish, she said, "They look so good together. He's such a handsome man."

"Nina is very fond of him, but . . . ."

"She looks so happy," Toula said.

"And healthier than ever . . . no more talk about becoming a nun." Pipina's voice had a soothing gravity.

Under his brand-new jeans, Danny wore a dark-blue bathing suit. Within a few seconds he had plunged into the pristine Aegean Sea and, like a young Poseidon, kept surfacing and diving, his body glittering in the midday sun. Squirming excitedly, he shouted from afar, "Nina, the water is delicious."

"You swim like a dolphin. Go to my father's island," she shouted back, pointing to the rock about five hundred feet from the shore.

Waving at him, she silently took the path that led to a tiny chapel at the top of the hill overlooking the sea. With sacred trepidation she lit two votive candles, one for Danny and one for herself, before the icon of Christ. She whispered, "Lord, I love him, and I know he loves me. Make known to us the path we must take."

As Nina retraced her steps, she saw Pipina bringing towels and a tray of sliced pears to the swimmer. He emerged from the sea, his shivering skin purple.

"You must be freezing," said Nina.

"It's much warmer in the water," he said. With a trembling hand, he lifted a slice of pear, took a bite, and offered the rest to Nina. She took a bite and kept it in her mouth, savoring its sweetness as she watched Danny drying himself. She felt a vicarious chill in her body. How much she wanted to take him in her arms and warm him up, but she couldn't do that in front of her aunt.

Pipina pointed to a gazebo next to the tavern. "Young man," she said, "before you catch pneumonia that might be a good place for you to change. Then we'll all have lunch."

After lunch, the couple took a long stroll by the shoreline. A narrow path, furrowed by the passing of goats and sheep, led them to a hilltop less than five hundred yards from the tavern. Under an old olive tree was a crudely made monument shaped like a boat, about six feet long. In place of a mast was a wooden cross bearing the inscription:

In Blessed Memory of Young Stephen
Drowned in a Storm, 1934.

Unaware that such a monument existed, Nina went into shock. Her eyes flooded with tears, and in her mind she saw her teen years, loving Stephen and wanting to marry him, despite her father's disapproval.

"Did you know Stephen?" Danny asked.

She nodded a silent yes and apologized for her reaction. "A sad story," she said. She made the sign of the cross and, holding Danny's hand tightly, led him downhill toward the inlet. Danny didn't want to probe. *Had he been her boyfriend? Why did she cry?* He comforted his curiosity by thinking, *These islanders are mysterious people. Even the happiest among them are apt to brood.*

Nina paused for a second and perused her surroundings. "Life on this island never changes," she sighed and stretched her arms. "It's forever the same . . . joys and troubles, tragedies, war, and worries."

"What are you worrying about?" Danny took Nina's hand gently.

"War. Young men taken away to fight against one enemy or another." She looked at him with sadness. Her eyes darkened. "I'm also worried about you leaving the island and never coming back."

Danny halted for a moment. "I can't think of my life without you or far from you."

"Really?" Nina replied with a sweet smile.

"That's how I feel. Maybe I have no right to make claims on you, but I want to be with you the rest of my life."

"Tell me more," she said with an inviting smile.

"Do you want to hear more? I love you. I want to marry you."

"You haven't even proposed to me yet."

With sparkling, pleading eyes he said, "Nina, will you marry me?"

Shrugging, she said, "You have to ask my father, and if he says yes, then I'll give it some thought. He reached out and took her hands into his own, drawing her closer to him. Momentarily, she resisted and pulled back saying, "Danny Cohen, I have the strongest feelings I have ever had. I fear what they will lead me to do." Nina felt stunned by the truth of her own words. She had admitted to herself what her heart had known since she first laid eyes on the young sailor's handsome face. And after that first kiss in her garden, her thoughts about becoming a nun had vanished. She wanted Danny Cohen to be her life's companion.

CHAPTER TWENTY-FOUR

LATE IN THE AFTERNOON Nina and Danny rode west on their way back home. Pipina lingered behind. She could hear her heart telling her, *They look so good together.* From a prominent point they watched the sunset, a golden lining behind the mountains. The landscape reflected their joy—rooftops shone, outlines of fences and angles of buildings were sharply delineated, the corn and wheat fields were rendered a relaxing green, fresh scenery from the artist's brush, recently varnished.

After a long ride they led the mares into the barn. They walked around the neighborhood for a while to stretch their legs and give Pipina time to catch up with them. Unaccustomed to horseback riding, Danny felt a slight ache in his strong legs and muscular tension in his whole body. He held on to Nina's hand, squeezing it with each step, but Nina suddenly pulled it away rather abruptly. She had seen Despina approaching from a distant narrow alley.

"What's the matter?" Danny asked. "You look scared."

"I didn't want that woman to see us holding hands."

"It's not her business."

"No, but in Moria there's a lot of meddling. And this woman, Despina, she can be vicious," Nina whispered.

Preceded by her perfume, the woman came closer, pretending that she was happy to see them. Danny's eyes followed her movements. She was wearing a short, tight, low-cut scarlet dress and high heels, and walked like a hooker, in a sort of imitation of those ill-reputed women he had seen once in the French Quarter of New Orleans. *She must be the one Tiny Tim visited,* he thought.

"You look like the perfect couple!" she said.

"Thank you," Nina said halfheartedly. Danny nodded politely.

"Well, shall I say congratulations, or is it not official yet?" Despina said with a seductive look. She had long suspected that Mourtos had strong feelings for Nina, and if she married this stranger, Mourtos would be totally hers.

Nina paid no attention to Despina, She waved a good-bye to her and, taking Danny's hand, she moved on.

Late that night, Pipina dropped into Nina's room to check that the windows were closed. It was a chilly night. Sitting up in bed, thinking over what had transpired on that day, Nina folded her hands around her knees, pursed her lips, and shook her head, seeking direction. Pipina sat next to her beautiful niece, caressed her hair and shoulders, and spoke softly. "Where are your thoughts, my dearest love?"

"Take a guess," Nina said.

"I could be wrong, but I think you are in love," Pipina said graciously. *The fruit is ripe, the harvester is here,* she thought. "The American sailor is a *palikari*, a handsome young man, and I can tell you love him. Don't pressure him to become an islander, one of the olive pickers. Trust in God and pray that He will show you the way. What is meant to be will be."

Deeply touched by her aunt's words, Nina let out a sigh of relief. "I love Danny, and I know he loves me. I would go with him wherever he takes me."

"Yes, dearest child, I'll miss you." Pipina's eyes concealed sad feelings with a simulated smile.

"I'll miss you, too, but I'll be coming back every summer to be with you and my father."

Pipina nodded, looking out of the window to hide her bittersweet emotions.

CHAPTER TWENTY-FIVE

EARLY NEXT MORNING, NINA entered St. Basil's Church to light a candle and pray. The sweet smell of incense and the artistic array of colorful Byzantine icons, etching the glory of the unseen, evoked a gripping feeling of piety. Not a sound or soul were in evidence. Only the periodic creaking of wood that supported the altar and the pews could be heard. The priest had not yet arrived. A lavender scarf covered her hair, and a silky feeling of joy over Danny's loving presence in her life filled her heart with gladness. Hands crossed on her breast, she felt the rhythm of her heart beating. The thought of Danny's looming departure someday evoked anxiety. But her thoughts were soon sidetracked by the sound of steady, swift footsteps. The priest arrived from a back door and appeared at the altar. She tiptoed to him and gently kissed his hand.

"Papavasile, good morning! I've come for confession," Nina said with hesitation in her voice, but the priest's kind face gave her courage. With fatherly love in his eyes, he invited her to come near the icon of Christ.

"Is it a sin to be so happy?" Her voice carried a tinge of worry.

"God made us for joy."

"But I have so much of everything," Nina said. "I am blessed with the riches of this world. My father and my aunt never deprive me of anything, and now God has graciously brought into my life a loving man. A beautiful man, Father! Already he has asked me to marry him. Believe me, I have strong feelings for him, but I'm afraid that this is too much to take in such a short time."

Previous confessions knocked at the door of her memory. It was with similar enthusiasm that she had told Papavasile about her decision to become a nun, a bride of Christ—and now? What about the orphanage she wanted to establish? Of course Danny had assured her that she did not have to become a nun to head an orphanage, a project they could start once they were married. Momentarily, she felt that she would disappoint her priest. But he interrupted her thoughts. "My child, there is a season for everything in our life. This is a time for dancing and loving."

"It's too great. Can such happiness last?"

The priest's presence felt like an apparition, his ethereal face radiating love that surpasses all understanding. *Had he just visited heaven and returned with such a divine glow?* Enveloped in his warm love aura, she heard his gracious words: "The cup of the Lord overflows with blessings." He looked at her in a fatherly way and smiled. "The Lord gives, the Lord takes away. Trust in Him, for even if all these gifts were to be taken away from your life, you would find His grace sufficient."

After confession, when he had read the prayer of absolution, the priest put his arm around Nina and, escorting her to the narthex, said, "Life moves faster than a weaver's shuttle. Live, love, laugh, and play while you can, before the evil day comes when sorrow fills our eyes with tears and our hearts with pain. Soon the cold winter snow will turn the green fields and the purple mountains into a great white shroud. There will come a time for sober thoughts, my child, but now is the time for singing and dancing."

Papavasile placed a golden cross strung on a chain in Nina's hand. "Give this to the man that you love. I have blessed it and prayed that may God bless your love." Gratefully she shook the priest's hand and kissed it. As she walked away, his eyes soberly followed Nina's steps. He was aware that the man she loved was engaged in a dangerous mission. Dan Cohen could be a wonderful man who might genuinely love Nina, but he also knew of his commitment to serve his country by doing his part in a secret mission. He glanced at the dome of his church from where Christ, the Sustainer of the Universe, conferred His perennial blessings, and clenched his hand around his bushy beard and said softly, "Who can fathom Your will, O Lord?"

CHAPTER TWENTY-SIX

CAPTAIN THOMPSON WALKED on deck with a slight limp in his right leg. The heavy cast was to stay on for another two weeks, until the leg was totally healed. Above his starched whites, lacquered gold buttons, and white gloves, with the ritual long glass tucked under his left arm, his tanned face glowed with anticipation. The pungent harbor breeze smelled good. At last, the stocky captain planned to make his debut on the island. He felt that a leisurely walk on dry land would benefit his injured leg. Momentarily, he stood on deck surveying the island through the glass. Last night's enthusiasm had reassured him that their mission was almost accomplished. Cohen's convincing message still echoed in his mind. *Captain, the previous night after midnight hours, when there was no soul around, the weapons were safely hidden under a trapdoor in the basement of Alexis' American Café. We need not to worry, Alexis swore. As far as the cargo of olive oil, the price was better than we had expected.*

Although the news was promising, the captain sensed that his first mate was skeptical. It was out of character for Cohen to be so out of spirits. When he had asked him last night what was wrong, Cohen swore that everything was just fine. Thompson was not convinced. Squinting as he sorted out his thoughts, he adjusted the long glass to his eye. He was not focusing on anything specific, but his mind raced, searching for an answer. Honest and direct as his mate had been, Captain Thompson knew that some serious issue was lurking behind this sailor's melancholic expression. He had no reason to be in control of the private lives of his crew. He felt confident that Cohen was a man of awesome strength and could combat any adversity.

After the oil deal had been sealed and signed, and the date of delivery to the *North Star* had been established, Dan Cohen requested another meeting with Cambas on Friday evening. He wanted to tell him that he wished to marry his daughter and ask for his approval. It occurred to him that it could be of benefit to run his thoughts by his good and trusted friend, Alexis.

It was only late last Thursday night that he met with Alexis in his American Café. He had trusted this man with a serious mission, the hiding of the weapons, and now he also wanted to share his own heart's secret. He was sure of his love for Nina and of her love for him, but he was not certain of the local tradition concerning the way to approach her father. Both men sat in a semi-dark corner of the café and began to talk. The café was empty. Alexis felt a special kind of joy being with his young American friend. Over a drink of ouzo, Alexis told Dan how honored he felt to be part of his mission. "Do not worry about the weapons. Trust me. In case something happens to me, Papavasile knows my plans."

"What plans?"

"If we have to use these weapons, we need men, don't we?" Alexis said, looking Cohen straight in the eyes. Silently, he sipped his ouzo, rolled his tongue in his mouth, and tried to speak with confidence. "Papavasile and I grew up in the same neighborhood, went to the same school, secretly we drank wine together, we have been friends for years. We parted only for a while: I went into the army, and he went to the seminary. So when I say trust me, I mean that the priest and I are determined to help you. We have already met a couple of times to discuss your mission. So far, we have compiled a list of brave mountaineers. They are men with little or no education, men inured to hardship and full of pride. They would defend Lesbos even with bare hands."

"Who would train them to use the weapons?"

Refilling his glass, Alexis let his smiling gaze fall on Cohen. "You won't believe it when I tell you what my job was in the army." He shook his head with pride. "I inspected and trained soldiers in the use of weapons." He gulped down his ouzo and Cohen saw flames of passion in his friend's eyes. "I can't believe that I trained people to kill. Crazy? Very crazy. The whole war game is insane. But that's what I did in defense of my country. And I'll do it again if Hitler gets any ideas about invading Greece."

"You're a devout patriot, Alexis, and I love you."

"Since I was a boy, we were taught in school that above any kind of love—of parents, siblings, mates, lovers—the love for one's homeland is the greatest of all virtues."

As Alexis was talking about his values, Dan Cohen was deep in thought about the danger in which he was placing Alexis and others. *Innocent people might die if they took up arms against the enemy. And here I am to tell Alexis about my love life?*

When he saw where and how well the weapons were hidden, Cohen felt confident that Alexis was not simply smart and crafty, but also determined to be a part of the *North Star*'s mission. "Pour me a little more ouzo," Cohen said.

Alexis jumped up, went to his counter, and rushed back with a full bottle. "Let's get drunk tonight," he said, refilling Cohen's glass, sensing something strange in the air.

"My dear co-worker, I'm already drunk, but not with ouzo," Cohen said. He had finally reached the stage where he felt he could trust Alexis with another secret.

"You called me 'co-worker'? I'm your friend. Just tell me what's on your mind."

"I'm madly in love," Cohen said.

Alexis giggled, happy to hear the news. "Now I know why you came to see me."

The two friends stayed up until dawn, discussing the possibilities of taking Nina to America or making their home on the island. Would Cambas approve of the marriage? And if he did, would he allow his only daughter to make a life far from Lesbos and leave her wealth behind? In his heart, Alexis wanted Dan Cohen to establish himself in Moria. He couldn't see parting from him. But realizing that a career was at stake, he said nothing, but busied himself behind the counter making two cups of fragrant Greek coffee. He inhaled the aroma and took a mouthful. His whole body vibrated. He brought a cup to Cohen and said, "Drink this coffee. It will clear your head."

"I feel numb," Cohen said.

"It seems to me that you have made a major decision."

"I believe I have, but I'm still anxious," Cohen said, energized by the coffee.

"You should follow the local customs. Go to her father and request Nina's hand in marriage."

Friday evening, Cohen went to Cambas' warehouse. Almost verbatim, he repeated Alexis' words. "Mr. Cambas, this evening I have come to you with a very special and personal request." Face blushing and heart pounding, he continued, "With respect and love, I come to ask you for your daughter's hand."

"For business or pleasure?" Cambas said, feigning a stern look on his face. Since the discussion with his sister and the priest about the close relationship Nina and Danny were enjoying, Cambas was, in fact, expecting him to come and ask for Nina's hand.

Dan Cohen was stunned. He did not expect such a question from a man he had come to admire.

Seeing the shock in Cohen's eyes, he smiled and said, "I didn't mean to offend you. I know you love my daughter. I also know that she loves you."

Cohen explained that he wanted Cambas' blessing, and that after the *North Star*'s mission was accomplished, he would be free to settle down with a wife.

"My American friend, you're a good man," Cambas said, accentuating each word, "but it seems to me that you have some unfinished business to attend to. And I don't want to see my daughter with a broken heart."

"The captain is understanding. I know he'll be willing to discharge me."

"Let's talk about this again tomorrow," Cambas said. "Meanwhile, I know that my dear sister has been planning for you and Nina some exciting trips." He reached out and shook Cohen's hand firmly.

Cohen took this as a sign of approval. *Now, how the captain will react is another hurdle to overcome!* he thought.

That night, Cambas called Pipina into his study and told her about Cohen's proposal. He managed to repress his real feelings from her. He did not want to tell her that the olive oil transaction was a cover-up for a secret mission that could spell danger for many on the island and certainly for Cohen. He did not dare tell his sister of the details the American sailor had confided in him. Proud to be an American citizen himself, he was willing to help them in any way possible. But exposing Nina to danger and to possible heartbreak was another matter. If the Nazis invaded the island and discovered that Cohen was involved in the weapons scheme, Cambas' family would surely be considered accomplices.

143

CHAPTER TWENTY-SEVEN

AT DAYBREAK ON MONDAY MORNING, the young couple, chaperoned by Pipina, once again headed toward the mountain. Their mares galloped briskly, and Pipina's donkey followed behind. The sun rose slowly and turned the white chapel of Saint Elias rosy-red. Dew sparkled everywhere, diamond-like tears of early morning reflecting the sun's love. Across the horizon a crimson color tinted the cliffs along the mountaintops. The sun's rays were warm, and a fresh-scented breeze lovingly caressed their faces. Cohen dismounted, patted the mares' backs, and helped Nina to the ground. He committed her elegant features to memory. *She will forever look beautiful to me.*

Nina reached out and linked her arm in his, and in that moment they were both excessively happy. Among the fragrant myrtle bushes was a cradle of grass, protecting wildlife. Cohen slid onto the green grass and pulled Nina with him, both of them resting on their sides, facing each other, while their eager lips and arms connected instantly. They kissed with fiery impatience, their chests and hips together as closely as nature allowed. His hand moved from her shoulder blade to her breasts, caressing them through thin silk, making them bud like lilacs.

Nina knew she should stop him and remind him that such delicacies could only be the fruit of married life. Instead, she breathed harder as her eyes glittered in anticipation of his next move. She had made the way clear and unencumbered. Her body felt liquid and hot, pulse driven. She acquiesced and stretched on the velvety grass alongside Cohen, holding his hand and looking at the sky. The far-off shepherd played a hauntingly beautiful song. The piping laced their thoughts with a melodic passion, triggering agonizing feelings in their hearts. Scary thoughts surfaced in her mind. *This handsome sailor was destined to go away. Should he place his seed of love in her, she would never be the same again, a mother, forever a mother, and he would never know. That could not be.* When she gazed at him, he looked at her with passion and inched closer. The urge to make love increased by the moment. His vision blurred, he glanced around. Pipina was not in sight. Either she had entered the chapel or she was roaming among the olive trees collecting herbs. Nina's eyes reflected heartfelt surrender. Cohen took her in his arms and kissed her, and she returned his kisses with equal passion, caressing the back of his neck and his ears. The thought that Pipina might see them had caused her to pull back gently. "The tea is almost ready. Come and have a snack," Pipina called from a distance.

"Aunt Pipina, we will be there shortly," Nina replied cheerfully. Her eyes looked like shiny black olives. She was glad to hear her aunt's voice.

Cohen could not wait to tell her last night's news. Tenderly, he clasped her face between his hands and said, "Last night I visited your father."

"And you didn't tell me?"

"There are many things I haven't told you," Cohen said in a teasing tone. His strong fingers crept behind her ears, her neck. He felt a thrill of pleasure at the sight of the torrents of dark hair falling on her shoulders. Again he kissed her and whispered, "Nina, you're most beautiful and I love you." With the charm of a woman in love, she closed her eyes, anticipating another kiss. As he kissed each of her eyelids softly, thoughts registered in his mind. *I would be justly called a fool if I let this gorgeous woman go. I want her to be my wife for life.* The warmth of their bodies called for lust. Aching with desire, he thought, *I would give up everything if I could only make love to her now.* But he didn't want to scare her away or, even worse, offend her. Storing his urges in a secret alcove of his thudding heart, he smoothed her hair gently and touched her eyebrows. Breathlessly, eyes misting, he kissed her more passionately, feeling the exuberance of the most loving woman in the world, one he could love forever.

Nina's natural shyness slowly died away. In total surrender in his arms, she said, "Well, Mr. Dan Cohen, tell me. Why did you visit my father, for the oil transaction?" She pursed her lips to hold back a smile.

"For business!" he laughed, as he recalled Cambas' response to his proposal.

Pinching his cheek hard, she asked, "Why are you laughing?"

"I'm not laughing at you. I just thought of your father's response."

"What did he say?"

"I said to him, 'Mr. Cambas, this time I have come to you with respect and genuine love to request your daughter's hand.' And he quickly replied, 'For business or pleasure?'"

"And what did you answer?"

"I said, 'Pleasure,' of course," Cohen said, biting his tongue to hide his real feelings.

Feigning annoyance, she pushed him back and said, "I'm going to join Aunt Pipina. You're not any fun."

"Don't you want to hear the rest of the story?"

"No!" Nina insisted, "I'm not interested," and pretended to walk away.

"I'm only teasing you, my love. Come sit next to me, please." He spoke of his visit to her father's office, reassuring Nina of his true intentions. "Your father likes me a great deal, and he did not reject my proposal. He said, 'Let's talk about this again tomorrow.'"

Excited about Cohen's meeting with her father, Nina felt great delight and could not take her eyes off her potential mate. The sound of his voice made her soul rush to her face, making it red and firing her desire.

"Oh, my love, I almost forgot," Danny said, and he reached inside his jacket and pulled out a small brown velvet box wrapped with a silk ribbon. "This is a little present for you. I hope you like it."

With a penetrating look, she said, "Daniel Cohen, what is in this box?"

"Open it," he said.

As she did, she saw a beautiful strand of pearls and screamed, "Dear God! You must have spent a fortune. These pearls are very rare and valuable, the best I have ever seen. Thank you!" She proceeded to put the necklace of pearls around her neck. "They are spectacular," she said.

"They are to tell you that I love you very much."

Touching her necklace, she said, "Danny, I love you, and I will love you for the rest of my life." Tears of joy rolled down her cheeks. My father will have to understand that. I know my father. His saying, 'Let's talk about this tomorrow' meant a definite approval." There was a charm in her voice that evoked growing excitement in Cohen's heart.

"I love you, too, with all my heart and soul, but as your father said, I have some unfinished business at hand. I must make some serious decisions. I plan to talk with the captain. Things will work out for us. I don't want you to worry."

He put his arms around her, and breathing her scent he touched her temple with his lips to seal his words.

"Nina, I'm going to leave the sea."

"Because of me?"

Cohen paused. "What if I did it because of you?"

"As happy as that would make me, such a decision has to come from the depths of your own heart," she said firmly.

"I've pretty much made up my mind." Nodding his head convincingly, he stood up and extended a hand to pull her up to him. Bodies warmed up and arms linked, they walked among wildflowers and plants. With each step on their way to join Pipina, they shared intimate memories from their past. Nina spoke of her mother's death when she was only three, and how her father had decided to return to Lesbos and never to marry again. She told him how Pipina treated her in a motherly manner. Cohen briefly referred to his father's death, then described how his mother had devoted herself to working as a waitress to put him through the Naval Academy.

Nina's eyes emanated compassion. "How old were you when your father died?"

With a deep sigh, Cohen said, "Almost thirteen. I forget exactly what he looked like. Sometimes I think Captain Thompson looks like my father."

"You must miss him a lot."

Cohen nodded, sadness evident in his face.

"How hard that must have been for your mother!" Nina said.

"We had to sell our home and move into a small apartment." His eyes darkened. "It wasn't easy for her."

"Our lives seem to share certain similarities," Nina said. "I lost my mother, and you lost your parents. I'm so sorry," Nina said, tightening her grip on his arm. "Nobody can replace a mother's love."

"But we cannot change our past, can we?" Cohen said.

"We can only accept it, and God gives us the strength to move forward," Nina said.

Quietly, they wondered how fate had brought them to this mountain at such a glorious moment.

Suddenly Nina asked, "Danny, why did you really come to Lesbos?" Studying his expression, she saw the sadness in his eyes. He didn't answer, and his silence brought doubts to her mind. *Does he have second thoughts about leaving the* North Star? "Tell me what you are thinking," she said.

He shook his head. Emotionally entangled with a woman of such warmth and understanding, he wanted to reveal everything about himself, his travels with Captain Thompson, his life, even his secret mission on the island. But the *North Star's* service to the United States government was serious business, and if Nina knew what it entailed, she would be truly scared. So he chose not to divulge this part of himself. "I'll tell you what I'm thinking," he said, clasping her hand and kissing it. "As soon as Captain Thompson's condition improves a bit, when the cast is off his leg, I'm going to tell him my decision. That's what I'm thinking."

"Dan Cohen, you're a wonderful man," Nina exclaimed.

"Seven years of sea travel is enough," he said, his mind racing again. *Perhaps Nina would like to make her home in America, a country with infinite possibilities. But would her father allow her to go away? Perhaps I'll make my home on the island and live happily with the woman I love.*

"My father has traveled a lot in his life. It's something I've always wanted to do, but Greek women do not travel alone. I've been to Athens, but I hardly call that travel," said Nina.

"Would you travel with me?" Cohen felt a little tug in his heart.

"It all depends."

"On what?"

"On whether or not we take Aunt Pipina along," she giggled.

"Why not? I like her. She's a good sport," Cohen said. "Has she ever talked about me?" He raised a curious brow.

"She agreed with me that you're a terrible man." Nina laughed, stroking his arm. "I'm only joking. She thinks you're a handsome man, a good catch." She gazed into his eyes and said, "I agree with her." She leaned forward and allowed her forehead to touch his lips.

"Strange things happen in life, Nina. The *North Star* is anchored in Lesbos. We met. And I'm in love with you." He grabbed both her hands and kissed them.

"And I am in love with you." Nina's heart did several somersaults. Her knees became weak, melting her into helplessness. Cohen held her tightly in his arms. The squeeze took her breath away. His lips brushed her hair, and his hands clasped her close to his body. She closed her eyes, and her mind soared over the Atlantic Ocean to America and back again to Lesbos. Again they kissed each other, breaking loose of all inhibition. Then they walked to St. Elias' Chapel, arms around each other's waist. Nina knew she would never be quite the same again.

Cohen said, "It's a miracle that you and I are together, America and Greece, on the top of the mountain of St. Elias."

"It's a miracle," Nina repeated and felt an exciting idea sneaking up in her mind. "Come." She took his hand and said, "I want to show you a miracle of nature." She pointed down the cliff. "The hot springs of the Gera Gulf are down there. The mares will take us there in ten or fifteen minutes."

"What about your aunt?"

"I'll tell her. She won't mind. But first we'd better sit with her and enjoy the delicacies she has prepared." As they drank mountain tea and ate delicious honey-soaked cookies sprinkled with ground walnuts and cinnamon, Cohen politely praised Pipina's excellent preparations for their outings.

Nina beamed, thinking of taking her Danny to the hot springs of Gera. She could not wait to step with him into the opalescent water and see his reaction. Finally, she told her aunt, knowing that she would never say no to her in anything.

Pipina agreed to the idea with an unsuccessfully concealed smile. *Things are getting serious,* she thought. "Oh, don't you worry about me," she said. "I need to roam around to collect herbs and mountain tea for the winter."

CHAPTER TWENTY-EIGHT

THE MARES KNEW THEIR WAY through the grove of stately olive trees. With instinctual dexterity they descended through a dangerous gorge, a sea of rocks that led to the gulf. Fifteen minutes later, Nina and Danny arrived at the hot springs. Three fountains in the shape of lions' heads poured an abundant waterfall of hot mineral water into the pool. Across the fountains were three windows that overlooked the Gulf of Gera. The pool was bordered with light brown marble plaques. Four high white walls sustained the vaulted dome over the pool. A small wooden door served as the entrance to the hot springs. Built three hundred years before the birth of Christ, these Roman baths had served the needs of the aristocracy and later the Byzantine emperors who vacationed in Lesbos. Although few people took advantage of the therapeutic springs, every October Nina visited this place with Pipina, who suffered with rheumatism. She loved to sit under the fountain and let the hot water fall over her shoulders.

Today, not a soul was around when Nina and the man she loved watched the thick vapor rising from the marble-bordered pool. Tightly they held hands, their bodies touching, aware that they were living out one of the most exhilarating days of their lives. They took off their shoes and socks, then silently descended three steps into the marble-paved pool. Their skin was hardly able to endure the heat and instantly turned red. Above them the rising steam filled the space, making it appear distant and ethereal. Cohen studied Nina's figure with the dancing eyes of a man who had been well trained in the art of looking at women. It was a precious, world-transforming stare. Pulling her toward him, he kissed her softly, tenderly, and he felt his mouth open and his tongue slip easily between her teeth. Their tongues met and tenderly spoke the silent language of love. He passed dreams into her and received hers in the whirlpool. In her kisses he discovered the ultimate pleasure a human body could yield. Kissing her eyes and her neck, he took his time, moving slowly as he memorized the shape of her face and throat. He wanted to make himself irresistibly attractive, so outwardly dazzling that she would never want to leave his side. Most of all, he wanted to be comely enough to be the admirable man that Nina Cambas would want to be totally hers. They sat on the edge of the pool in silence, legs dangling in the water, breathing hard through trembling lips, their eyes wide with discovery, each realizing what he wanted of her and what she wanted of him. Tenderly they snuggled closer.

"Oh, Danny," she whispered.

"My love."

Aching in the most sensitive area of her womanhood, she was seized by desire and fear. "I want you," she moaned.

"I want you, too, my love." He took her hand and squeezed it between his legs. He was invincible, not to be thwarted.

"Danny . . ." She grabbed him forcefully.

He could speak no more.

"I love you," she whimpered.

"I want to marry you, Nina."

But rooted deep down in her heart was a commitment to give up her virginity only on her wedding night. She said, "We have a lot to look forward to."

Cohen saw himself in Nina's enormous eyes. Unlike other women he knew, she was very special. He caressed her body, rubbed himself against her thighs gently. His face wore an expression of tenderness.

"Some day . . ." She lost what she was about to say as another thought crossed her consciousness. *How awful it would be if Danny didn't want to marry me after today!*

In sweet passion, he pulled her legs out of the water and began to rub her feet, pouring hot water over her toes. Firmly, he stroked her knees and thighs.

"It feels divine," she said, observing the veins of his hand. "Don't stop. Right there. Oh, God, what have you done to me? I'm losing my mind."

The echo of their voices and the roar of the cascade over the pool prevented them from hearing any other sounds. But Nina's face suddenly lost its color. She shrank with fright in her eyes.

"What's wrong?" he asked.

"There was a man's shadow at the window." She pointed, suspecting that they were being watched.

He jumped up and went to look out the window. "There's nobody there, I swear."

"Danny, I thought I saw a face."

"Maybe it's your fear."

"Aren't you afraid?"

"No! I love you." He took her in his arms and showered her with prolonged kisses.

CHAPTER TWENTY-NINE

DELICIOUSLY EXHAUSTED, Nina and Danny clung to the mares, who whinnied triumphantly as they climbed back up the mountain of St. Elias. Since they had met, Nina's personality gradually unfolded, and she now felt like a mature woman who was deeply in love and finally ready to make the ultimate commitment. Previous inhibitions had vanished; she felt an unexpected inner transformation, and the face of the earth had altered. She loved Dan Cohen unconditionally. Every cell of her body and soul loved him, nullifying obstacles in their way—his departure from Lesbos and the possibility of losing him.

At a distance, the snow-white steeple of St. Elias came into sight with its glittering cross against the sun. Whispering a prayer, Nina crossed herself, but sudden insidious, guilty thoughts crept into her mind and melancholy clouded the exuberance she felt at the hot springs. Devoted to God, she thought that by loving this man and letting him lust over her body, she had already committed a sin. She had tried to forget God and put human love higher. But one touch or word from the man she loved was enough to disperse such thoughts. She smiled, believing that God loved her through her Danny's love. She moved her mare closer to him and extended her hand. He kissed it, and she felt convinced that in truly loving a man, God made His love present.

Pipina had lit all the votive candles in the chapel and prostrated herself in front of every icon, while she whispered prayers and requests. When she came out into the sun, she looked younger. The day was fresh and bright, not a trace of cloud or mist in the sky. The gentle breeze caressed her face, reaching the depths of her aging heart, assuring her that life is sweet— and sweeter for younger people. Smiling, she welcomed her niece and the young American sailor. She had prepared a breakfast of homemade quince marmalade, *paximadia,* a type of toasted whole wheat bread, and *koulourakia,* buttery crullers. Danny and Nina helped her spread out a thick, colorful cotton blanket she had woven herself many years ago. Then she poured three cups of coffee.

"Aunt Pipina, you make the best cookies I've ever tasted," Danny said as he sat comfortably on the blanket with Nina beside him.

"Well, thank you," said Pipina, charged with joy that Dan Cohen called her "Aunt Pipina." "From now on, I'm going to call you 'Danny'. Do you mind?"

"Mind? Not at all, since you make the best cookies," he giggled.

"Wait until you taste my *galactoboureko*!"

"What's that?" he asked, although he knew, as Alexis had served this pastry to him and Tiny Tom.

"What the gods of Olympus used to eat," Nina said, winking at him as she dipped her *koulouraki* into her coffee cup.

"De-li-ci-ous," he said, munching on a *paximadi*. While Pipina's meal nourished them, the panoramic view rewarded their eyes, and the fragrance of nature sailed unceasingly into the uncharted canyons of their souls. After breakfast, they mounted the animals and slowly headed down the mountain.

"Don't worry, Aunt Pipina, we won't leave you too far behind," said Nina as the two mares galloped ahead. Indulging in her own reveries, Pipina tapped her donkey with a stick and shouted, "I'll catch up with you as soon as this beast moves."

Soon they approached the Roman aqueduct and could hear the sound of rushing water growing louder, but they could not see its source. Thirty yards from the aqueduct they stopped. To their left and behind a rock ridge they could see it, a beautiful waterfall spilling over a cliff's edge and dropping at least a hundred feet into a pool, a reservoir of the river. They neared a steep hill that brought them under the aqueduct. The mares neighed, alert eyes blazing, and Nina felt a strange chill shaking her body. A sudden thought crossing her mind made her face seem sad and her eyes a bit darker. *What if Danny decides to leave the island and never come back?* This thought kept haunting her, yet she did not want to worry him by divulging her fear. Forcing a smile and consciously reframing her thoughts, she said, "I was thinking how wonderful it would be to have our wedding under an arch of this aqueduct."

"Nina, as long as you want to be my wife, I don't care where we get married—at the top of a mountain or in the midst of the sea."

"Let's plan to have it here," Nina said, her heart pounding at the prospect of the unusual location for a wedding. She knew Papavasile would have no objection, for he loved her and her family.

For a long minute, he tried to read Nina's thoughts. As he perused the enormity of the aqueduct, and the two mountains that were bridged by it, he said, "It's a wonderful idea. We're going to have our wedding here where east and west unite, Greece and America, you and me."

"How did you think of that?"

"I don't know. I just think that our marriage will combine two worlds, and by having our ceremony under this huge arch, our union will last as long as these columns. Forever."

CHAPTER THIRTY

IN THE LATE AFTERNOON, Despina heard a loud and familiar knock at her door. In joyful anticipation she hurried to open it, but what she saw disappointed her—a face that had lost all color, disheveled hair, eyes red, revealing despair and rage. Never before had she seen Mourtos, the man she loved, this gloomy and unkempt, as though he had not slept for days.

"Mourtos, what is wrong?"

"Don't look at me like that," he shouted. "I don't need pity."

"Lord God," she whispered. "Come in."

As he entered the familiar room, Despina noticed his lack of interest in her. Listless, his bloodshot eyes were fixed at the open window as if he were waiting for someone special to pass by the alley, someone he would like to shoot.

Nina's imagination had not conjured up something strange at the hot springs. Mourtos, who had been stalking the couple from afar since early that morning, witnessed the love scene in the Roman baths. Fury had clouded his vision, and imagining events that did not really happen, he raced his horse among the olive groves on his way back to Moria. Squinting angrily and spurring on his horse, he arrived at the solution. *I must get rid of the American sailor. Otherwise I will never stand a chance of convincing Nina to be my wife.*

Once in Moria, he decided not to reveal what he witnessed to anyone. He plunged himself on a couch, ignoring Despina's seductive gestures.

"Can I bring you a drink?" she asked.

"Just leave me alone," he shouted again, not wanting any interruption of his thoughts: *I wished I had continued school and gotten some education. Perhaps I could have become a teacher, an engineer, a veterinarian. Then I would have been able to engage Nina in interesting conversations or talked to her beyond familiar things.* He lived with the nagging impression that had he been educated, Nina would have found him more interesting. But he had to quit school and support his mother. He was eight years old when his father, a hardworking quarry man, was killed in a dynamite explosion. After elementary school, Cambas hired him as an errand boy. In a few years, he had gained the oil merchant's respect and love. Cambas trusted Mourtos not only with his wealth but also with the well-being of his family. He had been the obedient and careful manager of Cambas' affairs until now, and he could never jeopardize his position.

Despina wanted to alleviate his despair. "Can I get you something refreshing? You look exhausted,"

"Poison," replied Mourtos curtly, shielding his face with his hands. A man of few words, he finally told Despina what he had witnessed at the hot springs. Seeing interest in her eyes, he felt slightly better.

"You mean Cambas' daughter was doing it with the sailor?"

"Don't talk like that," Mourtos said defensively.

"Sorry."

"Shut up. Just shut your mouth."

"Okay. But it hurts me to see you wounded like this," she said in a low, seductive tone.

"I don't want sympathy."

"Manolis Mourtos, you are too thick to notice who truly loves you."

"I suppose you do," he sneered.

"It's not the first time a woman has gone crazy over a man." Tears rolled down her cheeks. She felt defeated that her man had such strong feelings for

Nina Cambas, for her emotions were equally strong. She wished Mourtos could understand how she felt about him. She left the room and hid in her bathroom, weeping. *I hope that American sailor marries that bitch. Then Mourtos will have no choice but to be mine, totally mine.*

Alone in the room, scrambling for new schemes, his face flushed with increasing frustration, he punched his fists in his palms to keep his hands from shaking. *Dead or alive, the sailor has got to go. Then I'll stand a good chance with Nina.* The thought provided a ray of hope.

CHAPTER THIRTY-ONE

EXHILARATED WITH THE EXCITEMENT of the day, Cohen returned to the *North Star* to find the captain pacing the deck. Captain Thompson had lost a lot of weight, and his baggy whites were flapping in the evening breeze. His characteristic tan had faded, but his face retained that austere expression that prompted discipline and order. The spark in his eyes spoke of his satisfaction as he patrolled the vessel, thoroughly checking every rope, sail, and screw. Silently, Cohen followed by his side, but periodically he could not help looking across to the town. In the far distance he could discern the Roman aqueduct, where only hours ago Nina had suggested they have their wedding ceremony. Although back at his duties, he could not stop thinking of their excursion. The distant hills blurred before he brought his emotions under control.

Asking Cambas for the hand of his daughter in marriage seemed much easier than telling Captain Thompson of his decision. How could he possibly break his contract with the *North Star* and disappoint a man he had grown to respect and love? He had planned not to tell the captain the reasons he wished to stay in Lesbos. In his mind he had fulfilled the purpose of his mission. But the more he thought again about it, he saw this was the last thing he would do. He had made the decision that his captain was entitled to an explanation, and he was waiting for an opportune hour.

When they reached the new foremast, the captain placed a firm hand on Cohen's shoulder, the seal of approval. Highly pleased with the improvements, he said, "Great job, partner."

"Thank you, captain." He saluted, and they shook hands. Looking up, they surveyed the foremast.

"Soon we'll be sailing," the captain said.

"Yes, sir," Cohen said, heart anchored to the island, trying not to reveal how he truly felt about departure.

April's warm days slipped by as fluidly as graceful notes in a song. It was the Saturday before Palm Sunday. Since dawn, the *North Star* had been sinking deeper into the blue water of the harbor, weighed down by heavy cargo. Up and down the gangplank, barefooted workers carried goatskins full of top-grade olive oil on their shoulders and filled the steel barrels lined up on the deck.

Cohen took several photos of the oil carriers. He could hear the soft splashing of the liquid and the groans of the workers. He admired the swiftness and strength of the olive-dark villagers—unshaven, wrinkled faces baked by the Aegean sun, coarse black hair hanging low on their brows, untrimmed mustaches under long Grecian noses and eyes shining with determination. Their rugged trousers, patched with different fabrics, were rolled up above the knees so they could move rapidly without tripping over their cuffs. They took pride in a job well done.

The following Monday, the delivery of oil was complete. Cambas was happy that his tallest tree was to serve as a mast on the *North Star*. He counted the American dollars for a second time. The amount was correct, the price for the oil transaction was fair, and he was satisfied. Once the barrels were secure, Cohen went to the captain's cabin to report on the readiness of the crew and cargo. With a twinkle of satisfaction in his eyes, the captain observed the smoke curling from his pipe. He could tell that something was worrying his first mate, for his gaze seemed to be wandering.

On Tuesday morning, Cohen brought to the captain's cabin a number of photographs he had taken of the island. He studied the pictures, shaking his head with evident satisfaction. "Very good. I take it that you also have clear directions to these spots?"

"Of course." Cohen opened a manila envelope and pulled out maps of secret places and several names of people the priest had recommended.

"Guard these with your life," the captain said as he handed the material back to Cohen.

With trepidation in his eyes, Cohen held up his hand in protest. "Captain, you had better hold onto this envelope."

"Why?"

"I've made a decision . . . . I'm going to stay on the island."

"You're joking, I hope?"

"I'm sorry to disappoint you," Cohen said sadly.

"I don't want to hear this," the captain growled. "According to our contract, you have two more years on the *North Star*."

"But captain, I've made the most important decision of my life."

"I'm listening." Smoke puffed out from his pipe and mouth.

"I think I'm fulfilling my father's wishes. He wanted to return to Lesbos someday, but he never made it. Now I feel that same yearning in my soul. I want to make Lesbos my home."

"Too romantic, don't you think?" Then raising his voice, he said, "Are you out of your mind? Of course the island is beautiful, but you have a career ahead. What are you going to do here, become an olive picker? Besides, America is your home." The captain controlled himself from pulling rank on his first mate.

"America will always be my homeland," Cohen answered. "That's where I first saw the light. And you have been not just my employer but my best friend." His eyes brimmed with tears. "But there comes a time when a man must listen to his heart."

"A sailor must obey the commands of his captain. You know we are at war. You know you and I and the entire crew are now under the command of the American Navy." Thompson's face succumbed to sadness.

"I'm sorry, captain, but I have made up my mind. I'm going to get married to a woman I love and establish a home here."

162

With a sneer, the captain said, "So it's a woman. You give up your ship, your mission, for a woman? That's pathetic, Dan Cohen. I thought better of you." Picking up a different pipe, a huge polished ivory one, he nervously filled it with tobacco and lit it. Among curls of smoke and flame, he forced a smile and beckoned Cohen to sit in a chair opposite him. "Cohen, you're in love." The captain coughed, clearing his throat. "It's a sort of derangement that we men go through. You're almost thirty. It's understandable." Closing his eyes, he remained silent as he captured his thoughts. But his mind traveled to distant harbors, when he was younger. Endless images of ravishing beauties, young seductive females in every port, flashed on the screen of his memory. A part of him could understand the passions of youth, but another part was determined to keep Dan Cohen on his ship. *Cohen might be suffering from one of those crushes that sailors get when they hit a new port and get over the minute they sail away. The smell of the sea cures many passions. I have seen that happen to many men. Cohen will get over this feverish notion. Besides, I have plans for him.* While in the hospital and in excruciating pain, Captain Thompson had done some serious thinking. Enough travel! Possibly one or two more voyages for him, but the *North Star* was too young and too strong to retire. All it needed was a good and dedicated captain, someone with Cohen's management ability. He came back to the present. "Cohen, you know I need you on this ship. I know how good you are and know the remarkable job that you have done thus far. But I want you to listen, and to listen not with your heart alone, but with logic." He pointed to his temple with the end of his pipe.

Cohen nodded. He knew what the captain wanted, and he anticipated a strong argument from him.

"For you to make such a drastic decision, she must be an extraordinary woman."

Cohen nodded. "She is."

"Now. But once a woman becomes a mother, all her attention goes to her children first, and you come second. In fact, once a woman gives birth, forget it. She's wrinkles and sagging flesh all over."

"Captain, try to understand, I'm not in love with a body. I love this woman's heart and soul."

"I know." The captain drew deeply on his pipe, trying to repress his sympathy for Cohen's dilemma.

"Cohen," he said, his voice lowered, "let's not forget you have been commissioned by the Chief of Naval Operations of the Mediterranean Forces to take photographs of the island and to seek out allies."

"I have tried my best to do all that, sir." Agony in his eyes, he did not wish to disappoint the man he respected as a father.

"There's something else I'd like to tell you right now." He drew several quick puffs on his pipe. "I'm not getting any younger. In a couple of years, maybe in only one year, I'll want you to take over this ship. We'll split the expenses and profits fifty-fifty. How does that sound?"

Misty-eyed, Cohen remained silent for a long moment and then said, "That's a most generous offer, sir."

"Empty promises I don't make, but you've got to face facts, Cohen. If you jump ship, the sacrifice will be too great on your part. It would mean loss of your rating as a first mate, and far worse, you could be considered a renegade." He stressed every word, making sure that his last point about duty touched his mate's heart.

Cohen said, "Sir, what you have commissioned me to do, I have done thoroughly. Costas Cambas is the great Greek-American you met last night. He has a shelter and food supplies available. Alexis, the café proprietor, will do a lot of legwork. Thus far, all weapons have been safely stored by Alexis in a cavernous shelter under the café."

"What about a landing place?"

"Here it is, sir, Cara-Tepe, the Black Hill. There is a natural strip between two rows of trees. I have taken pictures of it. As I've said, all the photos have names and directions. Also, the Gera Gulf is a natural shelter for submarines. It cannot be seen from the air or sea."

"How could anyone find it?"

"Through Cambas. He speaks English well. He will contact Alexis. Papavasile, the local priest, is a staunch patriot. This trio of brave men have been working together for the past three weeks. Convinced that our mission is sacred, they will leave no stone unturned in their efforts to help. They have a network of freedom-loving people."

"I don't want to control your life, but in view of the fine work you have done, your presence among the crew is needed. Don't abandon ship."

"May I think about what you've offered, captain?"

"You bet."

Cohen saluted firmly and left. Outside the captain's cabin, he leaned against the railing and gazed at the island. At the foot of the shadowy purple mountains, the little houses looked cozy and welcoming. Cohen felt tightness in his chest, for Moria drew him like a magnet. Painfully torn between two equally powerful poles, his invincible love for Nina and his commitment to the captain paralyzed him. The faces of Nina and the captain alternated in his misty vision, pulling him in opposite directions. Either choice gave him no relief.

"Dear God, where do I go from here?" he whispered to himself. Still in a whirlpool of thoughts, he heard the disturbing sound of a whistle. He turned and saw the captain approaching with a forceful step. Obediently, the rest of the crew followed him. Cohen joined them, curious to hear what the captain wanted.

At the stern of the ship, Captain Thompson stood firm as his gaze surveyed the anxious faces of his men standing in a semicircle before him. He cleared his throat and said, "Gentlemen, you have today and the next two days, Tuesday and Wednesday, to get ready! Thursday at midnight we set sail."

"Pardon me, sir!" Cohen saluted. "The day after is Good Friday. Could we possibly delay our departure until Easter Sunday?"

"Please, captain," Tiny Tom pleaded, and the rest of the crew joined in.

"Enough carousing! We need to leave promptly."

"Two more days, captain, it's not too much to ask, is it?" Cohen stared straight into the captain's eyes, hoping he had reached his better part, his heart.

"You don't understand." The captain's eyes grew with concern. The latest news he had received on the radio frightened him. Hitler's mechanized forces had surrounded Salonica and were rapidly marching toward Athens.

———

EARLY TUESDAY MORNING, tormented by ambivalent emotions, Dan Cohen walked through the narrow marketplace of Moria on his way to see Nina. Eyes brimming with tears, his mind rehearsed words he would use to tell Nina about his decision. He agonized, but after his last encounter with the captain, he knew he had no choice but to sail with the *North Star*. He found Nina and Pipina in the dining area, busy cutting and sewing colorful material for Easter dresses. Initially it was Nina's idea, but eventually it became a tradition in the Cambas household to provide Easter dresses for the poor girls in Moria. At the sight of the sailor's uniform, the women put their fabric and needles down and stood up to give him a hearty welcome. Nina's heart pounded rapidly with feelings about the imminent departure of the *North Star*. She leaned forward and grabbed his hand, smiling to hide her fear that Danny's visit this afternoon might mean good-bye. Suppressing tears yet smiling, he announced his decision, explaining that it is his duty to obey orders. But he swore upon his parents' graves that he would return as soon as he could.

"Will you wait for me?" he implored, his sadness evident in his face.

Nina nodded a half-hearted yes, but unable to control her tears, she fell into his arms and wept.

"I'll be back my love, I promise. I want to make Lesbos my home and spend the rest of my life with you. Do you believe me?" he asked, in a tone of conviction. He wanted to return to Lesbos and marry Nina, but in the same breath he was afraid it might take years before he could come back, since Greece had now been invaded by the Nazis. Momentarily, another tormenting thought pierced his mind. *What if in my absence another prospective husband pursued her and convinced Nina to marry him?* Quickly he dismissed that ugly thought. *Nina loves me and will be waiting for my return.*

Seasoned in human emotions, Pipina witnessed with compassion the two tormented souls who loved each other dearly. She reached out and wrapped her arms around Nina and Danny and said, "Where there is love, there is no fear. That's what the Bible tells us." She pulled a white handkerchief from her pocket and gave it to Nina. "Now wipe your tears and be brave. Danny has to abide by the captain's rules, because he's a man of honor. But before you know it, he'll be back."

"Of course, I will," Danny said.

"Can't you at least stay until Easter Sunday?" Nina asked.

"The captain is determined to leave Thursday midnight," he said. "My colleagues and I begged him to stay, but he would not yield."

"Oh, I hate your captain," Nina said.

Pipina grabbed Danny's arm and said, "Well, young man, you've a long journey ahead. You'd better get Papavasile to bless your vessel and your whole crew."

Dan nodded in agreement.

On the way back to the ship, he stopped by the Cambas' olive-oil warehouse to break the news of his departure to Nina's father. They had a man-to-man-talk, and Cambas expressed his admiration that his son-in-law was a man of integrity. As the two men shook hands, Cambas said, "Don't break Nina's heart. Come back safe."

"Mr. Cambas, I made a promise to Nina and to Aunt Pipina, and now I make the same promise to you: Once my mission is complete, I'll be back. Lesbos will be my home." As both men hugged each other for a few precious seconds, Cambas kissed Dan Cohen on both cheeks.

Tuesday evening, Dan visited Papavasile and invited him to bless the *North Star.* He had persuaded Captain Thompson that a blessing would bring them good luck. He did this mainly to satisfy Pipina. Wednesday morning, many islanders swarmed near the ship to witness the event. With a cross and a sprig of basil in his hands, Papavasile went aboard, accompanied by Alexis, who carried a ceramic bowl of water and was followed by the Moria Quartet, who were dressed in their Sunday clothes. Curious observers lined the waterfront. Cambas and the mayor were the last to climb aboard. Pipina stayed at home to comfort her niece, whose despair over Danny's departure was inconsolable. Both women went to the balcony, where they could see the *North Star* through the telescope. The harbor was crowded with people.

"Protect, O Lord, Your people and bless Your inheritance!" chanted Papavasile, sprinkling the ship fore and aft with holy water. Likewise, he blessed the sea and the four points of the horizon, so that the winds and water would be favorable. He also sprinkled the crew, touching them on the forehead with the basil sprig as each of them came up to kiss the cross. Cohen felt shivers in his spine, and with tearing eyes he watched the priest. Humming the tune, the priest nodded to the quartet to take over the hymn. Complementing the priest's chant, Takis and his friends proudly took the cue:

Protect, O Lord, Your people and bless Your inheritance,

Grant victory to Your believers against their enemies,

And be present in their travels,

By the grace of Your cross and the Holy Spirit. Amen.

Captain Thompson was touched, mind and heart racing as he envisioned their long trip to America. Papavasile blessed Cohen and said, *"Kalo Taxeidi Paidi mou.* Safe journey, my son, and may the patron saint of sea travelers, St. Nicholas, protect you from any danger." Unfolding a small red velvet kerchief, Papavasile uncovered an icon of St. Nicholas and gave it to the captain. "Keep this in a special place on your ship. It will be a good reminder that you will always be protected. St. Nicholas is the patron saint of the sea travelers." The captain thanked the priest and bowed with gratitude as he received the icon.

After the ceremony, Cohen returned to town at the American Café to say good-bye to some of his friends and to express words of gratitude to Alexis for his friendship and cooperative spirit. Alexis had the usual pre-lunch appetizers of olives, pickled peppers, bread, and glasses of ouzo set out on a marble table in front of the café. Alexis, who acted as a waiter, was a picture of perfection in a white shirt unbuttoned at the neck, impeccably pressed black pants, and a smooth, close-shaven face and neatly trimmed mustache. The windows of his café were freshly washed and decorated. The narrow sidewalks, having been painted with newly burned lime, were snow white. The main street, store windows, and doors were garlanded with sweet-smelling myrtle and rosemary branches in anticipation of the Easter celebration. People moved about noisily, shopping and walking in all directions through the marketplace.

With a bear hug, Alexis invited Cohen to sit under the tree, where he had set a couple of wicker chairs. As they sat, Alexis' mother, Zographia, arrived with a covered dish and a folded apron.

"Mother, I want you to say good-bye to my new and dear friend, Dan Cohen. He's leaving for America tomorrow."

"Why Thursday night? The next day is Good Friday. Can you at least stay until Easter?" She looked at both men with a gracious, motherly smile.

"Sorry, but we have orders," Cohen answered affectionately.

"Well, if that's the case, may St. Nicholas and the Blessed Mother of Jesus protect you. And I hope you return some day." She put her arms around him, a mother's most loving embrace, and kissed him on both cheeks.

"Thank you," Cohen said. "What a beautiful mother you have," he said to Alexis.

"She's a treasure!" Alexis said, unfolding the apron and putting it on. He uncovered the dish and revealed salted sardines boned and steeped in vinegar and oil dressing. "A local delicacy!" he said.

They lifted their glasses, clinking them to seal their friendship. Alexis, repressing his sadness, said, *Stin-e-yiassou kalo taxeidi*, (*Good health and a safe trip*).

Grinning, Cohen repeated the customary salutation, "To your health also. Until we meet again," and took a sip of ouzo. "I'll miss you, Alexis," he said. While the ouzo did its work, Cohen saw a cunning look in Alexis' eyes, which was interrupted by a strange commotion. A number of people had slipped into the café, arms filled with covered baskets. Savoring his ouzo, Alexis pretended to ignore them, engaging Cohen with a light conversation about his trip.

"I'll miss you, dear friend, and I know another sensitive soul will miss you more."

Cohen nodded with a deep sigh.

"You'll be coming back, won't you?"

"I plan to marry her," he said. But before he could finish his sentence, he saw Apostolos the butcher going into the café with a huge *hot tapsi,* a covered metal tray, leaving a trail of spicy fragrance.

"Something smells delicious. What is it?" he sniffed.

Alexis knew that Apostolos had put in the local oven two spiced legs of lamb garnished with sliced potatoes early that morning. Feigning ignorance, he removed his apron. The twinkle in his eye revealed he had something up his sleeve.

"What's going on?" Cohen asked, sure that Alexis was plotting something.

"Just follow me. In Greece, you do as the Greeks do." In the back of the café, a group of men burst into a riotous screaming and cheering. *"Na zise O Americanos"* (Long and happy life for the American). Cohen could not believe his eyes. The backyard had been transformed into a colorful dining area. Two huge tables, placed together in an L-shape to seat thirty people, was covered with a light green lace cloth. In the center were three vases of flowers, and several ceramic platters that held whole lobsters, octopi, and other delicacies. Bottles of ouzo stood beside an army of thick glasses. Alexis rolled up his apron and threw it behind the marble counter, just missing the artist Gregori, who was eagerly helping with the preparations.

"Come, Gregori. Offer grace," said Alexis. Everyone stood and made the sign of the cross. Alexis leaned over to Cohen and whispered in his ear, "We purposely didn't invite Papavasile. He would never forgive us if he knew about the baked lamb. Holy Week is supposed to be meatless."

"We don't have to eat meat," Cohen whispered back.

"Don't be silly," said Alexis, aloud this time. "Travelers and the sick are excluded from the rule of fasting." He patted Cohen on the shoulder and added with a laugh, "You are the traveler, and we are the sick."

Alexis' comment made everyone laugh. Gregori was waiting for silence. In a surprisingly beautiful baritone, he sang a hymn from the Holy Thursday service.

While the glorious disciples were enlightened at the Last Supper,
Judas was darkened with the disease of avarice.
And to lawless judges he delivered Thee, the Just Judge.

Gregori's voice seemed capable of supporting the vaults of the weightiest melody. He made the sign of the cross again. "Bless, O Lord, the food and the drink of Thy servants. Amen."

Immediately, the merrymakers lifted their glasses in a triumphant outburst. "Safe journey, Danny Cohen. Favorable winds." They clapped thunderously.

It was at that moment that Mourtos happened to be passing by the café and heard cheers. He looked through the door and spat on the floor with rage. Unsettled, he walked away, whispering with each step, *"American sailor"* (Good riddance!). Jealousy still lurking in his heart, he hated his countrymen for showing such hospitality to an American sailor.

Alexis' voice rose above the joyous din. "Eh, fellows, this is Danny's day, so let's give him something to remember us. There'll be no glass or plate left unbroken in my joint today. *"Opa. Na zise O Dannys!"* (Long life for Danny!) They all drank a toast, wishing him a safe journey and asking him to come back someday. As the celebrants ate and drank abundantly, Alexis turned to Gregori and winked. The artist pulled down a long white sheet that covered the wall at the end of the backyard, revealing a beautiful fresco. A gray sailing ship was in the far background, and the smoke ascending from its smokestack formed the words: *I'll be back.* Part of the island was painted in dark green, and in the left foreground, a girl was waving a handkerchief with the inscription: *I shall wait for you.*

Cohen's eyes misted as he saw that the picture was meant for him. *"Efharisto, efharisto,"* he said, thanking Gregori. "What a great artist you are!"

"Take him to America," said Alexis. "He could become rich."

"Gregori is already rich," Cohen said.

At peak moments of the celebration, the participants picked up glasses and plates and threw them on the floor and shouted "*Opa.*" Alexis explained it was a custom that showed that no material object was more valuable than friendship. The table was still overflowing with food and drinks, and the floor was thickly paved with broken dishes and glasses. Now and then Gregori picked up a broom and swept up the pieces. Eventually, the revelers began to leave. The ebullient group of thirty diminished to five, and the afternoon slid into evening.

Alexis closed the door of the café. "I'll make a pot of strong coffee," he said. Cohen could barely keep his head up. Never before had he been feted by such a joyous group of simple folk, who hardly knew him. Never before had he drank as much ouzo. His head felt heavy, but his heart felt their love. The only way to reciprocate was to join them and be part of their lives. The thought of living in Lesbos someday gave him a feeling of unprecedented joy. His eyes sparkled as he gazed around the café. *This can be my America someday soon.* Still he had to say good-bye to Nina.

Alexis filled a cup of coffee and brought it to his friend. After a few sips of the potent brew, Cohen felt slightly revived. All of the glasses having been broken, Alexis continued to drink ouzo from a coffee cup.

"When you come back," Alexis said, "just the two of us will get drunk and celebrate for three days. Never mind these weaklings. Look at them." He laughed and pointed at Apostolos and Nikos. Dead drunk, the two could not keep their heads up or their eyes open. "Hey, heroes of Moria, this is not a hotel," Alexis' loud laughter woke them.

Gratefully, Cohen shook their hands. "Happy Easter, guys," he said. "I'll never forget you."

Butcher and barber responded, "Happy Easter, Danny," and with arms around each other's shoulders, hardly able to remain seated, they started up a song. Gregori grabbed an old guitar that hung on the wall and attempted to strum along:

> *Life can be unfair and so damn short,*
> *Cruel death comes too soon, the body to rot.*
> *But love lives forever, after we die,*

As flowers give fragrance, although they're dry.
Another glass of wine, let's all drink with Dan,
Make a sacred promise that we will meet again.

Gregori rested the guitar on a table like a mother placing her baby in a cradle. "Mr. American," he said, "come back to us someday. Come to the island of love."

Suits rumpled and stained, Nikos and Apostolos composed themselves and turned to Cohen. "Good journey and come back soon," they said, unable to keep their heads up straight.

"I'll be back, and that's a promise," said Cohen, deeply moved.

"Mr. Cohen, when you come back, Apostolos and I will get married," Nikos mumbled. "Of course, not to each other." He laughed. "He will marry a fat, rich widow, and I, a young divorcee." They all burst out laughing, and Alexis opened the door, pretending to kick them out.

"Out, you scoundrels, and don't go to Despina's tonight. Remember, it's Holy Week."

"After today," Apostolos said, "we're all going to holy hell." They went off laughing and singing. Cohen dozed off for a while on the leather sofa. Alexis covered him with his coat as Gregori gently strummed the guitar.

Returning from their evening serenade, Takis and his three friends peered into the café. When Alexis saw them, he eagerly said, "Come in, you little devils. Where have you been hiding? I was looking for you all afternoon."

As they entered the café, they saw the American sailor half asleep. In the corner was Gregori with a guitar in his arms. His saintly face looked sad.

"We need a little farewell song, boys," Alexis said and poured them a glass of lemonade. "Our American friend is sailing tomorrow."

"I know," Takis replied. "I asked him to take all four of us to America."

"Come on, sing him a song, and if you do it well, I'll ask him to take you to America." He chuckled.

"No lies, Mr. Alexis," the Moria Quartet replied.

Then, daring Takis said, "If you give us a little ouzo, we'll sing a new song that Patroklos finished this afternoon, sitting by the harbor and watching the *North Star*. It's really good."

"You've got yourselves a deal," Alexis said, and he poured a few drops into four little coffee cups. "This is all the ouzo you're going to get. Now sing that song."

Cohen woke up as he heard the young voices. He recognized Takis. "Hey, Americanaki, are you going to sing?"

"Gregori, join us with the guitar," Takis said. Softly strumming on the strings, Gregori gazed at their faces and effortlessly followed the quartet:

A ship will sail tomorrow,
Two hearts will tear apart,
Love will abide forever,
Songs from an angel's harp.
Darkness will be descending,
Years of evil, years of pain.
Good people may lose faith,
Wounds will be healed again.
God won't allow evil,
As humans may think,
He is a God of mercy,
Who tests our belief.
Would God ignore two lovers
Who might separate?
Love will bring them together,
Moria will celebrate.

Realizing that the song was written specially for him, Cohen said, "Thank you very much, guys. I'll never forget you."

When the boys left, Alexis said, "I will wait for you to come back someday to marry Nina."

"I will, and that's a promise," Cohen said firmly.

"She's not just beautiful," Alexis said. "Nina Cambas is the most kind-hearted and generous girl on the island."

CHAPTER THIRTY-TWO

WITH SLOW, CONTEMPLATIVE STEPS, men, women, and children headed toward St. Basil's Church for the Thursday evening services. Their conversations on the way were brief and subdued, while inherent grief filled the air. They anticipated the following day, Good Friday, a day of mourning, for once again the Son of God would die on the cross for the sins of His people.

Later that night at Cambas' villa, Danny and Nina walked hand in hand in the dim twilight, toward the small side gate by the sea. In silence, their souls sought ways to articulate their farewell, but their throats were tight and dry with the agony of love for each other. An intoxicating fragrance as they passed a gardenia bush caused a sigh, and Danny felt the appalling reality of his departure, of having to leave his Nina on this beautiful night. Arm tight around her waist, eyes adjusting to the dusk, he longed to be part of her mind's vision. In the vast sky he saw his favorite star, the North Star, but Nina's eyes reflected more stars. She looked stunning. Before they reached the gate, she nestled her head against Danny's chest, and they gazed at the sea.

Making an effort not to cry, she said, "Danny, how long will it be until I see you again?"

"Less than a year, if all goes well."

"I'll count the hours," said Nina, tears coursing down her cheeks.

"Don't cry, my love. I'll be back, I promise."

"I want you to know that even when you're far away I'll be with you," she said softly and bit her lip lest she burst into tears.

When Pipina, who had been following far behind, came closer, Nina and Danny were tightly embracing, holding onto their love forever. She looked away. It was not easy to conceal her sorrow.

"Nina, my sweet, Danny will come back," Pipina said.

Nina pulled back, preparing herself to say good-bye. She could feel a shiver penetrating her heart. "Danny, come back soon," she said. Giving him a quick kiss on the lips, she flew through the trees toward the house, sobbing uncontrollably.

Pipina walked silently down the path by Danny's side, clinging to his arm and feeling ten years older. She trembled and felt cold to the very bone, although the April air was warm.

"If I know Nina well, loneliness will be her companion until you come back," she said. "I fear for her life, Danny. She is not as strong as she appears. May God bring you back quickly."

"I hope so," he said. "I thank you for all your kindness to me, Aunt Pipina."

"Good-bye, Danny," she said, sighing. Her heart ached as she kissed him. "God keep you safe, my son."

Forcing back tears, Dan Cohen took a last glance at Pipina, hugged her, and walked away. He reminded himself of the strict rules of the ship and all the consequences that would befall him if he did not sail. He wallowed in confusion, hating present, future, and binding contracts. At the gate, he turned and looked back once more. Two small windows in the top story of the Cambas villa were lit up like sad eyes observing his fate. *Nina is probably looking for the* North Star, he thought.

Weeping, Nina leaned against the sill of her window, but nature's curiosity ran through her youthful body. She recalled the sailor's touch and scent. *Oh, what it had done to me!* She brushed her palms over her breasts, trying to recapture the exquisite sensation of Danny's fingers. But her own were somehow incompetent and left her wanting. Touching herself left her filled only with the desire to be held by the man she loved.

Darkness veiled the island, and only the stars, like chips of silver, winked in the deep blue sky. An agitated murmur of distant waves sighed their way into her sad heart. *Would I ever see him again? Why, Lord, could he not persuade his captain to let him stay? Couldn't he let the ship sail without him and make a life for himself on the island?* This last thought touched her reservoir of guilt. *How could I be so selfish? Dan also has feelings. I know he loves me. He will come back. I know it.* She comforted herself with these thoughts, but the cruel reality of separation kept her chest heaving. Hot tears blurred her vision. The harbor appeared like a cloud studded with flickering lights. She could no longer discern the *North Star,* but in her mind she could hear a musical humming, the Moria Quarter rising to a crescendo:

> *Death is bitter, the grave is dark,*
> *But separation breaks human hearts.*

Disturbing images paraded through Nina's mind: a heart-wrenching good-bye to young men drafted for war, leaving loved ones behind. *Will I ever see my Danny again?*

CHAPTER THIRTY-THREE

EIGHT BELLS THUNDERED in the harbor, signaling departure. Cohen shivered at the sound, for he knew the meaning. He took the road by the sea that led toward the harbor. Periodically, he turned and glanced at Nina's part of the town as his palpitating heart was torn in two directions. He trudged heavily toward the harbor, feet reluctant and unwilling. Doubting thoughts tormented him. *Should I jump ship now?* Waves lashed the rocks, the pungent fragrance of seaweed filled the air, and he felt the waves crashing at his feet, chilling his body. Weak and miserable, he walked up the gangplank and numbly entered his cabin. He rubbed his temples to suppress the nagging premonition that if he sailed tonight he might never see Nina again. If the *North Star* were attacked by enemy forces, his dream of returning to Lesbos would end in smoke. In his heart he made a decision. If he stayed on the island and the Nazis invaded, as an American sailor what would his destiny be? Would he end up a prisoner of war? How could he be of use to the woman he loved if he were captured? *Nonsense,* he said to himself, *you are not a coward.* He stood up, flexing his muscles in defiance of his thoughts. He felt a new vigor in his chest, a vitality, a life force that needed to take action. Dan Cohen felt taller and stronger. The idea of letting go of his mission made more sense. *If I block my feelings now, they will be lost forever. No power on earth can separate me from my love. I speak the language, I know the customs, I can work. All I need is to change my name back to its original form. If Daniel Papadopoulos was good enough for my grandfather, it's good enough for me. Papavasile is my friend. He can issue a baptismal certificate with my grandfather's name. What am I worrying about?*

These emerging thoughts fueled his courage to make a decision that brought relief to his mind. He decided to say good-bye to the *North Star*. Taking a last look at his cabin, he turned off the light. In the semi-darkness, he stuffed some of his belongings into a duffel bag and secured the buckles as he tested its weight. It was light. As he tiptoed onto the deck, he could hear his mate snoring, the dry cough of his captain in the next cabin, the murmuring of the waves, the beating of his heart, and the inordinate bustle of the harbor, which he had not noticed until that moment. He went off the ship and out into the sleeping alley on his way to the Cambas estate. Momentarily, he wished to find the gate barred. *Am I crazy?* He pushed the gate open. The hinges yielded with a mournful moan that left a frozen echo inside him. As soon as he edged his way through, trying not to make a noise, he caught sight of Nina's room. Sheets were hanging out of her window, airing. He was halfway between the sea and Cambas' garden, so he could not determine in the darkness if the silhouette in the distance was a person or an illusion. The moon peeped over the eastern mountains, and its beams spread a silver patina on the sea. The *North Star* could not be seen. He stopped, rubbed his forehead roughly with his wrist, and pressed his temples. *What will the captain think of me? The crew? My friend Tiny Tom?* But in leaving Nina behind, he felt he was abandoning half of himself. *What if I cannot come back? What would Nina think of me, a sailor who lied and deceived her?* His knees buckled at the thought. It was an excruciating feeling— an unfathomable crevice ahead, abysmal chaos behind.

Pipina was sitting in a white wrought-iron chair in the garden. Rubbing her back with one hand and wiping away her tears with the other, she stared at the sea. A dirge common to the islanders kept repeating in her head. As she smelled the saltiness in the air, she cursed: *Ocean, enemy of young women. Ocean, murderer of youth.*

Dark clouds drifted across the sky, swiftly covering the moon, and when they passed, Pipina daydreamed in her moon-bathed garden, conjuring up symbols out of the clouds, ignorant of the terror those clouds foretold. At this fateful hour, she hated boats and oceans. The whole world seemed cruel. Feeling the chill penetrating her aching bones, she rose and headed for the house, deeply concerned about how she could comfort her niece. But her thoughts were interrupted by running steps. Cohen had shut the garden gate and was hurrying toward her, gasping, "Aunt Pipina, Aunt Pipina, it's me, Danny. I'm not leaving . . . ." He dropped his duffel bag on the ground and reached for Pipina's hand.

Startled, Pipina hugged him. "My son, you really love her!" She cried tears of joy.

"With all my heart."

"God protect you," she said and held on to his arm. But an icy current sped through her whole body, leaving her numb. *What appeared a heroic act could bring calamitous complications.* She wanted to feel happy for her niece and the brave sailor who loved her so much that he was willing to abandon ship and sacrifice his career, but a lump in her throat prevented any exclamation of joy. With an agonizing heart, she said, "Danny, do you think you're doing the right thing?"

"What is the right thing, Aunt Pipina?"

"Oh, I don't know, my son."

"I love Nina. I want to be with her."

"I understand, but what about your ship?"

"They can manage without me."

"You know better," she said, shaking her head and staring at the sky as if to consult the stars. "I don't know how my brother is going to take this news."

"I know Mr. Cambas likes me."

"Oh, indeed he does, otherwise he would not approve his daughter marrying you." Her tone became cautionary. "But I'm not too sure he would like the idea of your leaving the ship."

"I hope I can talk to him tonight."

"Not tonight. He's not feeling well. He took two aspirins and went to bed at eight o'clock."

"Then tomorrow," Cohen said, bracing himself to contain his exhilaration.

"Let's go and find Nina. She must be still awake," Pipina said.

"Great," Cohen said. "I hope she is."

Danny triggered the tender region of Pipina's heart. She reached out and caressed his face, sensing his agony as her fingers touched his perspiration. The words of Papavasile's sermon echoed in her mind: *Love endures all things, believes all things, hopes all things. Love never fails.*

Nina, still tossing and turning in her bed, pulled the covers over her head to shut out the echoing sounds. She envisioned the ship slicing the blue waters of the Aegean and leaving Lesbos far behind. She imagined Danny's agony, his face blending with the clouded sky as he leaned against the rail of the ship and watched the silhouette of the island disappearing in darkness. She closed her eyes and felt his tight embrace. "My Danny," she whispered.

Apprehensively, Pipina and Cohen walked fast toward the house, Pipina leading the way. They went around to a back door, and taking deep breaths to quiet their tension, they both tiptoed to a private room. A kerosene lamp gave ample light, making visible two Byzantine icons hanging on the wall on each side of a large window that was covered by a thick brown curtain. The floor was covered with a white *flokati* carpet that ended near the fireplace. The fire Pipina had started earlier had dwindled, but she put a log of dry wood on it. Immediately huge flames brightened the area, giving a radiant flow to Cohen's face.

"Aunt Pipina, this is such a special room," Cohen said.

"This is my inner sanctum, a place of solitude," she said. "Now, my son, sit here and warm yourself and pray. It's a holy night and a long night indeed. I'll go and see if Nina is awake." He heard the trepidation in her voice.

Pipina knocked at Nina's door just before midnight, opened it softly, and said, "Put on your robe and follow me." There was a tremor of fear in her voice.

"What's wrong, Aunt Pipina?"

"Come, child."

Nina thought something must have happened to her father, but as she followed, Pipina walked past his room. "It's a good thing your father is a heavy sleeper," she whispered.

"Why? What's happening?"

"Quiet," whispered Pipina, putting a finger to her lips.

"What's going on?" Nina insisted.

"Come to my cell."

Nina's heart was pounding with apprehension. When she entered the room, she saw a dark silhouette against the bright light in the fireplace. As she came closer, she screamed, "Danny! Oh my God!"

"Hush, child!" Pipina whispered.

Nina hugged Danny tightly.

He said, "I've made another decision. I'm back for good."

"I can't believe it," Nina said as she held him. For a few moments they remained in each other's arms. Joy tears rolled down Nina's cheeks. Pipina left them alone.

"Did the captain grant you permission to stay?" Nina asked, eager to hear the details of Danny's change of plans.

Cohen remained silent. The image of the captain came to his mind, his austere yet benevolent face and piercing, brilliant eyes asking him to bridle his emotions. He could hear his captain's words: *Go to that woman if you genuinely love her, spend a couple of hours with her, but come back to your duties. Be a man of honor!*

"Will they be looking for you?" Nina suddenly said, instinctively pulling back, the worry evident in her eyes.

"They might, but . . . "

Pipina excused herself and left the lovers alone, still pondering Cohen's decision.

"Nina, look at me," Cohen said. He saw that she had lost her color and vitality and affectionately cradled her face in his hands. "I love you, and I came back because I love you. I want to protect you or take you with me."

"Take me on the *North Star*?" Nervously, she giggled. "You are not serious, are you?

"Of course I am. I'd take you to America, if you're willing to come."

"Danny, I love you, but I'm not ready to leave Lesbos." Concerned over his feelings, she went on. "My precious love, we talked about this before, and I thought you understood."

"I know your roots are here," Danny answered.

"It's not just that," she said. "It's my aging aunt and ailing father. They raised me, Danny. Try to understand. I feel duty-bound." Nina tried to hold back her tears.

"And you have plans to build an orphanage on the island."

"That, too. I made a promise to God."

"I understand, my love. That's why I've decided to abandon my career."

Nina swiftly fell into his arms and said, "And I am totally yours, Danny Cohen."

"If you don't come with me tonight, I have no choice but to stay and accept the consequences of my decision."

"Aren't you afraid?" she asked, serious concern in her eyes.

"My love, when I'm with you, I fear nothing. Can you believe me?"

"What if we were invaded by the Nazis? Would you be in trouble?"

"No. America has not declared war against Germany. Besides, I'm no longer Cohen. I'm taking on my Greek name, my grandfather's name, Papadopoulos. So I'll just be one of the Greeks on Lesbos."

"That may be a smart thing to do, but I'm still afraid."

"Of what?"

"I don't know," she said. "The enemy?" She shrugged, shaking off her conflicting thoughts.

Pipina came back and nervously fed the fire with dry wood. But realizing their need to be alone and talk, she said, "The night is long. I'm going to get you some warm milk and then I'm going to bed."

"Thanks, Aunt Pipina," Nina and Danny answered happily.

"Lower your voices. The walls have ears," she warned them.

The room was heavily draped in deep cherry velvet. A crackling fire burned sweet-scented olive-tree wood to warm the cold April night. Danny took another log and put it on the fire. Although there were two leather chairs in each corner of the room, they sat on the floor on a fluffy flokati, the wool rug. Over the mantle was a beautiful piece of embroidery, barely illuminated, depicting Jason and the Argonauts at sea. "That needlework was my mother's. She had made it before she married my father," Nina said sadly.

Danny drew closer to Nina, and kissed her softly and pushed his concern about Captain Thompson to the back of his mind. Then he took her in his arms, determined not to let her go. "God has blessed us, Nina," he said confidently. "Whatever life brings to us, we must accept it as His blessing."

His words surprised Nina. It was the first time she had heard Danny mention God. She took his hands in hers and caressed them. In his brilliant blue-green eyes, she could see herself and the reflection of the flames. Aware of the consequences of his decision, she felt the two arms that could crush the world, the lips that could inflame hers, and the heart that could engulf her own eternally. *He's totally mine,* she thought, and leaned her head against his shoulder.

The room grew warmer, and Nina rose to open a window. Fresh air, full of the fragrance of the spring flowers, filled the room. The sky was a clear, deep blue, dotted with stars. Porch lamps from the houses in the town cast a soft light over the simple streets. The town seemed deserted. Only the occasional barking of a dog and the croaking of frogs disturbed the peace of the night. Most of Moria's inhabitants were still at the midnight service of the Crucifixion of Christ at St. Basil's. The services this night were a dramatic ritual of solemnity. Out of the darkness, the breeze carried youthful voices from the church. Nina could just decipher the words: "Today is hung on the tree, the One who hangs the earth among the stars." Lingering at the window, she listened with mixed emotions. Never before had aunt and niece missed church on such a sacred night. Then, reaching a crescendo, the voices of the Moria Quartet could be clearly heard, evoking guilt in her heart:

As you lifted Your Cross, O Lord,
Fear and trembling fell upon the earth.
Creation itself suffered, seeing You on the Cross,
But You came to give us life, not death.
Loving Lord, glory to You.

Making the sign of the cross, Nina prayed softly, "Loving Lord, forgive our absence from your church tonight." Closing the window, she tiptoed back and sat beside the man she loved dearly. She said, "The quartet sounds so beautiful."

"They are great. I heard them today at Alexis' café," Danny said. "One of them called me Mr. America."

"Danny, please hold me," she said. "I wish you and I were in church tonight." She wanted God to bless their union. He took her in his arms, and she lost consciousness of everything around her except the great force of his love. In the light of the flames that leaped from the wood, she gazed into his eyes. Gently clasping his hands, she let them slide onto her breast.

"I love you," he whispered. "I'll never part from you, not as long as I live."

"Till death do us part?" she asked.

"Till death do us part," he vowed.

Nina placed her hands against his temples, feeling his pulse against her fingertips. Unbuttoning his shirt, she ran her fingers down his muscular, hairy chest and closed her eyes as a woman closes them when she sees the lips of her lover descending upon hers. Quivering, their lips fused in one pro-longed kiss. Tenderly, her hands glided over his cheeks, feeling his beard, his face rough and hot.

"You're more beautiful than ever," he whispered in the last flutter of the scented flames. The fire was gradually dwindling. He took her hands, kissed them, and pressed them against his chest.

"Come, *agape mou*," he implored simply, "rest in my arms."

With grace and tenderness, Nina reluctantly resisted the desire of her body. Face flushed and heart racing, she lay down on the rug. A sweet recollection of those ecstatic moments in the hot springs and a wish that they could reoccur caused her to shiver.

Sensing the change in her mood, Cohen leaned over and asked, "Are you okay, my love?"

She nodded a silent yes.

Nature and passion moved as one force, weaving the fabric of love. But Danny realized that he could not take advantage of Pipina's hospitality. She had made a sanctuary available to him. In full charge of his desire, he gazed at Nina. Her big brown eyes brimmed with tears. He could tell that she wanted him, but the risk of Cambas waking up and finding them in an intimate act was too great a risk. It could mean his banishment from Nina forever.

CHAPTER THIRTY-FOUR

A MESSAGE IN MORSE CODE left Captain Thompson unsettled. W. L. Bell, Chief of Naval Operations in the Mediterranean, ordered the *North Star* to leave Lesbos as soon as possible and seek refuge near Aivalic, a small Turkish harbor east of the Aegean Sea. Hitler's army had leveled and burned most of the towns and villages in the northern part of Greece, and that morning they had bombarded the island of Crete. Dan Cohen had not returned to the ship, and the captain paced the deck angrily. "Where the hell is Cohen? The lad is in love, and all the world has turned to blue skies and red roses."

"He should be back soon, sir." Tiny Tom said. The crew was ready for departure.

"And how do you know that?"

Tiny Tom was speechless for a moment. "Sir, I was just thinking. It's actually Friday morning. One more day, it will be Saturday, then Easter begins." He hesitated. "What I mean to ask, sir, is it possible we could stay here until Easter Sunday? Maybe Cohen will show up."

"We're at war, and you're talking about Easter!"

"Whatever you say, captain."

"Prepare to sail with or without Cohen." The captain's order was irrevocable. The mechanic emerged from a narrow hole in the deck, face filthy with oil and tar. He wiped the perspiration from his face with his sleeve. "Captain," he said, "everything is in shape, but the engine should run for at least another half hour before we cast off."

"We cannot wait much longer than that," instructed the captain.

Tiny Tom gasped. *I hope Dan comes soon,* he thought.

"Our next stop is Aivalic in Turkey," the captain said. "There we'll receive further orders. We might even have to change course on the way."

Tiny Tom and the mechanic listened intently.

"There's something else. The Germans invaded Athens an hour ago. The Greeks are fighting them tooth and nail."

"The Greeks are good fighters," said Tiny Tom.

"That's true," said the captain, "but they can't hold off the tanks and the German army."

"I bet Greece will last longer than France and some of the other European countries," said Tiny Tom.

Captain Thompson shook his head wearily. "Stop talking about things you know little about."

"Yes, sir."

"We weigh anchor shortly." The captain surveyed his crew. Then pointing a firm finger toward Tiny Tom he said, "We shall delay, but I want you to go to the local police station and ask for their help."

"How am I to talk to the police? I don't know the language."

"Find a way," ordered the captain.

———

An English-speaking policeman and Tiny Tom went straight to the American Café, where Alexis, still cleaning up the mess from Danny's farewell party, was the only person around.

"We know Cohen is your friend. We're looking for him. Do you know where he could be?"

Startled, Alexis set down his broom and asked, "What has happened? Isn't he on board?"

"The *North Star* is ready to sail, and Captain Thompson is waiting for him," Tiny Tom said through the interpreter, trying to read Alexis' expression.

"We said good-bye to him late this afternoon," Alexis said, smoothing his mustache with the tip of his tongue. He could guess full well where Dan Cohen was. He poured himself a drink, took a sip, and asked, "Gentlemen, may I offer you something to drink?"

"No, thanks," said the policeman. He nodded to Tiny Tom. "Let's go."

After they left, Alexis' worried look turned into a grin, thinking that his friend most likely was where he should be, with the woman he loved.

As they turned the corner half a block from the café, the two men ran into Mourtos. The policeman asked him if he had seen Dan Cohen. Tiny Tom agonized as the policeman explained that the *North Star* was about to lift anchor and the first mate was missing. Mourtos listened to the news, and his brain whirled with fear and anger.

He said, "It's a small island. You'll find him." His throat tightened as walked away. *There's only one place that American bastard could be. Let the police do their search, but I'll fish him out of Cambas' place and take him to his ship, dead or alive.* The thought that the sailor might remain on the island and marry Nina enraged him. Furiously dashing through the ebony night, wallowing in jealousy, he decided to visit Despina first. She always had room in her heart for him, but he also wondered if her vigilant eyes had seen the American sailor or if she smelled something brewing in Cambas' mansion.

"I've been waiting for you," she said in a voice that heightened Mourtos' dilemma. He was aware of her agenda, but his heart had plans that did not include her. Hands trembling, he lit a cigarette and paced back and forth, exhaling a painful sigh with the smoke. The floorboards creaked under his feet. "I think the American has jumped ship. They are looking for him, and I promised the police I'd find him," he lied.

"Why are you so anxious to find the American?" Despina asked, annoyed at Mourtos' eagerness. "Kick off your shoes and relax a bit. You look exhausted."

Ignoring her tender intentions, Mourtos shrugged his shoulders and went to her cabinet for a drink. He filled a glass with cherry cognac and gulped it down. Then he lied again. "There's a handsome reward if I find him." He stretched out on a chair.

"My Mourtos," she cooed, "is it the reward you're after or something else?" She came close and sat on the floor beside him, resting her chin on his knees and looking into his eyes.

"You don't know what you're talking about," he said.

"Nina loves this man. Can you understand what that means? She would be furious if she knew you were going to search for him."

"Nina's a fool. It's stupid to think of marrying a foreigner. 'Buy shoes from your own hometown, even if they are patched,' says the proverb. She should marry one of the islanders, someone she knows, someone trustworthy, not a sailor from another country who she hardly knows."

"Why do you care?" Her temples throbbed, knowing he was interested only in Nina.

"If you don't know why, you are a greater fool than I thought." He stood up and stretched his arms. He was tall, muscular, and strong as a titan. Despina stared at him scornfully, but her eyes welled with tears out of love for him.

"I know. You want Nina for yourself? Your vanity has made you mad. You are an even greater fool than me. A wealthy man like Cambas would never accept his servant as his son-in-law."

"You are a stupid whore." He struck her across the mouth and rushed out into the darkness. Mourtos intended to search every inch of the island, lift every stone in search of Dan Cohen, and get him back on the ship and off the island forever.

Betrayed, Despina wiped her bruised lips. She looked at herself in the mirror. Blood stained her teeth. "I swear I'll kill you, Mourtos," she whispered fiercely. With deliberation, she made the sign of the cross. Fury rising to a murderous pitch, she prayed, "Lord, forgive me, but I can't bear for another woman to have him."

Looking right and left, Mourtos marched briskly toward the eastern part of the town. Cambas' estate was a good place to start. Making his way down a twisting narrow alleyway, he stood before Cambas' gate like a giant. He could swear he smelled the scent of the American. He knew he was there.

One hour after midnight, he silently entered the garden. Smoke ascended from the chimney and a glow came from a side room. Strange! *Why would the fire be burning at such an hour?* Taking deep and prolonged breaths, he gained enough nerve to creep up the stairs and eavesdrop. With a tight smile on his face, he rapped on the door.

Danny and Nina jumped up from the flokati rug and hurriedly sat on the chairs, looking at each other with worry. The persistent knock grew louder. Flashlight in hand, in her white nightgown and with disheveled hair, Pipina hurried to see who could be visiting so late at night. As she passed by Nina and Danny in front of the fireplace, she put her index finger to her lips. "Quiet," she whispered.

"Who's there?" Pipina asked softly.

"It's me, Miss Pipina. There is a search party in the vicinity."

Pipina opened the door. "For whom?" she asked cautiously.

"If the American is here, I can take him to a place where he will be safe." Under the dim lantern light outside the door, Mourtos' face seemed sinister.

Pipina eyed him with intensity. "He's not here."

Mourtos shrugged his shoulders and said, "I'm only trying to help."

"I know," said Pipina. "I'm sure the American is safe wherever he is. Now, go home. Tomorrow is Good Friday, an important day."

"The police will be here any minute, Miss Pipina. They will search every inch of this house. I am here to help."

"I said go home!"

Mourtos turned away sullenly. "Very well, my lady. Very well," he said, descending the steps slowly, determined to spend the night in the immediate area and observe any possible movement.

CHAPTER THIRTY-FIVE

PIPINA SHUT THE DOOR behind her and closed her eyes tightly to collect her thoughts. *If Mourtos is serious about the police coming here, the American had better hide.* With a deep sigh, she leaned against the door. Concealing her suspicions about him, she told Nina, "It was Mourtos. He's concerned about Danny. There's a search party, so we'd better hide him."

"Please don't worry," Danny said.

Pipina, noticing concern in his eyes, asked, "Do you want to return to the ship, or have you other thoughts?"

"I've made up my mind. I'm staying. I can hide or disappear for a few hours," Cohen said.

Pipina took a good look at him. She saw determination in his face and she instantly knew what to do. She cleared her throat and said, "There is only one place where Danny can hide until the search is over and the ship is gone." Nina held Danny's hand tightly, concerned and wondering where such a place could be.

"Where, Aunt Pipina?" Nina asked.

"You are sitting on it," Pipina said with a sigh of concern.

Nina and Danny anxiously jumped up, unaware of what her aunt meant.

"My loving children, please step aside." Quickly, Pipina removed the flokati rug revealing a trap door, hardly noticeable.

Pipina's voice was serious as she began to explain. "Under this door there is a stone-paved tunnel that leads to the sea. It was built by an uncle of ours as a shelter and escape when the Turks occupied the island. Nobody knows about it except your father and me."

Nina could not believe that there was such a place where she grew up and knew nothing about it. She turned to Danny to see his reaction.

"Nobody would suspect that I'm hiding in there," Danny said. But his wish to convince Nina and her aunt that he had made the right decision was interrupted by sudden thunderlike knocks at the main entrance, followed by a harsh voice calling out, "It is the police."

Expect the unexpected and here it is, Pipina thought, and grabbed Danny by the hand.

"Whatever you do, Danny," Pipina said, "when the sun shines tomorrow, it should be a day of joy." Quickly, she removed the flokati rug and lifted the trap door. Nina gave Danny a warm hug and a kiss and said, "Be careful, my love."

Placing a firm foot on the first step of the ladder, Dan Cohen felt weak, less than a man. He began to project ugly thoughts upon himself. *What am I doing to myself?* He could just hear his mates' sneering remarks: *Dan Cohen, the lover-boy, is caught in* a *woman's web. Shame!* Captain Thompson would mock: *Are you a sailor or a snake? Too bad you're giving up your career for a woman. What a renegade you are!* Doubts clouding his mind, he nearly lost his balance as he waved good-bye.

Sensing his hesitation, Pipina handed him the flashlight and said, "Careful, Danny."

"Don't worry," he said and tried to dismiss his thoughts. The young lovers stole one more kiss as he descended the steps, and Nina leaned over the opening of the tunnel to ruffle his hair, hiding her fear in the darkness that was about to envelope the man she adored.

Nina helped her aunt close the heavy trap door over him, sealing the opening and pulling the rug over it. An excruciating feeling of loneliness engulfed her. She felt guilty, subjecting the man of her dreams to this humiliation.

"If the police come into the house, try to appear casual," Pipina advised. "Better yet, go to your room and get under the covers. *O God, why did I get so involved?* Now Cambas' household was under the dark shadow of suspicion. She made the sign of the cross. *God protect us from the machinations of the evil one.* Tiptoeing to her bedroom, Pipina realized what a dangerous scheme this could be. She wished that Dan Cohen had not come back this way.

Inundated with fear, Nina joined her aunt, and both women snuggled in Pipina's bed. They were unable to verbalize how they felt, knowing that Danny had made a sacrifice of his career at the risk of his life.

CHAPTER THIRTY-SIX

UNDER THE TRAP DOOR, Danny tried to light up the area with his flashlight. He could smell the dampness ascending to meet him. Feeling carefully for the shaky rungs, he moved slowly. Nervously, he fumbled for each step, hardly able to balance himself. He grabbed the rung above him, but the ladder suddenly cracked and shifted under him and the flashlight slipped from his grip. *Dear God, Nina, Captain Thompson, what have I done?* He felt himself falling backward into space and landed with a dull thud on the ground below as part of the tunnel wall gave way. He felt his bones crunch. The skin of his forehead was covered in a mixture of warm blood and sweat, which trickled into his eyebrows. An agonizing sigh brought a vague smell of mold into his lungs. Utter confusion, terror, and excruciating pain devoured him. Broken wood, stones, and bricks crashed down upon him in the darkness. Through the debris came the dim light from his lost flashlight.

Pipina heard the noise of the muffled cave-in. Propelled by her premonition that something had gone wrong in the tunnel, she ran to the fireplace and opened the tunnel door. Clouds of dust billowed out of the darkness. "Danny," she called. No answer came. "Danny!" she called again, but there was only dead silence. Carefully she used a log as a wedge to keep the trap door slightly open to admit air. In utter hysteria, she ran to her brother's room to inform him of the danger in his own house, but she halted in front of his bedroom door. She could not divulge what she had done behind his back. He would raise hell and never trust her again. Besides, she knew well that under this mighty merchant's show of confidence was a fragile man. What she had done for Dan Cohen could shock her brother so much that he might have a heart attack. She would handle the situation alone. The only person who might be of assistance, she thought, was Mourtos. She hated the thought, but had no other choice but to look for him and solicit his help.

In the quiet of the night, Mourtos had stealthily climbed back up Cambas' outer stairway after Pipina closed the door. He sat and schemed, wrestling with a lingering suspicion. *The sailor must be with Nina, and Pipina is an accomplice.*

Not long after, the door burst open, and Pipina came running out, an oil lantern in her hand. She saw a man curled up on the staircase. She could only see his back but she said, "Mourtos, is that you?"

"Yes, my lady. It's me."

"And what are you still doing here?" Pipina asked.

"Guarding Cambas' household," he said. "If the police show up looking for Dan Cohen, I can tell them that he is not here."

"But he is," she said and began to cry. "Mourtos! Come with me, but be very quiet." Pipina walked very quickly toward the sea.

"What's the matter? Is something wrong?" he asked as he followed her.

"Don't talk," Pipina said. Until recently he had respected her. But since Cohen's involvement with Nina, he had no favorable feelings toward anyone in Cambas' household. He hated them all.

In front of an array of thick bushes, she ordered, "Hold the lantern for a moment," and removed a huge myrtle bush from the mouth of the secret tunnel. With a ghostlike countenance she looked at him and said, "You are not to say a word about this to anyone, do you hear? I want you to swear to God." Pipina's guttural voice had such an ominous tone that she could convince the devil. She brought the lantern to his face; her uncompromising gaze blazed at him with rancor.

"Let me lead the way," Mourtos said protectively. Step by step, they silently groped their way along the narrow path that ended under Pipina's special room. Suddenly, Pipina screamed, "Danny, are you hurt?" There was no response. Cohen lay motionless on the stone-paved floor under the debris of the cave-in. In the dim light of the lantern, she saw blood on his face. "O my God," she cried. "He's badly hurt."

Mourtos held her back as she reached for Cohen's arm. "My lady, hold still, let me be of help." Eagerly, he knelt down and leaned over the motionless figure. His dark, glistening eyes moved like a raven's. He placed his ear over the heart. He touched Danny's throat to check his pulse, but in his mind he could only hear his own vicious voice, *American sailor, your days in Lesbos are over.* "My lady, he's dead. I'm very sorry," he said, feigning deep sadness.

Pipina leaned weakly against the tunnel wall. "Oh my God, dear God," she wept bitterly. "What have I done? I thought I was doing God's will by hiding him. I am the cause of his death. Strike me dead, dear God. I am a murderess."

"It's not your fault," Mourtos said with apparent sympathy. "Accidents happen. You had better get back to the house. If the search party finds us here, we could be in plenty of trouble."

"Maybe he's still alive," Pipina insisted.

"His skull is cracked open. There is blood and brains all over his face," Mourtos said. "It's a terrible sight, not one you'd want to remember. My lady, please get back to the house."

"How can I leave him here?"

"You must. I will help you," he said.

"When Nina finds out, it will kill her. My brother will never forgive me."

"Does Nina know about this?"

"No."

"Well, then, she doesn't have to know. Leave everything to me."

"What are you going to do?"

"Haven't I always been a reliable and a good friend? Now let me take you home. I'll take care of everything. Trust me," he said, eager to get rid of Pipina.

"Yes, yes, Mourtos, you are a good man. I'll always be grateful. I know you'll take care of everything. You always do." Her despair deepened and brought pain to her chest.

"Leaning on Mourtos for support, she mumbled, "Ill-fated Nina! Why, Lord? She lost her mother when she was a baby. She lost her first love, that beautiful boy Stephen. And now she has lost the man she wanted to marry. Why? What will I tell her? What will I tell her father?"

Mourtos could see by Pipina's expression that she had gone into terrible shock. Taking her by the arm in total darkness, he groped his way back out of the tunnel and to the steps to the house. Then he rushed back to the tunnel and found his way to where Cohen was lying unconscious. Again he knelt and put his ear to his chest. He could hear a faint, slow beat. Pausing to catch his breath before lifting him, he saw Cohen's hand flinch. He wrapped Cohen tightly in his coat, placed him over his shoulder, and carried him to the sea, where a small boat was anchored. Carefully, he brought him aboard. The sea had regained a calmness, and fog covered the shore. Ignoring Cohen's groans, Mourtos snatched up the oars and rowed the boat forward with all his might. As the mist thickened and spread over the harbor, no human eye could possibly see his vessel. Hurriedly, he rowed out into deeper waters. About half a kilometer from shore, he hauled in the oars. Dan lay motionless at the bottom of the craft. For a few moments, Mourtos let the boat drift in the foggy dawn. Determined to dispose of the American, he tied an old anchor around his feet with a thick rope, convincing himself that Dan Cohen was as good as dead anyway.

CHAPTER THIRTY-SEVEN

THE FIRST RAYS OF THE MORNING SUN had reached Cambas' estate when Mourtos knocked at the door. Pipina had waited up for him. Pale and fragile in the stark light, with swollen and red eyes, she had no strength to talk.

"I'm so sorry, my lady. The American is buried at sea and with him our secret," Mourtos said, simulating profound grief.

Pipina began to whimper softly. "It's all my fault. God is punishing me. It was my idea to hide Danny. But how did you have the heart to do it?"

"He was a sailor, and he would have wished it so. The poor guy had a horrible accident."

"It's a horrible nightmare. What will I tell Nina when she wakes up?"

"Tell her he decided to leave. A conscientious sailor could not shirk his duty after all."

"If I tell her that, she'll wait forever for his return."

"Then we must tell her that he is dead. She will mourn for a while, but time heals all wounds. Eventually Cohen will be a sad memory."

"Oh, how can you talk like that?" she said, her hate for Mourtos' cold and heartless attitude visible in her eyes. The past seven hours had made her a very old, very tired woman. "Just go home, Mourtos. It's still very early, and I'm exhausted."

Pipina found Cambas in his library unusually early this morning. His warehouse was closed on Good Friday. He was staring out the window at the harbor. The *North Star* had sailed away. He felt satisfied at having sold his oil for such a handsome price.

"A tragedy has occurred in our accursed island, dear brother," Pipina said and collapsed on a nearby chair.

"What are you talking about?"

"The American is missing since late last night."

"Sailors are survivors, don't you worry."

"This one is dead. I know he is."

"What do you mean? He was okay when he came by my office last night to say good-bye."

"He's dead, I say." Tears rolled down Pipina's cheeks.

"How do you know?" Cambas asked.

"Mourtos came last night to tell me that the captain of the *North Star* had asked the police to look for him. He thought he might be here. Later he returned to announce the sad news. The police found Dan Cohen lying on the rocks, dead," he said. "The ship took his body aboard and set sail after midnight.

"Something's wrong with that story," Cambas said. "I'll bet that this is all a scheme devised by that scoundrel, Cara-Beis. That snake is up to something evil because the Americans did not buy his oil."

Pipina persisted, "That's what Mourtos told me, that's what I'm telling you, and now I don't know what to tell Nina. You know how much she loved him."

"Pipina, if this story is true, I feel deeply sorry for Dan Cohen, such a wonderful human being, and I feel very sad for my daughter. But if it is what I think it is, I promise you I'll have the offender behind bars for life."

"What are we going to do about your daughter?" Danny's death haunted her. She felt a harrowing chill from her bones to the roots of her hair. Covering her head with a black shawl, she fled the house and half-stumbled to St. Basil's, where she sank into a pew and poured out her heart to the Lord. The familiar incense and the array of austere Byzantine icons at the altar evoked a gripping sense of guilt. "Strike me dead, Dear God. Our Danny's death is all my fault."

The church bell echoed mournfully to punctuate the dying stages of Christ. Good Friday unfolded against an unusually cloudy day. The peasants returned to their homes from the countryside, carrying Easter lambs on their husky shoulders. In town, flocks of fleecy lambs crowded the narrow streets. The ones to be slaughtered were marked on the head with red dye. Young girls carried baskets of flowers to St. Basil's, and the Moria Quartet rehearsed hymns to be chanted that night. Women brought white candles and sweet-smelling incense. This day, which marked the death of Christ, was the only day of the year the exuberant Greek spirit was subdued. But it was also a prelude to the ineffable joy of the Resurrection. Holy Week would be climaxed by Easter Sunday, the beginning of a week-long celebration.

CHAPTER THIRTY-EIGHT

GRIEF, BIG AS THE ISLAND of Lesbos, climbed up the front steps of Cambas' mansion, and his daughter didn't even see it coming. She moaned and tossed in her bed until dawn when her own scream *No-oo-ooo* woke her up from a nightmare. Gasping for air and groaning, *Let me go-oo-ooo,* in her dream she had seen Mourtos on top of her. He had tied a rope around her neck and was dragging her toward the sea. She touched her throat, feeling the pain, fingertips red with warm blood. The rope cut into her flesh. Mourtos's angry voice still haunted her: *Self-righteous whore, scheming with a foreigner behind your father's back. You'll pay for it.* Blinking and only half awake, she tried to distinguish between dream and reality as she lay under the covers catching her breath. The dwindling light from an oil-burning votive lamp in front of the Virgin Mary icon cast frightening shadows on the dark walls. Menacing images of angry faces blended into one huge silhouette of her father's manager. Tightly closing her eyes, she whispered, "Evil spirits must be after me."

"Oh, my God!" she gasped, raising herself into a sitting position. *My Danny is not still in the tunnel, I hope. Of course not. Aunt Pipina must have let him out and given him one of the guest bedrooms. What would I do without her?* She smiled. Pushing her horrible nightmare away, she thought, *Danny is still with me. He will be with me forever. I'll make him happy.* A reassuring presence, her cat, Apollo, lay heavily on her legs, oblivious to the world of humans. She reached down and pulled him gently under the covers, feeling his warmth against her. "Apollo," she whispered, "Danny is here. He'll be with us forever, and he's going to love you as much as I do." She hugged Apollo against her breast, felt his pleasurable purring, and indulged in a daydream of a glorious wedding, joy, travel, and life with Danny. But a persistent knocking at the main entrance interrupted her sweet dream. She wrapped herself in a red kimono and hurried to see who was there. She heard giggling outside. As she opened the door she saw two lovely girls dressed in purple, well combed and with radiant faces, each carrying a large basket of colorful flowers. "We've picked up these for the burial. Will you join us?"

"What burial?" Her lips turned pale.

"Nina, were you sleeping?"

"I just woke up," she answered.

"Are you forgetting what day is today? The burial of our Lord Jesus. We're going to decorate the *Epitaphios,* the tomb of Christ."

"Oh," said Nina, "of course, it's Good Friday. What's the matter with me? I must have overslept." Since her teens, every year at dawn Nina had joined the girls in gathering flowers to adorn the symbolic tomb. But since she woke up from her nightmare her mind had been only on Danny. *Was he safe? Was he alright?*

The church bells pealed in the distance. Pipina, ashen and drawn, appeared at the bottom of the stairs. At dawn she had gone to St. Basil's. When she saw the girls had awakened Nina, she frowned with irritation.

"Good morning," she said. Her voice sounded strangely harsh to her own ears.

"Good morning, Aunt Pipina," the girls said.

Pipina excused herself and entered the house.

"Nina, it's time for church," said the girls.

"No, I can't go." *I'll stay with my Danny. He'll need me today,* she thought.

"Oh, please come."

203

"I'm not feeling well. Maybe I'll join you later at the evening services."

"Good-bye, we'll see you tonight," the girls said and hurried down the stairs.

When the door closed, Pipina reappeared. "Child, you don't look well. You must be running a fever," she said, touching Nina's head.

"I don't know." Looking into Pipina's sunken eyes, she asked, "Where is Danny? Is he still asleep?"

"Better go back to bed. It's too early for anyone to be up."

Pipina went to her room and closed the door. Sensing that something was terribly wrong, Nina followed her. She found Pipina sitting on a stool by her bedside, weeping.

"Aunt Pipina, what is it?" She knelt and clasped her hands. They were icy cold.

"Forgive me, child. Forgive me."

"What is there to forgive? Where's my Danny?"

"It is all because of my foolish meddling. He is dead."

"No! I don't believe it!"

"It's true," she cried bitterly.

"It can't be true! Is this one of my father's tricks? Did he change his mind about our marriage? Has he sent Danny away?"

"No, child. I have already told your father. It was a terrible accident. He fell off the ladder into the tunnel." Pipina hid her face in her apron and cried inconsolably.

"If he's dead as you say, where's his body? I want to see him."

"It's not possible," Pipina said.

"Why?"

"It's a long story, child."

"I'm not a child. I'm a grown woman and deserve to know the truth. Aunt Pipina, please be honest with me."

"This truth is too painful for anyone to endure," Pipina replied.

"I don't care how painful it is. I want to know exactly what happened to my Danny. Did the search party seize him and return him to the ship?"

"I told you what happened, and it's all my fault, hiding him in that accursed and hellish inferno."

"Is that where he is now?"

"No," Pipina wept. "He was buried at sea."

"A sea burial? Whose idea was that?" Nina asked, eyes filled with indignation, shock, and burning tears.

Pipina remained silent for a long time, staring into space. Her eyes lost their luster. She could no longer speak.

The cruel reality of Danny's unexpected death coursed through Nina's veins like ice. She flung herself down on Pipina's bed and sobbed painfully.

"Oh, dear God. Dear God. Why? *Why?*" Fiercely, she pounded her fist on a pillow, and turning on her side, fastening her eyes on an icon of the Virgin Mary, she cried, "Please, Mother of Jesus, bring Danny back to me. Please . . . !"

The icon remained motionless; only the Virgin Mary's eyes looked back, seeming to drip with compassion. As the morning wore on, grief over Danny's death spread like a dark stain through the house. Dressed in black, Pipina covered her head with a black mantle. She draped a black veil over the icon and the mirror in her room. Delirious and remorseful because she felt responsible for his death, she became terribly ill and took to her bed, where she lay as if in a coma.

Nina, still in a state of shock, lay numbly in her own bed. The curtains were closed, leaving the room in darkness. She had no desire to eat or to pray. Her mouth was dry and she reached for the glass of water on her night table, but it was empty. She flung the glass against the wall, and hundreds of pieces of glass fell to the floor. Groans and moans of despair and fury burst from her lips as she pounded out her rage until she was exhausted and spent. "I love you, Danny. I miss you so much. Life without you is death." Conscience-torn, she lay in the dark, the back of one wrist draped across her forehead, wishing for death to visit her. Gradually she drifted into a deep sleep.

Overcome by sorrow, her father sat heavily in his favorite leather chair, unable to fathom the mystery of the death of such a young man. He had tried to submerge himself in his work, but his mind kept returning to the image of the good-hearted American sailor who had made Nina so happy. *How is she going to survive this tragedy?*

The next day, the Saturday before Easter, a devastated Nina sat in her room all day, avoiding the sunlight, feeling stabbing pains in her chest and burning sensations in her stomach, unable to unravel the mystery of her loss. But the physical symptoms were accentuated by another set of feelings. She felt horrific guilt for choosing love over church, hours before Good Friday! She thought that the Lord must have punished her by taking Danny. A painful sadness draped itself around her shoulders like an invisible but heavy quilt, the unrelenting and merciless grip of growing despair.

In her devastation, in the late afternoon she mustered enough strength to go to St. Basil's, where she spent hours prostrated before the Cross. When she finally raised her head, she saw the terrifying eyes of Christ watching her. Turning her sight upward toward his icon, she began to scream her anguished questions. "Why did you let this happen? Why did you bring Danny into my life? Why, why?" There were endless "whys" but no comforting answers. She wept and remained in church until her silhouette was swallowed up by the growing dusk.

CHAPTER THIRTY-NINE

HOLY SATURDAY brought about the annual aura of anticipation, Easter joy, and celebration. At sunset, church melodies interwoven with secular string music gave the town of Moria a festive spirit. Eating Easter breads, cracking red eggs, drinking wine, and dancing gave the islanders a feeling of rebirth and elation.

Takis and the Moria Quartet were planning an Easter party at the Mount of St. Elias, where they were going to eat hors d'oeuvres and secretly drink wine. As they walked by the harbor, all vessels were anchored, but there was an empty spot on the dock. Takis thought of the *North Star,* remembering bits of conversation he enjoyed with the American sailor. Shrugging his shoulders, he wondered how far they must have sailed by now.

Nina, wrapped in a black topcoat, head covered with a shawl, scoured the shoreline in a fierce search. *Perhaps the waves will return my Danny to the island, and then at least I'll be able to give him a decent burial.* But there was no sign of him anywhere. The Aegean Sea was a deep cobalt blue, as its murmuring wavelets sang a muffled dirge that offered no comfort to Nina. On her way home the landscape unfolded in full majesty. The sun cast an orange pall over the island, leaving a tinge of gold on the sunset sky. Trees swayed voluptuously as they overlooked the animal kingdom of goats and sheep, bleating as they swarmed toward the mountains. Dogs barked and hens cackled in every yard, familiar village sights and sounds, a sweet melody. But Nina felt the last of her hope draining away. She could not consider attending the midnight Easter services this year.

The sunbeams spilled into her room, piercing the center of her despair. But what about the man she loved? And what about her life among those who knew her? That night she slumped into her bed and buried her face in a pillow and wept. She saw ghastly images of Danny's body being thrown into the sea to be eaten by fish.

Before daybreak, a foreboding smell filled the air, a mixture of sulfur and gunpowder. She woke up thinking she had heard the distant roar of airplanes. Was her mind playing tricks on her? She could not tell. *Maybe the World War will end it all.* Brokenhearted, she closed her window and ran to Pipina's room.

Late on Saturday, St. Basil's was crammed full of festively dressed islanders anticipating the joyous midnight resurrection services. Papavasile, garbed in white vestments adorned with golden crosses, gave final instructions to his altar boys. From the altar ascended clouds of incense, as the Moria Quartet intoned pre-Resurrection hymns. Takis, eyeing his Eleni, who stood opposite the choir loft, felt the exuberance in his voice as he sang:

The One who once buried Pharaoh's army
Under the billows of the sea
Is now buried underground,
But let us rejoice
For soon He will rise and will be greatly glorified.

At the end of the hymn, all the lights in the church were extinguished, the total darkness symbolizing Hades, which was to be visited by the resurrected Christ. Then Papavasile, holding a glowing white candle festooned with a red ribbon, appeared in the pitch-black church. He chanted with a thunderous voice: *Come, all of you, and receive the light from the unwaning light and glorify Christ, Who has risen from the dead.*

Throngs moved forward to light their candles from the priest's candle, as joyous chanting gave new meaning to Christ's Resurrection. In utter exuberance, Papavasile patiently gave light to everyone and eyed the faces, whose moist eyes reflected the candle flame. Last to light her candle was Pipina, overwhelmed by grief. Her brother and niece had decided to stay home. Her teary eyes looked at the priest, hoping to glean some solace from his chant. As midnight approached, Papavasile kept an eye on an old clock opposite the bishop's throne. At twelve o'clock, he would chant the two-thousand-year-old hymn: "Christ Is Risen from the Dead," announcing the mystery of the Resurrection and reassuring all believers that beyond death there is a new and abundant life. But five minutes before midnight, the ear-piercing wail of nearby sirens shook the island. "The Nazis," someone said. "The Nazis," repeated another, and the word ignited fear and pandemonium. The people trembled in fear, then started rushing in all directions, disrupting the service. Papavasile gently told the congregation not to panic, but to pray for protection. "We are in God's house. He will protect us from any danger," he said, but many young people hurried to the exit, while others, paralyzed with terror, sought asylum near the altar.

Lighted candle in hand, Pipina stood undaunted in front of the icon of Christ and near the priest she loved. Determined not to leave him alone, she felt a surge of inner strength. Later she would report to her brother and Nina what she was about to witness.

A company of Nazi soldiers formed a solid wall of green around the church, while a squad of twelve helmeted men marched into the church holding machine guns. With lit candles in their trembling hands, the islanders swarmed closer to the priest. The quartet stopped its chanting and gaped in fright at the invaders. The icons creaked, and the church shook from the click-clack of Nazi boots on the marble floor. From a megaphone came a hoarse female voice: "Stay inside the church. Do as you are told and you will not get hurt." The woman, not more than twenty-five years old, wore a green uniform with a swastika emblem on the sleeve and long flaxen hair flowing out under a soldier's cap. She acted as interpreter. "The services are over. Return to your homes silently, stay indoors, and don't come out until nine o'clock tomorrow morning."

Takis and his friends towered over the interpreter and said, "We need another hour. The services are not over. These people have fasted for forty days in preparation for Holy Communion."

Oberst Lieutenant Conrad Otto Mueller approached the altar and, through the interpreter, shouted orders. His voice was harsh, the face under his cap hard and sharp as a hatchet. The interpreter, with equal pride and arrogance, informed the faithful that the Army of Occupation demanded unconditional obedience.

With blazing eyes, Papavasile stepped forward and glared at the commander. A candle in one hand and a cross in the other, he pointed at the icon of Christ. Momentarily, he thought he saw tears in the eyes of Christ. *Don't You worry, my Lord. In spite of these infidels, there will be a Resurrection service.*

Empowered by his thoughts, he turned to the invader and said, "I am a soldier of Christ. I cannot abandon the altar. The liturgy must be completed, for my people must receive Communion, the Precious Body and Blood of our Lord and Savior, Jesus Christ."

Mueller's face became a ferocious mask of anger. He grabbed the priest by his long beard and growled, "I said, the service is over. Do you want me to say it again?" The woman in the Nazi uniform translated the commander's words, adding her own emphasis.

"Let go of my beard," Papavasile shouted. "This is God's service in God's house for God's people. No one has the right to interrupt it."

"Do you know who you are talking to?" Mueller asked.

"I'm talking to an instrument of Satan who has decided to desecrate a holy place," the priest bellowed with increasing indignation.

The steel hand of the Third Reich held onto the priest's beard and pulled his face upward. Mueller said, "Do you want to be a hero?" The priest sighed deeply to conceal his rage, and turning to his congregation said with painful sadness in his voice, "My people, please return to your homes peacefully and pray. I will remain here for a while to finish the liturgy alone. Although the Moria Quartet already started to sing the anthem of Resurrection, 'Christos Anesti. Christ is risen from the dead,' Christ will not rise this year, not this spring." The priest blew out his candle wrathfully. As the flame was extinguished, his face darkened. The people obeyed him sadly. Scared and grief-stricken, the islanders trudged back to their homes, holding their extinguished candles in the dark. With angry eyes, they saw the ferocious faces of Nazi power controlling and guarding every street corner.

So began one of the darkest periods in all of Greek history. From the Yugoslavian border, Nazi tanks had moved through the Greek cities with invincible power. Their airplanes furrowed the blue sky, vomiting fire and showering death upon the innocent below. The scourge of Hitler's war reached even the little island of Lesbos.

CHAPTER FORTY

EIGHT HELMETED motorcyclists thundered uphill to the thirteenth-century castle, a cherished landmark in Lesbos. In an abrupt ceremony, they took down the Greek flag and replaced it with a swastika. Some people who happened to witness the event from a distance felt an emotional paralysis. Having no military defense, the people of Lesbos succumbed to the invasion. One had to look deep into their eyes to locate their subterranean defiance. But the naive Moria Quartet swore to defy the enemy.

"I'd rather be dead than live with the swastika waving from the castle every day," Takis said, determined to take it down at the first opportunity. During the midnight hours, Alexis distributed the weapons that the *North Star* had smuggled onto the island. Several young patriots enthusiastically picked up the shiny guns and headed toward the mountain crevices, eager to form a resistance movement. In time, Alexis would train them to be skillful fighters.

Under the pretext of illness, Alexis shut down the American Café, removed the American flag, the president's portrait, and any other items bearing American insignia, and stayed home for a few days. Meanwhile, he renamed it Alexis' Tavern and made a new sign for the café. Zographia, his mother, concerned for his safety, felt it was a wise move. Housewives feared for their lives as the rapacious Nazis entered each home, pillaging stored food, dishes, silverware, beds, sheets, and blankets. To feed the army, confiscating committees commandeered chickens, goats, and sheep, leaving families destitute and famished. By the second week of occupation, the arrogant army of the Third Reich had ransacked most of the houses, leaving behind only fear and misery. From the Cambas villa, they removed several priceless artifacts, carpets, tables and chairs, a telescope, and kitchen utensils. Speechless and without recourse, panic-stricken Pipina watched the invaders emptying her china closet and taking Nina's bed. Wrapped in a quilt, Nina pushed her way through the nameless invaders and went to her aunt's bedroom, aware that their eyes followed her. She was nauseated by them and feared they would return.

Caught between indignation and impending catastrophe, Cambas decided to be diplomatic with Oberst Lieutenant Mueller. He addressed him in English, and Mueller smiled. He was multilingual. Cambas made a deal: If his soldiers would leave his villa and his family alone, Mueller could take over his warehouse, which contained thousands of gallons of olive oil that could be shipped to his homeland. Temporarily satisfied with the deal, Mueller shook Cambas' hand. He accepted the offer of oil and promised Cambas that he and his family had nothing to worry about. They could remain in the villa safely.

Mueller toured the Cambas estate and found it exceptionally elegant. He met Pipina and Nina and politely greeted them in Greek. At the same time, machinations flourished in his Nazi mind. Mueller had a secret agenda. Once the olive oil had been shipped to Germany, he would make this luxurious villa his personal headquarters. Part of it could be an officers' club. As for Cambas' daughter, who presently appeared sadly indisposed, she might eventually become his girlfriend.

Much to Cambas' dismay, Cara-Beis, who had a smattering of German, soon profited from the Nazi occupation. He was employed as an interpreter for the army of occupation. In his youth, he had worked for three years as a cabin boy on a Greek cruiser operated by a German crew and had picked up a number of German words. In Moria, there had been no opportunity to speak

German, so now he had to work hard to learn the necessary vocabulary for his new job. As soon as the island had fallen into Hitler's hands, Cara-Beis became important, and the other islanders feared the evil he would do for personal gain. When they saw him riding in a jeep with three predatory-looking soldiers and pointing out certain houses that could be taken over, they began to worry about their destiny.

The third day the Nazis were on the island, they saw a jeep stopped at a freshly painted house near St. Basil's Church. Cara-Beis jumped out, thinking of himself as very special, and introduced the Nazi soldiers to the owners of the house. Feigning compassion, he interpreted for the frightened occupants: *The Army of Occupation needs a room in your house. If you are in possession of a radio or any type of weapon, you must hand it over now. The penalty for hiding radios or weapons is death.*

That same evening he addressed a meeting of Moria's nobles and made a serious pronouncement: *All civilians on the street for whatever reason between 6:00 p.m. and 9:00 a.m. will be considered saboteurs and will be shot on the spot.*

For the next few days, the town of Moria was a blur of numbing conversations. A memorial service was held at St. Basil's Church for Daniel Cohen. It was filled with an endless sea of faces, all sad and teary as they listened to Papavasile's Byzantine chant. No one knew what to think or what to say. Nina and Pipina, grief-stricken and dressed in black, stood by the priest.

Nina retreated to her bedroom. Dark curtains covered the windows, making it feel like a neverending night. Utter loneliness was her only companion as she tried to find comfort in the depths of her heart. But as each hour and each day passed by, she could not hide from the fact that her dreams and her most noble hopes had died. Eventually she sought solace near the One who she believed loved her.

Dark days unfolded. Terror and hunger threatened the besieged. Faces haggard and stomachs swollen, the once fun-loving folk were now forced by starvation to stand in bread lines for hours to buy stale, moldy crusts. Within a month, people would be dying of malnutrition. Epidemics of malaria and smallpox would accelerate the death rate. Famine and death lurked in every corner of Moria. The colorful island would become a cemetery, daily increasing in size, with charred walls containing the vanquished. Papavasile would spend several hours each day at the cemetery, officiating over one funeral after another.

Late one night, in spite of the curfew, Takis and his friends took a small lantern and went to the Mount of St. Elias in search of snails. Takis came home with a full basket. Happily his mother cooked them with onions and olive oil and made a meal for the family, but she saved half a dozen for Takis to bring to school for lunch.

On the way to school the next morning, Takis saw a Nazi soldier standing at the door of the big house of which he had taken possession, flapping his leather gloves against the palm of his hand. Takis avoided looking at him, lowering his eyes he walked past and increasing his pace.

"Hey, you. Come here." Takis heard the harsh order and turned to see a wiggling index finger beckoning him closer. In broken, heavily accented Greek, the soldier said, *"Yiati den les kalimera."* (Why don't you say good morning?)

Before he had a chance to reply, the soldier slapped him across the face with his gloves, repeating, *"Yiati den les kalimera?"* Takis' nose began to bleed. Blood trickled over his lips. He spat more blood on the ground. Under his breath he swore, *I shall seek revenge until my last breath.*

On Thursday, Ascension Day, on his way to the city of Mytilene, Papavasile caught sight of Stratis, one of his altar boys, a barefooted seventh-grader, taking a bottle of milk to his mother, who was sick in the Bostaneion hospital. A soldier on a bicycle whizzed past the priest and slowed down as he approached the boy. This bike had belonged to Takis; now it was a possession of the Nazis. Papavasile could not believe his eyes as he watched the soldier lift his boot and kick the boy into the ditch. Stratis screamed, *"Voithea"*. (Help!)

In his flowing robe, Papavasile stormed after the soldier. "You accursed son of the devil, why did you do such a thing to an innocent child?"

The Nazi sped off, laughing raucously, leaving the boy screaming. Blood gushed out of a deep cut in Stratis' shin, caused by the milk bottle, which had shattered. The priest knelt and wrapped a handkerchief around the wound.

"Father, I haven't done anything wrong," Stratis sobbed, wiping his tears with his sleeve.

"I know," the priest said and lifted the child into his arms. He carried him all the way to Mytilene. "Teach them justice, Lord Jesus," he prayed.

Nearing the city, Papavasile saw the red and black swastika waving from the top of the castle. His heart sank. *How long, my God, will these vultures suck the blood of our souls?* Stratis rested in the priest's arms, in increasing pain. Papavasile moved steadily, but his legs were feeling the boy's weight. Eyes welling with tears, he paused to rest by the sea, but the undulation of the waves brought to mind Dan Cohen's unfortunate burial in the sea, as well as a most painful confession he had heard not too long ago from Nina and her Aunt Pipina. *Has the* North Star *escaped into safe waters?* he wondered sadly.

On Friday morning it drizzled. From the trees, houses, and shops the water dripped like heavy tears. Most of the villagers preferred to stay at home, but Papavasile's ministry to the islanders drove him out of his rectory with a huge umbrella in one hand and a chalice in the other. He visited the ill and the dying, placing Holy Communion reverently between their parched lips.

Around 9:00 a.m., the rain stopped and the sun broke through the clouds. Papavasile visited the Cambas household. Pipina and Nina, who had been absent from church lately, were happy to see their priest. Gratefully, Pipina offered him a branch of an almond tree, a symbol of hope. As he thanked her, he noticed a few baby almonds among the leaves on the branch. Back at his rectory, he filled a vase with water, put the branch into it, and placed it by the window, exposing it to the morning sun.

From his window, he saw a woman in black hurriedly approaching his door. Recognizing her at once, he rushed to open the door. It was Stratya, a skinny, middle-aged woman who ran errands for people in Moria.

"What is it, Stratya? What brings you to my home this early? You seem distressed," he said as he invited her into the rectory. "Sit down, Stratya. I'll get you a glass of water."

"It's not water I need, Father. I need poison."

"Why are you so upset? What's the matter?"

She cast her pale face downward, and in a low, heart-rending voice said, "The infidels have killed your son. I saw his body lying by the fountain about fifty yards from Cara-Tepe, the Black Hill."

"My son, Christos, is dead? Why?" Papavasile dashed out into the street in search of his son. His anguished, unanswered cries echoed in the island's gloomy stillness. "Why? Dear Lord, why?"

CHAPTER FORTY-ONE

THREE DAYS AFTER EASTER, April 10, a dazed voice called out, "Where am I?"

"Danny! You spoke! You'll be okay. Oh, man!"

From a head wound up in bandages like a mummy emerged a guttural groan. "I'm dying of thirst."

A benevolent hand brought a tall glass of cold water and a straw.

"Who are you?"

"Danny, it's me, Tiny Tom, your friend."

"Tiny Tom, is it really you or am I dreaming?" He reached out and grabbed his hand, big as a shovel. "Oh, it is you."

"It's me."

"Where in God's name are we, Tom?"

"Somewhere in the Aegean Sea. I don't know exactly where."

"How far are we from Lesbos?"

"I have no idea. All I know is that we've been afloat for three days."

Dan Cohen breathed heavily and faded out. Tiny Tom covered him gently and smiled joyfully. *Lover boy, thank God you're alive!* Yawning, he sat next to his bed as vivid images paraded in his mind. Hours after midnight on Holy Thursday, after they had lifted anchor to leave Lesbos, Tiny Tom was standing at the lookout point when he spotted something moving. Training his powerful lamp, he saw a tiny vessel. "Ahoy, there! Are you in trouble?" he shouted. The *North Star* started to slow down.

"I've found someone. I think he's one of your men, but he's badly hurt," came a voice from the small vessel.

Tiny Tom shouted back, "Bring the wounded man over." *I wonder if that's Cohen,* he thought.

Mourtos had tightly wrapped Cohen's body in a sailcloth, attached an anchor to his feet, and was ready to plunge him into the sea. *The days of the American sailor are over. He will no longer present a threat to me. And Cambas' daughter will be mine.* But when he heard the sound of a ship's bell, and through the mist he saw the lights of the approaching vessel, he panicked at the possibility of being caught in the act of drowning the sailor. With shaking hands, Mourtos removed the sailcloth, untied the knots that secured the anchor to Cohen's feet, and yanked off the cross from around his neck. *At least this cross might be my lucky amulet to bring me closer to Nina,* he thought.

Effortlessly, Tiny Tom lifted the wounded man aboard gently and instantly realized that it was his mate, Dan Cohen. "He's ours," he said to the man, who had come aboard.

"I found him lying unconscious on the rocks," Mourtos said. "He must have had a bad fall. I don't know. He may even be dead.

"He's a hardy one. He won't die easily," Tiny Tom said.

Captain Thompson heard the commotion. "Why is our vessel slowing down? What is going on?"

"Dan Cohen had a bad accident, sir. I knew something had gone wrong." Tiny Tom said. "This islander found him on the rocks."

Excited to hear about Cohen, the captain said, "Don't just stand there. Invite the man aboard and give him a reward."

"No, thanks. I'm glad I was able to help." Mourtos jumped back into his little boat and picked up his oars. He wanted to leave, lest the captain require details of Cohen's accident. As he rowed away, the captain's voice thundered, "Tell the Greek authorities on the island that the American sailor has been found."

"I will. I will," Mourtos said, forcefully plying the oars.

Semiconscious, bruised, and exhausted, Cohen was carried by his mates to a place where they removed his clothes and wrapped him in thick cotton blankets.

Two days later, Dan Cohen opened his eyes, and through the gauze dressings, he saw he was in a spacious cabin with a line of cots, clean covers, and freshly painted walls, quite unlike the quarters of the *North Star*. He no longer smelled the flowers in Cambas' garden or Nina's hair. Only the smell of iodine permeated the air and filled his nostrils. There were several other patients, and two light-complexioned nurses in whites moved around silently. An abundance of light came through small round windows, and the fresh sea breeze blended with the medicinal odors.

"Hi, Danny. Welcome back to life," Tiny Tom said.

"Where are we, big man?"

"We're alive, and that's all that's important. And you, lover boy, you're lucky. You had a bad fall."

"Where? What happened?" He tried to lift his head, but the pain made it impossible. His head was bandaged, and his left shoulder was bound in heavy plaster cast.

Shrugging his shoulders, Tiny Tom said, "Man, I don't know." He propped his friend's head up with two pillows.

"How did we get here?" Cohen asked.

Tom whispered, "We're in the hands of Nazis. We're prisoners."

"Are you serious?" Cohen whispered back.

Tiny Tom shook his head. "Don't even look outside the window. We're guarded by two green-helmeted crocodiles, and they are not holding toys. He shaped his hands to form a gun and imitated the sound of a machine gun. *"Rat-tat-ta-tat!"*

"Where is everyone? Captain Thompson? What kind of boat is this?"

"This is a German hospital ship. The captain and rest of the crew were taken prisoners. We never made it across the Aegean. Tiny Tom sighed. "I think we're near Crete. A nurse told me."

"How did we get here?"

"Easy, friend, and speak softly. You aren't well. Your shoulder blade and four ribs were broken. You had a beauty on your head, a great gash. Honestly, I didn't think you'd make it."

Cohen's body ached all over, but he said nothing. Tiny Tom stood up and looked out of the porthole. Rubbing his palms together, he said, "We thought you'd decided to stay. You know, with that gorgeous creature you had spent time with. We looked everywhere for you. Just as we weighed anchor to set sail, someone brought you along in his rowboat."

"I can't remember a blasted thing," Cohen said.

"The man said he had found you lying wounded on some rocks near the sea. Don't you recall anything?"

"Nothing."

From under the mattress, Tiny Tom pulled an item wrapped in a thin towel. He unfolded the towel and showed Cohen the icon of St. Nicholas. "Do you remember this?"

Cohen blinked. "What is it?"

"Remember? Your priest friend gave it to the captain."

A strange shiver shook Cohen's body, as Tiny Tom explained what had occurred on the day of their departure from Lesbos, while Cohen stirred restlessly on his cot, now and then raising his right hand to touch the bandages. Slowly, Cohen began to piece together memories of the island. Vaguely he recalled coming back and telling Pipina that he had decided to stay. Pipina had brought warm milk and cookies by the fireplace. Nina looked more beautiful than ever on that Holy Thursday night. They had lain on the thick rug and watched the dancing flames. Over and over again, he tried to reach out to her but a sleeping numbness spread through him like a drug, and he was again enveloped in silence and darkness.

Then he recalled the terror in Nina's eyes as the loud knocks on the door disrupted their intimacy. Then a raspy voice. Pipina and Nina helping him to hide. The ladder to the tunnel crumbling beneath him. All was darkness and dust after that. In confusion, he tried to remember the face, and gradually it was before him. He saw raging insanity. He was sure it was Mourtos. Blinking to maintain consciousness, Cohen turned and grabbed his mate's hand. "What else has happened, big man?"

Tiny Tom explained softly, "You were in such a bad shape that Captain Thompson decided to return to Lesbos and take you to the hospital where they had taken care of his fractured leg. But as we approached the island, a Nazi submarine seized the *North Star*."

"What about all the maps and pictures I had brought aboard?" Cohen asked anxiously.

"All ashes. The Nazis set the *North Star* on fire. The Aegean Sea was in flames as the barrels of oil exploded. Man, it was like Fourth of July fireworks in America."

"Where are the rest of crew?"

"I don't know. I'm only here because I bribed a Nazi officer to let me stay with you. I gave him your camera."

"You gave my camera to an enemy?"

"I had to."

"Thank you," Cohen said. "At least we're together." He was grateful.

"But I have no idea where they're taking us," said Tiny Tom.

"Any hope for escape?"

"Escape? You can't move."

"I want to go back to Lesbos," Cohen said emphatically.

"How? By swimming? We're at sea."

"I don't care where we are. I need to find a way to get back to Nina."

"Danny, the Nazis invaded the Aegean islands, including Lesbos."

In anguish, Cohen asked, "Do you know what happened to Nina? Will I ever see her again?"

"Get some rest now. You're exhausted." Tiny Tom covered him, then lay down on the nearest cot. As he stared at the ceiling, a vivid recollection put the sweetest smile on his round, now bearded face. He remembered that unforgettable day when Despina brought him into her home. Having been away from port for months, he made endless love to her, and she responded to him like a lioness. If he had been able to speak her language, he might have married her. He closed his eyes and mumbled, "Despina, Despinaki."

"Where are we headed, Lord?" Cohen prayed softly. "Please protect my Nina."

He brought his hand to his chest to touch the cross Nina had given him. It was missing. *Now I know what Nina meant when she talked about the strength we derive from God. Because of her faith and perhaps her prayers, I have survived. O God, help me get back to my Nina.*

CHAPTER FORTY-TWO

HEAVEN AND EARTH MEET each day in the town of Moria. The clouds hang low over the rolling green hills forming the spine of the island. But on the morning of April 29, 1941, the sun hid behind a dark cloud, not to be seen for some time. Papavasile was about to bury his only son, the ultimate pain a parent can endure, witnessing his child's funeral. A veil of profound grief shrouded the population of Moria. The ground was soft and damp like volcanic ash, and the vegetation was thick and dark. The singing of the birds had faded away, and Moria looked eternally sad. For Papavasile, this day was a living hell. He saw his own son in a coffin being lowered into the grave. His wife and daughter, their hearts cruelly wounded, wept. Groaning in her soul's agony, Christos' mother exhausted herself, tearing at her face and hair. As the priest held her hand to prevent her from beating her chest, she released a mournful wail: "My precious child, light of my eyes, who wrought this cruelty?" The dirge of the afflicted parents at the graveside overwhelmed the swarm of sympathizers. No eyes stayed dry. Next to the grief-stricken parents stood Pipina and Nina, heads covered and dressed in black. Since Cohen's loss it was the first time they had ventured out of their home to mingle with people, as respect for the grieving priest compelled them to attend the funeral. As much as they felt Papavasile's pain over the loss of his son, the deeper source of their tears was Cohen's burial at sea.

Mourtos leaned against a pine tree and observed the burial service, keeping a predatory gaze on Nina and Pipina, who were crying incessantly. He was the one who carried their secret, and in the past few weeks he had been scheming. Cohen's alleged death was going to cost them more than they bargained for, and he would make sure they showed their generosity.

When Nina returned home in the late afternoon, a thought brightened her mind. *Do we really die, or do we live on in the heart of those who love us?* Feeling a tinge of comfort, she decided to knit the trim around the neck of a pullover she had intended to give to Danny. Now she planned to wear it and think of Danny holding her. Under a dim light she sat on her bed and attempted to knit, fingers moving nervously, sighing and weeping.

Seeing that she was awake, Apollo jumped on the bed and rubbed against her knees, purring and moving closer to her. She pulled him into her arms and kissed his nose. "Apollo, my Danny is alive in my heart and will always be there because I love him." Outside, it became dark. Emotionally exhausted after the funeral, she fell asleep.

———

Through the month of May, at the end of each day Mourtos would return to the estate and update Cambas on the progress of the pruning and fertilizing of the olive groves. Pipina would make the customary demitasse coffee for the men and then leave to attend to household tasks. Mourtos' boots, with leggings and iron-tipped heels, were always shined, a quality of perfection Cambas liked in his manager. As a hardworking man, he was in Cambas' good graces. The imported trees he had planted for Cambas had developed into a much-envied olive grove. His salary had been doubled.

Each time they sat together to discuss the latest news about work, Mourtos felt validated by his boss. *I'm becoming a definite husband candidate for his daughter*, he thought. But one evening, something made Cambas' head turn. When Nina joined her aunt in the kitchen, Cambas didn't like the lusty glance his manager directed at his daughter. With his eyebrow raised, he cast on Mourtos a serious, almost suspicious look that visited Mourtos later that night and left him sleepless. Vividly he remembered the first time he flirted with the idea of marrying Nina. It was when she had just come back from Athens, where she attended a graduate school for girls, the famous Arsakion. From the minute he laid eyes on Nina, now a full-grown and wonderful woman, the other girls of Moria became unimportant. Only in critical moments of anger or frustration did he find solace in Despina's arms. From her, he had received good training in the enjoyment of his manhood, but he was oblivious of her deeper feelings and the thoughts she entertained for him.

On Friday evening, June 8, Cambas was not at home when Mourtos returned from the olive groves. After his demitasse, he lingered in the room talking to Pipina about the fortieth-day memorial service for the priest's son. Because of her strong feeling for Papavasile, she tried to temper the conversation. Mourtos reminded Pipina of her promise, *I'll never forget you,* on the night he found Cohen supposedly dead, and took care of his body.

"Of course," Pipina recalled. "I've never got around to giving you something."

"Something?" Mourtos asked, and pulling his worry beads out of his pocket, he fumbled with them nervously.

"I'll be right back," Pipina said.

Pipina had an impromptu meeting with her niece, and they agreed to give him a sizable reward in the fervent hope that he would keep his mouth shut. Dressed in black and with eyes swollen, Nina came out of her room holding an oriental box made of cedar and studded with mother-of-pearl. As she handed it to Mourtos, she saw the greed in his eyes. A silent yet visible, *Is this all you are giving me,* was written on his face. But as he opened the box he saw a large number of gold coins that Nina had inherited from her mother. He clasped both hands around the heavy box. *They must be very valuable.* "Thank you, Miss Nina. I shall never forget you." He bowed twice and left.

At his home, Mourtos eagerly counted the coins. Seventy-five pounds sterling. Converting gold into drachmas was difficult, and he could scarcely figure out how much money he had just acquired, but he felt rich. *There must be more where these came from.* He made up his mind to get the rest of the gold before the Nazis got to Cambas' coffers.

As time marched on, Mourtos grew taller in pride and fantasy. He invented reasons to talk to Pipina and Nina. However, a thought kept nagging at him: *Cambas had given his warehouse with the olive oil to a Nazi officer. In return they allowed him and his family to live in the villa. But what if one of the offices was attracted to Nina?* He realized that to win her affections, he had better behave like a gentleman, not like a peasant. It was then that he began visiting Nikos the barber once a week and having his hair trimmed to perfection. After work, he showered and dressed in freshly pressed clothes. Gradually he gave up smoking and became an avid reader. Apart from studying the newspaper every day and updating Cambas with the events of the war, he wanted to get some education, so he borrowed books from the little library of Moria.

"What's all this reading about?" asked Cambas.

Mourtos explained that besides physical muscles, he needed to develop his brain muscles while he was still young. "I never had a chance to go to high school. It's about time I read one or two books."

Cambas, who was usually perceptive about everything around him and even far from him, could not remotely conceive that Mourtos was obsessed with his daughter and was prepping himself for the position of his son-in-law. Pipina began to suspect his frequent unannounced visits, especially when those visits occurred while her brother was out of town. One day she said to him, "I prefer that you visit only when Mr. Cambas is here."

Pipina wasn't the only one whose suspicions were aroused. One afternoon, the barber entered the butcher's shop and told Apostolos that Mourtos, who lately has been grooming himself, was trying to impress Cambas' daughter.

"I thought he was going after Despina," Apostolos said.

"I even asked him if he was in love. He blushed all over, winked at me, and said, "Nikos, my dear friend, some day I will marry that girl, whether Cambas likes it or not."

227

"Despina will kill him," said Apostolos. "Each time she buys lamb chops, she says, 'For my man, Mourtos.' Lately she has spread the word that he plans to marry her."

But Mourtos, instead of going to Despina's house for her familiar delights, changed direction. The thought of pursuing Nina's love reverberated in his mind, but a current of insecurity pierced his heart. He decided to go to his home and figure out a plan. *How he could best approach Nina and propose marriage to her?* He knew he could not wait too long. Mourtos had a consistent fear that his lie about Dan Cohen being buried at sea could catch up with him. Dan Cohen might return to Lesbos to reclaim his love. Then what? Still, he comforted himself by thinking that with the Nazis occupying the island, the American sailor wouldn't dare to return. At least for now!

One morning he woke up unnerved. He had a dream that the *North Star* was just arriving at the harbor, only it was quite small. Many people came to see the ship, including the Moria Quartet. Takis began to play his harmonica as Dan Cohen descended the gangplank. Mourtos awoke drenched in sweat. It took a few long seconds to come to his senses. "What I have to do, I must do it quickly," he said to himself.

CHAPTER FORTY-THREE

PIPINA NOTICED A STRANGE LOOK in Mourtos' eyes when she told him to harness the mares and have the carriage ready early on Tuesday morning. He did exactly as he was told, but he observed the movement in the Cambas household. Dressed in a light gray suit, Cambas paraded between his study and the living room, his shined shoes squeaking with every step. He kept looking at his watch and waited for Pipina, who had entered Nina's room, pleading with her to accompany them to St. Raphael's Shrine.

Gaunt and austere, Pipina emerged from Nina's room, crossing herself. Covering her head with a black shawl, she told Cambas, "She's not coming. She made up her mind that, at least for a whole year, she would not appear in public places."

"She's still grieving," Cambas said, pursing his lips in sadness.

"We need to pray for Nina," Pipina said.

My sister could be right. We need to pray for Nina, Cambas thought. He had mixed feelings about religion. He attended church, but he was not as devout as his sister. Yet today, he was hoping that his daughter would come to the shrine with them, simply to get out of her room. Of course, he could not let his sister travel alone. Silently, brother and sister started on their journey to Thermi, a town eighteen kilometers from Moria. Perched on a picturesque, steep mountain was the shrine of St. Raphael and a large reception room for guests.

On that Tuesday morning, June 30, the feast of the Twelve Apostles, more than a hundred people attended the services at the shrine. Never in his wildest imagination did Cambas think he would enjoy the long liturgy his sister had imposed on him. To his surprise, he began to hum the Byzantine melody, and in a state of spiritual stupor, he did not notice the passing of time. Pipina could hardly contain her joy. "Praise the Lord," she said under her breath. "A prayer answered. My brother seems to have seen the true light."

Many faithful islanders were visiting the shrine, some among them being handicapped. Sitting in a back pew, Cambas had to swallow his pride when he saw a man on crutches fall in front of the icon of St. Raphael, crying, "Help me!" All eyes focused on the lame man who, after a few moments of silence, stood up, staggered a few steps, then threw his crutches away. A teenager who stuttered and a middle-aged deaf mute woman approached the icon. The priest laid his stole on their heads and prayed. Both became well. Witnesses of these miracles crossed themselves, crying tears of joy. *Christ continues to perform miracles through His saints,* Pipina thought.

"This is a place of magic," Cambas said.

"It's place of miracles, dear brother, take it from me."

"It's their faith that makes miracles happen," Cambas said.

"Maybe that's what we need, faith," Pipina said.

At the end of the service, Archbishop Iakovos, who knew Cambas, invited him and his sister to stay for coffee. Cambas was not given a chance to decline.

Pipina nudged him with her elbow and said gratefully, "Thank you, Your Eminence, we are honored."

"Must we spend the whole day here?" Cambas asked her when the archbishop moved away.

She eyed the clock on the church wall. It was 11:00 a.m. "I don't think we ought to decline the archbishop's invitation."

Cambas lowered his voice. "We need to get back." He loosened his tie and exhaled. He felt thirsty. "And what about Nina all alone?"

"She's a big girl. She can fend for herself," Pipina said.

"You're a shrewd manipulator, dear sister."

"St. Raphael may get upset if you say bad things about your sister."

"I'm not afraid. Saints don't scare me."

"You saw the miracles! St. Raphael can also cause you trouble if you upset him."

"Nonsense," said Cambas, standing up to leave the shrine. He longed to roam among olive trees, fill his lungs with mountain air, and drink some cold spring water from a nearby fountain.

CHAPTER FORTY-FOUR

ON THAT SAME DAY, Mourtos decided what he wanted. Knowing that Nina had stayed home, he lingered around Cambas' barn, cleaning it and stacking the hay for a long time.

Later, he went for a haircut and for a shot of cognac to relax. Around noon, holding three red roses, he strolled to Cambas' villa, and after a few deep breaths he rang the back doorbell. His heart beat faster when, through the screen door, he saw Nina in her father's leather chair, doing needlepoint. Sun rays piercing the window rested on her hands, making them luminous. He stood with his weight on one hip, left hand tucked inside the stomach flap of his britches and right hand holding the roses. He noticed how resolutely Nina approached the door, really annoyed at the sight of him. Hundreds of images raced across his mind too quickly to grasp. He knew her father and aunt were hours away. Gazing at her, not just his visual senses were affected. He actually felt genuine love in his heart. He wanted and had determined to make this woman his mate. Impatiently he waited, but she wouldn't open the door. His glance fell on the sweet-smelling roses he had brought her, and he felt energy emanating from them. He could hear his heart pounding, and tongue-tied, he blushed. "I brought these for you," he said, eyes glowing in pleading anticipation. He had spent some time grooming himself for the occasion. Hair freshly cut, a light brown shirt open at the neck to display his hairy chest, freshly pressed khaki pants, shiny army boots, and a wide leather belt held his nervous stomach tight.

"Mr. Mourtos, what do you want?" She unlatched the door with hesitation.

"Why 'Mr. Mourtos' all of a sudden?" He looked askance and smiled. "I have a first name, you know." He handed her the roses. "I've just come to see you. It has been weeks since I saw you last." He watched her put his roses on the table and resume her needlework. He sat on a chair across from her. Choosing each word carefully, he attempted small talk and offered to take her for a ride to picturesque parts of the island, although he could sense her disinterest.

Eyes on her needlework, Nina said, "I understand how much Aunt Pipina and my father appreciate you."

With a peculiar glare, he said, "I, for my part, love your family very much." He felt perspiration rolling down his spine. He smiled. "Remember how I used to carry you on my shoulders when you were a little girl?"

"I know you love my family," Nina said. Feeling a surge of strength from within and wanting to stifle any feelings he was nurturing for her, she said, "Certainly we are fond of you, too. But I wish you would realize how painful it is for me, missing the one I loved so much and having to live with the thought that I will never see him again."

Feigning sympathy, Mourtos said, "Sorry, Miss Nina. I think I'm beginning to understand."

"And you know what's most painful to me?" Nina continued, with a firm tone in her voice but controlling her tears. "It's the way my Danny died and the way you buried him. How could you have the heart to do it?" True indignation suddenly rose in her eyes.

"It wasn't easy for me. But I had to do what I thought was my duty, to preserve the reputation of your father."

"The reputation of my father? But how could you tell that Danny was dead? He fell and he could have just fainted, or maybe he was in a coma."

"I'm not stupid, Miss Nina," he countered. "His skull was cracked open. Blood was gushing out. I kept my ear right on his heart for a long time. I felt all his pulses. There was no life in him. By the time I carried him to the shore, he was ice cold." Mourtos' face had that pensive look that said, *I hope she believes me.* "I was also worried about something else," Mourtos said.

"What is it that you mean?"

"If the truth ever came out that Dan Cohen died in your home, your father might be blamed for his death." Mourtos stood up, keeping his balance with difficulty. The cognac had entered his brain. "But you can count on me. That will never happen." He rested his hand on her shoulder.

Shocked by his gesture, Nina stood up defiantly. Repelled by the smell of liquor on his breath, she pulled back and went to the back door. "Please go now, Mr. Mourtos."

He grabbed her wrist firmly. "Only God knows how much I love you. I want to make you happy, Miss Nina. Can't you believe me?"

"I've had enough happiness in my life. Please go before I get more upset. Besides, I have important things to do."

"Not yet, my dear, dear Nina," he said. "I know I'm poor, but my wealth is here," he pointed to his heart. "Honor and pride are my only wealth, and I want to marry you." He released her wrist. "Do you understand? I promise to make you happy," he said with tearful eyes.

"I know you're an honest and hard-working man, but marriage is not in my plans." She tried to speak to him kindly, anything to get him out of her sight. A nagging fear convinced her of the danger of being alone with him. Again he reached out to stroke her hair with the tips of his fingers, whispering, "Oh, my precious Nina, you are a most beautiful woman." Simply touching her and smelling her hair ignited his passion. He had cornered her like a small bird in a cage, but she moved quickly aside, gasping angrily and giving him a ferocious look. "Mourtos, go home. Soon my father will be here, and you will be in plenty of trouble."

"Okay, I'll go, but someday your grief will be over, and then you will want to get married, dear Nina. Believe me."

"Never!"

"If you would only give me a chance, I could make you love me."

She shook her head. "Go home. I'm very upset right now." Inching away from him, she managed to open the screen door. Mourtos seized her arm, and as he touched her skin he felt the world disappear. Forcefully, he pulled her to himself. "Don't play the saint," he snarled. "I saw you naked at the hot springs. Do you know what happens to a man who sees the woman he adores in another man's arms? I could have killed him."

Realizing it had been Mourtos' shadow that had passed by the window when she and Danny were at the hot springs, Nina jabbed her elbow into Mourtos' stomach, escaped his grip, and ran out of the main entrance. From the top of the stairway, she glanced around. Everything seemed quiet except for the rustling of a few dry leaves scudding across the phoenix mosaic. Like a thunderclap, Mourtos appeared behind her. "Where do you think you're going?"

"You must go, Mr. Mourtos," Nina insisted.

"I'm not good enough for you, am I?"

"Go away, and don't come back unless my father or my aunt is at home."

"I want to marry you. I'll make you very happy, the happiest girl on the island."

Nina didn't say a word.

Despina had been watching from among the trees and bushes, keeping out of sight. She had known where to look for Mourtos; indeed, she had been stalking him since the moment he had left the barber shop, and sure enough, there he was, chasing his boss's daughter. She tiptoed and hid under the marble staircase, she listened to him pleading.

"Cohen is dead. Do you understand?"

Scared, eyes filled with tears, Nina looked around for a way to escape. Mourtos unbuttoned his shirt and pulled out a chain, on which hung a cross. "Look!" he said, bringing it close to her face. "I'm wearing his cross. Let me take his place. Please, Nina, I've been in love with you ever since you were a teenager."

Nina recognized the cross that Papavasile had blessed, her gift to Danny. She put her hands up to her mouth, wanting to scream, but she had no voice. Her throat felt scorched and her stomach tight.

"Why are you silent? I'm young, strong, and hard-working. I'll be faith-ful. I'll be good to you. What else do you want?" he pleaded.

Nina descended a couple more steps, and Mourtos reached gently for her arm. "Let me be the one to take care of you."

Nina's horror increased when she found herself in his grip. She could not get past him. "Alright. Please," she gasped. "I need time, one or two days, to think this over. Okay?" She hoped to calm him down so that he would go away. *If only my father would show up now.* He was her only hope for rescue.

Mourtos was caught off guard, but he was not about to wait for some-thing he could get now. He reached to embrace Nina, but she had dashed past him down the stairway and fled among the trees. Mourtos chased her, stumbling down the staircase. He swaggered, steadied himself, and leaned against the banister, looking for his prey.

Under the shade of the trees, Nina hurried to the plaza where she had sunbathed happily for so many summers. Looking around her and seeing no sign of Mourtos, she sat down in a lounge chair to catch her breath. A refresh-ing breeze caressed her face as she burst into painful sobs. She did not know where to go. She thought of Papavasile and St. Basil's Church, but her feet felt like lead.

Behind the marble stairs, Despina made the sign of the cross. She had watched Nina flee and Mourtos awkwardly follow. He was up to no good. She knew what she needed to do. Her face was ablaze with fury. Holding a shovel in her hand, she felt strong and determined. She surreptitiously stalked Mourtos as he pursued Nina. The sea breeze whipped her dark gray skirt above her tanned thighs.

As he ran, glancing right and left in search of Nina, Mourtos felt a short-ness of breath as something that was not so much desire as it was an insane possessiveness flooded through his body. In a moment of intense jealousy, he was ready to kill anyone who touched, claimed, or attempted to take Nina away from him. He wanted to own her, and nothing was going to stop him from it. He loved her more than anything else in the world, and she was des-tined to be his wife.

As his angry eyes darted around, he tottered and stumbled among the rocks and shrubbery. His head became heavy, and he missed his footing and fell down. He sensed someone behind him. "Nina, is that you?" He looked up and saw a blurry silhouette, a voluptuous figure with large buttocks and big breasts holding a shiny object. He smelled her perfume and recognized who she was. Shock! "Despina, what are you doing here?"

Despina lifted the shovel high and plunged the sharp edge into his skull. "You bastard. If I can't have you, nobody else will." For a second time, the shovel cut through the air and crushed Mourtos' head. The waves crashing against the rocks drowned out his agonized groan. He drowned in his own bloody vomit.

Crossing herself, Despina threw the shovel into the bushes and stole quietly through the town. As she stepped through her door, she looked back down the long alley. Nobody had seen her. No one had followed her. Feeling safe, she crossed herself gratefully.

Another huge wave crashed against the shore. Nina shuddered, but all at once her fears disappeared. Mourtos hadn't followed her. Mentally exhausted, she sat gazing across the Aegean Sea. The rhythmic murmur of the waves brought comfort. Arms folded tightly over her breasts, she felt relief. Afraid that Mourtos may still be around, she would not go back to the house for a while. Apprehensively, she stretched out on one of the wicker chairs, staring at the sky. Still in shock, she could not believe that Mourtos, her father's trusted manager, would dare to make such advances. It was hard to push him out of her angry thoughts.

The moisture from the sea penetrated her bones. She began to walk back home, scared that Mourtos might still be hiding somewhere along the way. But her fears vanished instantly when she heard the noise of the carriage and the neighing mares arriving at the barn. She rushed to meet her father and aunt, wondering with each step whether she should tell them about Mourtos. *If my father knew what his manager had attempted to do today, he would kill him.* She decided not to reveal the ugly event she had experienced that day.

CHAPTER FORTY-FIVE

SPIRITUALLY CHARGED, PIPINA'S FACE glowed over yesterday's visit to St. Raphael's Shrine. The services and the miracles she had witnessed calmed her soul, giving her new hope for her niece and brother. Early this Wednesday morning, she took a quick look around the house and saw everything was intact. Nina, with her arm around her cat and her head cradled in a feather pillow, was sprawled across her bed sound asleep. Pipina knew that her niece needed a few extra hours of sleep. She made a pot of fresh mountain tea, poured two cups, and took them to the balcony, where her brother was reading a newspaper. Savoring the tea, they gazed at the harbor. Out of the corner of her eye, she recognized the troubled look on her brother's face. She asked no questions, for she knew the source of his worry and his periodic depression. It was not just the loss of his warehouse, which he had given to the Nazis. It was not just Nina's loss of her loved one that worried him. Pipina had an awareness that a deeper wound in her brother's heart had not yet healed. *What he confessed to me more than twenty years ago was still nagging at him. He should have confessed to a priest as I suggested. But he didn't believe that a priest could relieve him of his pain.* Such thoughts were in her mind, but she preferred not to mention them to him.

When he returned from America with Nina, a motherless baby, Cambas was inconsolable. He wanted to die. One night, his sobbing woke Pipina up. She dashed into his room to see what was wrong. After she calmed him down, he said, "I have committed murder, Pipina. I killed my wife." In shock, Pipina asked, "Did you have a nightmare?"

"Sit down and listen," he said, and between sighs of guilt, he poured out his heart to his sister.

Nina was eleven months when Mercina became pregnant again.

I don't want another child, I shouted angrily. Do something about it.

Do what? she asked innocently.

You know what, I told her.

You mean, you want me to have an abortion? she cried.

Anything. We just can't afford another child.

Costa Cambas, my husband, how can you be so cruel?

Mercina, my twenty-six-year-old wife, was devastated.

The next day, she consulted a neighbor, who told her how to do it. She went ahead and pierced herself with a clothes hanger. She got an infection. At the hospital, she said she did not want to see my face anymore. She died a most horrible, slow death. Pipina, I caused her death. God should punish me.

Compassionately, Pipina said, "God does not punish. It's our sins that punish us. You have carried this burden long enough. It's time to seek God's forgiveness. Go to Papavasile and confess."

The screeching of two crows startled them. Two blackbirds, soaring over the villa, glided onto a tree, and then a whole flock noisily descended on the ground. Pipina's heart began to pound from fear. Blackbirds were a bad omen. But Cambas said, "The crowing signals wind or rain, and we need rain badly. It's good for the olive trees." Pipina wanted to scare them away. *Maybe there's a dead animal lying somewhere near.* She decided to go in the garden and look around. As she walked and looked around, the crows noisily flew away. What she saw made her scream in utter hysteria. She was horrified when her eyes met the lifeless body. Coming a bit closer, she recognized Manolis Mourtos sprawled between the rocks and a tree. Dried blood covered his face, and green flies swarmed around his nostrils.

Cambas, hearing his sister nightmarish screams, dashed down the stairway and ran to her side. From the window, Nina saw her father and aunt and rushed down to join them. At the sight of Mourtos, she burst into bitter tears, wishing the earth under her feet would crack open and swallow her up.

"I wish I had gone with you yesterday," said Nina.

"Child, what do you know about this?" Pipina asked.

Nina told them of Mourtos' unexpected visit and his advances, but knew nothing about his death. Awestruck, Cambas looked at his sister, who was inconsolable, and said, "Neither God nor His saints can rescue us now. We are doomed. This is no accident. I could be accused of killing Mourtos."

"Perhaps it was a bad fall," Nina suggested. With conflicting feelings, she looked to her father for solace. He took a last glance at his manager, shook his head, and sighed, wondering what effect Mourtos' death would have on his life. *There could never be another Mourtos; he was like a son to me.* His voice cracking, he said, "Let's get back to the house. I must notify the police."

Escorting the two women, with his arm around their shoulders for support, he spied the shovel coated with blood lying under a bush. Careful not to touch the bloodstained metal, he clasped the handle with a handkerchief. It was the steel shovel he had purchased in Athens. He meant to use it in Nina's rose garden, but he never did. He wondered who had thrown it under the bush. He surveyed the area, looking for clues. It was surely the murder weapon, but he could not know who had done the deed or why.

Within the hour, the news of Mourtos' death had spread throughout Moria. *A murder on the Cambas estate!*

"A poor peasant with rich ambitions," remarked the barber.

"Who do you think did the job?" asked the butcher.

"Who knows?" replied the barber, clipping his scissors in the air and shrugging his shoulders.

Despina answered her door to find a policeman on her step. "What's wrong?" she asked nonchalantly.

240

The policeman sensed something odd in the tone of her voice, a tinge of fright. "Ma'am, I need to ask you a few questions," he said. "Would you mind coming along to the station with me?"

"What for?" Despina asked. Her face was drained of all color.

"It's about the death of Mourtos."

"Mourtos is dead? I can't believe it." She sounded shocked.

"It's no secret that there was a relationship between you, that he often came to your house."

"Of course he did. We planned to get married someday soon."

"I'm sorry," said the policeman, pointing to the street. "You'll have to tell your story to the sergeant."

Despina gasped. "Officer, what's going on? If Mourtos was found dead on the Cambas estate, what am I being charged for?" Realizing she had said "found dead on the Cambas estate," she adopted a haughty look to intimidate the policeman. There was a long silence as they stared at each other.

"Just follow me," he said.

At the police station, Despina feigned innocence. "Sure, there have been many men after me, but there was only one I gave my heart to, Manolis Mourtos, may he rest in peace." She whimpered and crossed herself.

"Where were you yesterday afternoon?" the sergeant asked. In his eyes, a woman with her reputation was a natural object of suspicion.

"Cleaning and washing. Come and see. My wash is still hanging out to dry."

The officer who had brought her to the station said, "Miss Despina, when I came to your door, you remarked, 'If Mourtos was found dead on the Cambas estate, what am I being charged for?' Remember?"

"I do," she replied defiantly.

"Would you mind telling me how you knew where Mourtos died?"

"A premonition, I guess," she answered.

"Premonition? Or were you, in fact, involved in the murder?"

"Officer, how can you say such a thing? Why would I kill the man I loved and whose child I am carrying?" She drew her fingers over her belly.

Amazed at Despina's revelation, the policemen withdrew a few steps and looked at each other, filled with doubts and suspicion.

"I suggest you remain in Moria until further notice," said the sergeant, pointing a stiff finger at the door.

Despina insisted that the wake be held in her home. Papavasile granted his permission. She confessed to the priest how much she loved Mourtos and how they had been planning to wed within the year. Eventually, she also confessed that she was pregnant with his child.

When Mourtos' body was brought to Despina's house, it was stiff and arched, the tongue sticking out between the teeth. She painstakingly cleaned his face with hot towels, shaved him, bathed him, rubbed his skin with aloe, and wrapped his whole body in white sheets and flowers, covering his head with one of his red kerchiefs.

That night, many islanders attended the wake to pay their last respects. They found Despina weeping in her bedroom. She draped mirrors and pictures on her walls in black and hid Aphrodite's statue in a closet. It was her favorite symbol of love. Two professional mourners she had hired sat on wicker chairs on either side of the corpse in the living room. But when the islanders left, she chased them out of the house. A deep silence and the smell of trampled flowers prevailed in the room. The only sign of Mourtos' tragedy displayed by Despina were the black dresses she would wear for the three months following his death.

The following day, the islanders saw the coffin pass by the marketplace as the pallbearers carried Mourtos to the cemetery. The whole procession exuded the air of a ritual performed so many times that everyone knew exactly what was expected. The road leading to the cemetery was thick with respectably dressed men and women, who walked toward the newly dug grave that was to be Mourtos' final resting place.

Cambas, his sister, and his daughter were waiting at the gravesite, bewildered by the mysterious murder. Pipina hung onto the words falling from the priest's lips as he chanted: *Blessed is the way in which you shall walk today . . .* words that knocked on the door of her heart. Pipina's mind became a babble of emotions. At the sight of Mourtos in the coffin, she felt despair, unbearable guilt, and pity. Her heart leaped in her chest, and she could not lift her hand to make the sign of the cross. She had loved Mourtos like a son since he was a boy, and at one time or another, she had naturally thought of him as a potential husband for her niece.

In a dark gray dress studded with tiny white butterflies, Nina attended the funeral for the eyes of the people. With mixed emotions but without tears, Nina glared at the open coffin. Hands folded over his chest lay Manolis Mourtos, another man who wanted to marry her, now dead. *Had I accepted his proposal, he could have been the happiest man on the island. But how could I? God gave me only one heart, and already I have given that one to a very special man.* She looked upward at the traveling clouds, hoping that her Danny was watching.

Tall cypress trees towered over the ceremony. St. George's graveyard was hauntingly sacred. With bowed head Papavasile continued the service: *All human things are vanity, for they don't exist after death. Neither wealth nor glory can accompany us into the next life.* His voice was plaintive, immensely evocative, profoundly sad. His message was a cry, a dirge from one who did not understand death but accepted it as a calling of man by his Creator, Who has prepared a place for all humans where there is no pain, no sadness, no sighing, but a life of everlasting love and bliss.

Then the mourners walked past the open coffin and viewed Mourtos for the last time. Despina paused to look. Her face was blank. To cover up her lack of grief, she burst out in hysterical weeping. Two women, who seemed to be present for that purpose, carried her away from the grave. Out of nowhere appeared Cara-Beis. He was the last person to pause at the grave and bow over a promising young man who had good intentions but bad fate. Seemingly sad, he put his arm around Despina, who was not surprised to see him.

CHAPTER FORTY-SIX

EMOTIONALLY DRAINED, NINA could not contain herself. Peering through her bedroom window, she saw the garden, once like paradise, now veiled in brooding despair. Gloom and melancholy hung thick in the air. Dark clouds shrouded the sun before its setting. After sunset, she trudged to St. Basil's Church to look for the priest. Perhaps he could forgive her sins and unwitting errors, and restore her innocence. Choked with trepidation, Nina entered the church slowly. The array of icons, the glow of the burning candles absorbed her thoughts. The only person in sight was Papavasile, lighting the altar candles. She greeted him with a deep bow and a trembling heart. He beckoned her to approach.

"Father, I'm the cause of so much tragedy. I need to confess," she wept.

"My child, allow yourself to experience the grace of God."

"Is there salvation for me?

Sensing her torment, Papavasile answered, "Now you're in pain, perhaps even angry with God, and also afraid. But a broken heart is a sure road to salvation."

"I don't know what to do." Tears ran down her cheeks.

"You're in the right place," Papavasile said. "It is God who will give you the strength to endure these critical days."

"How much more can I endure, Father? My burdens are more than I can bear, and I have no strength left."

"God molds us according to His love, not according to our fears. Trust in His mercy, and let Him guide you."

"My days are dark. I see no future."

"God has a plan for each of us. We need to pray for patience."

Physically numb, Nina stood beside Papavasile. He focused on the icon of Christ as he whispered prayers she could hardly hear. A violent gust of wind howled outside. Dark clouds rumbled ferociously. The narrow windows of St. Basil's rattled, and the chandeliers shook. As her frightened eyes looked up at the swinging chandeliers, she saw the austere eyes of the Sustainer of the Universe, Christ's icon, in the dome. Struck with guilt, she clasped her hands tightly around her neck. She gasped as her pearl necklace broke and the pearls scattered all over the dark marble floor. She interpreted the broken necklace as a bad omen. Papavasile could see that she wanted to flee the church and leave the pearls where they lay.

"Don't leave, my daughter. Collect your pearls and make peace with God." She picked up each pearl with trembling fingers. She brought them to her lips and tearfully kissed them.

"My necklace was a present from Danny at the time he promised me marriage."

Papavasile nodded sadly. "Pray that God's will may be done. In time, His divine love will soothe your pain."

His prayers and admonitions echoed in her ears as she walked back home, minutes before the Nazi curfew. As she neared the iron gates of her home, she saw a man coming toward her. Although in uniform, she could tell he was not a Nazi soldier. Nina had become accustomed to their ubiquitous, menacing presence, yet she still felt a strange fear as she realized this was Cara-Beis, a Nazi accomplice and a traitor to his people. She did not want his prying eyes gazing at her. After he had passed her, she quickened her pace. Once inside the gates, she looked back, half-expecting to hear the thin, short figure calling after her. A shiver of fear raced through her veins, but she kept on walking.

That night, Nina could not sleep. Tossing and turning in bed, she gazed at the icon of the Virgin Mary, which shone behind a votive light. The compassionate, inviting eyes in a gracious face compelled her to make up her mind. *I must make a decision. I must make a decision,* she thought, not knowing why, but an ardent inner desire guided her thoughts.

At dawn, she woke up with a surge of energy and made up her bed quickly. She donned a white dress of raw silk, trimmed with royal blue velvet around the neck and sleeves, and a matching velvet belt. Combing her hair, she looked at herself in the mirror. Whatever she had decided overnight gave her a feeling of inner peace. In her mind she could still hear the priest's prophetic voice from the night before, quoting St. Paul, *We have no city here in which to stay; we seek the heavenly one.*

Nina approached the icon and whispered, "Mother of Jesus, many times I went to your convent when I was happy. I have been blessed with everything, a father's love, wealth, security. Yet I felt even happier when I visited the convent. I wanted to become a nun, but I fell in love, incurably in love. I could not help it. I thought I had found happiness in loving a wonderful man, but I lost him one fatal night." Tears welled in her eyes and distorted her vision so that she saw a brilliant wreath around the icon. She blinked to recapture her thoughts. "I want to serve you, Holy Virgin Mary, Mother of Jesus. Please, accept what remains of me, and I shall praise you as long as I breathe."

In the next room, as Cambas was shaving, he accidentally knocked down and shattered the mirror hanging on the bathroom wall, spraying the floor with tiny splinters of glass. He sighed, hoping to hide the evidence from his sister. Pipina never missed an episode to which she could attribute some symbolism. He knew she would have said, "A broken mirror betokens seven years of misfortune." *A nonsensical superstition,* he thought. Then, seeing his disjointed image reflected in the shards of glass, he shivered. For a split second, visions of men in green uniforms and dark helmets marched in front of his eyes. Face downward, pale as sulfur, he emerged from his bedroom. Wearied by his manager's death on his own property, he muttered, "The saints are dumb and lifeless, and God is too distant to hear our prayers."

Despair was lurking in his soul. Since the Nazi invasion he had been sleeping badly, disturbed by nightmares, and his heart palpitated irregularly.

Today, as he plodded into his library, the strange shadow of his own cruel fate seemed to follow him. Pipina, toting in a tray of coffee and toast, interrupted his thoughts. She poured a cup for herself and sat opposite him on the leather sofa. Paintings, tapestries, pictures on the wall, everything in the room seemed sad. Speechless, Cambas sank into his chair to savor his morning coffee, reading his newspaper to avoid any conversation with his sister. Suddenly, Nina entered her father's world with a worried look on her face. Her determined eyes shone with fervor. Carefully searching for the right words, she said, "Father, Aunt Pipina . . . I have something important to tell you."

She joined her aunt on the sofa. Pipina had a premonition about today and anxiously waited to hear what her niece was about to tell them. Although a part of her believed that we all live under grace and no one escapes God's plan, another part of her was worried about Nina's life.

Cambas smiled pleasurably at his daughter, the one precious treasure left in his life, now in glowing splendor, sitting near him. Taking the last sip of her coffee, Pipina said, "Well, don't keep us in suspense. Tell us."

"Father, Aunt Pipina, I have made up my mind. I am leaving home. I am going to St. Mary's Convent. I have decided to become a nun."

"Wait a minute! What about us?" Sadness sprang into Cambas' eyes. "Nina, I'm begging you to carefully consider what you are about to do."

"Allow the child to speak," Pipina said.

"Father, I have made a decision. It's all very clear in my mind."

"Do you think you'll find happiness in such a life?" he asked.

"Yes, I do."

"In a convent?"

"There is happiness in prayer and solitude," Nina said.

"My dear child, happiness is in life itself, with its adversities and its pleasures."

"And Nina has had plenty of them," Pipina said, shooting her brother a grimace of annoyance.

"Life is a shadow, a dream. At times, a nightmare," Nina said.

"I realize it has been a nightmare lately." Cambas paused in serious thought. "Feel my hand." He laid his hand on Nina's. Its touch affected her painfully. It was hot and dry and trembling. A father's attempt to hold onto his only daughter was at stake. "Is this hand a shadow, a dream?" he asked urgently. "This hand, this body, this world, this life, all are to be explored and enjoyed. They are realities, not shadows." He pulled his hand back. "Nina, we've had tragedies, but we are still alive!"

Pipina shook her head, restraining her emotions. She thought of Nina's decision as God's plan and felt relieved. At the proper time she was going to persuade her brother to allow Nina to live her life as she chose. She did favor and admired the monastic life, but would not divulge her feelings to her brother yet.

"In my heart I'm already a nun. I am resolved to enter the convent and enjoy a life of peace and prayer. I've had enough of this world," Nina said with determination.

"My sweet child," he pleaded in a softer voice, "are you running away from something? Is there anything you would like to tell us?"

"Costa," Pipina advised, "you and I have been blind to Nina's wishes. We wanted her to find a nice young man and get married, as if marriage was the only means to happiness. But a man came into her life and . . . ." Pipina sighed. "She always wanted to become a nun. I don't know why, but she did." Pipina's eyes widened with courage to curb her brother's ego. "It's time that we both stopped trying to control human destiny."

"A father knows everything, all the secrets of his child," Nina said, meaning that Papavasile, her spiritual father, knew all her secrets, for she had confessed all the events of her life to him.

Pipina knew that her brother did not know all the details of Cohen's disappearance. But she felt comforted knowing that Nina had confessed everything to her priest. She also knew that the Sacrament of Confession restored a person's peace of mind and integrity.

"Then your decision is final?"

"Yes, it is, Father."

Tears rolled down his cheeks at the realization that his daughter had finally succumbed to her yearning to become a nun, a life he had many times tried to dissuade her from choosing. Having no other recourse, he resolved, "Yes, my child, I'm beginning to believe it is God's will."

Pipina wept.

"Oh, thank you, Father. Thank you, Aunt Pipina." She kissed them, and then she, too, wept. But she sensed some relief as they put their arms around her and kissed her. It was the kiss of love.

Throughout Moria it soon became known that Nina, the daughter of the wealthiest man on the island, was to forsake the world of wealth and enter monastic life. Elderly women praised her courage. *Blessed Nina, she's such a nice girl.* Zographia, Alexis' mother and Pipina's dear friend, said, "Nina will ultimately be a saint." Others, including Despina, wagged their evil tongues.

CHAPTER FORTY-SEVEN

MEMORIES OF MOURTOS haunted Despina at night in her solitary bed as the ice in her heart melted. She thought she had once loved him, but now she knew that her heart held pure hatred. There would be no more false tears for him. He was but a vile serpent who deserved his fate. Mourtos had betrayed her. He was after Cambas' wealth and his daughter.

Despina convinced herself that Cambas was guilty of complicity in the crime because he had allowed his daughter to associate with a foreigner even though he knew Mourtos was in love with her.

Before Mourtos' death, one morning when she'd soaped herself, her breasts had felt firm and her belly significantly swollen. Despina had monitored her body, aware that she was pregnant, but definitely not by Mourtos. *A woman always knows who the father of her child is.* She was sure. Something serious had happened the night she made love to the tall, bullheaded American sailor, Tiny Tom, the one with the blue eyes and crew cut. But why had she not pursued him more seriously? Simply because he was too big and he could not speak her language? The second time she had missed her period, she knew. This child was the sailor's, and he was long gone. It was then that she became more persistent in her pursuit of Mourtos. *The child ought to have a father.*

Mourtos will have to believe that it's his. But now, with Mourtos in his grave, Despina would have to search for another father.

Thoughts of Cara-Beis wrestled in her mind. He was ugly and she knew of his machinations, but he seemed to have ambition and his deals promised security. If he would only catch her bait, she would no longer share her body with anyone else. For all she knew, the child in her womb could be his, if he would only take her word for it.

One day when Cara-Beis came to her house to offer his condolences about the loss of her boyfriend, Mourtos, she found herself closer to him, admiring his features. In her intrigued eyes, he even appeared handsome that day. Like everyone else in Moria, Despina was also aware of the power Cara-Beis had gained since the Nazis occupied the island. He was a volunteer in the German army. It was a known fact that he had become a Nazi accomplice. In fact, he wore high boots and a faded Nazi uniform with no insignia. Tight around his waist were a belt and an empty holster. His eyes were watchful and resolute, and his face, tanned by the sun, had acquired a metallic hardness. Although he loved his mother, with whom he lived, the people of Moria suspected that he was capable of selling her to the Nazis for a personal gain. But Despina had no interest in his political proclivities.

Grateful that he crossed her threshold, she lavished on him ample charm. Cara-Beis took pleasure in developing his relationship with her. He knew that she was vulnerable, so he could use her for his purposes. He remodeled the house she had occupied since her younger years, where the feared eyes of the saints on the walls still fed her adolescent terrors, and he decorated it with precious paintings he had plundered from wealthy families. He brought her a new bed with a brass headboard, a vanity, and peach-colored curtains. Overwhelmed with his generosity, she almost felt the impulse to confess her secret to him, but instinct told her that Cara-Beis was a cunning bastard who someday could use her confession against her.

251

Forty days after the death of Mourtos, early in the morning, Despina took a long perfumed bath and pampered herself as usual. She felt no tinge of guilt. She put on a tight corset and dressed meticulously. The thought that in another seven months she would give birth gradually began to burden her. She would be the mother of the child of an unknown American sailor who had left the island oblivious of the results of his actions. She put a red ribbon around her hair, perfumed herself, and started toward the marketplace in search of Cara-Beis. At the same time she hoped her presence in the marketplace would quell any possible suspicion of her crime in the minds of the islanders.

She almost bumped into Cara-Beis as she rounded the corner of a street where the Albanis Bakery divided the marketplace from the residential area. "Well, well, oil merchant. What are you doing up and about so early in the morning?"

"Oh, it's you, Despina." Cara-Beis surveyed her. She came close to him, flashing her seductive eyes at him and brushing her breast against him. He scratched his unshaven chin and said, "I'll see you over the weekend."

"Why not tonight?"

"No. I can't. I'm busy."

"The news I have to tell you will make your ears burn."

"Okay, okay. I'll see you tonight."

Later in the afternoon, Despina heard the hoarse voice of Panagos the peddler in the street, praising his fruit. She ran to her door. She wanted quince. *I'll make a quince pie that will send Cara-Beis instantly to heaven.*

Panagos carried a huge basket on his shoulders.

Despina asked, "How can you carry that heavy weight? What happened to your donkey?"

"Those infidels, the Nazis, killed my precious donkey," he said sadly.

"Why?"

"Could I ask a Nazi soldier why? They kill humans."

"Poor Panagos," Despina said, selecting six huge quince and helping him put the basket back on his shoulders. "I'll help you to buy another donkey," she said.

"Thank you, Miss Despina, you are a good woman," he said and went on his way. Carefully she peeled the quince in crescent-shaped slices and arrayed them in circles in a baking dish. She sprinkled a cup of brown sugar over the dish, a thin sprinkling of cinnamon, and drenched it with cognac before putting it in the oven.

After dinner that evening, Cara-Beis was leisurely eating this dessert and Despina was rehearsing in her mind what information she would give him. She offered him another slice of the pie, thinking, *I would train Cara-Beis to be the best father for my child.*

"It's time to trim your beard again," she said.

"My beard is just fine."

"You need me, Cara-Beis, more than you need any other woman in the world."

"Why?" He pulled her close, the lust evident in his eyes.

"Because I know things you'd die to know."

A drink in one hand and Despina in the other, he tried to unbutton her dress. Affectionately, she slapped his hand.

Cara-Beis, set his glass on the floor. Taking Despina in his arms, he carefully placed her on the sofa. It creaked as he laid down next to her. He touched her breast, kissed it, and then gave her a prolonged kiss on the mouth. She sighed as she caressed the crescent scar on his face.

"Let's sit up. I can't breathe," Despina said.

They both sat up, then he kissed her again and moved closer. She took a firm hold of his hands. "What do you make of it?"

"Make of what?" Cara-Beis' eyes widened curiously.

"Mourtos' death in the Cambas garden."

"I don't know what to make of it." Cara-Beis shrugged.

"Isn't it obvious?" Despina asked, putting her hand into the left cup of her bra and pulling out a tiny velvet pouch. "Look at this," she said. Cara-Beis took the pouch. Thinking it was a sort of amulet, he asked, "What is it?"

"It's a cross. I found it around Mourtos' neck as I was cleaning him up before he was placed in the coffin."

"So?"

"You know how to read, don't you? Read the inscription on the back of the cross."

Eyes moving from Despina's glowing face to the shiny cross, Cara-Beis read, *For Danny, Love forever, Nina.* He handed back the cross and said, "So, both Nina's lovers are dead. I don't know what you want me to do about it."

"They are dead and we are alive, full of life, Cara-Beis, and I know you to be a smart merchant. So think hard."

"What am I missing?" he asked, his face taking on a seductive look. She moved closer to him, allowing her thighs to show. "Listen carefully. Mourtos found the American dead on the rocks. Correct?"

"That's the story I've heard." Cara-Beis showed signs of interest.

"Mourtos was not the honest man I thought. He was after Cambas' daughter, or should I say, after Cambas' wealth. I could tell he was obsessed with the idea. So when he realized that Nina was in love with the American, and Cambas had already approved of him as his son-in-law, Mourtos decided to get rid of him."

Cara-Beis, pursing his lips tightly and squinting his eyes, listened with increasing interest.

"Then he began to go after Nina forcefully, although he knew she was grieving over her lost love. So one day in her fury, she got rid of him. Isn't it obvious?"

"Are you making all this up?" Cara-Beis scratched his beard, smoothed his mustache, and forced a grin as his mind raced faster than his tongue. "Keep talking, Despina, I like what I hear. You are a good storyteller."

"Well, Mourtos was found dead on the Cambas property. That's a fact," Despina said. "Who else would kill Mourtos but Nina Cambas?"

Cara-Beis' face flushed red. Fiercely, he whispered, "Woman, with this kind of information I can crucify Cambas, the wealthy bastard. You and I could move into his famous villa."

"You can do more than that," said Despina, realizing that she had won Cara-Beis' favor.

"More?"

"Yes. I know you have connections. Information is very valuable to the Army of Occupation. Correct? Suppose you reveal that Cambas' daughter was engaged to an American spy, Danny Cohen, a Jew?"

Cara-Beis knew what he had to do, which made him feel needed. Bringing information to the Nazis would improve his status, and there would be a reward for him. He could not wait.

"I'll be back," he said, getting up to leave. Despina followed him to the door, combed his hair with her fingertips, and brushed the lint off his shoulders. "I know you will," she said alluringly. *My child will need a father*, she thought.

CHAPTER FORTY-EIGHT

THE DAY OF THE ASSUMPTION of the Virgin Mary, August 15, Nina
was to enter the convent and become a bride of Christ. The sun shone without a cloud in the sky. It was a rare day of joy in Moria, a celebration the
Nazis grudgingly allowed and now guarded carefully. The local population
attributed a redeeming meaning to Nina's commitment to become a nun.
After all, she was well respected in the town of Moria. Besides being the
daughter of a wealthy man, a pillar of support for his town, she was the niece
of Pipina, a reputable woman who excelled in charity work for the benefit of
the entire island.

A swarm of people of all ages dressed in festive clothes came to Cambas'
home. They wanted to follow Nina on foot, up the hill all the way to the convent. Pipina, wearing a black dress and a cover over her head, and Cambas,
in a gray suit, white shirt, and black tie, escorted Nina out of the villa. She
was dressed in a white gown befitting a bride. Brother and sister maintained
a serious look. Something of a mysterious nature was happening in their lives;
they were unable to understand Nina's decision.

Papavasile chanted, "Archangel Gabriel stood amazed when he saw the
beauty of your youth," a hymn in praise of the attributes of the Virgin Mary.
Altar boys bearing a cross and lit tapers followed the priest. Behind them

marched the Moria Quartet, which chanted Byzantine hymns, nurturing a spiritual feeling among the crowd. Bouras, a member of the quartet, leaned over and whispered in Takis' ear, "Why would a young and pretty woman want to become a nun? Is she mentally sick?"

Takis said, "I don't understand why. Maybe there is a reason."

"Beauty buried alive in a convent. What a waste! She could have made a man very happy," Bouras said.

"Maybe this is her answer to her loss. Everybody in Moria knew she was in love with the American sailor."

The streets were filled with the fragrance of rose water that the people had sprinkled out their windows. Others tossed rose petals as Nina passed by their houses. Waving her hands at the crowds to the right and left, she greeted them, concealing her nervousness with a festive expression on her face. The people responded to her with great zeal. Walking along slowly like an empress of the past, her white gown made her look enchanting. Her unique charm and beauty were irresistible.

The excitement of the moment flushed Nina's cheeks. Trailing through clouds of smoke from the incense, she pushed any tinge of sadness behind her. Even Cambas began to feel some relief in his heart. He looked around with pride. Had he been giving her away in marriage, the moment would have been his happiest, but what was destined could not be avoided.

Young girls accompanied Nina, often touching her gown and smiling. A sacred aura of peace and vitality streamed from her whole presence. "The joy of Christ shines upon her face," said Pipina. Even armed Nazi soldiers who strategically fringed the crowd seemed impressed by the strange pageantry. During the hour-long walk, hundreds of people joined the procession.

When the crowd reached the convent, they stood on either side of the gate, making a passage for Nina. Cambas wept as he embraced and kissed his daughter. Pipina, concealing her tears with a smile, hugged and kissed her niece, wishing her God's blessing. Convinced that this was God's plan for her, Nina lifted her hands, blew a kiss to encompass the throngs with her love, and walked through the gate.

In full garb, Mother Superior reached out with open arms to receive her, but something unexpected occurred, causing havoc. A roaring noise filled the air, and a jeep emerged from a cloud of dust. Two stern Nazi soldiers, a Greek policeman, and Cara-Beis jumped out of the vehicle.

With dignity and courage, Cambas approached the policeman and asked what was the meaning of their presence. But he felt the weight of a club on his shoulder and was roughly pushed aside. He watched the motions of the one who seemed to be in charge, one of the Nazis, a fair-haired, arrogant man in his late thirties. Under his helmet, big sunglasses covered half his austere face. The skin of his nose was peeling. Cambas was shocked, unable to figure out what the Nazis were after.

Acting as an interpreter, Cara-Beis said, "Nina Cambas, in the name of the Occupying Forces, you are under arrest."

"On what charges, Mr. Cara-Beis?" Cambas asked.

"Soon you'll find out, Mr. Cambas."

The voices of the assembled grew into madness. "A curse has befallen among us," some women screamed. Nina's girlfriends withdrew, scared. *What has Nina done to be arrested?* Pipina fainted. Zographia tried to revive her, as other women broke into hysteria. Perplexed at the turn of events, Papavasile told the quartet to stop chanting and asked his people not to panic. Some of the daring islanders surrounded the jeep, hoping to fend off Cara-Beis, a *donkey in a lion's skin,* but the Nazi officer stood erect next to him, club at hand and eyes reflecting their defiance. More Nazis appeared on the scene to begin their amusement—humiliating the innocent population, who feared them.

Although Costas Cambas vehemently protested the arrest of his daughter, Nina was taken to a jail for women, and he was detained at the police station for further investigation.

That night, Nina sat in a dank, filthy, subterranean cell with her hands bound behind her back. A group of women with untidy hair and ragged clothing encircled her, buzzing like hornets around a nest. They had spent the day sleeping, and now, full of energy, they were about to initiate their new roommate.

"Aren't you Pipina's niece, Nina?" asked one of the inmates. The rest of them moved aside.

"Yes, I'm Nina Cambas. How do you know me?"

"Lopa is the name. My real name is Penelope. I remember you. You were a sweet little girl with pigtails, but look at you now! A full-grown woman!"

"Yes, accused for no reason and in jail," Nina whimpered.

"I know you're not one of us. And I heard you were about to get married?"

Nina nodded with a bittersweet smile.

Penelope sat next to her on the floor.

"Pipina is a wonderful woman. A beautiful soul," Penelope shook her head with an evident feeling of gratitude. "I used to run errands for her, and she never left me unrewarded. She gave me money, food, and clothes. Many times she asked me to rub her back with alcohol. It used to ache when the weather changed. What a nice woman. Is she well?"

"Not too well, I'm afraid," Nina said sadly.

"That's what happens to good people. They suffer. May God grant her a quick recovery." She crossed herself. "Nothing happens to leeches like me."

"Don't say such a thing about yourself. We don't really know God's will."

"We surely don't," agreed Penelope.

"Why are you here?" asked Nina in a childlike tone.

"Girl, I wanted to ask you the same question. What brought you to this hell?"

"I have no idea."

Yawning, Penelope said, "Let's talk about it tomorrow. We're both tired."

Penelope lay down next to Nina and closed her eyes. Penelope had killed her husband, and shame and guilt over her crime brought her close to someone she believed to be innocent. "Good night, Nina. I hope tomorrow is a better day for you."

"Thank you," Nina said. Protected by her new friend, she attempted to sleep, but a clamor of sadness and pain echoed in her brain, keeping her awake.

She had no idea what the charges against her were. Around midnight, Costas Cambas was escorted back to his home by two policemen.

Determined to destroy Cambas at any cost, Cara-Beis drafted some derelicts, talking to them of equality and explaining how sharks like Cambas had become wealthy by exploiting the innocent poor. "The wheel of fortune is turning; the time has come to upgrade ourselves," he told them. And Cara-Beis, wedged between those two grinding rocks, the plutocrats and the Army of Occupation, felt capable of producing results—flour and bread for everyone, even positions in the barracks. They believed him.

The next day, a policeman and a Nazi soldier with a machine gun slung across his shoulder brought a summons to the Cambas villa, announcing that Saturday morning at nine o'clock the civil court would convene to deal with the charges against his daughter.

CHAPTER FORTY-NINE

WHEN LESBOS FELL into the hands of the aggressors, parasites like Cara-Beis had a field day. From a busy jack-of-all-trades, a man of ill repute, Cara-Beis changed into a man in a uniform, a Nazi volunteer. Despina managed to trim his wild beard with great effort and a pair of old scissors. There were many men in Moria who considered him a lecherous opportunist. He fabricated what he had gathered of the *North Star* with the information he received from Despina into an insidious plot to annihilate Cambas and go after his wealth. Bringing these allegations to German authorities gained him the position of Public Prosecutor. He had spent the previous night with Despina, scheming and speaking of his determination to destroy Cambas. When he lost the oil deal with the *North Star,* he swore he'd make Cambas pay, and now he was making that happen..

Despina knew where to add spice to her conversation with Cara-Beis. "No wonder Nina is where she is," she said. "Cambas let his daughter whore around with the American sailor, most likely a spy. I used to think he was a decent man."

"If I had a daughter, I would have her barbecued and fed to the dogs rather than allow her to be with a foreigner," Cara-Beis said.

"I understand how you feel," Despina said. She combed his hair, smoothed his beard, and kissed him.

On Saturday morning, the day after Nina was arrested, a commotion erupted outside of St. Basil's Church. By ten o'clock, a large number of spectators had assembled in front of the church. A chubby, balding man with thick glasses resting on the end of his big nose banged his gavel to bring the noisy crowd to order. He wore a black robe, indicating his position as judge. Two intimidating Nazi soldiers in full gear stood guard on either side of him. On his right, arrayed on a wooden bench, were six stony faces with raised eyebrows, angry eyes, and thick mustaches. These men were the refuse of Moria, whom Cara-Beis had promised positions at the Nazi barracks. Lambis, Cara-Beis' friend, a notorious scoundrel, sat in the midst of them. A member of the jury, he, like Cara-Beis, was eager to render his form of justice. The two wicker chairs on the left of the judge were for Nina and her father.

The judge pounded the table with his gavel once more, and two Greek policemen and four Nazi soldiers accompanied Cambas and his daughter into the public court.

Pipina, mentally and physically ill over Mourtos' death and her niece's arrest, felt too weak to attend court. Cambas had asked Alexis to send his mother to watch over her.

Pale in her soiled prison garb, Nina waited for the trial to begin. Cambas reached out to her and held her by the hand. "Are you alright?" he asked.

She nodded, but her mouth had the bitter taste of bile. When her father saw the Nazi soldiers and their machine guns surrounding the curious spectators, a premonition disturbed him.

"I'm glad Aunt Pipina is not here," whispered Nina.

"We haven't done anything wrong," Cambas said, and suddenly frowned when he saw Cara-Beis seated pompously next to the jury.

Cara-Beis, avoiding looking at the accused, rose from his seat and mingled with the crowd. He mumbled a few words to some of his collaborators and sneered at others, as the crowd in front of St. Basil's swelled.

At 10:30 a.m., the judge looked at his watch, and with a grimace, nodded to the policemen. One of the sergeants-at-arms called the court to order. But the crowd continued to stir until one of the Nazi guards fired into the air.

The roar of the machine gun echoed around the plaza, and the incandescent spitting could be seen. But apart from an instinctive ducking, there was little reaction from the crowd, not even a cry.

Despina, winking at Cara-Beis, inched closer to him. Replacing Mourtos was not easy. Now her options were limited to one. She was responding to her primitive instinct for support and protection. Cara-Beis was better than nothing. Renouncing the idea that she had once loved Mourtos, she took pride in Cara-Beis, now her partner, for they had engineered a shrewd scheme.

"It's our day," he told her, his eyes wide with delight.

Exhilarated, Despina brushed her breast against his arm and wished him good luck as he returned to his place near the judge. From his superior, privileged position, Cara-Beis was able to perceive the fear that Cambas and his daughter were feeling. He saw Nina cross herself and thought, *Neither God nor the devil can save you now, rich bitch.*

Silence finally prevailed. A dark cloud covered the sun to the relief of the watching crowd. More clouds gathered over the southern part of the island, carrying a breeze. The judge looked at the sky, and Cara-Beis said to himself, *That's all we need now. If it rains, court activities will be suspended.*

From the corner of a tearful eye, Nina saw the devastation in her father's face. The loving father who denied her no material comforts had initially refused to understand her yearning. Surely, he did not want her to become a nun. *I cannot blame him,* she thought. *I, too, am at fault. I fell in love with Danny and forgot about the convent. I should have listened to my inner voice. Had I become a nun, I would not be part of this madness today.*

But hindsight faded as Cara-Beis, the prosecutor, stood and read the accusation in a vociferous voice: "Costas Cambas opened his home to an American spy, Daniel Cohen, allegedly a Jew, who spoke English, Greek, and German. Cohen was seen photographing key areas of the island, under the direction of Mr. Cambas and his daughter. Cohen had established a close relationship with some key people in Moria."

Cara-Beis gazed at Alexis and Papavasile, who were standing on the right side of the crowd. Taking a sip of water, he continued: "Still under investigation is a large oil transaction between Cambas and the *North Star*, which conceivably involves collaboration. Nina Cambas, once a candidate for monastic life, was seen with the American spy in remote parts of the island. Suddenly the spy disappeared without trace. He was reported to be dead. But the source of that report, Manolis Mourtos, is now dead himself, murdered on the Cambas estate. Allegedly, Mourtos knew secrets related to the spy and was killed to ensure his silence."

Leaning against a pine tree, Alexis kept a sharp eye on the crowd. Sighs of anguish and anger swept across their faces as the judge nodded to Cara-Beis to proceed. Unable to control his rage, Alexis withdrew from sight with concern. He was fearful because the weapons the Americans had brought ashore were still hidden in his café. *I'll poison that Cara-Beis, so help me God.*

"Miss Nina Cambas, what happened to Daniel Cohen?" Cara-Beis asked.

Nina shook her head. She did not know how to answer.

"Perhaps you are hiding him or you have helped him to escape or you persuaded Mourtos to make up a story that he found him dead on the rocks and delivered him to the *North Star.* Yes?" His eyes had the riveting attraction of a snake.

Nina did not respond.

"What about Manolis Mourtos, your father's manager, who obviously knew your secret, and who wanted to be your lover? You killed him in your own garden!" Cara-Beis saw despair on the face of his prey.

"No, I did not," answered Nina.

Cara-Beis pulled a box wrapped in a towel from under his chair and opened it. He grabbed a few coins, and they glittered as he let them drop one by one into the box.

"Do you recognize this box and these gold coins, Miss Cambas?" he persisted with a sneer. "You had been bribing Mourtos. Didn't these gold coins come from you?"

Nina shivered. Every cell of her body froze, and her heart palpitated violently. All too well, she remembered the box. Nina stood up and surveyed all the faces before her. Most of the eyes looked back in shock, others were sympathetic, but some smoldered with suspicion. A deathly silence permeated the air. She felt helpless and scared by the changing spirit of the spectators. But a glimpse at Papavasile, who finally sat prayerfully among his people, gave her courage and hope. Beginning with the part she had played when her aunt hid Dan Cohen in the tunnel, Nina confessed to everything up to Mourtos' mysterious death. She described the events in detail.

When Nina finished, Cara-Beis arched his eyebrows and sneered. "It's a good story. We are touched, but why didn't tell us earlier that you hid your American lover?"

Shocked by the litany of events, the audience stirred, and eyes of pity and compassion gazed at Nina.

Cara-Beis said, "It would interest the court to know that you have been going to church every night since Mourtos' death, although there have been no services."

Nina sat down and remained silent.

"Obviously, your conscience bothered you, and forced you to go to confession. Correct?"

Papavasile, who was moving restlessly in his seat, pulled at his beard indignantly. Cara-Beis spotted him. "Bring the priest to witness," he said arrogantly.

"No," Nina screamed.

"That won't be necessary," said the judge, yawning. He sensed falsehood in Cara-Beis, but afraid of losing his prestigious position, he was not about to thwart him, for he knew Cara-Beis was in league with the Nazis.

Once more, Cara-Beis stood up, coughed to clear his throat, glanced around, bowed before the judge and the Nazi soldiers, and lifted his hands toward the audience. "Your Honor, respected authorities, ladies and gentlemen," he pulled a white handkerchief from his left pocket and wiped his forehead. "Let me tell you what really happened. I have researched the story." He pointed at Nina in an accusing manner. "Allegedly the American did fall from the ladder, as you say, but that doesn't matter. What does matter is that Cohen was a Jew and a spy. This makes you, Miss Nina Cambas, and your father, Costas Cambas, accomplices."

Cara-Beis lifted a wooden box, opened it, and tilted it, first toward the judge and then toward the audience. He had removed these weapons, souvenir revolvers, from a storage depot where the Nazis kept items confiscated from Greek-Americans on the island.

"Weapons. American weapons. Aren't these some of the weapons your American lover brought to Lesbos?" Cara-Beis insisted.

"No, no," protested Nina. "I know nothing about weapons."

"Yes. You concealed a spy who brought weapons."

"My aunt hid him because I loved him. We were to marry," she cried.

"Then you bribed Mourtos to hide your secret, didn't you?"

Alexis snuck away and returned to his café, wondering on the way if Cara-Beis, the snake, had slithered into the secret place and found the weapons. He was terrified, for his skin was at stake.

"Why was Mourtos able to buy himself all sorts of things and spend money like never before?" asked Cara-Beis.

Everyone turned to see Nina's reaction.

Shifting nervously on the wicker chair, her eyes were filled with fear.

"That money came from you, did it not?"

Nina nodded. "Yes. But . . . but . . ."

"It's true," thundered Cara-Beis. "You bought his silence. You, and no one else, killed Mourtos. Unable to bear your horrible secret, he threatened to tell the authorities what you had made him do. You crushed his skull. Then your guilty conscience compelled you to seek shelter in the convent. You wished to cover your crimes in a nun's cassock. Isn't that what happened?"

When she tried to protest, Cara-Beis shouted her down. "Your Honor, the story is clear. Nina Cambas is guilty."

"She is innocent. Innocent, I say," shouted Papavasile, pushing his way through the crowd and insisting upon being a witness. The judge told Cara-Beis to quiet down as Papavasile took the witness stand.

"My people," Papavasile said, lifting his hands, "listen carefully. Nina Cambas is innocent. Believe me, she has committed no crime. If we sentence her unjustly, God, the Righteous Judge, will punish us somehow."

"Father," Cara-Beis bowed his head and in a humble voice he said, "do you think anyone as clever as she is would confess murder to you? But even if she did confess, you cannot reveal it, for you are a priest and under oath. Correct?"

"That's right," answered Papavasile, "but you, Mr. Cara-Beis, are wrong."

Suddenly, the fierce scream of a woman arose from the crowd. It was time for her to play her part in the scheme, which she had rehearsed for many days. Cara-Beis, who purposely did not look at her, felt relieved. Despina, now pregnant, was to bring their plot to a climax. She approached the judge and glanced at Cara-Beis, who nodded approvingly, concealing a smile. Despina pointed at Nina. "Your Honor, that girl bewitched Mourtos. She cast a strange spell over my man. She tried to take him away from me, and then she killed him."

The judge cleared his throat and nervously unbuttoned his shirt. He watched Despina suspiciously and said, "Go on."

Dressed in black, Despina tried to stand tall and proud. Her voice lapsed into a pitiful tone. "Everyone here will agree that Mourtos was a good man, Your Honor. I knew him well. I took care of him." Then she said softly, "And, regardless of what some people think of me, I was to be his wife. We were to be married." She pointed to her stomach.

Cara-Beis, simulating sympathy, shook his head and kept eyeing the jury, conveying the subtle message *Cambas' daughter is guilty* and hoping to evoke their sympathy for Despina, who had began to cry. "Your Honor," she said, "I carry his child." She pointed a wrathful finger at Nina and said, "First she stole the man I loved from me, and then she killed him. Speak no evil of Mourtos here," and turning toward the jury, she added emphatically, "let judgment fall upon . . . her!" Members of the jury shook their heads, clearly thinking, *What a sad situation!*

The islanders were accustomed to regarding a woman as a helpless quarry who had no way of defending herself against the passions of men. Seeing sympathy for Despina in the judge's eyes, Nina hid her face in her palms and wept.

Exasperated, the judge stood up and said, "The court is adjourned. The jury is to see no one and speak to no one until two o'clock this afternoon, when the verdict will be read and the sentence will be pronounced." As he prepared to leave, the crowd broke into pandemonium.

By the appointed time the jury had reached a verdict. The judge concluded, "Nina Cambas is found guilty of murder. Her sentence is life imprisonment. Mr. Costas Cambas, within a week from today, must find a new residence. His villa shall be the headquarters for the Army of Occupation. Court is adjourned."

The pounding of the gavel on the table signaled a fatal day for Costas Cambas and his daughter, Nina. In shock over her sentence, she fell into her father's arms. He did not need many words to explain what he felt. One was enough: rage. Nina, sensing his pain, grabbed him by the hand and said, "Father, I remember that Mother Superior at St. Mary's once said, 'Evil always seems to triumph, but we need to wait patiently and trust God.'"

"Wait?"

"Yes, wait and trust in God's ultimate plan. At the end evil is always defeated."

"You see that imbecile?" Cambas turned his head toward Cara-Beis. "That is an evil man, but I think I can get him to do something good at least once in his life."

"Don't even go near them." Nina saw Despina clinging onto Cara-Beis. *Birds of the same feather,* she thought, and she knew in her heart of their conspiracy.

Cara-Beis scarcely raised his eyes when Cambas, towering above him, confronted him. Shrouded by pride and greed, he was to listen to a man whose life he had just destroyed.

Menaced by a spirit of revenge and resignation that he had never before experienced, Cambas made an irrevocable decision to save his daughter at any price, even at the cost of his own life.

He took a deep breath, and with a ferocious look he demanded, "Why have you done this to my daughter?"

"She is guilty, isn't she?" Cara-Beis asked arrogantly.

"You know she is not."

"Do I?" Cara-Beis smirked.

"I'd like to kill you, Cara-Beis, but I wouldn't want to dirty my hands with your filthy blood."

"Mr. Cambas, you are through. Your days of wealth are over."

"Name your price, you filthy pig."

"Everything you have, and I mean everything." Cara-Beis narrowed his eyes to accentuate his demand.

"It's yours," replied Cambas. "But all the Nazis have left me is my house and my olive tree groves. Take both, but first make sure my daughter is set free or prepare yourself for your funeral." Eyes inflamed with indignation, Cambas thought, *Someday I'll have you put behind bars.*

"I won't fail you, Mr. Cambas," said Cara-Beis. Pulling a folded piece of paper from his pocket, he pointed. "Sign here, and I promise your daughter will be set free."

"You had everything all worked out, didn't you?"

Cambas read the document in disgust. With a last loathing glance at Cara-Beis, he signed the contract.

Shorty after, a torrential downpour descended upon the island. The people, drenched to the skin, scurried through streets and alleys to return to their homes. Most of them could not believe that a delicate, loving young woman, daughter of a highly respected citizen and brought up by a much-admired aunt, could have committed such a heinous crime.

CHAPTER FIFTY

FOLLOWING THE SECULAR COURT'S decision, Papavasile, deeply disturbed by the unjust sentence of innocent people, approached the authorities at the police station and in utter humility begged them to allow Cambas and his daughter to spend a night with him at his rectory adjacent to St. Basil's Church. He emphasized that it was his priestly duty to prepare his people spiritually for what lies ahead in their lives.

Seeing the look in the priest's eyes, the stationmaster granted his wish, but assigned two policemen to escort the prisoners to the rectory and to guard it overnight.

Cara-Beis, now speaking the language of wealth and presumed influence, persuaded the Nazi officials that life imprisonment in a convent would be most appropriate for Nina Cambas. It would evoke higher respect toward the occupying forces in the indigenous population. "Since childhood, she has shown abnormal signs," he said. "Meanwhile, St. Mary's Convent might be the most secure place for her. But if anyone should be punished, it should be her father. Costas Cambas must be charged for extending hospitality to an American spy, using his daughter and involving himself in anti-German activities."

The next morning, the Nazis dispatched two armed guards, Cara-Beis as an interpreter, and two Greek policemen to the priest's home, where Cambas and his daughter were temporarily staying. Papavasile answered the unexpected pounding at his door.

"We're here for Costas Cambas and his daughter!" the policeman announced. Cambas heard his name and called out, "We're here." He came to the door to see who wanted him. Shaking and in fear, his daughter followed him. She put her arms around him and cried inconsolably. Cara-Beis intervened and said to the priest, "Father, you may escort Miss Nina Cambas to the convent. The policeman, one of these two guards, and myself will accompany you to see that you arrive safely." Showing his importance, Cara-Beis mumbled a few words in German to the other guard, and then nodded to the policeman, who put handcuffs on Cambas. "Mr. Cambas, you will be coming to the police station with us," he said coldly.

At the sight of her father in handcuffs, Nina cried and once again put her arms around him, not wanting to let him go. Papavasile came closer to father and daughter, and with a cavernous embrace he said, "May God keep you under His grace." He kissed them both on the cheek. Seeing Cambas in handcuffs and being led away, Cara-Beis shook his head and grinned, satisfied that his plans were now complete.

Nina, emotionally beaten, followed Papavasile and their escorts. She was wearing a plain white dress and sandals, soon to be replaced by a novice's long white cassock and black shoes. Before they left, the priest sent word to Pipina and her friend Zographia, who hurried to walk with them to the convent. In black long dresses, the two women walked beside Nina. Several of her former classmates followed the little procession, commenting about Nina's new fate. Nina felt the eyes of the spectators upon her. She waved at those who wished her good luck and greeted her from their windows. The moment she saw the convent in the distance, she struggled to push Danny's memory and their plans to marry away. Choked with emotions, her glance fell on Cara-Beis and she wondered why the court had accepted his testimony so readily.

When they arrived at St. Mary's Convent, they went directly to the chapel. Lit candles arrayed in symmetry in front of the icons and the sweet-smelling incense set Nina's soul on fire. Her face was radiant, and she could feel her heart pounding, articulating words only she could hear and understand: This is where you belong. This used to be your innocent wish . . . Papavasile put on red vestments and the pectoral cross to offer a prayer. Intensely pale and sad to the core, he felt a hard lump rise into his throat as he guided Nina to the front of the altar. Biting her tongue to curb her feelings, Nina conducted herself so well that she did not lose her composure, not even when Mother Superior dropped the cross that she tried to put around her neck for her initiation into the monastic life. A vital strength that she understood as God's grace surged within her soul. She saw Mother Superior, who stood in front of her, arms outstretched, as if they were the arms of her Aunt Pipina. She felt the presence of love. It was warm and inviting. Contemplating God's ineffable mercy, she was unaware that the spectators thought of her as an exceptional being who was sentenced unjustly and was now entering a life of solitude. Offering a brief prayer, the priest gave her a new name, Anthusa. When she heard the name, her whole being felt a pleasurable warmth. She liked the name, for it meant the "Blossoming One."

Later in the day, Papavasile hurried to the police station to inform Cambas that Nina had been escorted safely to the convent and solemnly received by Mother Superior. As the guard opened the narrow door of the cell where Cambas was being held, the priest's mouth fell open in horror. Cambas lay on the floor, his face purple. The shock of the past few days had proven too much for him. His heart had stopped. The priest fell on his knees in prayer and touched Cambas' face. It was icy cold. "O Lord, Thy will is an abyss that no human can fathom," he whispered. *How am I going to tell Pipina and Nina?* he thought.

"*Rizospastis*" (The Rootbreaker), the only newspaper in Lesbos, published the following obituary:

OIL TYCOON DIES AT 66

Born on July 7, 1875, in Smyrna, now Turkey, at seventeen Costas Cambas immigrated to America, where he made his fortune. Upon the death of his wife, he returned to Greece with Nina, his three-year-old daughter, to live with his only sister, Pipina Cambas. Cambas owned the largest olive groves on the island. A pillar of power behind her brother, Pipina devoted her life to raising Nina. Cambas attributed his success in the oil business to his sister's support and wise counsel. He was buried in a plain mahogany coffin on September 8 at St. Panteleimon's Cemetery in the capital city of Mytilene. Throngs attended the funeral. Wreaths and flowers were laid near the white marble grave where Costas Cambas lies under a large white cross and a sea of yellow pansies. Among the ecclesiastical dignitaries participating in the funeral services were Archbishop Iakovos of Lesbos and Papavasile, who delivered a brief eulogy, praising Cambas' virtues, his dedication to his homeland, and his philanthropic endeavors. Cambas is survived by his sister, Pipina Cambas, and his daughter, Nina, an ordained nun renamed Anthusa. She resides in St. Mary's Convent.

CHAPTER FIFTY-ONE

WITHIN THE CONVENT'S CONFINES, Sister Anthusa, wrapped in a novice's white cassock, her shorn hair covered in a black veil, felt sad and lonely. In her younger years, what she had perceived to be a paradise of prayer that *eye has not seen nor ear has heard* was not present in the convent. For the first few days, she did not want to leave her room. Every day with a grimace she looked around the room in the dull gray of the growing dawn that snuck in around the window. This was not her bedroom in her father's mansion.

At noon, Maria, a young novice, brought food of bland boiled vegetables, cracked green cured olives, and dry homemade bread. Sister Anthusa took a glance at her meal and shook her head. She had no appetite for anything on the tray. Around 5:00 p.m. the carillons rung, calling the nuns to Vespers. The sound interrupted her loneliness. Wondering what to say to God in her evening prayers, she put on her veil and peered through the window. Two by two, the nuns walked toward the chapel. The young novices, eager, intelligent girls, clad in white cassocks, moved graciously as they eyed their surroundings. But Sister Anthusa felt distant and emotionally unavailable. Life had not worked out it as it should have.

Although it deflated her romantic notions of "forever," now she had to accept that love really is forever on a spiritual level, not on a physical one.

Her grieving heart prevented her from talking or sharing her pain, lest others would not understand how she really felt. Looking toward the sky, she wished to escape her body and soar up high to seek the one she truly loved. She looked at the deep blue of the Aegean Sea. She wished to witness a miracle by divine power, and from the depths of the water see her Danny emerge and swim ashore. She would run along the beach and receive him. But the melody of the nuns' voices reached her ears, and reality returned to haunt her. She walked slowly to the chapel and went in. The service had already begun.

Gradually, Sister Anthusa learned to intone her own prayers under a cloud of incense, but part of her felt that God's throne was too high to hear the anguish of her soul. Her life of wealth and excitement had become a sad memory. Pressing heavily on her heart, as well as on her feelings for her lost love, was now the shock of her father's unexpected heart attack and death. Losing three loved ones in such a short time was a heart-wrenching experience. *How was she to find the strength to move on with her own life after three major tragedies?* she wondered. Was there an essential meaning behind inner turmoil? There were moments when she felt grateful for the transient love she had had in her life, the experiences she had shared with her loved ones.

Attending church services every evening brought her some peace, for there was comfort in the melody of the nuns' voices, the fragrance of the incense, and the sacred environment of saints in the Byzantine iconography that filled the chapel. As the incense permeated the chapel one evening, her vision blurred, among the hazy images of saints surrounding her, and she remembered the agony she felt that harrowing day when Pipina announced Danny's death. Her teary eyes became riveted on the icon of the Crucifixion of Christ, as depicted on the right of the altar. She could hear the echo of the voice of Mary, who stood by the cross: *My Son who is not my Son, if this be of God, may God give us patience . . . but if it be of man, may God forgive him forevermore.* Wiping the tear that rolled down her cheek, Nina thought, *The one who once rested against my breast is now in God's presence.*

In the early spring of 1942, a tidal wave of smallpox and malaria swept the island of Lesbos. St. Mary's Convent organized an emergency infirmary in an old warehouse within walking distance of St. Basil's Church. Mother Superior assigned Sister Anthusa to be in charge of the infirmary, where the sick died daily. She considered this an appropriate position for Sister Anthusa, who had a record and who had been fortunate to escape life imprisonment. *Taking care of the sick and dying might be atonement for her sins,* thought Mother Superior.

Sister Anthusa labored so feverishly among the dying that she repressed feelings about her former life. In comforting and helping the suffering, she discovered a new meaning in being a nun. Between famine and plague, hundreds of people prematurely met their Maker. Everyone knew that the famine was caused by humans—the Nazi invaders had confiscated all the food supplies. But what was the cause of the plague?

Some sisters, including Mother Superior, believed the plague had come upon Lesbos as a punishment from God. One rainy night when Sister Anthusa, because of physical and emotional fatigue, decided not to attend evening services, Mother Superior visited her cell and said, "It may be that your unconfessed sins are causing this calamity on the island. Repent, child, and confess."

Sister Anthusa was shocked. "Should I mock God and confess something that I have not done?"

Mother Superior stared at her with determination in her eyes. "May God have mercy upon your soul, Sister Anthusa." Angrily, she left. From that day forth, Sister Anthusa knew no peace. She wandered in the convent garden and looked at the flowers. She watered them and carefully tended them, and in the process she meditated, comparing her happiness with theirs. They blossomed, bloomed, faded, and died. So Sister Anthusa, yesterday the daughter of Costas Cambas, Nina the envied one, today finally a consecrated nun, felt destined to blossom, bloom, fade, and die in the garden under God's watchful eye. The thought that she and God knew of her innocence breathed moments of comfort into her heart. Yet subconscious feelings of guilt surfaced to evoke some doubts. *If I had not fallen in love, if I had not been selfish in wanting Danny Cohen to remain on the island, if I had not ignored Mourtos' feelings, then I would not have been in this emotional hell.* As she pondered

276

the "ifs," she said to herself, *Maybe I'm the catalyst of the calamity in Lesbos and deserve to suffer.*

After Mother Superior's accusation, Sister Anthusa did not want to attend church services. She stopped visiting the infirmary and tending to the sick. She had no appetite, only fatigue and guilt, which caused her to lose weight and become pale and drawn. Resentment surfaced within her, affecting her physically; she felt hate for everyone and everything, which followed her in her sleep. As her vitality diminished, sacred services agitated her, and she no longer wanted to attend church. Mother Superior sent word to Pipina about her niece's condition, and late one Saturday afternoon, Pipina and Zographia entered the main gate of the convent carrying two baskets of food.

"You look like Mary and Martha, Lazarus' sisters," Nina said with a faint smile as she invited Aunt Pipina and her friend into her cell.

"Child, you've lost weight," Pipina said.

"Is this how they make saints out of you here, starving you to death?" Zographia said in wonder.

The presence of the two women and the smell of the food brought an unexpected change to Nina. The chicken soup was still hot and tasty, and she longed to eat. After a few spoonfuls, Nina said, "Aunt Pipina, you haven't lost your touch."

"Thank you," Pipina said.

"How is Apollo?

"That silly cat!"

"Is he okay?"

"More than okay. He's adjusted to Zographia's house, but once in a while, he goes back to our villa. I don't know what the attraction is there."

"But that's his true home."

"Maybe I should bring him here."

"Great! Mother Superior would kick us both out of the convent."

Zographia rolled her eyes and mumbled a few unkind words. She did not like Mother Superior's stiffness. Seeing how much Nina savored the food, Zographia wanted to cheer her up a bit more. Perusing the cell and looking outside the door lest someone should be listening, she said, "Now that you are a holy person, I have to confess a personal secret to you."

"What?" Nina asked, curious.

"When I saw you several times in church, Mother of Jesus, I said to myself, *There is a beautiful girl. I wish my son Alexis was a bit younger. They would have made a perfect couple.*"

"What a nice thing to say," Nina said and looked at Aunt Pipina, who seemed amused at her friend's naive ambition. She knew Alexis was a rascal.

"The way you take care of Alexis, he will never want to leave home," Pipina said, and both women laughed.

As the women rambled on, Nina stared out the window. Her mind traveled to the man she loved and had lost one dreadful night. She visualized herself back home, walking barefoot in her garden. In a flowing nightgown, she tiptoed on top of the phoenix designed in colorful pebbles at the entrance to her house. Under her feet crunched the dry autumn leaves, which were swept away by a sea breeze, revealing the huge bird with outspread wings. *If the mythical Phoenix could return to life from its ashes, why couldn't my Danny come back from the sea?* Indulging a brief fantasy brought a momentary comfort. She sighed deeply.

When Pipina and Zographia left, Nina fell on her knees before the icon of the Virgin Mary and cried: "Lord Jesus, these thoughts are in my brain. Please forgive me and restore the joy of Your salvation in my heart."

CHAPTER FIFTY-TWO

THE AUTUMN NIGHTS wrapped the island in blue darkness. The soil, the rocks, and the timbers of the boats were still warm from the summer sun. The water breathed slowly and deeply. When the sounds of the day were stilled, the liquid tongues of the sea could be heard lapping the sands and hollow rocks. Then the moon would rise above the olive trees, the expanse of the sea, the boats, and the high cliffs. On one such beautiful night, September 7, Sister Anthusa escaped the vigilant eyes of the nuns and walked on the beach alone, although she knew this was against monastic rules. Ocean spray stung her flesh with a pang of keen delight. It was a vivid feeling of bliss, and it refreshed her soul. The moon vanished behind a cloud, and when it reappeared, it threw a handful of silver rays upon the statue of Sappho that stood on a cement platform at the edge of the beach. Here she had sat one evening with Danny, and they had eaten roasted chestnuts.

As she walked back to her cell, she whispered, "Miracle Worker of the Universe, take me to my Danny tonight." The nuns and novices were in bed as she stole surreptitiously through the darkness. That night, she was possessed by a fierce desire to throw her arms around the man she loved and could not get out of her mind and tell him, "I am forever completely yours, body and soul. Take me, wherever you are, down to the depths of the sea or to the heights of heaven."

Rays of the full moon brightened her face. Her eyes blinked, creating many images. What a miracle it would be if she could wake up in Danny's arms and find that she had been having a nightmare, that Dan Cohen had not died and had not been buried at sea. Then he would take her to St. Basil's Church. She would be dressed in a white wedding gown adorned with pearls, the church would be decorated with flowers and hundreds of lit white candles, and the Byzantine icons would smile as she and Danny, hand in hand, approached the altar. Papavasile, in his colorful vestments, would perform the sacrament of marriage. Melodiously, he would chant, "Whoever God has joined together, let no man put asunder."

In the late afternoon of Wednesday, September 9, 1942, Mother Superior entered Sister Anthusa's cell with a firm step, a perfect image of authority and intimidation, and spoke between clenched teeth. "Sister Anthusa, it's about time you started to obey the rules," she said emphatically. "You have been missed at services. For more than a year you have been an ordained nun with serious responsibilities. Show your humility and repentance and attend church regularly. To fail to do so is to break our monastic vows, and I will not allow it."

Sister Anthusa gave no sign of response or reverence, remaining immobile and staring at Mother Superior with unseeing eyes. Inner torment, conflict, anger, and confusion whirled in her psyche.

"I won't stand for disrespect," Mother Superior lashed out, "nor am I going to allow you to ruin the reputation of our convent. Either you return to the life of prayer and daily devotions, or we'll have to send you back to where you came from."

Sister Anthusa felt Mother Superior's words blistering her brain. *We'll have to send you back to where you came from* meant lifetime imprisonment. She knew she had better follow the rules. Like an actress, she would have to play the role with dignity, trying to think about anything except Danny. In painful mourning, she looked up at Mother Superior. Could she make her understand? Eyes fiercely fixed on the older woman, she wanted to scream, but she managed to restrain herself.

"You are being tempted, dear child," Mother Superior said. "You must pray and fast."

"Do not pressure me, Reverend Mother. Can't you see that I'm not well?"

"Not well or guilty? If you are sick, then you must go to the hospital."

"Sick is the word," retorted Sister Anthusa. "Sick of you, of your constant pressure and lack of concern of how I feel."

"Insubordinate and lacking commitment, that's how you feel. You must repent and confess. Our whole island suffers because of your unconfessed sins. Innocent people die daily because of you."

Wrath and hysteria mounted within Sister Anthusa. Enraged, she dashed forward, grabbed the water pitcher from her night table, and hurled it at Mother Superior, missing her by only a few inches. The pitcher smashed against the wall, and hundreds of fragments scattered on the floor.

"Unless you repent, you shall perish," Mother Superior screamed and ran from the room.

"Oh, go to hell," Anthusa said, and instantly covered her mouth with both hands, feeling deep shame for using such disgraceful language. Frantically, she paced her cell like a caged beast. Every inch of the cell was ugly and depressing. She sat down on her cot in a whirlpool of emotions. Her eyes settled on her white veil, which hung over her black robe on the wall. She stood still and stared with fiery eyes. Scorn bordering on insanity formed in her mind. Pointing at her garb, she snarled, "You, the veil of purity, mask of sinners, refuge of the weak-willed." Her voice started low and rose in pitch with each word. "You were supposed to give me solace. Why haven't you? Why?" she sobbed. She pulled her garb off the wall, tore it apart, and threw it on the floor. "I don't need you anymore," she cried, kicking it aside. "You are nothing but a dishrag." Her throat grew thorns with the strain of rage. "Instead of healing my wound, you have poisoned my heart. Don't you know that I'm innocent? Don't you know that I was accused unjustly?" As she attempted to kick at the torn clothes, she stumbled on the broken pitcher and fell down in a crumpled heap. She could not even move her hand to ease the wracking pain in her temples.

As she lay motionless, the mist in the depths of her brain dispersed. With her swollen eyes shut, she took deep breaths and saw herself as she had been a moment before. Her ears echoed with the violence of her voice. The fiery inferno was fading away. "O my God, what has my sinful mouth said? The devil must have taken over my soul to torment me. How could I be so wicked?" As she reached for the torn garments, she whispered, "Forgive me, Lord. Forgive me." Quickly, she gathered the shreds together and brought them to her lips. With a painful effort, she sat up, still dazed. Rolling the veil and her cassock into the shape of a baby she began to rock the bundle in her arms and croon over it. "I know you will forgive me," she whimpered. "You know I did not mean what I said. My good and precious veil. My sacred robe, symbol of humility. I love you." She wept deliriously, then drew herself upright below the vigil light. She hung up the cassock and over it carefully placed her white veil. "Near the icon of the Virgin Mary is where you belong," she said.

Spent and weak, she sprawled across her cot. Her temples pounded like a hammer beating upon an anvil. She reached for the water pitcher, but it lay broken in a hundred pieces on the floor. Hardly able, she dragged herself to the open window. The breeze from the pine forest felt cool, and the fragrance was a balm to her soul. She gazed at the grass, a green velvet carpet bordering the convent, and breathed easier. As the sun was about to touch the mountain, nature in all its magnificence stretched out before her. She could breathe more easily now as she tried to grasp something of the earth's beauty and heaven's majesty.

Drained through and through, she whispered a verse from the Communion service: "Into the splendors of Your Holy Temple how shall I, unworthy, enter? Cleanse me O Lord, and save my soul." Guilt-ridden and eyes welling with tears, she watched the sun rolling gloriously over the western mountains. Physically exhausted, she turned away from the window. A tumult rose within her. Like a kaleidoscope, her mind's eye rotated blurry images—Stephen, her first love, wrestling with huge waves; Dan Cohen, holding her tight in the hot springs; and Mourtos, with a bleeding face, lying in her garden. Unable to resist the onslaught, in a choking voice, she screamed, "Blood. Blood." Her knees buckled, and she saw flames on her veil and drops of blood dripping from it. Trying to extinguish the flames with bare hands, her fingers became blood red. As the setting sun shone through the stained glass in the upper part of her window, bathing the veil in a deep crimson color, her eyes had created the apparition of flames and blood. When the last sunbeam vanished into dusk, she realized it was only an optical illusion. *Is God sending me a message?*

Beneath the icon of the Virgin Mary she knelt in prayer. *I am tired. I cannot stand the torment of my soul much longer. O Lord, let Your handmaiden depart in peace.* She sobbed in utter dejection. The chimes rang for the office of Vespers. She had no desire to attend chapel. When the melodic chanting of the nuns reached her ears, she wallowed in pain. *I have cried unto You, O Lord. Listen to my supplication. God, where are You? Why have You abandoned me? You have been so silent. Why do You torture those who love You?* Burning tears streamed down her cheeks.

CHAPTER FIFTY-THREE

DETERMINED TO GET RID of Sister Anthusa, Mother Superior sent a message to the priest asking him to intercede. Early next morning, Papavasile entered Sister Anthusa's cell, and after a few fatherly amenities he begged her to tell him what she intended for her life.

"Is something serious bothering you?" he asked.

"I have confessed everything to you."

"Tell me, child, is there is anything you, perhaps, have forgotten to confess?"

Raising her pained eyes to Papavasile, she saw a face shadowed by doubt and grief. She realized that he, too, did not fully understand her. Disappointed, she asked, "You, Father, who are God's holy man, even you do not know the truth when you hear it?"

Sister Anthusa gazed out of the window, focusing on some distant world where her soul journeyed, feeling a deeper sadness, a new feeling of separation from God. Papavasile tried to comfort her. "Sister Anthusa, your pain and my pain are not the only pain in this world. When we are in pain, it's hard to think of a God who loves us." He asked her to face the icon of the Virgin Mary, where a flickering light conveyed ineffable grace. He clenched his hand around his gray beard. "Our whole nation is suffering. Last winter,

260,000 people died of starvation. In Moria, so far we have lost 185 people, 10 percent of our population. I go to the cemetery two or three times a day, burying young and old who have died of disease, hunger, or betrayal. People are horrified each time the Nazis kill someone who they say violates their rules. Just yesterday, two Nazi soldiers snatched away Eleni, the orphan, Bouras' sister, and nobody knows where they took her."

"But what did she do?"

"Nothing. She had gone to draw water from the village well. They found her alone and . . ."

"She is a young girl?"

"No more than sixteen, but she looks older."

"I hope they didn't hurt her." Sister Anthusa made the sign of the cross.

"Someone removed the swastika from the castle, and the Moria Quartet has disappeared. Cara-Beis spread the rumor that they probably did the job and are hiding."

"What if they find them?"

"I hate to think of it. They may suffer the same fate as my son." The priest placed his hand compassionately on her shoulder. "If you are innocent, you need not fear what others think. But if you feel guilty . . ."

"I'm not guilty," cried Sister Anthusa. "Why can't you believe me?"

"My daughter," he said, "be patient with me. I am also human, but God is love and forgiveness."

Sister Anthusa grew a bit calmer. The words *love* and *forgiveness* pacified her inner warfare. The priest's voice was soothing and fatherly.

"God's ways never fail. We need not cry for any special recompense for days of despair or discomfort. Either we accept the challenge that God is good, or we die in despair."

"I have always believed in God's goodness. I have done no evil, Father." The veins on her neck swelled as she spoke.

"Sister Anthusa, it must not matter to you whether I believe you are innocent or not. You must learn that God's grace is sufficient for you to regain peace."

"You said those same words to me almost two years ago."

"I remember. Those were happy days for you," said the priest.

"I always had a fear that those happy days would not last."

The priest listened solicitously. "Why, child?"

"I don't know. I just had the feeling."

"Sometimes we create our own fate."

"Sometimes we cannot help but do so," said Sister Anthusa. "We are motivated by an invincible force, like love."

"Love, Sister Anthusa?" The priest shook his head. "Love, like war, is easy to start and difficult to bring to an end."

"And we suffer the consequences. But why has God afflicted me so much?

"Nobody knows that."

"It seems that one misfortune succeeded another misfortune in my life. Whoever I loved, I lost. Nothing has happened in my favor. Why? A man came into my life, we loved each other. You know that story. He was a good man, Father, and one tragic night I lost him. Now I cannot get him out of my mind."

"I understand," Papavasile said, sadness visible in his sunken eyes. His priestly heart searched for words of comfort. "Hard times are not only about losing a loved one, as painful as that is, my dear sister, hard times are about losing spirit and hope. It is then that our dreams dry up. There is a reason behind every event in our lives."

"What could be the reason behind the events in mine?"

"I don't know all the answers, my child. I don't know why the innocent suffer, why there is war and pestilence, earthquakes and floods, hunger and disease, or why children die. Why did the Nazis invade our land? There are millions of whys, and we don't have as many answers." Papavasile rose, getting ready to leave. "At least you're safe here. Now in prayer and contemplation learn whether or not God's grace is sufficient for you."

"But my misery knows no end. I desire only a peaceful death."

"The path of bitterness and the path of forgiveness are set before you. You must choose one. I can only say that if you choose the right path, God will

286

reveal to you the meaning of your sorrow." Papavasile made the sign of the cross over Sister Anthusa's head and blessed her, saying, "May our Lord grant you His peace." He excused himself and left.

On his way out of the convent, he met with Mother Superior and suggested that Sister Anthusa be left alone. "Be patient with her," the priest advised. "She's hurting and needs our prayers." He walked to the chapel, where he fell on his knees and prayed at the altar. *Most events in our lives serve some purpose, dear Lord. But what is Sister Anthusa's purpose in life?* He felt powerless even in his prayers.

———

For three days Sister Anthusa remained alone. On the fourth day, she asked for food and for permission to resume her life as a nurse at the infirmary. She felt that time would bring peace, and the thought caused a spirit of reconciliation with God to flow through her veins and ease her soul. *Evil, pain, suffering, losses, seem to be aspects of life that most humans go through. And I'm part of the human race,* she thought, and shaking her head, she crossed herself as she pondered on her condition. *The priest said that someday we will know the answers.*

Tending to the sick and the dying became increasingly demanding, leaving her physically weak. She tired easily, ate very little, and lost more weight, which was not apparent under her cassock. Mother Superior, after the priest's advice, began to be sympathetic toward her. She suggested Sister Anthusa return to the convent at three o'clock in the afternoon and not work late hours. She respected Papavasile's words, *Be patient with her,* and she even prayed for the restoration of Sister Anthusa's health. Mother Superior also recommended that Sister Anthusa should take a brief walk by the sea twice a week after the evening service for some fresh air, but never alone. She insisted that she be accompanied by another sister.

One Saturday evening Sister Anthusa roamed around the garden meditating and reminiscing. It began to drizzle. The roses seemed to weep, the myrtles sighed, and around the fence the narcissus dressed in black caused her vision to darken. Her misty eyes saw nature veiled in sadness. God had offered her this place of peace and prayer. What else could she want for the remainder of her life? A nun's daily ritual was her constant reminder: *May the ending of life be painless, shameless, and peaceful, that we may render a worthy account before the judgment throne of God.*

Along the shore she could hear the murmuring sound of the waves. Although she had been by the sea the evening before, she decided to go again this evening, alone, ignoring Mother Superior's order. She felt the need for solitude. The sea reflected the pale moon, giving her an extraordinary feeling. As her shoes dug into the sand, she sensed a familiar fragrance in the air. She had smelled the same scent the previous night, but in the presence of Sister Maria, who accompanied her, she made no fuss. *Was I hallucinating? I smelled Danny's scent, the scent of American soap.* At the spot where she and Danny had been before, the scent had been intoxicating. Tonight, her feet, as if they had a mind of their own, took her back to the shore. The smell of the sea aroused memories almost forgotten. Holding her breath, she looked around. *I must be losing my mind.* She felt a sudden shiver electrify her spine. She drew her veil around her face and hurried back to the convent. Joy radiated from her face. *Danny may be dead, but his soul is hovering over the island. He wants me to be with him someday. I know it.*

———

Week followed week, month followed month, and Sister Anthusa's monastic life marched into its third year. Even in the summer heat, it was pleasant to walk by the seashore, always with Maria, the young novice. Feeling the caresses of the Aegean Sea invigorated her. The passing years had not harmed her looks. She still possessed a stunning face, although it was a bit pale, the striking eyes, the Sapphic nose, the perfect lips, the slender and taut figure of youth.

All the while she had managed to repress her true thoughts and feelings about her life, but by the end of August 1944, her attitude had changed dramatically. The days had shortened and grown cooler, and whenever she walked by the sea, her body and soul felt stronger. She felt an inner confidence and strength that she understood to be God's power within her soul.

Unaccompanied one Saturday evening, as she walked and meditated, she felt light as a feather, heavenly. Emotionally, her heart stopped aching completely. Exalted, she tiptoed back to the convent, but was shocked to see Mother Superior standing by the gate. Seeing her angry grimace, Sister Anthusa's exuberant feelings completely evaporated. She realized that trouble was ahead.

"Sister Anthusa, where have you been?" Mother Superior said. Her voice was harsh, her glare disapproving. Orders had been disobeyed, and she was determined to do something about it.

Chest heaving, Sister Anthusa replied, "Nowhere."

"Don't lie to me," Mother Superior snapped.

"I'm not lying. I was walking along the shore breathing a bit of fresh air."

"But you were there last night alone and again tonight alone."

"Yes, I was, and I'm going to go tomorrow night alone and the night after, because it makes me feel better. The vastness of sea makes the presence of God real to me."

"Nuns never walk alone, do you understand me?"

Silently Sister Anthusa returned to her cell, feeling sentenced to life imprisonment. That night she could not sleep. She tossed and turned, pushing away thoughts of her past that had once again became present. She pondered on how insignificant her turmoil was, compared to the horror of Danny's death. She visualized his body being thrown into the ocean, without flowers, candles, or a funeral service. Morning was taking longer to come.

At last, another night had ended, another day had begun.

In the distance, the chapel carillons pealed, inviting the nuns to attend the Sunday morning liturgy. The sun rose in full glory, and the doves cooed as Sister Anthusa sat sadly by the window of her cell and peered outside. She had no desire to attend church this morning. She listened to the bells chime, and as the beautiful sound faded away it made her think of the infinite potential of the sound of music to reach the end of the world. It was a moment of ecstasy, and she wished for her death, that she might be with her Danny forever. *What life has separated, death will bring back together,* she thought. The longing for union with Danny, the joy of a celestial marriage, haunted her every waking hour.

CHAPTER FIFTY-FOUR

ON SEPTEMBER 10, 1944, the Nazi troops left Lesbos, and by the end of the month, they had completely withdrawn from Greece. At their departure, the country was utterly devastated. Dan Cohen and Tiny Tom, who had been incarcerated in the Averof prison, were now free. Thinner and with long untidy beards, dirty and hungry, yet free and joyful, they roamed lost in the streets of Athens, trying to locate the American Embassy. Tiny Tom talked only of steak and potatoes, apple pie heaped with vanilla ice cream, and steaming coffee.

Wandering through the ruins of the city, Dan Cohen sought comfort in his thoughts. The island of Lesbos and the love of his beautiful Nina were fixed in his mind. *But why she did not answer my letters? I've written to her again and again,* he thought, *yet not a single word in reply. Maybe my letters never reached her.* This reason had sustained him through three years of Nazi dominance and cruelty.

An American army base was temporarily established in Faleron, a seacoast area. Dan Cohen and Tiny Tom found relief and direction there. New uniforms, underwear, shoes, and some cash were supplied while they made arrangements to return to America. During a check-up by an army doctor, Dan Cohen requested permission to stay in Greece for at least another month.

"I need some time to recuperate." The American Embassy granted permission, and three days later, the two comrades, holding back their emotions, decided to part ways. They knew why Cohen was staying. Tiny Tom boarded the next boat to England, and from there he would take a four-engine aircraft to New York.

Dan Cohen's life was set on an irrevocable course. He was determined to return to Lesbos and claim his love. *She may have married someone else,* he worried, *but I still would like to see her once more. I'll take that chance before I return to America.* His heart beat harder at that thought, and he felt a sharp ache in his temples.

For the journey from the harbor of Piraeus to Lesbos, the only boat available for Cohen and several other released prisoners was an old vessel with weathered timbers and faded paint. As he once again sailed the Aegean Sea, he tried not to think of the executions and tortures he had witnessed during the Nazi nightmare. Hundreds of men died terrible deaths in the concentration camp of Haidari, outside of Athens, where he and the rest of the *North Star* crew had initially been imprisoned. After three months, he and Tiny Tom were inexplicably transferred to the prison of Averof, a less threatening place. Here, Dan was permitted to write letters. It remained a mystery to him what had happened to the rest of the crew.

About an hour after Dan and his companions set sail, the north wind gave the Aegean a relentless whipping. As they were passing Cavo Doros, the seaman's hell, the sea roared against the prow, and massive waves tossed the boat around like a cork. The small group aboard cowered in fear. Four tall, skinny boys in tattered clothing stood by the stern, teasing each other and trying to sing liberation songs. Cohen couldn't believe his ears or eyes. It was the Moria Quartet. He hurried toward them. "Guys, I know who you are! You sang at the blessing of the *North Star,* as we were about to depart from Lesbos. Remember?"

Puzzled, Takis, the leader of the four, took a look at Cohen. After sizing him up from head to toes and shaking his head in disbelief, he turned toward his friends, thinking, *Without that red beard, he certainly looks like that*

American sailor we knew, but he is dead. His friends raised their shoulders, uncertain what to say. Then daring curiosity and persistence surfaced, and he said, "Oh, I remember years ago, a boat came to our island, and there was an American sailor who was friendly. He looked like you, but he did not have a beard."

"That's me."

Taking another profound look at Cohen's blue eyes and blond hair, he said, "If you are that sailor, you're supposed to be dead! Everybody in Moria thought so."

"I almost died," explained Cohen.

"The four of us had a narrow escape, too. Three years in Haidari, a living hell." Lest Takis begin to tell about life in the concentration camp, his three friends walked away.

They did not want Takis to start recounting the scary experience, when that fatal night he removed the swastika from the castle of Lesbos, and how they tried to escape by boat, but they had been caught and sent to Haidari.

Cohen wanted to know if he or his friends knew anything about Costas Cambas or Nina. Seeing the concern in Cohen's eyes, Takis shook his head. He knew too well what calamity had befallen the Cambas family, but he did not want to upset him.

Once the sea calmed, the quartet connected again and caused a great deal of commotion, telling jokes and mimicking the Nazis. When the island came in view they screamed out, "Lesbos! Lesbos! Here we come!" As the boat came closer, the excitement increased. Joyful shouts filled the air. The passengers sang, "Lesbos, you are still breathtaking. Glorious mountains descend in graceful lines to the coast, quenched by the crystal waters of the sea, and the silvery light of the moon spreads joy all over thee."

Standing at the prow, Cohen felt like a passionate schoolboy returning home for summer vacation. He wanted to join the innocent young men of the Moria Quartet, to scream and shout with them, but his tongue was dry. Instead, he remained alone, anticipating the unknown. In his imagination, he saw Nina waiting for him, walking in her garden and tending her roses.

Gentle waves like mermaids carried the boat much closer to the island. Cohen could now see the cemetery. It seemed much larger than he remembered. An enormous army of tombstones, half-drowned in the soil, paralyzed him. *Many people must have died in Lesbos,* he thought. He remembered Gregori, the artist who had painted the fresco in Alexis' American Café and wondered if he were still alive. What about Papavasile, the priest? Or Alexis, who had helped his secret mission? Every face and every event of his life on the island came back in detail. Gregori's voice resounded in his ears as the murmur of the waves took on a plaintive note. On the last day the *North Star* was on the island, Gregori prophetically sang:

> *Years of darkness will descend*
> *Years of evil, years of pain*
> *Good people will lose faith*
> *But human wounds will heal again!*

"Will they heal again?" Cohen asked himself. His return to Lesbos brought an acute sadness. He strained his ears to hear even an echo from the town of Moria, but in vain. The jubilation of the crew annoyed him. He was tired and anxious. The pulse in his temples throbbed, and he clasped his hands tightly around the rope that was tied from the top of the mast to the prow. *Will I find my love well? What if her father and Pipina persuaded her to marry someone else?* How was he to approach Nina this time, especially if Takis is right and they all believe he is dead?

Upon arrival, the passengers stormed out of the boat and streamed though the streets and alleys of Moria toward their families. The night was clear, a half moon white against a velvety dark blue sky. Moria had lost three hundred of its two thousand citizens to starvation caused by the Nazi invasion.

Dan Cohen passed the former German barracks of Cara Tepe which had been sacked and reduced to ashes. He walked down shabby streets and saw that Moria looked emaciated, like a very old woman with disheveled hair and tattered clothes.

Carrying a daffodil bag containing his few belongings, he walked like a refugee along an alley so narrow that the balconies of the houses almost met.

He had passed this way many times before on his way to Cambas' villa. There were no fragrant flowers, no human figures leaning curiously against the railings to watch the passersby. The wind whistled fiercely, a mournful spirit, tossing thousands of dry leaves down deserted streets. There was not a soul around.

Suddenly the sound of footsteps drew his attention. He saw two dark figures at the end of the alley. A dog began to howl, straining his nerves. Mournfully, the belfry clock tolled ten. Only a few flickering oil lanterns in some of the houses cast a soft light on the streets. The moon rose higher, but its light was faint and overshadowed by clouds. More clouds, driven by the south wind, floated above the hills and valleys, ready to drop tears upon the charred earth. What had been full of colorful life and beauty now seemed dead. Profound loneliness caused Cohen's feet to grow heavy. The silence amplified the sound of his footsteps as he quickened his pace. Something was terribly wrong.

Between anxiety and excitement, he began to wonder whether it was wise to visit Cambas' villa at such a late hour. But he could not wait for a whole night to pass. Nina had already waited too long for him. The closer he came to her home, the clearer her image became in his mind, stirring his emotions. He saw her glowing eyes, her smiles, her beauty. He could not wait to put his arms around her and kiss her. When he reached the villa, he found the iron gate half-open and the lamp over the entrance unlit. He pushed the gate, and the rusty hinges crumbled and clouds of cobwebs were broken and fell apart. Weeds and grass grew in the cracks of the pebble-paved entrance, and creeping creatures had made their nests in the crevices. Covered by leaves, the mosaic of the phoenix could hardly be seen. There were no lights on in the house, and the whole place was unkempt. He rushed up the steps and knocked on the front door, but there was no answer, He knocked again and then pushed the door forcefully. It cracked open, and a ferocious German shepherd barked furiously, startling Cohen. The animal's eyes were hostile, and his mouth was drawn back viciously, baring sharp, yellow fangs. *What if some of the Nazis are still here?* Cohen shivered. But a sudden cry that sounded like a human voice sent him hurrying down the stairway, heart beating with intense fear. For a few seconds he stood on the pebbled pathway and brushed the dry leaves aside with his foot. His eyes were now accustomed to the pale moonlight, and he could see that the phoenix was intact. *This mythical bird dies, and in four years, out of its ashes, it rises, alive again,* Nina's voice echoed in his ears. *Am I the symbol of this bird? A survivor of the Nazi nightmare, a man thought dead? But where is my Nina?*

Cohen looked up to the sky, an infinity of fatigue in his eyes, and then began to retrace his steps, but a cat's meow made him pause. Skeletal and hardly able to walk, the cat came closer to him, meowing pitifully. Cohen squatted and scratched the cat's fur. Gently, he took the animal in his arms and felt saddened and comforted by the sound of its purring. "You are Apollo," he whispered, "but what has happened to our Nina and her family?" Tenderly he put the cat down and tiptoed into the garden. The olive trees, the pride of Costas Cambas, were gone. Nina's rose garden and the bushes were wizened and dry. Heart sinking, hopes collapsing, he pushed on. The once beautiful pond was now a yellowish-green muddy marsh. Its waters were turgid and filthy, filling the air with an unbearable smell. He nearly lost his wits when someone lurched out from behind a tree. The little moonlight showed an emaciated figure, bowed and old, wearing a torn Nazi jacket and cap. Two deep lines were etched around his mouth. Smallpox scars marked his face, and his cheeks had caved in, devoured by the dreadful disease. On his face was fixed an expression of profound grief. What he had greedily hoarded was no longer of any value. Cohen recognized him as the man who tried to sell him olive oil.

"Where's Nina? What has happened to Mr. Cambas and his sister?" Cohen asked. The man shook his head.

"And what are you doing here?"

"All gone. All gone," said Cara-Beis, his eyes wild. He collapsed on the ground.

CHAPTER FIFTY-FIVE

MENTALLY NUMB, Cohen walked along a familiar path parallel to the river. In the darkness of the night he could scarcely distinguish the landmarks he'd hoped would guide him in the right direction. In the distance, he could make out the silhouette of the aqueduct. Hope and strength forced him to grope his way for a quarter of a kilometer to Papavasile's house, adjacent to the church. *If the priest is alive, he may be the only reliable source of information about Nina and her family.* Apart from an emaciated dog resting against an empty table, the town was desolate. Crickets and an occasional rooster's crow disturbed the silence of the night.

Cohen knocked at the door. There was no answer. He knocked again harder. The door creaked open, and the priest appeared with an oil lantern in his hand. "Who are you and what do you want at this hour?" There was fear in his voice.

"Father, I'm Dan Cohen, the American sailor. Don't you remember me?"

In disbelief at the sight of a bearded young man in army fatigues and boots, the priest hesitated. "But you are not Danny the sailor, are you?"

"I am he, Dan Cohen, Father Daniel Papadopoulos' grandson."

Now convinced, Papavasile placed the lantern on a little table near the door and put his arms around Cohen affectionately. "Danny, my son," he said, his eyes brimming with tears of joy, "welcome back. I thought you were . . . dead."

"I know," Cohen said.

"This is a miracle! But why are we standing out here? Come in my little house! I'm so glad you are alive and back in Moria."

As they walked inside, Cohen said, "It is a miracle, Papavasile. The Nazis blew the *North Star* into pieces, and the crew and I were taken prisoners."

"Horrible," the priest sighed, again wrapping his arms around the resurrected sailor. "And I performed several memorial services in your name." Suddenly the priest's face took on a sad look, thinking of the death of his son, Christos. But a new image quickly crossed his mind, giving him a smile of relief. *God sent Danny Cohen back to be my son.*

"Papavasile, I am alive. I refuse to die until I kill that evil man, Manolis Mourtos, who attempted to drown me. Forgive me, Father, but I'm determined to do it."

"Leave revenge to God, my son. Mourtos is already dead. His life came to a dreadful end. Someone unknown killed him. It's still a mystery to the authorities."

"Then God has spared me the sin."

"Come, let's sit. You must be very tired and hungry."

Though Cohen was exhausted, he was still delighted to see the priest in his humble yet heartwarming surroundings. Together they entered the simple room that Papavasile used for prayer and meditation, a carpeted cell with old pictures on the walls. Cohen sat on a cot by the fireplace, as Papavasile threw a piece of wood on the fire and got out a flask of wine. With a trembling hand, he poured out two glasses and offered one to his God-given guest. "Drink this. I haven't much else to give you at this hour. It's the wine I use for Communion." The priest settled himself on a huge pillow, his disbelieving eyes fixed on Cohen as he savored the wine. His bearded face glowed with joy.

Cohen was overwhelmed at the priest's warm reception. After a brief silence, he decided to speak, but his voice sounded sad. "Answer me just one question, Father. Is Nina Cambas alive?"

"Danny, my son," said the priest gently, "alive she is. Now, rest on this cot, and we will talk in the morning."

"How can I rest if I don't hear a word about Nina? Tell me, where is she? Did she get married?" he asked, anxiety widening his eyes.

"She's in the convent, married to Christ." The priest sighed.

"I thought she loved me and wanted to marry me."

"Indeed she did, but she believed you had died."

"Don't spare me the details, Father. I'm glad that she is alive. I want to know everything."

Papavasile shook his head. "Well, as you may recall, three years ago, the *North Star* set sail Thursday after midnight. On Good Friday, the news spread throughout Moria that you were missing, and the captain asked the police to search for you. By noon, Mourtos had told the police that he'd found you lying dead on the rocks and had delivered you to the captain."

"That's not what happened, Father."

The priest said, "The whole town of Moria believed that you probably had a bad accident and died. Nine days later, Pipina asked me to offer a memorial service for you. But the person who suffered the ultimate pain was the beautiful woman who loved you, Nina Cambas."

"Is that why she resorted to the convent?"

"There is more. Mourtos was found murdered on the Cambas estate, and Nina was accused of the murder."

"Oh my God, that could never be, not Nina," Cohen said, shaking his head.

"I knew Nina was innocent, but that venomous snake, Cara-Beis, a Nazi collaborator, convinced the Army of Occupation that Nina killed Mourtos because he knew she was hiding an American spy."

"And that spy was me?"

"That's what was said. Cara-Beis engineered all of this deviousness to destroy Cambas, and he succeeded."

"But why? Where is justice in this world?"

The priest raised his shoulders and said, "Evil people do evil things. Betrayals and corruption have become rampant in our times."

"I saw Cara-Beis earlier tonight. I went directly to Cambas' villa hoping to find Nina there. Instead, I found that evil man. He looked like a dying leper. The whole area seemed deserted."

A few silent seconds elapsed, and Cohen asked in agony and anger, "How did Nina end up in the convent?"

"Nazi accomplices coerced the judge to sentence her to life imprisonment. But her father offered his estate and all his olive groves as a ransom, and Nina was set free under one condition. She had to live within the confines of the convent."

"It's still life imprisonment," Cohen said.

"Thinking that you were dead, Nina found solace at St. Mary's Convent. It's a place of peace."

"And how is her father and her aunt?"

"After the tragic events, her father had a massive heart attack and died. Poor Pipina is not too well, but she lives with Alexis' mother, who takes good care of her."

"This is all a nightmare. How unfortunate and how painful for Nina," Cohen said.

"Unfathomable is the calamity that fell on Cambas' life." Emotional fatigue taking over, the priest gave a couple of long yawns. He caressed his beard and said, "Now, let's both get some rest, and we will talk again in the morning."

"It's almost morning, Father." Forcing a smile, Cohen took off his boots and stretched out on the cot, hardly able to keep his eyes open. Shortly after he dozed off, the priest placed a blanket over him and made the sign of the cross, praying for peace.

Cohen woke at dawn and found Papavasile sitting beside his cot, smiling graciously. He handed him a mug of strong mountain sage tea sweetened with honey. He took a sip and felt the hot fragrant liquid warming his chest and stomach. Gratefully, he looked at the priest, and mastering sufficient courage he said, "Papavasile, I have come to marry Nina. I want nothing else in life."

"Be patient, my son. There is much that you should know."

"I understand, and I also meant to ask you about my uncle."

The priest shook his head sadly. "Barba-Thanos died a year ago. I'm very sorry. We had three hundred deaths in our little town." He fingered his beard in an effort to think what else he could say. He leaned back in his straw-padded chair, casting his eyes on his sunburned hands, folding them together in a way that suggested contemplation. Yet his mind recollected that these hands, which had blessed hundreds of people, one dark night picked up a bayonet, joined the army of liberators, and fought the enemy with determination. He smoothed his beard to submerge that fatal memory, wishing it was only a nightmare.

"Our island lost thousands of people. Death from starvation is a most horrible way to die. I buried hundreds of people." Tears filled the priest's sunken eyes. "And someone killed my son."

"Christos is dead? Oh, Father, I am so sorry." Cohen reached and grabbed the priest's hand and held it fast.

"Do you remember how Christos took you around and introduced you to certain people in Moria?"

"Of course I remember. Such a good-natured young man! I'm very sorry." Cohen bit his lips, unable to find words that could comfort a father who had lost his only son.

The priest nodded and forced a smile. "But God has given me another son . . . my daughter married Dimitri, a fine young man."

"From Moria?"

"No, from another town of Lesbos." The priest sighed and pain surfaced in his face, thinking of the loss of his son. "Danny, if you were here . . ."

"All this time, I have not slept without that wish. I wrote to Nina countless times with no response. I have spent three years in a prison outside Athens. I saw death, murder, and torture . . . ." Cohen's voice trembled.

"Like a plague," the priest added, "the Nazis devoured our life, sucked the very blood of our souls. Rapes, murders, and countless deaths."

Cohen's thoughts gravitated around Nina. *What must she have been through?* Deeply concerned about her, he finally said, "Father, I want to see Nina."

The priest shook his head. "I don't think you can."

"Why? I love her. I want to marry her if she still loves me."

"If it is God's will." The priest continued to comb his snow-white beard slowly with his fingers, trying figure out what was really God's will.

"I have seen enough of God's will," Cohen protested. "God is blind and deaf and has no heart for human suffering."

"My son, you are angry, but we cannot blame God for our misfortunes. He gives us strength to endure them." The priest's prophetic look and his words penetrated Cohen's heart.

"Papavasile, please forgive me. I have seen too much pain and suffering in the last three years."

"I'm sure you have." The priest stood up and, taking Cohen by the arm, he pulled him up gently and said, "Come with me, I will take you to Nina."

"You will?" Ecstasy beamed in Cohen's eyes.

In the streets, occasional drops of rain moistened the air, sending a chill through the bones. Cohen changed into a U.S. Marine uniform he had carried with him and, wearing the shiny boots provided by the American Embassy in Athens, walked with anticipatory joy beside the priest, who followed a steady pace. Within five minutes they stood in front of a big building. It was a temporary infirmary that Moria's nobles had made available. People moved in and out, carrying bottles of medicine, boxes of food, and ceramic pitchers of water for the sick. Cohen and Papavasile stood unnoticed near a low wall and gazed through a window overlooking the sick.

Cohen's heart leaped and his body jerked when he spotted Nina bending low to feed an elderly bedridden woman.

"This is what she does all her waking hours, and they adore her," whispered Papavasile. "In this service she bears her cross and has found God. Can't you see it in her face?"

Cohen took a prolonged look. The sight of Nina dressed in her white cassock evoked a heart-piercing sigh and accentuated his yearning for her. The urge to jump through the window, grab her in his arms, and take her away was overwhelming. But the priest's hand on his shoulder held him still.

Both of them watched Nina, who was busy caring for her patients, caressing their heads, tucking them into their beds, and giving them a smile of hope. Effortlessly, she tiptoed among the sick, feeling much at home in their midst. She did not shrink from contact with them and showed no feeling of revulsion at their touch. When her eyes chanced to meet any of their searching eyes around her, seeking her attention, she smiled, recognizing that they were all children of God who wanted to be loved.

"Her face is so pure and beautiful," Cohen whispered.

"Just like the face of the Blessed Mother herself," said Papavasile.

"Father, what is she saying that makes the sick smile?"

"I don't know. I think it's her presence."

"Aye," said Cohen, a whimper in his voice. Tears streaming down his cheeks, he reached out and touched the priest's hand. "May I at least go and see her?"

"No, my son." The priest wept and embraced him.

"Forgive me, Father. I love her more than ever. I want her. Can't you understand? I want to make her my wife, to make her happy. She has had enough grief and misery in her life."

"I'm sorry. That cannot be."

"Why, Father? Of all people, you know best the crosses we have borne." Cohen could see discomfort in the priest's face. "Why such a terrible fate, Father?" he went on. "Isn't Christianity a faith of love? Why so much pain for Nina when I have so much love to give to her and want to provide a new life?"

"Someday we shall know the meaning of pain. Then, perhaps we shall be glad we have suffered. There is nobility, purpose, and splendor in suffering, my dear son, Danny. God has a plan for each one of His children."

"What's God's plan for Nina? What's God's plan for me? Tell me, please. I want to know." The priest's words evoked doubts in Cohen's mind. Watching from afar, he saw the sick and the suffering in the infirmary, as Nina graciously tended to them. He had the impression that only at that instant had these ailing souls begun to exist. Then, something mysterious occurred inside him that uprooted him from his own time and carried him adrift through an unexplored region of his soul. While Nina continued treating her patients, he stood there with an absorbed look, contemplating their condition until his vision blurred. With a deep sigh of resignation, he asked, "Father, what do you think I should I do?"

"I don't know."

"I want Nina to be my wife. I love her."

Papavasile shook his head, took a last look at Nina, and then grabbed Cohen by his arm. "Let's go back to my home. We need to think this over. Better yet, let's go inside the Church of St. Basil and pray to God for some direction. No one has recognized you yet. Stay hidden at my home for a while and pray." After a last glance at the infirmary, both men walked away silently but in serious thought.

Suddenly the priest stopped and turned toward Cohen. "I just got an idea." There was a glitter in the priest's face. "Tonight, I am going to write a letter to the archbishop of Lesbos, who resides in the capital city of Mytilene, telling him about the seriousness of your circumstances and appealing to his leniency to release Nina from her vows. He is the only one who can grant this to a nun and give approval for marriage."

Jumping for joy, Cohen said, "Could you possibly go and see him, instead of writing to him? Person to person it may be faster."

"Protocol dictates that a priest who wishes to see the archbishop must first write a letter and make his request. You can be assured that my letter will be delivered into the hands of the archbishop by nine o'clock tomorrow morning. I'll send it with my son-in-law, Dimitri, for expediency and safety. Tomorrow evening, I will visit him in person. May the Lord be on our side."

In an entreating voice, Cohen added, "Pray for us, Father. Honestly, I don't know what I will do if the archbishop refuses your request."

Papavasile invited Cohen to stay at his home. It so happened that his wife wanted to spend a few more days with their daughter and there was no one else at his home. By the time he showed him the room that used to be his son's, each of them had seen the other in a way they never had before.

Cohen, realizing what this priest was planning to do for him, could not be grateful enough. His expression conveyed an aura of warmth and maturity.

"Papavasile," he said, "you are a great man. How happy and grateful I feel to be in your presence."

"You are my spiritual son, and I'm glad to have you back in my life." For a long day they chatted as father and son. They had bonded for life. The abundance of events during the last three years in their lives lay between them like mines. But they stepped gingerly over and around them, choosing courage and faith to get them through this critical time. Before he said goodnight he reached over and put his hand on Cohen's shoulder and squeezed it gently. "Danny," he said looking him in the eyes, "I feel for you. I want you to pray hard, for tomorrow evening I will go see the archbishop. He is our only hope."

Cohen nodded a silent *thank-you*. That night, conflicting thoughts kept him awake for a long time. What if the archbishop did not dispense Nina from her monastic vows? There could be no marriage. What if Nina is so committed to being a nun that she doesn't want to get married? Then even the archbishop's approval wouldn't matter.

After Dan went to bed, the priest in his study, under the flickering oil lantern, struggled to find the proper words to compose a persuasive letter, stating the reason and urgency for his visit. For a few seconds, he put his pen down and scratched his beard to process his thoughts. A sudden realization hit him like a thunderbolt. *Even before I visit the archbishop, it is imperative to inform Sister Anthusa that Dan Cohen is alive and back in Moria. How else could I ascertain her feelings for him?*

CHAPTER FIFTY-SIX

LATER THAT NIGHT, Mother Superior entered Sister Anthusa's cell, carrying a little girl in one arm and an oil lantern in the other hand. Her whole being was shaking with emotions she would have a hard time explaining. Sister Anthusa was awake, sitting on her cot meditating. Startled at the unexpected sight, she asked, "Whose child is that?" Her tone of voice was firm but caring.

"Despina's little girl," said Mother Superior, and handed the toddler to her. "She's almost three years old, an innocent little girl."

Sister Anthusa held the child in her arms. Once she had a dream of establishing a home for orphans and neglected children. She saw the child's face, red with the rash of smallpox and dying of fever. A pug-nosed baby, with half-closed blue eyes and blond hair, she was certainly not a Greek child. "Dear and beautiful child, God have mercy on you." Affectionately she pressed the child against her breast and, staring at Mother Superior, she asked, "Why have you brought this child to me?"

Tears rolled out of Mother Superior's eyes, and she bit her lip nervously. "Forgive me, my daughter," she said pensively. "Despina is dying a dreadful death, and she confessed that she killed Mourtos in your garden. I am so sorry for what I thought of you. So sorry . . ." She fell on her knees in front of Sister Anthusa and cried inconsolably. "O God," she said. "I promised her I would bring her little girl to you. She begs your forgiveness and wishes you to bless her child. If this child survives we will raise her here in our convent." Then she pulled a folded kerchief from her pocket and gave it to her. "Despina gave me this and said it belongs to you. She also wants you to have this letter."

Sister Anthusa, still holding the child on her lap, unfolded the kerchief and instantly closed her eyes in shock. "O dear Lord," she whispered. Tenderly, she refolded the kerchief, kissed it, and put it inside her cassock, next to her heart. It held the cross that Mourtos had snatched from Danny's neck. She held on to the letter but did not open it. A gut reaction convinced her that only the priest should know about this letter. It could be a confession. Looking compassionately at the child and shaking her head at the surprise, she managed a sweet smile.

Maria, the young novice, entered the cell and found Mother Superior on her knees and Sister Anthusa cradling the baby in her arms and humming "Lord Jesus, Son of God, have mercy on this child." The little girl seemed in a coma. She breathed lightly.

"How sick is this child? Will she be okay?" asked Maria.

"Help me up," said Mother Superior. "This child is half dead."

Maria assisted her, and they both helped Sister Anthusa to stand with the child in her arms. All three turned toward the icon of the Virgin Mary on the wall and bowed. "Let us pray," said Mother Superior. "Better yet, let's go to the chapel."

Despina's dying confession traveled like fire throughout the convent. All the sisters at St. Mary's were alerted. In an endless procession, they marched toward the chapel. which was aglow with many votive lights and candles, and smelled of burning incense. Sister Anthusa and the child, assisted by Maria the novice and Mother Superior, entered last. Spontaneously the sisters gathered around the dying little girl. The angelic voices chanted in exceptionally melodic voices: "*Kyrie Eleison*" (Christ have mercy). Sister Anthusa knelt before the icon of the Holy Mother of Jesus. She held the baby in her arms, and all the sisters knelt around her, chanting:

> *O Lady Theotokos, Mother of God,*
> *Receive our humble prayers,*

And deliver this child from all illness and pain.
Most Holy One, Mother of Jesus,
You are the comfort of the afflicted,
You are the healer of the sick,
You are the protector of the orphans.
We place our hopes before you,
Guard this child with care and save her.

Suddenly the child burst into a loud and endless scream. "She must be starving. Maria, warm up some milk." Sister Anthusa laughed with happiness. "Lord be praised. The child will live." Joyfully the sisters returned to their cells praising the Lord for the child's miraculous return to life. Maria caringly took the little girl in her arms and brought her to her cell to feed and care for her that night.

Despina was in another part of the convent dying by the minute. As she sensed her end was near, she asked to see Sister Anthusa. Mother Superior was already by her beside, inaudibly offering prayers of forgiveness. When Sister Anthusa arrived, Despina began to cry, "Forgive me, please, Sister Anthusa, I have wronged you badly. Forgive me." She wept as she faded away.

CHAPTER FIFTY-SEVEN

OVERWHELMED BY DESPINA'S CONFESSION, Sister Anthusa slept peacefully. Her innocence had finally been revealed. She felt happy that even Mother Superior apologized for accusing her falsely. But during the night she woke up and some disturbing thoughts kept her from going back to sleep. Often she had heard the slogan that time heals all wounds, and once she believed it. But she realized that her wound had left a sensitive and aching scar. Vividly, she brought back the memory of the few romantic moments she and her Danny cherished that accursed Thursday night before the sudden intense knock at the door caused panic.

Sister Anthusa wept for what seemed a long time. When her tears finally ceased, the thought of Despina's little girl momentarily soothed her pain. She felt the urge to visit her, but it was still early and she didn't want to disturb Maria. How much she longed to tell the story to her father confessor, Papavasile, but she decided to wait for the right time. She put on her cassock, covered her head with a scarf, and went straight to the chapel, feeling grateful for last night's episode.

On the eastern horizon, the fleeing darkness was replaced by a pearly luster, and the Moria roosters were shrieking an earlier welcome to the dawn. At top speed, Papavasile headed toward the convent, eager to tell Sister Anthusa about Danny. He felt an unprecedented exuberance at the thought of the American sailor and of the possibility of a once much-anticipated marriage. He was aware of his vicarious joy. Dan Cohen represented his son, Christos. It seemed that his son had come back to life. *God brought Danny back, another son to bring me joy,* he said to himself as he increased his pace.

Dawn was starting to break over the mountain peaks, the colors of early morning sunrise beginning to identify against the ashy gray of the escaping night. It was too early to disturb the morning routine at the convent, so he thought of going first into the chapel to pray alone. Weathered by the plague of war, pestilence, and emotional pain, with skin the hue of winter mountaintops, the priest sat in a back pew, staring at the altar screen, which held life-size paintings of saints, patriarchs, and prophets. What words could he use to tell Sister Anthusa about Cohen's return?

It happened that he saw a statuesque black figure standing in front of the icon of Christ. Movement and whisper spoke of a nun in prayer. *Strange that she would be alone at such an early hour,* he thought. It was Sister Anthusa, who, after three profound prostrations before the altar, crossing herself and thanking God for the little girl's recovery, was ready to return to her cell. The spark in her eyes reflected a lighter heart, a feeling she always experienced after a heartfelt prayer. Her steps were gentle but firm. But she was not alone in the chapel as she thought. With the steely gaze of a person in shock, she realized that it was Papavasile unobtrusively sitting in the pew. It seemed as if a figure in one of the old icons at the altar had come to life and stepped out to pray. Joyfully she approached him. He stood up, and Sister Anthusa bowed and paid the traditional respect by kissing his hand.

"Papavasile! What brings you to St. Mary's so early in the morning?" she asked.

"God's will, I hope. But I'm glad to find you here."

"I'm glad to see you here, too, for I have the most astounding news to tell you." Firmly, she held onto his hand with evident excitement.

"And do I have some good news to tell you!" He smiled. The priest's countenance had taken on a cherubic glow, hinting at some unconcealed mischief behind his glittering eyes, making the nun curious.

310

"Father, you go first," Sister Anthusa said, unable to imagine what could possibly be the priest's good news.

"A priest is trained to listen. Let's hear your news first," he insisted, still weighing the words he would use.

Unaware of the priest's extraordinary news, Sister Anthusa elaborated on the previous night's events. She told him about Despina's confession on her deathbed, and Mother Superior's sudden change of heart about her. But the astounding news was about the miraculous recovery of Despina's very sick child. "Despina left a letter for me, which I have kept unopened in my cell, hoping to let you read it first."

"Praised be the Lord," said Papavasile. Taking her hand into his own, they walked silently together back toward the flickering vigil luminary on the altar table, their faces radiating feelings of joyful anticipation. "Let's stand here in front of the icon of Jesus. We both need the blessing of our Lord Jesus Christ," said the priest, eyes focusing on the icon. Reverently he revealed his part of the news, the true story of Dan Cohen.

Sister Anthusa's knees buckled. She nearly fainted, deluged by a whirlpool of emotions. She was not sure if she was having a dream or if she was awake. Could this be part of a beatific vision, soon to dissolve? After a few deep breaths she said, "Father, is what you are telling me the truth or are you testing my faith?"

"Dear sister, Dan Cohen is alive, well, and lucky to have survived the cruel Nazi imprisonment. Now reclaiming his original name, Daniel Papadopoulos, he is back to Lesbos and is staying at my home." The priest waited for her face to light up in excitement, but it didn't. In fact, a frown crinkled between her eyes and she shook her head. *Can this be true?*

In a few carefully chosen words the priest in one breath told the nun what she needed to know. Deep sunken eyes reflecting strong emotions and brimming with compassion, Papavasile said, "He's back, Sister Anthusa, because he loves you and wants to marry you."

"How could that be? I'm in my third year . . . ."

"I know, an ordained nun for three years . . . but let me be direct. Do you still love this man? Do you want to marry him?"

"Ask me if I ever stopped loving him."

"I know, true love never dies, but do you want to marry him?"

Sister Anthusa remained silent for a long time and kept looking at the icon of Christ.

"What are your thoughts?" the priest persisted.

"I'm considering my vows, my commitment to St. Mary's, my plans to establish a much-needed orphanage on the island, and last but not least, I'm concerned about the big scandal I would cause among our people."

"We cannot design our lives according to people's comments. And the orphanage? You don't have to be a nun to establish one."

"Papavasile, it seems that you want to see me married."

"What I want is to see you happy. But you need to search your inner self and see what it is that you truly want."

"I know what I want, Father. But would the archbishop ever release me from my monastic vows so I could have the sacrament of a church marriage?"

"That I don't know, but I do plan to visit him today and ask him."

With her eyes riveted on the eyes of Jesus in the icon, her mind conjured up an impromptu prayer: *Lord, it has been a lonely life here. Let it be over soon. I cannot tell my sister nuns that my heart never stopped loving the man I lost on that ill-fated night. They would not understand. But You do, and You have sustained me over the years. You have known my wish all along. Now, my lost love is back. Please grant me a life with him, and I shall be grateful until my last breath.*

Then, falling on her knees, she put her head on her folded hands and let her mind float freely. She didn't consciously pray, but rather became an intrinsic part of the ethereal atmosphere, an ineffably sacred experience. Never before did she feel so much at peace with herself and so removed from pain. Her eyelashes lowered, her eyes closed. "Thank You, my Dear Lord," she whispered.

The priest, crossing himself, placed his hand on her head.

From her kneeling position, Sister Anthusa turned and looked at him. "Thank you, Father. Whatever the Holy Spirit guides you to do, do it quickly, please."

CHAPTER FIFTY-EIGHT

PAPAVASILE TRAVELED ON FOOT six kilometers to Mytilene with a gait a younger man would envy. From afar, he spotted the old castle of Lesbos and sighed with relief. The Greek flag waved victoriously in the breeze. The Nazi swastika was gone, and Nazis no longer occupied the island. "Good riddance," he whispered to himself. He grinned because he had participated in that last bloody battle against them, and he felt fortunate that he had been spared on that dreadful night. *How could I have fought so valiantly? It couldn't have been me, the priest who used the bayonet to kill! The Archangel Michael must have entered my body and fought the enemy with his own sword.* That thought brought comfort to his heart.

The last glow of sunset bathed his long beard and his flowing cassock as he approached the hilltop where the archbishop's luxurious villa rested, overlooking the Aegean Sea. The September evening felt cool and invigorating. A young deacon who served as the archbishop's private secretary met him at the door. The priest took off his hat, shook his hand, and asked, "How soon will I be able to see His Eminence the archbishop?"

"A barber is trimming his hair now, and then he has to take a bath. He had a busy day and is very tired. He needs to rest," the deacon said unemotionally. "Why don't you come tomorrow or another day?" he suggested.

Papavasile's blood rushed to his ears and his face turned red. Thinking of the agony and anticipation of both Dan Cohen and Sister Anthusa, who awaited the archbishop's decision, he raised a fierce finger and said, "I must see the archbishop tonight. It's urgent. Do you understand? He did receive my letter early this morning, didn't he?"

"Yes, he did. I'm not so sure he's going to approve . . ."

"Please inform His Eminence that I'm here."

Rolling his eyes, the deacon looked at the priest and said in a demeaning voice, "I'll see what I can do." Sharply he turned away and went inside.

The priest waited at the entrance for a long time. A half moon hung overhead. Combing his beard with his fingers, his memories began to transport him to a time when he had come to see the archbishop for another reason.

It was a dangerous time for the island, and he wished to inform him that he intended to join the brave liberators and fight the enemy. The archbishop, holding onto his staff with pontifical authority, said, "Impossible. You're a soldier of Christ, you can only fight the unseen warfare of the demons."

"Too many priests do just that, Your Eminence. We need fighters to overthrow the legions of demons who have been destroying human lives every day and turning our island into a cemetery."

"And you're going to abandon your cross and pick up a weapon?"

"The cross will always be in my heart. But I want to fight by the side of our young men and give them courage."

"I hear revenge in your voice, Papavasile. I know some infidel killed your son, and I don't blame you for feeling angry. But remember what the Bible has to say: Revenge is mine, says the Lord." For a most painful moment, Papavasile's gaze was fixed on the archbishop's face, but the archbishop's eyes looked elsewhere. He knew of Papavasile's impeccable character and nurtured strong feelings for his priestly integrity.

"Your Eminence, it is not revenge that I seek."

"As the spiritual head of the Church, I cannot permit you to join the liberators."

"It's not permission I need. I need your blessing, Your Eminence." Defiantly *he walked out of the archbishop's office, filled with determination. His homeland had many priests, but not enough fighters.*

While waiting at the entrance, the memory of that visit with the archbishop revitalized him. He smiled. When the deacon finally returned, with a frown of arrogance, he said, "His Eminence will see you now, Father, but please make your visit brief."

"I understand," said the priest.

Behind a huge mahogany desk, surrounded by leather-bound books and colorful icons, sat the ecclesiastical giant who controlled and determined the spiritual welfare of the entire island. With a glance over his spectacles, the archbishop said, "Blessed be the hour. Papavasile, welcome. Please, be seated."

"Thank you, Your Eminence."

"Your spirit continues to be restless. Why is it that you always make such unusual requests?"

"You know too well that often unusual things happen in the service of our Lord."

"I wonder about that," the archbishop said with a grin. "But a priest picking up weapons and joining the liberators, do you call that a part of your ministry to the Lord? Where does 'Thou shall not kill' fit into your priesthood?"

"You are right, Your Eminence. I should have listened to you and stuck to my priestly duties. But I could no longer see my people tormented by Nazi deprivation and cruelty. I hope you have forgiven me for disobeying you," Papavasile said, with an uncomfortable throbbing in his neck and temples.

Grinning, the archbishop quoted the book of Ecclesiastes: "For everything there is a season, and a time for every matter under heaven: a time to be born, and a time to die, a time to kill and a time to heal."

"About the letter, Your Eminence,"

"Oh, I know," the archbishop said, "God grant that I am sufficiently prudent to say no to such an absurd request." He accompanied his words with a little laughter to conceal his reluctance. In his mind, he had decided to say, *I will not allow such a thing.* Fumbling with the gold pendant hanging

315

from the thick chain around his neck, he lightly fingered his beard, skeptical. His eyes, which could see through the human psyche, were looking straight at Papavasile. *Is this priest out of his mind?* "I've read your letter carefully. I'm sympathetic to this American sailor who was captured by the Nazis, and so on and so forth, but Sister Anthusa is now the bride of Christ. Besides, I have received glowing reports of her remarkable service to the sick and dying. Her mission is far more important than a marriage."

Papavasile's shoulders tightened, and the skin around his ears prickled. He was solemn, and had a pensive air with a mournful glow on his face that was the color of autumn. *How can a celibate like you and all the other archbishops and bishops in our Church ever understand human love?*

"She is a fully ordained nun committed to her vows. She is already in the angelic order. Nobody can take her away from God's side."

The priest's eyes brimmed with agony, which the archbishop saw instantly. "You and I, Papavasile, cannot possibly violate the rules of the Church."

"Are there violators where there is genuine love?" the priest said solemnly.

"I sympathize with the situation, but rules are rules and they must be obeyed."

"Your Eminence, you are the archbishop of Lesbos and all the Aegean islands, the shepherd of the largest flock in our country, the spiritual leader of a million souls. But, if you will please forgive my boldness, you don't understand that unique emotion of the human heart, which is love."

"And love for Christ is of less importance?" His grimace spoke of disapproval and power.

"Your Eminence, our Lord can do with one less bride."

"It must have great meaning for you, too, that you took time out of your busy ministry to describe love so dramatically in your letter."

Papavasile gazed at him in utter reverence and said, "I wrote about what I believed to be God's love."

"You're confusing human and divine love," the archbishop said firmly.

"Am I, Your Eminence? Forgive me, but that's a strange thing to say. I don't mean to sound irreverent, but I believe human and divine love are two sides of the same coin."

"No wonder you expect me to annul her vows and allow her to marry the American sailor. It's not possible."

"For a love as pure and powerful as theirs, the Church will not make a sacrifice and let Nina Cambas be free to marry the man she loves?"

"Nina Cambas no longer exists, dear Father. She is now a bride of Christ, Sister Anthusa. Indeed, as her name implies, she is blossoming in grace. She will live to do good things, and she will be loved by many people."

Realizing that his dialogue with the archbishop was turning into a power struggle, Papavasile decided to win or to die. He eased himself out of his chair and knelt in front of the archbishop, the pillar of power he had respected and served all his life.

"Please, Your Eminence, don't say no to Dan and Nina."

"Why are you so persistent? I don't understand."

"Dan Cohen survived the horrors of Nazi cruelty. He returned to marry the woman he loves. He is an exceptional human being, honest, strong, and I happen to love him like a son."

The archbishop dragged himself out of his chair and moved slowly around his desk. Age and arthritis made him seem brittle, but when he spoke at any audience, however small, people paused to listen as if Moses had come down from Mount Sinai carrying the Ten Commandments. He put his hand on Papavasile's shoulder, simulating compassion. "Our Dear Lord sends us many afflictions. You must be missing your son very much. It was indeed a tragedy, a great loss. But He sent you another blessing. The man who married your daughter seems to be one of the finest men on the island. Indeed, I was impressed with the way he spoke and behaved when he brought me your letter this morning. I also remember his melodic voice when he chanted in one of my Pontifical Services at St. Basil's."

"Yes, Dimitri does have a good voice and he is a good son-in-law," the priest said, unable to control the tear that rolled down his cheek. He wiped it away. "I'm very sorry, Your Eminence."

"What is it now, Father? Please get back in your seat."

The archbishop took his seat again, and the priest with difficulty got up and sat. He cleared his throat and reverently said, "You mentioned that our Dear Lord sometimes sends us many afflictions."

"Yes, I said that."

"I want to see Your Eminence make one sacrifice."

"What sacrifice?"

"Dispense with the monastic vows of Sister Anthusa. Let her be Nina Cambas again and allow her to marry Dan Cohen, whose real name is Daniel Papadopoulos, a grandson of Father Daniel Papadopoulos, who I succeeded years ago at St. Basil's."

Startled, the archbishop pulled himself straight back on his chair in a posture of defense. He had no intention of yielding.

"I realize you will suffer some personal discomfort, presumably because you will violate a rule made by humans," Papavasile went on.

"You are asking me to sacrifice my principles?"

"For the sake of love, yes," the priest said, looking undaunted at the archbishop, who looked invincible. "We all have to make some sacrifice in our life. I have made my share, Your Eminence." The priest began to shake. He closed his eyes and lowered his head.

"Papavasile, are you feeling well?"

"I still hurt, and need healing . . ." he replied, ready to cry.

"In the name of Our Lord, tell me what's hurting you." The archbishop's face took on a solicitous look. Only he was empowered to hear his priests' confessions. This much he was willing to do, for it gave him a feeling of power and superiority.

"Your Eminence, a few minutes ago you said how impressed you were with my son-in-law, Dimitri."

"Of course." The archbishop felt instantly relieved. Getting the priest to talk about his son-in-law and his daughter was a good way to change the subject from Sister Anthusa.

"He and my daughter are very happy together."

"You must be happy, too."

"I am, but . . ." A hesitation in the priest's voice and a frown made the archbishop wonder.

"'But . . .' Finish your thought. Is there something else you want to tell me?"

The priest nodded yes. There is an untold story behind my daughter's marriage. Does Your Eminence wish to hear it?" Obviously he wanted to tell his story and reveal the sacrifice he had made in his life, hoping that the archbishop would consider making a sacrifice himself, dispensing Sister Anthusa from her vows.

In a tone of sadness the priest said:

About a year and a half ago, during Lent, one Friday evening I was hearing confessions. Last in line was Dimitri, a young man in tears. "The Lord loves and forgives those who repent, my son. But what makes you cry?" I asked.

"My crime is unforgivable," he replied. "I have killed." His face was contorted with pain.

"God's mercy is immeasurable. Were you in combat?"

"No, Father. I killed out of rage. I got crazy when a Nazi soldier killed my father."

"Why, what did your father do?"

"Nothing. One of our goats went near the Nazi barracks. My father tried to get the goat out of the area and a soldier shot him. When I found out, I broke a window and started a fire in a building where Nazi officers lived. After that, they stalked me. During the day I hid, and at night I came out for revenge. I was determined to kill at least one Nazi to get even. One moonless night, while I was hiding in an empty cistern by the fountain near the Nazi barracks, I thought I smelled sulfur, the scent of a Nazi uniform. The running water ceased. *The Nazi soldier is drinking water at the fountain,* I thought and peered out to see him leaning over. At once I jumped on top of him and went straight for his throat. He struggled to free himself, but my hands clenched like steel bands around his neck. When I finally let go, he was dead. And if my crime wasn't bad enough, I pulled this chain with a cross from his neck and left his strangled body, like a dog, on the fountain curb. Just then I realized that I had a killed a young man by mistake, not a Nazi soldier. Then he pulled a cross out of his pocket on a broken chain, and gave it to me. Seeing the cross, I nearly had a heart attack. It was one of the crosses that I give to young people on special occasions. When I put on my glasses to read the inscription on the back of it, to my shock I realized it was the very cross that I had blessed and given to my own son, Christos, on the day of his graduation from high school.

"The pain was unbearable, Your Eminence. That is the trauma I've learned to live with."

"So, it was not a Nazi soldier who killed your son?"

"No. It was Dimitri."

"Did you tell him it was your own son he had killed?"

"No, my tongue became tight."

"Well, what did you do?" The archbishop's curiosity shone in his weathered eyes.

"It was a dreadful moment. A volcano of emotions erupted within me. Rage roared in my throat. My knees buckled. 'Kneel,' I said, and I knelt next him, looking at the effigy of Christ on the cross behind the altar. In a blinding flash, I realized my conflict. I was the spiritual father to this penitent man who desperately needed forgiveness and the natural father of a dead son."

With a worrisome glance the archbishop said, "How did you react?"

"The face of Christ, bloodstained from the crown of thorns, in compassionate agony glowed in the vigil light," Papavasile continued. "I turned and looked at the face of my son's killer. His eyes were red from crying. I pointed at the cross and whispered, 'Dimitri, He is the One who forgives. You are forgiven.' At that moment, I felt ethereal, without an angry thought in my mind."

"I guess this is the joy the angels experience in heaven when a sinner repents of his sins," said the archbishop, and reached out to touch Papavasile's hand. "You are an extraordinary priest."

"Not extraordinary, just another piece of clay, living and serving under God's grace."

"I don't know if I can bear to hear another story like yours, but tell me, what happened to Dimitri after his confession?"

"Do you really want to know that, Your Eminence?"

"I do. I do. You have triggered disturbing feelings in me."

"My intention was not to disturb Your Eminence."

"I know what your intention was. Just continue."

"Shortly after Dimitri's confession, he came to me, looking for a job. He had no one. His father had been killed, and his mother had died of tuberculosis. I let him clean the church and run errands. As it turned out, he was also a good cantor. He helped me a great deal with services, weddings, baptisms, and funerals. Since I had lost my son, I began to treat Dimitri like a son.

"My wife also liked him, and many times she had asked me to bring him home for dinner. At that time, I saw a change in my daughter. She came out of her grief for her brother. Once again, she blossomed and acted like girls do when they are ripe for marriage. Dimitri and my daughter fell in love, Your Eminence. I talked it over with my wife, and we agreed that this young man, the cantor with the good voice, whom we had grown to like a lot, would be a good son-in-law. Of course, my wife had no knowledge of his confession."

"And you allowed Dimitri to marry your daughter?"

"Yes, Your Eminence."

The archbishop's eyes looked moist, tears ready to flow. He did feel moved, but tears were a sign of weakness he could not accept. Graciously, he stood up, removed the golden chain with the precious pendant from his neck, and placed it around Papavasile's neck. "You ought to be the archbishop, not I. All my training and studies in theology have not given me as much as you have given me this evening. Thank you for a great lesson."

"Your Eminence . . ."

"Please, just call me brother, and forgive my arrogance."

Papavasile leaned forward to kiss the archbishop's hand, but the archbishop pulled it back. Standing firmly, he put his enormous arms around the frail body of his priest and kissed him on the cheek.

"Whatever you are about to do, do it quickly."

"You mean . . . you'll grant . . . ?"

"Permission granted. Go to St. Mary's and inform Mother Superior about my decision."

"Your Eminence, you are a saint."

"I don't know about that, but let me know the day and the hour. I'll be there myself to bless the marriage."

Speechless, Papavasile embraced and kissed the archbishop on both cheeks and left. As prophet Elias was snatched into heaven in a divine chariot, so did Papavasile feel instantly propelled by an inner force that shuttled him through the busy marketplace of Mytilene on his way back to Moria. It was nearly eleven at night when Papavasile returned to his home. Tired, war-bitten, but still a winner, aging but ageless, he was in a state of unprecedented ecstasy, floating in the air, not knowing whether he was walking on earth or in heaven. The archbishop's approval breathed a new life into him. He reentered a war-weathered microcosm where his son had been killed, and where he had buried hundreds of people victimized by starvation. In his eyes, Moria was riddled with pain and deprivation, orphans, widows, sick people. But at this hour, overflowing with joy, he saw Dan Cohen as his own son who had risen from the dead. God had sent him back as a reward, a comforting ray of hope to restore and renew life in his hometown.

Papavasile found the American sailor in his study, on his knees before an icon of Christ. The room was dark, and only a small olive-oil light burned in a corner. Dan Cohen, gazing imploringly into Christ's eyes, appeared transformed into an ethereal state. When Papavasile neared and touched his shoulder, he stood up, feeling the ache in his knees.

"Father, I didn't even hear you coming."

"Danny, my son, your prayers have been answered."

Silently, he fell into the priest's arms and wept. But the priest said, "It's time for joy. Early tomorrow, we'll go and find Nina. Now get some sleep."

The two men were alone, in a home fragrant with sweet basil. Over a glass of wine, the pillar of faith and the brave sailor sat opposite each other and exchanged stories. The priest was careful to refrain from talking about his own personal ordeal, the death of his son. Inner joy made him look at the sailor.

"Papavasile, I can close my eyes, close them this instant at this very joyful moment, and my brain still comes alive with the horrendous, unspeakable images of heinous crimes the Nazis performed against innocent people."

"Danny, nothing shocks me anymore. I have reached a point in my life where I am seized by an utter conviction. If we humans do not turn our direction toward our God and see each other as His children we'll destroy ourselves."

Fixing his gaze on the priest's gentle face, Cohen asked, "Why is it that humans turn against their own kind?"

"The mystery of man—avarice, envy, greed, thirst for power and control, these are aspects of humanity that violate our lovely planet."

"What's the answer, then?" Cohen asked, his eyes widening in anticipation of priestly wisdom.

"Danny, you know the answer."

"I do?"

"Of course you do, my American friend. We go back to God by loving each other as God loves us."

Danny smiled, wanting to hear more.

"You have returned for your love. God is love. But it's past midnight, so let's get some sleep. We'll have plenty of time to talk tomorrow."

The night seemed long, filled with excitement and wonder. Danny visualized Nina dressed in white garb, behind the walls of St. Mary's Convent, and wished he could be with her now. But the thought of how she would react when they met kept him awake. The priest had a point. He had to be patient until morning.

Dawn tinted the sky, finding Danny without having had a wink of sleep. But he did not feel tired. Little sparrows twittered on the pine tree by the window. He stood before a small mirror and shaved his beard. As he rubbed the skin on his face, he felt younger and revitalized. He noticed his sideburns had turned gray. *A sign of maturity,* he thought. Then a cruel thought crossed his mind, needle sharp, pressing on nerve cells, activating fear. *What if Nina decides to remain a nun? She has always wanted to be a nun, even as a teenager.* These thoughts brought a shade of sadness to his face, but a knock at his door interrupted them. It was Papavasile, who had already finished the office of Matins, a daily ritual, and was ready to go.

It was a glorious morning. The men walked vibrantly by the sea, joyful feelings, like branches intertwined, supporting them as they pursued their goal. They arrived at St. Mary's at sunrise. The eastern mountains across the Aegean Sea were dipped in auburn. A thin vapor arose over the sea, penetrated by the life-giving sun. Bright sun rays made the moisture-dripping olive trees appear to be adorned with diamonds.

Morning prayers had ended and sisters, two by two, emerged from the chapel bustling with inspiration. Danny's eyes searched for Nina. Dressed alike in their white cassocks and with their heads covered, the sisters appeared identical, making it difficult to distinguish which one was Nina. His temples throbbed and his heart beat rapidly. Papavasile recognized Maria, the novice in a white cassock, and he beckoned her to come closer. Maria's eyes widened when she saw Dan, but the priest placed a finger on his lips. Silence! Maria told him that Nina, Sister Anthusa, had left services a few minutes earlier and this morning was probably taking a stroll by the seashore alone.

"Go to her, Danny," Papavasile said. "Run!"

CHAPTER FIFTY-NINE

MOTHER SUPERIOR WAS PLEASANTLY surprised to see Papavasile. Her heart nurtured a special place for him, and he knew it. Over the years, she went to him for her personal confession or for a friendly chat and often sought his advice about pressing issues pertinent to the convent. He was always supportive.

"I'm glad to see you, Father," she said with a warm smile. "Will you join us for coffee this morning?"

"Thank you, but I need to have a little private talk with you," he said with a twinkle in his eyes. Mother Superior sensed that he had something serious to discuss with her.

"Then we can have coffee on my balcony."

"Splendid," he replied.

Mother Superior entered the cafeteria and took two ceramic mugs of coffee. "Please follow me," she said. Her study led onto a balcony garlanded with evergreen vines and colorful flowers, azaleas and tall geraniums. Below, ardently rolled the blue Aegean Sea, sending up a soothing breeze. She thought it would be a good opportunity to open Despina's letter that Sister Anthusa had given her and share it with Papavasile.

As he savored the coffee, Mother Superior pulled a yellow envelope out of her pocket and gave it to him. It was sealed.

"What's this?" he asked.

"It's from Despina. Sister Anthusa and I thought it might be a serious document, and that you should have it."

Papavasile tore open the envelope and pulled out a handwritten letter. "I think you should read it," he said with a grin, eager to tell Mother Superior the good news after she had read the letter.

With a sweet grimace, she put on her spectacles, cleared her throat, and began to read the letter, periodically looking up to see his reaction:

Dear and Benevolent Soul:

My last hope is that benevolent eyes will read this letter and pray to God to forgive me. I grew up without a father and my mother worked as a maid. When I was eight, a cousin raped me. He threatened to kill me if I didn't do what he wanted me to do.

Childhood years are cloudy, faded scenes I don't want to remember. In my late teens, I made home into a brothel, with kisses from strange mouths, curses, orgies, quarrels till dawn, diseases and injections, a frenzy of lust. I sought shelter in Moria, but God's curse followed me. Men used me and I used them, searching for a good one to marry. Still nobody wanted to make a home with me. Only Manolis Mourtos seemed sincere, but he, too, had given his heart to someone else. I still wanted to marry him, but he betrayed me. Then my fury surpassed my reason. I killed him. I'm sorry I did. At the court, I lied when I said I was carrying his child. That was a scheme I devised with Cara-Beis, a scum and collaborator with the Nazis. On one of those crazy nights, I conceived the child with a tall American sailor when the North Star *was anchored in Lesbos.*

If my little one survives this epidemic, let a loving couple adopt her, but don't ever reveal to her who her mother was. A rotten plank of a sunken ship, I have wasted my life. Please pray for my tormented soul.

Despina

"That's a painful letter," said Papavasile. "All we can do is pray that God may have mercy upon her soul." Shaking his head, he knew of Despina's reputation in Moria, and when he was informed of her last confession to Sister Anthusa, he felt genuine pity for her. "How is her little girl?" he asked.

"Well, she's out of danger. She's a sweet little bunch, but she wants to be held all the time."

"Are the sisters taking turns?" he laughed.

"Not really. She's very attached to Maria, the novice who loves playing mommy, so I let her."

"God must have a plan for that child," Papavasile said with a sigh of relief.

"Well, we'll keep her here until God reveals His plan to us."

The priest smiled. It was time to speak about God's plan for Sister Anthusa. Taking the last sip of coffee, he said, "In proper time, our Lord reveals His will to all of us. All we need is patience and prayer to pave the path that brings us closer to Him."

"Indeed," she said. Her face radiant, she was anxious to hear what God had planned for this particular visit.

Papavasile informed her of the archbishop's decision. In view of the extraordinary, tragic circumstances, he had released Sister Anthusa from her monastic vows, and upon her consent, he had granted her permission to marry Dan Cohen. Mother Superior nearly fell off her chair and became pale. With a trembling hand, she kept crossing herself. She whispered, "Great are You, O Lord; in wisdom You rule Your world." She knew her obedience to the archbishop was absolute. "May God's will be done, Father," she said, pressing her lips together, eyes turned toward the sky, unable to utter a word about her true feelings.

Papavasile gazed at Mother Superior, trying to read her mind. He suddenly realized the premium put on hierarchy by believers. It was the power that utterly shocked Mother Superior and the sisters at St. Mary's when they heard the archbishop's decision. *Never in Orthodox Church history had a dispensation and permission to marry been granted to a nun. Perhaps never before did the Church have an archbishop like Iakovos of Lesbos. A giant ecclesiastical power who could move mountains. This day he had decreed, and his orders had to be obeyed.*

"Perfectly clear, deep blue Mediterranean sky," Papavasile observed. "God's infinite space where His angels rejoice over human happiness."

"What's written in God's book cannot be unwritten," Mother Superior added, realizing her inner joy for Sister Anthusa's new destiny. "Now she may find peace and a new purpose in her life."

"When it is God's will, human and natural laws are subject to change," Papavasile offered. Fatherly, he looked at the aging virgin, monastic discipline personified, and said, "My dear sister in Christ, true love knows no boundaries, and true love is God. I hope you find it prudent to tell the rest of the nuns what God's love is all about."

"It will be difficult to justify Sister Anthusa's . . ."

"You don't need to justify anything," Papavasile said. "All you have to say is—or if you prefer, I'll tell them that one of their sisters is going to fulfill God's will in married life. Simply, God gives us freedom of choice."

"If I said that, I might lose all my nuns!" Mother Superior burst into laughter.

"Think positive. If that should happen, we'll have a few more young families. You know, war, famine, and Nazi cruelty have reduced Moria's population."

"You're not against monastic life, Father, are you?" she giggled.

"Would I be here if I were?" the priest said. He saw a cunning look in her eyes as he prepared to leave. "It's time to get to work."

"And we have a wedding to plan, don't we?" she said. "I had better get my sisters emotionally ready."

"And I need to get my congregation prepared." Heartily, he shook her hand. "Time for celebration."

CHAPTER SIXTY

WHILE PAPAVASILE WAS STILL with Mother Superior, Dan Cohen anxiously roamed by the shore, hoping to meet Nina. In the distance, he noticed the familiar sight, Sappho's statue, veiled in morning mist. Trudging behind a dune, he waited with increasing worry, wondering how Nina would react to their meeting. How would he feel? What would his first words be? The area appeared deserted, and flocks of seagulls, nature's excellent navigators, descended into the sea for their morning forage.

Wrapped in her black cassock with her head covered tightly, Sister Anthusa took the constitutional, a walk that nurtured her soul. The chill by the sea was penetrating, but she felt a tinge of warmth. The sun had just begun to ascend in the eastern sky, above the gaunt mountains of Asia Minor. Focusing on the shimmering golden disc that suddenly leaped through the mist, Nina thought, *The mythical phoenix rose from its ashes. The love of her life has risen from the depths of death and appeared again in her life. It is true. Dan Cohen is back. Papavasile has seen him, touched him, and has kept him at his home until the archbishop decided our destiny. But what if the archbishop said no? Then, if I defied his orders and got married, the Church would never accept me. I'd be an outcast.* Sauntering slowly toward the pure white marble of Sappho, she thought, *I would still want to see my Danny and tell him that I've never stopped loving him.* She picked a handful of seashells as she strolled along, and with a child's curiosity she paused to examine them and gave each one a name.

Then she heard a call: "NI-I-INA!" *Is my mind playing tricks on me?* But once again she heard the familiar vibrant voice calling her name.

"Da-a-a-anny," she screamed, overwhelmed by a tide of emotions, and tried to move forward, through the veil that held them separate. To her consternation, she ran into a power that would not allow her to get closer, as if some magnetic force increased in direct opposition to her effort, deflecting her back into the convent.

"Da-a-an-ny . . . where are you?" Her heart aching in anticipation and joyful fear, her eyes searched the area. Glancing over her shoulder, she saw a tall man running along the shoreline, haloed by misty breeze. He sped toward her against an unseen wind.

"Yes . . . oh yes!" Wiping her eyes with her veil, she kept coming closer with uncertain steps, until a wave flowed over the hem of her cassock and shoes and laced them with sand. She stopped. He stopped. Twelve feet away from each other, both stood still in disbelief. Was she hallucinating? Face blanched, heart wild, shore spinning around, she stared at him in love and ecstasy. The six-foot American sailor, hale and vital, stood before her—impeccable khaki uniform, broad shoulders, copper skin, blue eyes, bleached brows and hair, and those lips she had kissed so long ago—as if he were ready to grab the helm of his ship.

Dan Cohen studied Nina, the woman he had loved and dreamed about for three long years, and found her as beautiful as ever. The sea breeze ruffled her cassock, chiseling the lines of her body. Although cloaked in a nun's attire, she remained ravishing. The gleam in her eyes pulled him closer, but he hesitated to reach out, grab her in his arms, and sweep her off her feet. *I don't want to scare or insult her; besides, she is a nun.* His silence was raising a brick wall between them.

"Danny! . . . God Almighty! Blessed Mother! You're alive!" Delirious and delicious joy welled up in her, and she jumped, floating slowly up into the air, falling gently into his embrace. Wrapped in each other's arms, they felt safe from any external force. The sea breeze kept kissing them, as God's breath that gave them life together. Stunned, she whispered, "Oh, my God! I've had a feeling you were alive, but where were you all this time?"

"A Nazi prisoner."

"Oh, my God!"

"It was a horrifying nightmare."

For a few seconds, oblivious to the fact that evil eyes might be looking at them embracing, and what a scandal that would cause, both remained motionless, each hearing the other's heart pounding. Gently, she stroked his mustache with her fingertips; soft, thick, honey-colored whiskers framed his lips and she had to resist the urge to kiss him. He had the bearing of a man who had been a sailor for a long time. She was pressed against a soft khaki shirt that smelled of the sea, and his rough cheek felt warm and alive. Her hands did what they had done many times before, what they had ached to do since the night of his accident. During these delicious moments of their reunion, their hearts danced to the lyrics of love, pushing time aside, until reason interfered. This present ecstasy could be turned into an emotional volcano if they had to part again.

"Nina, my love, I'm back and I want to marry you." He held her forcefully, but she pulled back, stiffened, as if struck by lightning. Her eyes widened in disbelief.

"What are you trying to tell me?" he asked with a concerned voice.

"Danny! Could what is happening to us be just a dream? If it is, I don't want to wake up." She looked at him, shaking her head no. Her agonizing eyes forced back her tears. The cloak of celibacy, the commitment to be one of the brides of Christ, stifled her surging emotions.

Noticing her hesitation, he said, "Nina, is there any part in your heart that still loves me? Tell me the truth." There was a haunted look in his eyes. *What if she can't go through with it? What if she chooses to remain a nun? The convent walls and the sacred monastic life may have provided a security that she cannot abandon.*

"Of course, there is love. I love you with all my heart and soul," she said, ready to burst into tears. "But I don't want Mother Superior to have a heart attack or tarnish the reputation of St. Mary's Convent. Besides, I doubt if the archbishop will ever . . . ."

"The archbishop already said yes, and he plans to attend our wedding. Can you believe it?"

She pulled her veil down. She no longer had the long hair Danny remembered, but minimal streaks of gray added grace to her face.

"Danny Cohen, how do you know all that?" she asked with a skeptical grin.

"Papavasile." Danny tilted his head, eyes expressing gratitude. "And you know what? Right now he's with Mother Superior announcing the archbishop's decision in favor of our marriage.

"Incredible," Nina said. "Papavasile convinced the archbishop to grant me dispensation from my vows? I can't believe it." Tears of joy flowed down her cheeks. Nearly tongue-tied, she managed, "But . . ."

"There is no *but,* my love," he said in a firm voice. "Tell me, in spite of what has happened in our lives, will you marry me?"

"I'll marry you, my sweet Danny, even if they tie me in chains or excommunicate me." Then she kissed him with all the passion she had been keeping inside for three years. The sun climbed higher in the clear sky, casting ceaseless warmth upon their bodies. With open arms, she engulfed the man of her dreams, burying her nose under his rough chin and feeling his strength as he held her. In a moment of ecstasy, she could not resist the thought that God had reunited them. *Whoever God joins together, let no human put asunder.* But she also wondered about Mother Superior's reaction. *What would she think or say when she saw us together?*

Holding hands, they wandered along the sand, and by force of habit, gravitated toward the statue of Sappho. The sky hung in a tranquil perfection of blue and white. It seemed like yesterday that they had sat on the same cement pedestal three years ago. The murmuring of the wavelets attracted their attention, but their minds still pondered upon the irrevocable yesterdays. Nina linked her arm through his and said, "When Mourtos told Aunt Pipina and me that you had died and that he had buried you at sea, my life became a living hell."

"I think he intended to drown me."

"Let's not talk about him. I want to hear about you," Nina said.

"Didn't you receive any of my letters?"

"Letters? What letters?"

"I wrote to you from the Averof prison. I bribed a Nazi soldier to mail my letters to you. You didn't receive any of them?"

Shaking her head, she said an angry and tearful "No!"

"Every day I was thinking and talking to you through those letters. Like an icon, your image was ever-present before my eyes. Instead of praying to God, I prayed to you, knowing that you were so close to Him. And when the Nazis interrogated me and threatened to kill me, thinking that I was Jewish because of my name, all I could think of was you, my Nina."

"If I'd only received just one of those letters and had known that you were alive . . ."

"Either the Nazi soldier threw them away or my letters fell into the wrong hands."

"It doesn't matter now, my love. You are here." Nina reached over and kissed his eyes. "True love transcends all losses," she said.

"The priest told me about your father. I'm so sorry."

"There was a mockery of a trial. You could never imagine his humiliation, his pain. I was accused of Mourtos' murder. I was also accused of harboring an American spy, a Jew by the name of Dan Cohen. Oh, Danny, it's too painful to rehash. Evil just took over Moria."

Danny wanted to know the whole story, but Nina could not bear to reveal all of it just yet. She preferred to speak of her Aunt Pipina, who was in frail health since her brother's death and didn't care to talk much. Zographia took meticulous care of her, and Nina visited her once a week with her novice friend, Maria.

She turned to him with a radiant smile, and said, "And do you know who keeps Aunt Pipina going?"

Danny lifted his shoulders curiously.

"Papavasile!" she said with an air of gratitude in her smile. "Monday, Wednesday, and Friday he brings a special lentil soup that his wife makes.

Aunt Pipina calls it soul soup. But she also cherishes his visits." Nina's female intuition told her that Aunt Pipina nurtured a special love for Papavasile.

"Do you think I could visit Aunt Pipina today?"

"I'm afraid the excitement might give her a heart attack. She's so fragile," Nina said with a charming giggle.

"I really want to see her."

"Of course you can visit her. Seeing you might be medicine. Maybe we could go together, after I meet with Mother Superior," Nina said. But the forthcoming encounter with her gave her the chills. She wished that Papavasile would be still there for support when she returned to St. Mary's.

"Do you want me to come with you to the convent?" Dan asked.

"God, no! I'll handle this meeting alone," Nina answered with simulated confidence. "But before I see Mother Superior, I need to go to our chapel and offer a prayer of thanks to God."

Danny said, "Good idea. And I'll go find Papavasile. He may tell me about his meeting with Mother Superior."

As they both stood up and prepared to part, Nina said, "Danny, take me to America."

Gently, he clenched both her hands in his own and asked, "Do you really mean that?"

"Yes. Take me anywhere, to a new place where no one knows us, and we know no one." They strolled toward St. Mary's, holding hands.

"I'll take you anywhere you want." He squeezed her hand. "Whether we live in America or in Lesbos, the only thing that's important to me is our love for each other. We can build a place here in Moria. If we choose America for our home and family, we can still return once a year to reconnect with the place where we met."

Elated by Dan's idea, Nina said, "That sounds great. We can spend our summers on the island. You know what I plan to do with my father's property once I get it back?"

Absorbed by every word she uttered, Danny halted to hear her plans. He wanted her to be happy and he felt determined to go along with any of her wishes.

"Papavasile reassured me that now that the war is over, I can reclaim my father's estate. With a bit of remodeling, it can be a perfect home for the orphans of the entire island."

"Isn't that what you have always wanted?" His voice shared her excitement.

"Another dream to be fulfilled," she said.

CHAPTER SIXTY-ONE

PAPAVASILE'S BEARD AND ROBE billowed in the evening breeze as he hastened to important store owners, asking them to participate in the wedding. In his thoughts, Moria was about to celebrate a monumental event. He told Alexis, "I want you to be in charge of the food arrangements."

"My dear priest and father, for Danny the American, you can count on me. And I'll even get my mother busy. I know how much she loves Nina."

"Good idea," the priest agreed, and hurried on to make the next call.

"Get the Moria Quartet to sing at the ceremony," Alexis shouted.

"Are they back?" the priest asked.

"They are. Brave kids!" Alexis said.

By the time the priest finished his rounds, he had a large list of volunteers. Among them was Apostolos the butcher, who offered to kill a calf he had secretly fed for months in a secret stable behind the Roman aqueduct. Nikos the barber went to his father-in-law, a vineyard owner, and secured two barrels of wine. Panagos the peddler twisted his thick mustache with pride and said, "For Nina Cambas, I'd give my life. Fruits, vegetables, and salads, I'll provide all that. It will be a day of joy."

Sitting on a marble bench in St. Basil's plaza, the four friends were waiting for the priest. When they saw him in the distance, Takis began to play his harmonica, as the other three sang:

> *Children of the wind, sing your nation's joy.*
> *The invaders disappeared, no longer fear.*
> *Machine-guns cannot control our destiny.*
> *No more fears, no more tears.*
> *Do you hear dear friends? Free is our nation.*
> *People of Moria, young and old time for celebration.*

"Time for celebration, indeed!" shouted Papavasile and dashed over to them. He put his arms around them, eyes brimming tears of joy, and said, "Welcome back. I've missed you a lot. My church services were dry without your voices, but I thank God you're alive and back in Moria."

"Your prayers kept us alive," Takis said and kissed the priest's hand. The others followed suit.

The priest, taking another look at them, said, "My Lord, look at you! You have grown a lot thinner but taller. You are men! But I hope you can still be my choir."

Takis said, "Father, we're ready."

"Come to St. Basil's. I have a request. I want you to rehearse the hymns for the wedding ceremony with me."

"Wedding? Who's getting married?" Takis asked, heart pounding, afraid that it could be his Eleni.

"The American sailor is marrying Cambas' daughter."

Surprised, the four friends said, "But isn't she a nun?"

"The archbishop granted her special permission to marry," Papavasile said as they entered the church. A gleam in his eye hid some ineffable secret as his fingers fumbled through his beard in contemplation. Whispering a prayer, he was lighting candles when suddenly he noticed someone at the entrance.

Zographia, Alexis' mother, bent over with the weight of a big bundle, trudged in the direction of the priest. One of the boys offered to help her, but she made a motion indicating that she didn't need their help.

The priest said, "Zographia, what in the world are you carrying?"

"My sins, Father," she chuckled.

"What sins? You're a saint," Papavasile said, and he really meant it.

"I guess the halo around my head is showing," she laughed.

"We're going to have a glorious wedding," Papavasile said.

"So I hear. And I'm going to dance," Zographia said, dropping the bundle into a chair. She took a profound look at the boys and smiled. "You're the singing boys."

"It's the Moria Quartet," Papavasile said.

"My God, you're so tall, I didn't recognize you."

"They are going to sing at the wedding."

"Good," she said, unfolding her bundle. "I've brought twelve silk tablecloths. They were my dowry, but I want Nina and her man to have them."

"I told you, you're a saint." Papavasile wrapped up the tablecloths and gave the whole bundle to Takis. "Take this to Alexis. He will need to cover the tables on the wedding day." He turned to Zographia and said, "Your son is an angel."

"I wouldn't go that far." She laughed.

The four boys took off, singing on the way, but Alexis' mother lingered behind to see Papavasile alone. She told him that she had a handmade wedding gown of natural silk. A well-known seamstress had made it for her daughter. She wanted Nina to have it. Papavasile remembered when Zographia's daughter had died of a perforated appendix, seven years ago. She would have been twenty-seven. Embracing the grieving mother, he gave her a warm hug and a kiss.

"When I see Cambas' daughter dressed as a bride," she said with a sweet smile, "I'll think she's my daughter."

"Will Pipina be able to attend her niece's wedding?"

"She will be there, even if I have to carry her."

An unprecedented spirit permeated Moria. The dark clouds of fear and sadness had finally evaporated. In joyful anticipation the islanders looked forward to celebrating a wedding. They had adopted Dan Cohen and Nina Cambas as their own offspring and vouchsafed to make their wedding the happiest on the island. For a whole week, volunteers worked day and night to prepare the festivities.

The Moria Quartet went door to door asking for cups of flour, eggs, and homemade butter, which Zographia planned to knead into twelve large buns. The four friends helped Alexis to bring chairs and tables to the aqueduct, and silverware and dishes from his mother's household and from other neighbors. They arranged chairs and tables in the form of an amphitheater. The tables, they covered with Zographia's dowry, added classic uniformity to the seating arrangement.

A local carpenter built a platform and an altar in the midst of nature's elegance, near the waterfalls. Papavasile placed a gilded Bible and a cross on the altar table. The Roman aqueduct towered behind the altar, soon to hear sacramental prayers and songs of love.

CHAPTER SIXTY-TWO

LIKE A BIRD'S NEST concealed among cypress and pine trees, behind St. Basil's Church was a four-room stucco habitat with a trellis making an awning in front of it. This cozy little house belonged to Alexis. The exterior was whitewashed with shutters blue like the Aegean Sea. He had painted the interior light green and the bedroom pink. It was his hideout for afternoon siestas or for special guests. When Papavasile asked him if the groom and his bride could stay there until they established their own home, Alexis agreed wholeheartedly and asked his mother to give it a thorough cleaning.

On Friday, October 11, 1944, as the sun was sliding behind the mountains, six rosy-cheeked maidens in cream-colored gowns carried gifts from their precious trousseaus—bedding, blankets, pillows, sheets, sofa covers, underwear, bathrobes—all embroidered or woven by their own hands. In a joyful procession, they brought these to the bridal home-to-be.

Zographia cheerfully received the gifts and arranged them in prominent areas of the house. Clean and neatly decorated with local bric-a-brac, the bachelor's dwelling became a mythical little palace "suited for lovers," Alexis' mother said, beaming with pride.

When Papavasile came to inspect the progress, he found Zographia setting a small table for the groom and his bride. Next to a bottle of wine were two covered dishes of cheese, two glasses, dark homemade bread, and a big bowl of grapes and apples, topped by a huge polished pomegranate, the symbol of fertility.

"Monday morning, I'll have chicken soup ready," Zographia said.

"You think of everything." Papavasile said.

With a twinkle in her ageless eyes, she said, "Father, you know the newlyweds, especially the groom, need strength after the first night of their wedding."

Papavasile knew what old Zographia implied and with a grin he said, "You sound so happy."

"The whole town is excited," she said, "and I'm planning to dance."

Affectionately, he looked at her eyes and his heart melted. His thoughts lingered on their losses. Zographia had lost her only daughter, and he had lost his only son. Both surrendered to the memory of what once was and could no longer be. But their mission in life had continued in spite of the ultimate pain they had experienced as parents. *Life is a mosaic of bittersweet experiences,* the priest thought, shaking his head. "It's going to be a great wedding," he said, and as they gazed at each other, both were aware that their shared vicarious joy for Nina and Danny represented their lost children. On the brighter side, he remembered Zographia's tenure as a teacher. Most of the adult population in Moria had gone through her classroom. She had given a lifetime to educate the youth of Moria, and with pride she mentioned the names of several students who excelled. Among them was Nina Cambas. The Moria Quartet were her last students before retirement, and "the most mischievous ones," she said.

On Sunday morning, the priest announced to his people in church that all preparations were ready and that the wedding would take place at three o'clock in the afternoon. Nina Cambas and Dan Cohen had requested that all the inhabitants of Moria, young and old, be invited. An aura of joyful commotion enveloped the congregation. Papavasile suggested that by two-thirty at the latest everyone should be gathered in the church plaza to accompany the bride and the groom.

At two o'clock that afternoon, in two different parts of the town, prenuptial rituals were simultaneously taking place. At the convent, on a marble-paved plaza, Nina stood in her silk bridal gown, looking stunning, like a Greek goddess of the past. A group of sisters in black cassocks, some novices in white, and several of her former classmates eagerly formed a circle around the bride. Mother Superior, assisted by Maria, served almond cookies and cherry juice. After all present had been served, Maria began to sing traditional verses as six bridesmaids in peach-colored gowns encircled Nina and tried a variety of dance steps.

Mother Superior watched the festive scene with a smile, but her mind was elsewhere. The thought of the archbishop's leniency evoked warm feelings. She felt not just simple compassion for Nina's tragedy but also genuine concern. The sisters, who knew of her rigidity, had noticed a radical change of heart since the day she had witnessed Despina's confession and the miraculous healing of her child. Never before had Mother Superior felt as happy, and momentarily she was tempted to join the dancing bridesmaids. But her early programming and her present position as the head of the convent held her back. *If only her father and aunt were here, Nina's happiness would be complete,* she thought. She turned to Maria and said, "Sing, dear nightingale, sing." Maria obeyed the command and began:

> *Beautiful Nina is our bride,*
> *In pure silk dress all white,*
> *Giving herself to man with love,*
> *Abundant blessings from God above.*

In chorus, the nuns sang the refrain:

> *Sweet bride, O sweet bride,*
> *You're our island's joy and pride.*

More spectators joined the dancing, as the song continued:

> *Today a wedding takes place,*
> *In God's own verdant garden,*
> *The moon is marrying the sun,*
> *Before His holy altar.*

Sweet bride, O sweet bride,
God grant you a joyous life.

Nina, smiling gratefully, approached the participants, and kissed and thanked each one. A pleasant sensation traveled through her whole body as she thought how the Lord whom she loved and worshipped had answered her prayers. She thought of Danny and wondered how he was reacting to the local customs.

There was more cheer and commotion at the other end of the town, where the groom was getting ready. Dan Cohen had just finished bathing and was still naked when Alexis knocked at the door of his own private little mansion.

"Danny, open the door. Some friends are here and want to come in to help you dress," Alexis said.

"Thanks, but I don't need any help," Danny said.

"It's necessary," Alexis insisted.

"Well, I'll be out in a few minutes." He wrapped a towel around himself and cracked the door open.

"Alexis, what's going on?"

The Moria Quartet burst in, followed by three young men about Danny's age, Nikos the barber, and Alexis, who was holding a roasting pan.

Alexis beat the pan once for attention and said, "Listen, my American friend, in Greece, you do as the Greeks do. You have no choice. Just surrender yourself and enjoy."

"I'll feel strange, somebody else dressing me," Danny said.

"We won't look," Alexis said and laid the roasting pan in front of Danny's feet. This was a Greek custom that Danny was just learning about: The groom-to-be must stand in a roasting pan so his friends can symbolically roast him with poetic humor.

"Now step in here and let us do the work." Laughter began, as each person knew what to do. As soon as they had finished dressing him, Nikos, snipping his scissors in the air, trimmed Danny's hair and mustache to perfection. Alexis held up an old mirror so that Danny could see himself. Not being allowed to touch anything, he looked in the mirror nervously, as the young men around him began teasing and joking.

"Now you look like a groom," Alexis said.

Danny turned to Alexis and said, "Now I know why you remained a bachelor."

"Why?"

"You didn't want to go through all this fuss."

"That's not it. I just couldn't give all this charm," he pointed to himself, "to one woman."

Everyone laughed, and Danny said, "Alexis, I'm a lucky man to have a friend like you." He smiled. But a sudden thought of his friend Tiny Tom, who he wished was present and could be his best man, caused a sad expression that Alexis noticed.

He said, "Hey groom, it's time for singing."

"Did you say singing?" Takis asked, elbowing the rest of the quartet. Everyone encircled Danny, who was still standing in the roasting pan, and Alexis began the song:

> *Groom, O handsome groom,*
> *Be careful with the big bam.*
> *Your bride is a delicate maid*
> *Don't overload your gun.*

Giggling, the quartet sang:

> *O bridegroom from the U.S.*
> *Time has come to say YES.*

Lust gleaming in his eyes, Alexis pointed to the pink bedroom prepared for the newlyweds and winked at the young men around him. "Oh, I almost forgot," he said, setting the mirror down. From the top shelf of a nearby closet, he pulled out a jar. The barber, who was now massaging Danny's face, asked, "What is it you've got up there, dirty old man?"

"It's my secret potion for the groom," Alexis explained with a cunning glow on his face. He dug out a spoonful and stuck it in Danny's mouth.

"Sweet and delicious," Danny said. "What in the world is it?"

"An old recipe from way back, from my great-grandfather, whose name was also Alexis. Ground pignolia nuts and walnuts, mixed with spring honey and cognac."

"Alexis, you're up to something," Danny said.

"Potency and endurance!" Alexis said. "A woman can have seven orgasms during one intercourse, but a man can have only one, you understand? And this makes me mad. Why did God do such an injustice to man? Two hundred and eighteen bones in a human body, so why didn't God put a tiny bone where we need it most?" Alexis sounded deadly serious, but everyone around him was laughing loudly.

Danny's laughter lasted the longest. "I want to hear more about this miraculous potion."

"Two tablespoonfuls before the wedding ceremony, and two more a half hour before you and your bride are about to . . . you know what I mean."

Danny gladly welcomed this endearing preparation offered by friends. His heart quivered at the thought of the imminent meeting with his bride.

CHAPTER SIXTY-THREE

ON OCTOBER 13, 1944, ST. BASIL'S CHURCH was to witness yet another miracle. Nina and Danny, accompanied by dozens of friends, arrived from different directions. Papavasile welcomed them and joined their hands, determined that today's ceremony would be exceptionally impressive.

Altar boys dressed in white robes and holding lit tapers led the procession, while a cantor and the Moria Quartet sang hymns. Papavasile, holding a gilded prayer book, walked behind them. Six bridesmaids and six ushers kept the way open for the bride and groom, while two six-year-old girls sprinkled rose petals along the road to the aqueduct. A private coach decorated with flowers followed the crowd. Papavasile had arranged that Pipina and Zographia would arrive in style. With a nervous smile and moist eyes, Dan Cohen held Nina Cambas' hand, feeling her rapid pulse. Her gown, with its long white train, set off her fine-boned fragility—the delicate jaw, chin, nose, and adorable lips shaped like the petals of a rosebud ready to blossom. Dainty features made Nina's dark-lashed eyes appear even larger than they were, as did the style of her hair, which was partially hidden under the customary lace veil.

Ebullient, the couple glanced at each other, eyes reflecting wonder: *Is this a magnificent dream, unfolding in the mansion of Paradise?* A breeze coming from the wind-hewn olive trees caught Nina's veil, but she brushed it back with a charming sweep of her hand. As she smiled at her peers, her face looked younger. Finally, the aqueduct came into view. They heard music, an awkward testing of instruments, bouzoukia, violins, and trumpets. Thick smoke ascended behind the aqueduct, blending a fragrant spicy smell with the mountain air. In addition to the young calf that Apostolos had promised, he was roasting six lambs on skewers between a cage of trees.

As the bridal party took their places on the platform, Papavasile cued the musicians to play wedding music. With the awesome aqueduct as a backdrop, Nina and Danny approached the altar table solemnly. The echo of the music soon faded away, and silence prevailed among the attendants. The rough rumble of the waterfall gushing on the rocks could be heard in the background.

Birds soared through the air and landed in the trees, chirping autumn melodies. Alexis, Apostolos, Nikos, Pipina, and Zographia had taken prominent places at the foot of the altar, adjacent to a fragrant display of pastries.

Pipina, dressed beautifully in black, watched the priest. Occasionally, she leaned lightly against Zographia, wishing Nina's father were there to see his daughter as a bride. Today, her normally pale face seemed darker against the whiteness of her hair. Zographia was glad to see her friend rise to her feet without help. In the midst of the crowd, her dress sparkled, and the gleam in her eyes mirrored the joy she felt witnessing God's ineffable miracle: Dan Cohen had risen from the dead to marry her niece, who adored him. Making the sign of the cross, she whispered into Zographia's ear, "God has granted me the ultimate bliss." Noticing the glowing expression on the priest's face, Pipina felt the greatest comfort in her heart. *As I depart from this world, before I close my eyes forever, in my last breath, it's the face of Papavasile I would like to see.*

Through the silvery olive trees, the sun's rays veiled the altar platform with ample light, enveloping the bride and groom in dazzling splendor. All of a sudden, the disturbing sound of an automobile made all faces turn. Who could it be? An unusual sight in this part of the island, a black Mercedes, leaving a cloud of dust in its wake, made its way toward the aqueduct.

Papavasile recognized the vehicle and winked at the bridal pair with a smile. *Archbishop Iakovos was keeping his promise.* "Nina and Danny," the priest clasped their hands together, "the archbishop is here to bless your marriage."

"Oh, my God," Nina's eyes welled with tears of elation.

"My love," said Danny and offered his handkerchief. "I can't believe what's happening."

"Danny, do you know what this means? We'll be married for good and forever."

"Aye," he said, bowing gratefully at the archbishop.

In splendid vestments, the archbishop commenced the sacrament of holy matrimony in a melodic voice. Papavasile responded, intoning matrimonial petitions and prayers, and ending with the Biblical verse: *Whoever God joins together, let no man put asunder.*

Parallel to Pipina, like a flock of blackbirds, three rows of nuns were watching the ceremony. Mother Superior, in the front row, wanted to be noticed by the archbishop. Next to her sat Maria, holding a little girl on her knee and trying to keep her quiet. But the little one insisted upon making noises: Da-D-Da.

Only a week ago, Nina and Danny had become godparents of the little girl and named her America, in honor of Tiny Tom, her father. To silence her chatter, Mother Superior tenderly pinched the girl's snub nose and placed a finger to her lips. *This is definitely not a Greek child—blue-eyed, curly blond hair—but she has certainly brought new life to St. Mary's,* she thought and crossed herself in gratitude, wishing that the child's father would someday show up to claim her.

Excited about the wedding and still a novice, Maria was thinking how wonderful it must be to be in love. She was happy to see Nina marrying the man of her dreams. *If a man ever loved me like Danny loves Nina, I would not mind marrying him.*

Mustering all his strength, the archbishop chanted, "O Lord our God, with glory and honor, crown Your servants Daniel and Nina." The cantor and the Moria Quartet, in their cheerful voices, repeated the verse in harmony while the archbishop placed the crowns on the heads of the couple, symbolically establishing a new kingdom on earth, with Danny and Nina as the new royalty of a new home in Moria. Joyfully Danny looked at his bride, squeezed her hand affectionately, and asked, "My love, are we married yet?"

"Aye," said Nina.

Feeling blessed, Danny and Nina joyfully embraced the archbishop and Papavasile and thanked them. They felt deep gratitude for these two clergymen, whose sacrificial love helped them to fulfill their dream. Papavasile took Danny's and Nina's right hands, and holding them tight together for a few seconds and smiling, he said, "Love never fails."

First in line to congratulate the newlyweds was Pipina. After kissing her niece with tears of joy, affectionately she put a ring on Danny's left hand and kissed him. It was her brother's ring. Her loving heart wanted Danny, her new nephew, to have it. As Danny touched it, he trembled with emotion. He felt grateful for marrying the woman of his dreams and for now being part of Cambas' legendary life, a new life in Lesbos.

EPILOGUE

NINA CAMBAS AND DANIEL COHEN, now Mr. and Mrs. Papadopoulos, stayed three months at Alexis' little palace while they built their own house beyond the aqueduct, in the midst of olive and pine trees, a stone's throw from the waterfalls.

Meanwhile, Danny was able to secure grants—Greek War Relief and Restoration Funds from the American government, and remodeled the hot springs of Gera into an elegant spa resort. Next to the spa he built a first-class motel, which became an attraction for the people of Greece and other European countries and a source of income for the islanders.

Apostolou, the mayor of Mytilene, granted Danny permission to develop a fishery in the gulf of Gera. He brought seeds from Japan and developed oyster beds. In time, he built facilities where men and women processed and packaged the oysters and canned sardines. The whole area of this picturesque gulf was home to a lucrative industry, Cambas-Papadopoulos Enterprises, which provided employment for an increasing number of the island's population.

In the spring of 1945, the Greek government returned properties that the Nazis had confiscated to their rightful owners. Nina reclaimed her father's estate, which she restored and converted into an orphanage. The archbishop helped her select appropriate personnel to run the home for orphaned boys and girls. When the inauguration took place, he named the orphanage Idrima Pisteos and Elpidos, the Institute of Faith and Hope. Twice a week, Papavasile visited the orphans, and his spiritual guidance and presence offered new hope.

Intimate friendship had developed between the priest and the young married couple that cut through all the hurts and the injustices of their troubled past. The ruins that World War II left behind were gradually restored by the redeeming power of love and a commitment to a better life.

In one of their encounters, Nina and Danny informed Papavasile that Despina's little girl, America, soon might have a father. Danny had written to Tiny Tom in America telling him about Despina's confession, and that he was the father of her child. Tiny Tom replied with a special delivery letter. He would be visiting Lesbos in April during Easter vacation.

On April 23, 1945, Tiny Tom returned to Lesbos to visit the newlyweds, but he primarily came to see the child that was allegedly his daughter. When he saw little America in the arms of Maria, he stood in awe. To his surprise and delight, she had his features, his eyes and the shape of his face, his pug nose and fair hair. She was a miniature of him. He was also impressed with the way Maria cared for the child. Somehow he felt that Maria's face looked like his mother's. *If only Maria could speak English I'd marry her now,* he thought.

When Maria handed him the child, her heart began to palpitate intensely. *This is America's father? What a huge and handsome man!* she thought. Although it didn't take long to like this tall American, she did not want to give up the child that had given her a purpose in life. But she was also happy that America would now have a father. *Of course America needs a mother, too,* she thought.

Danny and Nina told Tiny Tom that Maria had been the only one who mothered his child since Despina's death. He thanked her profusely and offered her a handful of money, but she refused to take it. During his stay, Tiny Tom visited the convent to see his daughter for a few hours every day. Seeing how affectionately Maria treated America, he began to like her a little more each time. *I wonder if she would like to be my daughter's mother.* With

Danny as his interpreter, he asked Maria if she would share her life with him. He wanted to marry her and bring her to America.

Eagerly, Maria sought the priest's advice about the possible change in her life.

"Maria, you are still a novice, you still have a choice," Papavasile told her, and suggested that it was a good idea. The three-year-old girl already called her "Mama," and he had seen how responsively Maria took care of her. He felt that marrying Tiny Tom would be a blessing for the little orphan, and that Maria would have a comfortable life in the United States. *I wonder what Mother Superior would say this time,* the priest thought.

"Father, I would like to marry this man," Maria said, "but how am I going to talk to him, not knowing his language?"

"Where there is love, you don't have to speak the language," the priest said. "In time, you can teach him a little Greek, and he can teach you English."

On the Wednesday after Easter, Tiny Tom married Maria in St. Basil's Church. Nina was the maid of honor and Danny was the best man. Papavasile performed the sacrament of marriage in utter solemnity among a small group of friends including Alexis, Apostolos, Nikos, and the Moria Quartet. Two weeks later, the three joyful faces of Maria, Tiny Tom, and America said good-bye to Danny and Nina and to the island of Lesbos. Freehold, New Jersey, became their new home.

ACKNOWLEDGMENTS

As always in writing a book, I am grateful to a number of people. *The Phoenix* owes its final form to the editorial department of Crossroad Publishing Company and for the hard work of Jane Cavolina and John Zmirak, who did their best for its completion. My thanks to Gwendolin Herder, President of Crossroad Publishing Company, who found that this novel convincingly carries the theme of true love. I am grateful for her enduring support in publishing my four other psychological/spiritual books, as well as a historical novel, *One More Spring*. Pat, my ever-loving and precious wife, makes possible the long hours that I spend at the computer writing. She is a vital source of strength and encouragement in my life. Blessings and thanks to my loving children, Mersene, Michael, Basil, and Katina; my grandchildren, Nicolette, Andrew, Stacey Mercene, Peter Andreas, and Victoria Patricia; and my great-grandson Hudson. I dearly love you all and hope that someday each of you will visit the Greek island of Lesbos, where the story of *The Phoenix* takes place.

ABOUT THE PUBLISHER

The Crossroad Publishing Company publishes CROSSROAD and HERDER & HERDER books. We offer a 200-year global family tradition of books on spiritual living and religious thought. We promote reading as a time-tested discipline for focus and understanding. We help authors shape, clarify, write, and effectively promote their ideas. We select, edit, and distribute books. Our expertise and passion is to provide wholesome spiritual nourishment for heart, mind, and soul through the written word.

Joan Ohanneson

Hildegard of Bingen

Lady of the Light, Woman for the World

A Historical Novel

Paperback, 288 pages, ISBN 978-08245-20182

Joan Ohanneson brings to life the "feather on the breath of God"—Hildegard of Bingen, the prophet who shattered stereotypes of women, saints, and even God. An eminent visionary, Hildegard influences the fields of medicine, music, ecology, and theater to this day. This gripping "memoir" includes the saint's own vivid accounts of her visions and thoughts.

Ohanneson interweaves the events in Hildegard of Bingen's life with her illuminating written works to create a vital and intense characterization of the fascinating woman who in her humble yet authoritative way spoke to the power of the God and changed the Church forever.

"*Hildegard of Bingen* is a compelling, novelized account of Hildegard's life and work. Ohanneson stays true to historical fact, but brings a depth of personality to her subject that makes the centuries drop away as one reads."

—*Milwaukee Journal Sentinel*

Support your local bookstore or order directly
from the publisher at www.CrossroadPublishing.com

To request a catalog or inquire about
quantity orders, please e-mail
sales@CrossroadPublishing.com

 The Crossroad Publishing Company

You Might Also Like

Peter Kalellis

Why Have You Abandoned Me?

Discovering God's Presence
When a Father Is Absent

Paperback, 204 pages, ISBN 978-08245-26283

An intimate look at troubled or distant relationships with parents—particularly fathers—and offers spiritual and therapeutic solutions for healing the wounds of abandonment and living a healthy, fulfilling life. Informing psychology with his signature compassion and forgiveness—for both self and family—Kalellis reveals how a strong belief in the Heavenly Father can help sons and daughters understand their earthly parents, while freeing themselves from the feelings of abandonment they might have carried from childhood into adulthood.

Support your local bookstore or order directly from the publisher at www.CrossroadPublishing.com

To request a catalog or inquire about quantity orders, please e-mail sales@CrossroadPublishing.com

The Crossroad Publishing Company